Sinister Secret
An Alexis Parker novel

G.K. Parks

Copyright © 2022 G.K. Parks

A Modus Operandi imprint

All rights reserved.

ISBN:
ISBN-13: 978-1-942710-32-5

For mom and dad

ONE

"It's about time you showed up, Alex." Eddie Lucca lifted his jacket off the adjacent chair so I could sit. "I figured you were going to cancel again."

"I owed you dinner." Truthfully, I owed Lucca my life. Dinner was just easier. "Mark Jablonsky might have mentioned you've been dying to see me. I would have figured after almost dying, you would have realized it's better when you don't see me. Refresh my memory. Were you always this dense? I thought you had it more together when we were partners."

"I haven't lost a step. I hope you haven't either."

That didn't sound good. "What's going on, Lucca? What's so important that it requires a face-to-face meeting?"

He picked up his glass and took a sip of water. "We've had dinner plans on the books for a while now. You just haven't bothered to follow through."

"I've been busy. Cross Security isn't exactly a walk in the park."

"Don't give me that. I've seen where you work. It doesn't get much cushier than that."

"Whatever you have to tell yourself, but it isn't easy. Far from it." I eyed the glass in front of him. "Still not drinking?"

"After everything, I thought I should take it easy on the liver." He gestured at the menu. "Don't let me stop you. Order whatever you like. You're paying."

I looked around. "Where's your wife? Isn't she joining us?"

"Not tonight. Our babysitter backed out at the last minute." He peered behind me. "Where's your fiancé? I thought you were bringing him with you."

"Can't. He's in California."

"Wow, when you chase them off, you don't mess around."

"You know what they say. Go big or go home."

"Is everything okay? I was just joking."

"No, it's fine. We're fine."

"Glad to hear it. He's definitely the best part of you."

"No argument there." I picked up the menu. "Let's get this over with. What do you want?" When my question was met with silence, I looked up. Lucca wasn't studying his menu. He was studying me. We might not have worked together very long, but I knew him. "Mark said you wanted to see me. I'm guessing it wasn't so I could buy you an expensive steak."

"I'm thinking lobster."

"Whatever." I put the menu down. "Did the babysitter really cancel?"

"Why do you always have to look for trouble, Alex?"

I could play the first name game too. "Cut the bullshit. What is this about, Eddie?"

"I need a favor."

"Do you want one of my kidneys?"

He grinned. "Are you serious?"

"I don't know. But if I'm giving you a kidney, you're paying for dinner."

"I don't need a kidney, but I was hoping you could help me out with something work-related. A victim from an old case has resurfaced. She reached out to me a couple of months ago. She says she's in trouble. I thought this might be something you could handle."

"What kind of trouble?"

"I'm not entirely sure."

"I'm going to need a little more than that."

He grabbed the folder from the empty seat and slid it toward me. "Do you remember the Lightning Killer case, or was that before your time?"

"I remember seeing a notice or two when I was still a probationary agent. Why? What does that have to do with this?"

"Daria Waylon, the woman who reached out to me, was his final victim. She believes someone's been watching her. She's afraid he's back to finish what he started."

"Is there even the slightest possibility she's right?"

"I don't see how. We stopped the guy. He can't hurt anyone else."

"Are you sure?"

Lucca gave me an annoyed look. "Absolutely. I was there when he went down."

"How did you catch him?" Maybe they'd collared the wrong guy.

"I'd just started working in the D.C. office when the serial killer was in the midst of his spree. The behavioral analysts had come up with a profile, but we didn't have any suspects. The killer moved around too much. The only clue we had as to where he'd strike next was in the photos he sent of his next victim. He wanted us to scramble to find her before he could kill her. He moved from city to city, making it damn near impossible to locate him or his victims. He never stuck around in one place long enough to strike twice. That's why it took so long to catch him. When we received his last photo, we tracked him down via the 35 mm film he used. He worked analog to make things harder and printed the photos himself, which ending up biting him in the ass. Once we figured out where he was buying his film developing supplies, we got him."

"If it was that simple, someone should have stopped him sooner."

"I'm not saying luck didn't have a lot to do with it, because it did. You know how this job works."

"It's better to be lucky than good. What happened after you caught him? Did he confess? Was the case solid? How about the evidence?"

"We had everything."

"Still, judges overturn convictions all the time. Do you think he could be out on parole, or maybe he escaped from prison?" The last thing I needed was to piss off a serial killer.

"It never went to trial."

"Why not?"

"Because he's dead."

"Are you sure? This wouldn't be the first time someone came back from the grave."

"I saw him die with my own eyes. It's not possible. He's in the ground."

"Okay, but if someone's terrorizing the Lightning Killer's final victim, it begs asking, are you sure you got the right guy?"

"Yes, I'm sure. I was there when we busted through Daria's front door and found him basking in what he'd just done. The water was still dripping down his chest. He hadn't even pulled her out of the tub yet. He reached for a gun, and two agents and three cops shot him." Lucca closed his eyes, swallowing. "He landed right on top of her. I can still hear the splash. We pulled them both out, but he was already dead. She wasn't breathing and didn't have a pulse. I don't know how long she was underwater, but she was down for several minutes. The EMTs worked on her the entire ambulance ride to the hospital. By some miracle, they got her heart beating right before the doctor called it."

"Wow."

"Yeah. That's one night I'll never forget. Her parents were bereft when they arrived. They had so many questions. They made me promise to make absolutely certain the man who hurt their daughter couldn't do it again. I double-checked everything with the coroner just to make sure we didn't screw anything up. We had his prints, DNA, the murder weapon, the camera, everything. He was in the midst of drowning her when we arrived on the scene. There's not a single doubt in my mind. The man who attacked Daria is worm food."

"If that's true, who do you think is watching her now?"

"I have no idea. She called the police before she contacted me, but they couldn't help her."

"Why not?"

"They didn't find any indication she's being followed. But stalking's hard to prove. She thought I'd come up with something, but I haven't yet."

"Why did she reach out to you? Is it because you worked the Lightning Killer case?"

"It's because I promised I'd keep her safe."

"Never make promises you can't keep," I said.

"It's a good thing I fully intend to keep this one. That's why I'm asking for your help." From the way he winced, I wondered if saying those words caused Lucca physical pain.

"What does this guy look like? Does she know what he wants? Has he made any overt threats?" I thought about what Lucca said. "Why does she think the Lightning Killer's back?"

He hesitated, suddenly finding his menu fascinating.

"There's more to the story, isn't there?" I asked.

"The attack left Daria with a few impairments. She doesn't remember anything from the night she almost died. She doesn't remember the attack or the Lightning Killer. She only knows him from the photos she's seen. She remembers how she felt before the attack happened, how things had gone missing from her house and how she always felt eyes on her. The same things are happening again. Of course, she knows he's dead. But she can't quite shake that feeling. Since this is what happened last time, she thinks he's back to do it again."

"So you think someone else is terrorizing her, but she's gotten it into her head it must be the Lightning Killer returning to finish what he started?"

"Something like that."

"Do we have a description?" I asked.

"Not a good one."

I didn't like that answer either. Lucca wasn't usually this cagey. "What about a copycat or crazed groupie? Maybe the Lightning Killer had an apprentice, someone who's decided to pick up where he left off."

"I don't think so."

"Why not?"

"It's been a few years. Why would someone like that wait so long to surface?"

"He could have been incarcerated or institutionalized. He could be active military. Maybe he just got back stateside."

"That's a stretch, even for one of your theories."

"That doesn't make it impossible."

"Just improbable."

Before either of us could say anything else, the waiter came to take our orders. Lucca opted for a lamb chop. "I thought you wanted lobster," I said.

"Lamb reheats easier. I'm not sure I have much of an appetite."

"Make that two," I said to the waiter. He left without another word. "Daria survived one psycho, and now she's being stalked by another one. Do you think your fancy FBI badge might be enough to convince this creep to back off?"

"It's not that simple. We don't know who he is."

"Daria doesn't know him?"

"No. I've tailed her a few times, but I've never spotted anyone. The same's true of every cop and agent she's spoken to about this. No one's found any evidence to back her claims." Lucca nodded down at the folder I had yet to open.

"Have you tried staking out her house?"

"That was the first thing I did. I even called in a few favors and had some guys at the precinct keep an eye out. They never spotted anyone."

"How exactly is this guy terrorizing her?" I asked. "Phone calls and e-mails can be traced."

"He hasn't communicated with her."

I leaned back, realizing most of what Lucca told me didn't make much sense. "Daria claims someone is watching her. She calls the cops, but they don't do anything. So she calls you. You look into it, but you can't find anything. What exactly is this unsub doing that has her so freaked out? Has he left threatening messages in her mailbox? Keyed her car? Broken her windows?"

"None of the above." Lucca turned his attention to the table, picking up his fork and polishing it with his napkin.

"All right, spill. What am I missing?"

"I'm not entirely sure the guy she's seeing is real."

"You think she's making it up?"

"No," he shook his head for emphasis, "but she has some issues. The attack put her in a coma for a few weeks. She has permanent brain damage and memory problems. Her vision and hearing are partially impaired too. Almost dying has left her with a lot of anxiety. She's doing the best she can, but the police don't necessarily believe her. They think she's crying wolf. It might not be the first time this has happened."

"Jeez." I eyed him. "Do you believe her?"

"She believes it," Lucca said. "I checked her townhouse. I even spent a couple of nights camped outside her place. I didn't see anything suspicious, but I don't know. I might have missed something."

"You said the police checked too."

"That doesn't mean much. Not in cases like this, not under these conditions."

"Do you think there's a legitimate threat?"

"Probably not, but what if I'm wrong? I promised her she'd be safe from now on. I told her I'd keep her safe. What if someone is watching her, waiting to strike? I can't let that happen again. I just can't. Surely, you of all people must understand that."

"I do, but I never thought you did. If our roles were reversed, what would you tell me to do in this situation?"

"C'mon, Parker, for once in your life, don't be a hardass."

"Did you cross any lines on this one, boy scout?"

"No."

"Are you sure? It's not uncommon for victims to fall for the guy who saved the day."

"You know me. I'd never take advantage like that."

"When did you get married?" Lucca and his wife had a two-year-old daughter named Grace. But I wasn't sure how long they'd been married before she arrived.

"This anniversary will make it six years." He stared at me. "Don't do that. I didn't cheat on my wife. I would never cheat on my wife."

It was equally common for the white knight to fall for the damsel in distress, but I didn't share that with my former partner. He'd attended the same lectures and seminars at Quantico that I had. "I never said you would. I was just curious." But when we worked together, I'd gone to extreme lengths to avoid details of Lucca's personal life. He knew I asked for a reason.

When I fell silent, he nudged me. "Daria needs someone who will make her feel safe again. I don't know if someone's out to get her, but I can't take that chance. Not after she's already suffered so much. I was hoping, as a Cross Security employee, you could do some digging and put her mind at ease."

"What are you thinking? A 24/7 protection detail? A personal bodyguard?"

"Whatever you can swing."

"I'll have to talk to Cross and see who's available. I'm guessing this is a pro bono assignment."

"Charity's good for the soul."

"I agree, but I'm not sure Cross will see it that way. His biggest concern is usually the bottom line, not eternal damnation. But I'll do what I can." Lucien Cross would not be happy about this. He already hated that I often worked freelance for law enforcement. Lucca's request might be unofficial, but my boss wouldn't see it that way. And he had a thing about working murder investigations. The serial killer aspect made two strikes. With an unreliable witness, that made three. Luckily, after my last case, he owed me. Big time.

"You should investigate. I trust you. You have good instincts. If I missed something, you'll find it."

"Flattery will get you nowhere." I was already committed to helping Lucca. But as his former partner, it was my job to bust his chops a little.

He gave me that hardened FBI stare of his. "Come on. You owe me."

"A lot of that going around," I muttered.

The waiter returned with two steaming plates. I moved the folder to the side, so he could place my dinner in front of me. "Fresh pepper?" he asked.

"No, thanks," I said. Lucca shook his head, and the waiter retreated back to the kitchen. I picked up my fork and knife and cut the meat. "Maybe I should have ordered liver."

"Parker," Lucca growled.

"Relax. I'll do it. You know I can't say no to you."

"Since when? You used to tell me no all the time."

"I never told you no."

He rolled his eyes. "Fine, but you never listened. Apparently, that hasn't changed. You always did what you wanted, when you wanted, consequences be damned."

"You know how I am with a case. It's just how I'm wired." Sometimes, I wished I could turn it off for everyone's sake. "Why did you go through this whole song and dance routine? You could have brought this to me at work and cashed in your chit. We didn't have to meet for dinner." I shoveled a bite into my mouth and chewed. The lamb was tender and perfectly seasoned. Once reheated, it wouldn't be as good.

"How else was I going to get you to talk to me? You were ducking my calls."

"Because I wanted to avoid dinner. Things go sideways when we're in close proximity to one another."

"You need to get over your neuroses. I know you're afraid of what will happen if we work together again. But nothing's going to happen. No one's going to get stabbed or shot."

"You can't be certain of that."

"If something happens, that's not on you. Agreed?" He chuckled. "What am I saying? Of course, you won't agree. You have the worst martyr complex I've ever seen. It's always your fault. Aren't you working on that in therapy?"

"I'm not in therapy."

"Really?" He looked surprised. "You should be."

I'd been attending group meetings in a church basement, but Lucca didn't know about that. At least, I didn't think he did. "I'll do this on one condition." I pointed a finger at him. "The same rules apply to you. If something happens, it's not on you either. Agreed?"

"But I promised her."

"I know. But you did your best. Now step aside and let a professional handle it."

TWO

After parting ways with Lucca, I returned to the office. At this time of night, the place was practically dead. Most Cross Security investigators did their best to maintain normal business hours. The security teams were out on assignment, so only the skeleton crew of techs and medics remained.

I grabbed a cup of coffee from the break room, stowed my leftovers, and settled in behind my desk. The file Lucca had given me was massive, so I moved to the couch and coffee table.

The first thing I had to do was make sure the Lightning Killer was dead. According to FBI records, Andrew Holland was the infamous serial killer, and he'd been killed by responding officers. OPR had cleared the agents involved in the shooting, as had the PD's internal affairs unit. Holland was the only other person at the scene besides Daria. When officers and agents entered, he pulled a gun and was killed.

That went along with Lucca's retelling of the events from that night. But I didn't doubt that's what happened. I just wondered if Holland was the notorious serial killer. The FBI and local police departments never found much in the way of forensic evidence. Holland hadn't left fingerprints or DNA behind at the other scenes. But since they'd interrupted him mid-kill, they'd found all kinds of things inside Daria's apartment.

I looked at the other crime scene photos. The Lightning Killer had drowned each of his victims before dressing them and posing them like dolls. Each of his victims' apartments was immaculate, which meant he'd cleaned up everything when he set the scene. That explained the lack of prints and DNA, but it didn't sit right with me.

Flipping to the end, I examined the photos taken after Holland's death. The FBI had found eleven photographs depicting each of the previous crime scenes inside Holland's car. The clerk at the camera store positively identified Holland. Surveillance footage had a rough approximation of what the killer looked like, but it wasn't enough for facial recognition to get any hits.

A few stills had been printed and were included in the file. I picked them up and looked at them. Each had been taken in a different city, but the killer always wore the same red sneakers. Those were the same sneakers Holland wore the night he attacked Daria.

I put the photos down and picked up the report. As I suspected, after Holland's death, the techs combed through every bit of footage they could find. The man with the red sneakers had been stalking Daria for an entire month before he struck. He'd even gone so far as to break into her apartment when she was out.

I had no idea what he'd taken. I couldn't find the details included anywhere in the report, but surveillance footage showed him sneaking in through her fire escape window while she was out. He'd invested a lot of time and effort when it came to stalking his prey. If Daria was being stalked now, whoever was terrorizing her was following Holland's playbook.

All Holland's planning and preparation paid off since it took the authorities so long to catch him. He'd killed eleven women over the course of two years before he was stopped. If they hadn't figured out he was printing his own photos and tracked down the equipment purchased to a store in the metro area, he might still be killing.

That left me with one major question. Since Holland wasn't terrorizing Daria this time, who was?

Getting up, I went to the computer. Keying in Andrew Holland's name and alias, I hit enter and leaned back while Cross Security's extensive database populated my screen with dozens of hits. The Lightning Killer was dead, but that didn't mean his antics hadn't caught the attention of some other psycho who hoped to emulate the serial killer or complete his legacy.

While my computer found tons of search results, I familiarized myself with everything the Bureau had on Holland, but since they hadn't known much about him until he was caught, they didn't have any details regarding his known associates. As far as the FBI was concerned, Holland worked alone.

He never strayed from the victimology. He always chose female artists in their mid-thirties. The type of art varied, from painters to clothing designers to commercial artists. But the women were similar enough. Each had attended art school and was on the rise. Unfortunately, none of them attended the same art school, which made figuring out how they'd gotten on Holland's radar even more difficult.

Holland was an art school dropout who specialized in photography. Whatever caused him to leave art school was probably the same thing that helped him decide on his victims. After all, nothing was more frightening to a man than a successful woman in the same field.

In his early twenties, Holland had been arrested a few times for vandalism, larceny, and illegal trespass. He'd gotten a fine and some community service each time. While these offenses seemed minor, they were prerequisites to stalking, terrorizing, and eventually killing his victims.

I searched every police report I could find, even going so far as to place several late night calls to other jurisdictions and fudging on the details concerning my identity in order to get the specifics. But Holland had never been arrested with anyone else. He'd always been brought in alone, and the police had no reason to believe he was working with anyone when he was tagging billboards or wandering into unlocked buildings.

Returning to the file Lucca gave me, I read the rest of the case report. Holland picked his targets and watched them, finding ways into their homes and cars without them noticing. He'd take objects, clothing, or tools of their art, probably to keep as trophies or to test the waters. All the missing items had been discovered inside Holland's mailbox. Instead of traveling back and forth, he'd mail the items to himself for safe keeping. That was a smart move, at least until he was caught. The tiny voice in the back of my head couldn't help but think that'd be a great way to frame someone. But I was paranoid and a bit delusional, so I let the thought pass.

Given how Holland played with the FBI agents assigned to capture him, I assumed he did the same with his victims. He broke into their homes and took something they'd be sure to miss, either to confuse or scare them. After all, knowing someone had been inside one's house was all sorts of creepy.

He waited for them to be most vulnerable and drowned them. Then he photographed the murders, like it was just another art project. It was sickening. And he did it over and over again as he worked his way across the country, growing ballsier as he taunted the FBI by sending them photos of his future victims. But without the victim's name or location, facial recognition never got a hit before he struck.

I skimmed each of the entries the computer spit out. The news media had gone crazy. Prior to his capture, their profiles varied wildly. But everyone agreed on one thing; the Lightning Killer worked alone.

It was hard to argue with that kind of consensus. But I had to be certain someone else wasn't involved. Daria insisted the killer was back. Maybe she was crazy, and maybe I was just as crazy for believing her. But I told Lucca I'd do my best, which is what I was doing. So I started my search where this began for Holland—art school.

Social media hadn't been as prevalent back then, but it still existed. The few photos I found of him were taken in various art studios. I couldn't find any personal photos or private images.

Picking up the phone, I dialed Amir's extension. He was one of Cross Security's technical experts with advanced training in forensic and computer sciences. He normally didn't work nights, but the boss had him working late this week on a top secret project. So I hoped he'd still be around.

"What can I do for you, Ms. Parker?" Amir asked.

I explained the situation. "I want to know if Holland was close to anyone. Someone might be acting on his behalf by terrorizing his final victim."

"I'll see what I can find. Do you need a rush on this?"

"Sooner would be better than later."

Amir made a humming noise. "Does Mr. Cross know you're working on this?"

"Not yet." I still had to ask Cross if he could spare a security team to watch Daria, but that could wait until tomorrow, after I had a chance to suss out the legitimacy of the threat.

"Once you get his approval, I'll bump this up the list. You have access to the lab and our resources, but your cases can't be prioritized over Cross Security's. And you know Mr. Cross's stance on murder investigations and police matters."

"This isn't either."

"Maybe not now, but it was at one point. I want to help, but I have to follow orders."

"I understand."

"I'll give it a quick look and let you know if I find anything within the hour."

"Thanks, Amir."

While Amir was digging into Holland's personal history, I did some searching on my own. I had worked this gig solo before. I couldn't let all my skills go to waste.

An internet search on Andrew Holland's name turned up plenty of websites. True crime was big business. People were fascinated by unsolved murders and highly publicized killings. Dozens, if not hundreds, of podcasts, shows, books, and movies were dedicated to such things. And not everyone who followed this stuff did so innocently.

The Lightning Killer was a known celebrity among the true crime crowd. The majority of these podcasts and message boards reported and dramatized the events, increasing the scare factor. Most of the people who frequented these places were amateur sleuths or crime drama junkies. I dismissed those easily enough, but a few posts glorified Holland's kills.

The most vocal weren't always the most dangerous, but since Daria believed the killer was back, any one of these fanatics could be responsible for her recent unease. Sickened, I called Lucca.

"Parker?" He sounded as though he'd been asleep. "Is something wrong?"

I looked at the time, wondering how it could possibly be after midnight. "I'm e-mailing you a list of websites. You should run the administrators and anyone who's active in the comments. From what I've read, some of these whack jobs act like Holland's a god." I rambled off several handles while I typed them into the e-mail, figuring Lucca might not remember this in the morning. I continued scrolling through the posts and comments, but I didn't see Daria's name or address listed anywhere. The details concerning Holland's final victim had been withheld from the media for security reasons and had been sealed and redacted from public documents. Gaining access to that information would be difficult but not impossible if someone knew where to look.

"Hang on a sec." Lucca came back after checking the message I sent. "Yeah, I already explored those possibilities."

"And?"

"None of them have gotten close to Daria."

"How can you be sure?"

"It's called the worldwide web for a reason. Only one or two of these wackos are in the city, and the few who are haven't gone anywhere near Daria. I ran them each down, including alibis for the dates and times she claims to have seen someone watching her."

"Are you sure no one tracked her down and came here

to find her?"

"I already exhausted that possibility, but I'm glad you're taking this seriously."

"I told you I would."

He yawned. "Will Cross swing a protection detail?"

"I haven't asked yet."

"Don't wait too long."

"It's fine. I got this. Go back to sleep, Lucca. I'll see you tomorrow."

He grunted good night and hung up.

Parker, what have you gotten yourself into this time? the voice in the back of my head asked. I didn't have an answer. All I knew was I had a debt to repay. But I didn't like pissing off serial killers or serial killer wannabes. I'd done it enough in the past, and I'd learned my lesson.

Drumming my fingers against the desk, I scanned the entries on my screen for a few more minutes before giving up. The internet was full of vitriol. But most people were all talk and no action. It was usually the quiet ones who caused the most damage.

I'd just picked up the file to see if it contained any information on Daria Waylon's next of kin or potential witnesses when my phone rang. I fished it out of my pocket, smiling when I saw the name on the caller ID.

"Hey, beautiful," James Martin said, "am I calling too late?"

"Not at all." I dropped onto the couch, glad to hear his voice. "How was your day?"

"Better now." I could hear him smile. "Today was like pulling teeth. Two steps forward, and four steps back. I don't understand why things aren't getting done. No one wants to give me a straight answer. You'd think I wanted to know something complicated. All I asked was if they wanted to move ahead on this project and what the timetable might look like."

"It's corporate America. You should be used to getting the runaround by now."

"I'm used to the usual bullshit, but this is something else. They're all a bunch of indecisive morons."

"What's the problem?" I asked.

"No one has the balls to pass on the project or to sign on. They have to think about it or present it to the board or get approval from their stockholders. It's ridiculous. I'm starting to think this is because no one wants to be tied to the scandal with Lucien Cross."

"But that was resolved. He was cleared."

"I know, but it's complicated."

I licked my lips. "Do you think your history plays a factor in this?" Martin had been wrongly accused of killing a woman on his yacht. His name had been cleared quickly, but since his business partner, my current boss, had recently found himself in a similar predicament, business tycoons might have taken notice. Who would want to go into business with two wrongfully accused killers, well, besides me?

"I don't know."

"Why don't you forget it and come home?"

"You want me to give up?"

"No, I want you to come home. I miss you."

"I miss you too. How was dinner with Lucca? I'm sorry I couldn't make it."

"Lucca blindsided me by asking for a favor."

"Should I be concerned?"

"If I say yes, will you come home?"

Martin laughed. "You miss me that much?"

"Not you. Marcal and Bruiser. Your valet keeps the fridge stocked, and your bodyguard's always good for a sparring match. I'm not sure how I survived so long without them."

"Rosemarie said you haven't been home at all since I left."

"How would your housekeeper know? She only comes to clean every other week."

"Alex," Martin said in that tone that meant he knew exactly what I was doing, "how are you? Really? Do I need to come home? Because I will."

"I'm okay."

"Are you sure?"

"Yes."

"Good. Are you still planning on flying out this

weekend? I can't wait to show you the house in Malibu. It's incredible. You're going to love it. And I have a surprise for you."

"You know how I feel about surprises."

"I'm sure you'll enjoy this one."

"Like the last surprise you brought me when you came home two weeks ago?" I snickered at the memory. "Because I don't think that counts since I wasn't particularly surprised."

"But you enjoyed it. Multiple times, if I remember correctly."

My cheeks heated. Luckily, no one was around to see me blush. "So did you."

"I most certainly did."

"Do you want to know what I'm wearing right now?" I asked, my voice husky.

Martin chuckled. "You can't distract me that easily. We were discussing our weekend plans. Are you flying out to see me? We said we'd alternate every other week. It's your turn."

"I don't know yet."

"How can you not know, especially when you miss me as much as you do?" He snorted. "Wait, I'm sorry, I meant to say especially when you miss Marcal and Bruiser. Because they'll be here too."

"I know, but this thing with Lucca might get in the way."

"Don't let it."

"I'm not sure that's an option. Why don't you fly back this weekend instead? It sounds like you could use a break."

"I have meetings Friday and Monday. If I do, we won't have much time together. Plus, if the Board hears I'm in town, they'll want an update on the progress I'm making, and I'll lose half of Saturday doing that, like last time."

"Don't you update them during the week?"

"Every damn day. I'm still working East Coast hours, so I spend the first part of my day on the phone with Luc Guillot and everyone else at the flagship MT building, getting updates on the things I'm missing before everyone else shows up to work. And then I spend the rest of the day running things at this branch and looking for investors for my new project. No matter what I do, it never feels like enough."

"Workaholic."

"Says the woman who's been camping out in her office ever since I flew back to L.A."

"I'll make a deal with you. When you come home, so will I."

"Does that also apply to the house in Malibu?" he asked.

"We'll see."

"I'll be waiting."

THREE

By morning, I was convinced Andrew Holland had worked alone. Amir's search hadn't found anything, and none of the supposed internet experts on the Lightning Killer had any theories to the contrary. That left three possibilities. Daria was being stalked by an unknown suspect. Andrew Holland's ghost was haunting her. Or she was imagining the entire thing. I knew two of those weren't true. I just wasn't sure which two.

I stood behind Lucca, surveying my surroundings. Rows of townhouses lined both sides of the cul-de-sac. From what I could tell, this was your typical suburban neighborhood. It wasn't particularly upscale with its cracked sidewalks and peeling paint, but it was a safe place to live.

"Did you ring the bell?" I asked.

"I know how doors work. Just give her a minute. She's probably eating lunch," Lucca said.

"You're the one who set up this meeting. Maybe you should have waited until later in the afternoon."

Even though I couldn't see his face, I knew he rolled his eyes. "This was the only time I could get away from work," he said.

"What kind of case did Jablonsky assign you?"

Lucca glanced over his shoulder. "You'll never lose that itch."

"What itch? I'm making polite conversation by taking an interest in your life."

"Sure, you are."

The heavy door banged open. The hinges squeaked loudly. The woman on the other side flinched. She rubbed her right ear, making the large silver hoop hanging from her earlobe jangle against the smaller gold hoops hanging beside it while the tortoise shell glasses flopped up and down on her nose. She had a small jade colored stud in her left nostril.

She stared up at the top hinge. "I need to get that fixed." She looked at Lucca, her mouth opening in a wide smile. "You heard that, right?"

"Yep." Lucca stepped closer, squinting at the hinge. "It didn't do that the last time I was here."

"I know, but it rained. The door always sticks when the humidity is high. I must have gone a little crazy tugging on it and knocked something out of whack."

Rain? It hadn't rained in the last two weeks, but I kept my mouth shut. Maybe she didn't use her front door that often.

"I'll take a look at it before we leave." Lucca stepped to the side. "Daria Waylon, this is my friend, Alex Parker."

She swallowed uncomfortably, her smile tightening. "Nice to meet you."

"Likewise," I said. Lucca warned me she was skittish around new people. I kept my hands at my sides and didn't move toward her.

"Alex was my partner when I originally transferred here from D.C. She works private security now. She's one of the best. I think she can help."

"I remember. We discussed this on," she bit her lip and turned around to look at something behind her, "Monday."

"That's right," Lucca said. "Is it okay if we come inside?"

"Oh," Daria blinked a few times and stepped backward, "right. Come in. Just wipe your feet."

Lucca rubbed the soles of his shoes on the welcome mat before entering her home. "How have you been these last two days? Has anything else happened since we spoke?"

"I heard scratching at the window last night, but I didn't see anyone. I called the police station, but the patrol officer didn't find anything out of the ordinary."

"Did he check outside your window?" I asked, following Lucca's lead and checking the bottoms of my shoes before stepping inside. First impressions were important.

"He says he did." Daria glanced out the window. "You can ask him yourself. He's been out there ever since."

I turned, seeing the nose of a police car poking out from around the corner. "I'll do that after we have a chance to speak."

The front door led to a narrow hallway, which branched off in two directions. To my right was the living room, which opened into the dining room and circled around to what I assumed must be the kitchen. The living room and dining room were pristine. Not a single thread was out of place.

Daria led us past these rooms and down the hallway, glancing back every two steps. Ten feet later, the hallway ended in a large room. Another hallway jutted off to my left, leading to the bedroom and bathroom. From here, I could see a washer and dryer built into an alcove in the wall.

Daria slumped into a desk chair, swiveling to face us. The desk in front of her was covered in piles of fabric, sketchbooks, and planners. A three foot by six foot whiteboard hung on the wall beside her desk. It had been sectioned off with black tape to make a monthly calendar. A stack of journals sat on a nearby folding chair. She reached for the top journal and flipped back a few pages. Using her finger, she scanned the lines.

"Did anything else happen?" Lucca asked after she had time to read.

"That was it. Just the scratching at the window. The cop said it was probably a blowing branch. He didn't find any footprints or anything. No signs of tampering."

"That's a relief," Lucca said.

Daria frowned at him. "Great, so I'm insane." She sighed. "More insane."

"You're not insane."

Daria climbed out of the chair and went into the kitchen. She picked up a half-eaten sandwich and took a bite, wiping the mayo from the corner of her mouth. "Would you guys like something to eat?"

"No, thank you," I said.

She pointed to the coffeepot. "Help yourselves. I made that fresh, just for you."

"Thanks." Lucca grabbed two mugs from a nearby cabinet. He filled them, replaced the pot, and opened the fridge to grab some milk. Based on his behavior, he must have spent a great deal of time here. "Milk or cream?" he asked me.

"Either."

He poured a splash of half and half into each mug and handed me one. Then he took the pitcher of iced tea out of the fridge, filled a glass, and put it beside Daria. I cocked an eyebrow at him, but he shook away my unasked question.

While she ate, I wandered around her square kitchen. It had two openings. One led to her workspace, and the other led to the dining room. The view from each opening could make a person think she was looking at two separate homes.

"Alex," Lucca patted the chair beside him, "maybe Daria will give you a tour later."

"Right, sorry." I sat down while Daria finished her lunch.

"Don't be." She blotted her lips with the napkin. "I get it. I must look and sound like a crazy person."

"Not really."

"Well, I feel like one."

"Do you want to tell me what's going on?" I asked. "Eddie's already filled me in on the basics, but I'd prefer hearing everything from you."

"What is it you do exactly?" She reached for a pen and a pad of sticky notes.

"A little bit of everything," I said out of habit. Lucca nudged me beneath the table. He'd warned me the previous night to be as straightforward as possible. "I'm a private investigator. I work for Cross Security."

She scribbled that down, as if it might be on a test later. "Phone number."

I gave her the number for Cross's main line, and then I gave her my cell number. "I've provided protection and security before."

"Like a bodyguard?" she asked.

"Yes."

She stopped writing and focused on Lucca. "Has it come down to this?"

"I don't think so, Dar. Nothing indicates you're in danger, but you said you don't feel safe. I wish I had more time and resources to devote to this. But I don't. Alex is the next best thing."

I resisted the urge to comment.

"That's because no one believes a threat exists." She chewed on the end of the pen. "The police said my risk is low. They ran an assessment."

"So did I," Lucca said. "Alex will too, if you'll allow it."

Daria leaned back in her chair. "I know what I saw. He was outside my window. I saw him. I've seen him more than once. Following me on the street. Waiting for me when I come home. He only gets so close before backing off. He's playing with me. I know it. I can feel it." She peered into the main room, which she used as her workspace. "Things are starting to disappear again. A pencil here. A piece of fabric there. I don't think I've misplaced them or forgotten about them. I think he took them, just like last time."

"Daria," Lucca said, his voice firm but gentle, "we've been over this. Andrew Holland, the Lightning Killer, is dead. He can't hurt you again."

Defiance reflected in her dark brown eyes, but she didn't argue. Instead, she brushed her long, raven-colored hair back behind her ear, revealing a hearing aid. "Are you sure?"

I had asked Lucca the same question the night before, but just like the night before, he said he was.

"That means it's someone else." She quietly cursed. "You know, this sucks. It's not bad enough one psycho nearly killed me, but now some other lunatic wants me dead. Do I have a sign on my back or something?"

"We don't know enough yet to reach that conclusion," Lucca said.

"Right." She dragged out the word. "Because no one believes me."

"I didn't say that," Lucca insisted.

"No, but you think it." She folded her arms over her chest, challenging him to deny it.

"Ms. Waylon," I interrupted, "can you describe the man you've seen following you?"

"He looks just like the man who ruined my life. He has light brown hair, and these dark, penetrating eyes. They're blank, soulless. They give me the creeps. That's how I know it's him. No one else has eyes like that."

"Was he tall?"

"I guess, but not freakishly so."

"So, not a basketball player?"

"No." The timer on her cell phone went off, and she pulled it out to check the notification before typing something and tucking it back into her pocket. "That's one thing I don't understand."

"What?" I asked.

"Basketball."

It was my turn to laugh. "You and me both."

She gave me a genuine smile, warming to my presence. "Good, because I thought it might be due to the brain injury."

I pulled a notebook out of my purse and jotted down the guy's description, which made her smile even more. "Was he fat? Thin?"

"I'd say average, but he looked strong. Athletic. Menacing."

"What was he wearing?"

"When?" she asked.

"The last time you saw him."

"That would have been last week, outside my bedroom window. He had on a red cap, red and white tennis shoes, a long black trench coat, and dark-colored cargo pants."

I wrote it down. "I'm impressed. Witnesses rarely

remember hair color. You seem to remember everything."

She snorted cynically. "Eddie didn't tell you?"

I glanced at my former partner. "What?"

"I have a lot of trouble forming new memories. I have to make notes on everything, just so I'll remember if I ate or took a shower. I don't remember what he wore, but I can still read." She pointed to the fridge where she'd written the time, date, and location of her last encounter. It included the man's clothing and description. A few other sheets had been stuck to the fridge, detailing her earlier encounters. "As soon as he left, I wrote it down so I wouldn't forget. Just like when you leave, I'll write that down too. If I read it enough and review it enough, some things eventually stick. Not everything is a black hole, but a lot is."

That explained the squeaky hinges on her front door. "I can't imagine how difficult that must be. I'm sorry this happened to you," I said.

She let out an ugly laugh. "Oddly enough, that is one thing I can't seem to forget."

I turned to study her notes, copying down what she'd written instead of asking more questions. "Do you recall anything about these other encounters?"

"Flashes mostly. The red on his shoes sticks out in my mind. He always wears them, but the rest of his ensemble changes. But I recognize him. I know him. I remember drips and drabs about the man who did this to me. The person I keep seeing, that's him. His clothes and car might change, but it's still him. I can't shake that, just like how I can't shake the way seeing him again makes me feel. The only way I can describe it is like waking up from a nightmare. You know how scared you are, but you're not sure exactly why."

"Are these the only notes you made?"

"No, I have more. Lots more."

"May I see them?"

"I made copies for you. They're on my desk."

"Not to sound insensitive, but how do you remember that?"

"I've seen them at least a dozen times since I put them

there. Repeated exposure leads to memory formation. Once you take them, I'll probably look for them a few times before I remember you took them, which is why I make notes. It's weird how my brain works now, but it's gotten better over the years. The doctors think my mind is finding ways to compensate for the deficit. When I first got out of the hospital, I couldn't hold on to anything for more than a matter of minutes. Now it's hours or days. Depending on the situation, sometimes, long-term memories form." She held up her phone. "Do you mind if I take a photo? I trained myself to put names to faces. It helps my brain form connections faster."

Lucca had explained her flashcard method of remembering people by looking at photos and quizzing herself on the facts. Eventually, it'd stick, just like multiplication tables.

"Go ahead." I waited for her to take the photo.

Daria checked the screen, tapped against it, added a tag, and tucked it away. "What do you think about this? Now that you know how it works, how my brain doesn't work, do you still want to help me?"

"I wouldn't be here if I didn't." But my internal voice had doubts. Daria couldn't be certain of herself, so how could I be certain of her? Lucca warned me about this last night, but we figured it'd be best to put Daria's mind at ease. Now, I wasn't sure that was even possible. "Would you mind showing me around?"

"Sure, follow me."

"I'll take a look at the front door while you do that," Lucca offered.

Daria gave him a puzzled look. "Why?"

"The hinges squeak," he said.

"Oh," she shook her head, "right." But the befuddled look didn't fade.

Shaking it off, she led me through the immaculate dining room and into the living room. From there, we looped around to her work area before she led me toward the bedrooms. She pointed out the guest bathroom, linen closet, laundry alcove, and the guest room.

"You said you heard tapping at the window last night.

Where were you when that happened?"

"In bed."

"Do you remember that?"

"Yes. Traumatic things stick. The tapping happened when I was getting ready to fall asleep."

"Did you have your glasses or hearing aid in when this occurred?"

She stared at the floor, shaking her head no. "I know how that sounds, but I heard something out there. I'm sure it was him."

"How is your vision and hearing?" I asked.

"I can get around the house without my glasses, but I can't see my cell phone screen without them. My hearing's only impaired on one side. I can hear, just not well."

"What about the other times you saw him lingering near your home? What were you doing then?"

"The time before was right after I got out of the shower. I had my glasses on, but the window was fogged up. Maybe I hallucinated that too," she said cynically.

"I never said that, Ms. Waylon. I'm on your side. I want to stop whoever's doing this."

She searched my eyes, trying to determine if she believed me. "You can call me Daria. Mrs. Waylon's my mom." She flipped on a light, revealing her bedroom. "Let me show you where I was when it happened. These last two times, he's been in the backyard, right near the maple tree."

I froze in the doorway while she approached the window. Her bedroom looked more like her workspace. But it wasn't the rumpled bedcovers and notebooks everywhere that gave me pause. It was the religious shrine along the back wall. Religious icons hung on the walls and were propped up against the mirrored back of her two-tiered dresser. Statues of saints lined the top tier of the dresser, their eyes staring down at us. Symbols were painted on the ceiling and were carefully sewn into the throw rugs and various tapestries.

She turned, realizing I wasn't behind her. "Alex?"

"Sorry, I was just admiring your devotion. That's quite a collection."

She frowned at the figures. "It's not for us to understand. Like everyone says, it's a miracle I survived. Still, I'd like to know why all this shit happens."

"You and me both." I went to the window. Her backyard was small. Tall wooden boards separated the connected yards along the back of the townhouse. But only on either side. The back remained open. Near the end of the property stood a tall, red maple tree. None of the branches were low enough for a person to climb, but the trunk was thick enough and positioned close enough to the fence to allow a person to remain undetected or slip away quickly if spotted. I didn't like it.

I went into her bathroom and peered out the small window next to the counter. From beside the tree, a person could see clearly into the bathroom. And since Daria only had a sheer curtain hanging over the window, it'd be easy to see inside at night.

The tour continued. The second floor was smaller than the main level. It contained two smaller bedrooms. One had been converted into a storage area, where she kept her holiday decorations and some workout equipment. The other she used as an art studio. The loft, near the staircase, had a couch and TV.

"Do you spend a lot of time up here?" I asked.

"Some. Just to work, mostly."

I peered into the upstairs bathroom. The windows on this level all had blinds, which were closed. "What's that?" I nodded to a closed door.

"The utility closet. Aside from cobwebs and cables, you won't find anything in there."

"All right, let's see if Lucca's made any progress on the front door. Then I'll check outside and see if there are any structural weaknesses. From in here, everything looks good. But you could use some thicker curtains in your bathroom."

"I have some. I just haven't bothered to hang them."

"You should get around to doing that sooner, instead of later."

"Okay." She took out her phone and set a reminder. "What happens after that?"

"After you hang the curtains?"

"No, after you look around outside?"

"I'll speak to the patrol officer. If he doesn't have anything helpful to say, I'll check with the precinct before going back to the office. I'm going to do everything I can to find the guy you keep seeing."

She scribbled something down on her stack of sticky notes. "That sounds like a plan."

FOUR

The cop outside didn't have anything to say, not that I thought he would. If someone had been outside Daria's house, he was long gone by the time the police arrived. I didn't find anything to contradict the officer's findings, but Lucca asked me to be thorough. So I was being thorough.

At the precinct, I picked up a copy of the 9-1-1 recordings and the reports the responding officers filed each time Daria called for help. According to police records, the precinct hadn't received any 9-1-1 calls from Daria's address prior to two months ago. But in the last six weeks, they'd received eight calls. They were convinced she was crying wolf.

I understood why they'd think that. Each time officers investigated, they never found any evidence backing her claims. When they spoke to the neighbors, no one reported seeing anything out of the ordinary. But Lucca didn't think Daria was making this up. Even I could tell she believed it. Unfortunately, that didn't mean the threat was real.

"The lady lives alone. Maybe she's just scared," the cop who responded to her first 9-1-1 call said.

"I'd be scared if I spotted some menacing figure following me. If some creepy guy in a trench coat was hanging around outside your house in the middle of the night, wouldn't that freak you out?"

He held up his palms. "Look, Ms. Parker, I'm not saying I know what's going on. All I'm saying is we get a lot of crank calls. Each time we investigate one, it leaves someone else who needs our help at risk. And the way it's looking, Ms. Waylon's seeing nothing but ghosts. You find something solid, bring it to us, and I'll be happy to investigate further."

"I get it. I do. But this isn't a normal situation. Daria's scared. Her feelings are genuine, even if her mind's a little foggy on recalling details. She's been through a lot. You need to cut her some slack."

"We're trying." But he was getting tired of this. "When we have the resources available, we leave a patrol unit outside her place to keep watch. That request came from the FBI field office. I'm guessing she has friends in high places. Is that why Cross Security's looking into this? Did she hire you?"

"Not exactly."

"Why the interest?"

"The FBI asked us to look into it too." That wasn't completely true, but Lucca worked for the OIO, a branch of the FBI, and even though he asked for a favor in an unofficial capacity, as far as I was concerned, Lucca was always on the job.

I went back to the office to see what I could dig up. None of Daria's neighbors had reported suspicious activity in the last two months. Aside from Daria's 9-1-1 calls, no one on that street had requested emergency services. In fact, no crimes had been reported in the area in the last six months.

I hadn't noticed anything suspicious when I looked around outside her house. Nothing indicated she was under surveillance. The only one watching her was the patrol unit outside. If someone was stalking her, surely, one of the cops would have noticed something. But no one had.

Frustrated, I leafed through the intel Amir had compiled, but research on a dead man wouldn't result in a hot lead. I closed the files and rubbed a hand down my face. Resisting the urge to pace, I filled my lungs and started building a profile on Daria Waylon.

The only way to find her stalker was to learn more about her. However, since the attack, Daria had done all she could to vanish into obscurity. I'd need to figure out who she was before Holland flipped her life upside down.

Daria had been an average student from a small town. Her mom and dad owned and operated a fast food franchise. They'd encouraged Daria to pursue her dreams.

She'd graduated from a well-known art institute in D.C. She'd been one of the premier fiber artists. Her work had been on display in galleries, and she'd been featured in various modern shows. Some of her more elaborate pieces had sold for thousands of dollars. As an up-and-comer, she'd been featured in art publications—magazines, blogs, and podcasts. That's probably why Holland targeted her.

Daria didn't have any prior run-ins with the law. As far as I could tell, she'd never crossed paths with Holland. But the art world was tight-knit. They might have met at some point, but I had no way of knowing that. From what I gathered, they didn't have anyone in common. If they did, the FBI would have found it.

"Focus," I scolded myself. I had to figure out who wanted to harm Daria, not who already had.

Daria had been attacked six years ago. Her life today looked completely different from her life back then. She only kept in touch with a few of her friends, but Lucca had already checked into them. Her parents came to visit every few months. In fact, they had returned home the day before Daria first noticed someone watching her.

Could that be a coincidence? I was conditioned not to believe it, but I couldn't fathom how her parents' departure correlated with an unknown stalker. However, if these sightings turned out to be nothing more than her imagination, her parents leaving could have triggered her somehow. Perhaps she was freaked out to be alone.

Unwilling to leave a stone unturned, I looked into her mom and dad. After finding their home phone number, I dialed. When Christina, Daria's mom, answered, I introduced myself. "There's no cause for alarm, Mrs. Waylon," I said. "I'm Eddie Lucca's ex-partner. He's one of the FBI agents who worked the Holland case."

"Yes, I remember Agent Lucca. Is something wrong?"

"Daria reached out to him recently. She thinks someone's stalking her. Since I work for a private security firm, Lucca asked me to provide protection for your daughter and assess the threat."

"I've spoken to Daria. You don't need to get dragged into this, Ms. Parker. There is no threat."

"I'm sorry. I don't quite understand."

Christina hesitated, weighing her words carefully. "This isn't the first time Daria has seen that monster. Ever since the attack, she's different. Her memories are fuzzy. We've taken her to doctors, specialists, and psychologists, hoping someone can do something. It's been a struggle. She'd been doing so well for so long. I thought she was finally over the hump, but after our last visit, she spiraled. I've been trying to convince her to move back home, but she doesn't want to give up yet. She says once the police catch this man, she'll be okay. But we all know there is no one for them to catch."

"You sound certain."

"I am." Though, her words sounded remorseful. "Unfortunately, this is the third time she's called me, frantic that someone has been inside her house. Usually, when this happens, her dad and I visit for a few days and show her everything's okay."

"Is that why you came to see her two months ago?"

"It was."

"And?"

"This time was different. We couldn't convince her no one was out to get her. In fact, she got mad at us because we didn't believe her. She told us to leave and that she'd figure something else out. I'm sorry she dragged you and Agent Lucca into this. Daria needs help. She shouldn't be on her own."

"She seems more than capable of living alone," I said.

"Physically, she is. Psychologically, I'm not sure. She's afraid all the time. It's no wonder she's seeing and hearing things again. The doctors said that could happen. Part of it could be repressed memories resurfacing, but my daughter's always had a very active imagination. When she gets anxious or stressed, her mind conjures up some scary things."

"I see."

"Don't misunderstand. I don't think she's making this up for attention. What she's seeing and feeling is very much real. But this wouldn't be the first time she's seen things no one else does. Her doctor warned us this could happen from time to time. He says it's best to let it run its course, so she can come to grips and recover from some of the trauma that demon inflicted on her."

"Is she under doctor's care now?" I asked, wondering if Lucca knew any of this.

"She has regular doctor's appointments every four months and still sees her psychiatrist once every two weeks."

"Do you know if she's mentioned her stalker to any medical professionals?"

"I'm sure she has, but since they haven't contacted me, I can only guess that means they do not believe her sightings are cause for alarm. I wish she'd just move back home. It'd make it easier on everyone."

"Doesn't Daria have a life here?" I asked, feeling defensive over a woman I only met a few hours ago.

"She does. And I don't want to take that away. I really don't. To be honest, I'm grateful. It's a miracle she survived. It's amazing how far she's come. She's strong, but I just don't know if she'll ever be able to overcome this. That sick bastard is haunting her. She sees him. Hears him. Feels him. He's nothing more than a vengeful spirit with unfinished business. I wish I knew how to free her from his grasp. We've tried everything, but he always comes back. When she moved out of the apartment where it happened, I thought she'd be free, that the evil was tethered to that place, but it seems it went with her. He went with her."

"There is another possibility to consider. Someone else could be stalking your daughter."

"No, you must be mistaken." From her tone, Mrs.

Waylon wouldn't hear of it. Daria wasn't the only one traumatized by the attack.

Deciding it was best not to argue, I switched gears. "Have you or your husband had any problems at home or in your community?"

"No."

"Do you have any money or drug issues?"

"Of course not. We're good people."

"I don't doubt that, but I had to ask. I'm sure you understand." I circled my desk. "Have you had any problems at work?"

"Not that I can think of."

"Did you fire any employees recently?"

"We haven't fired anyone."

"What about upset customers?"

"We always get a few, but nothing serious."

"Has anyone made any threats?"

"No."

"How many people know about Daria's circumstances and condition?"

"Everyone does, especially around here."

That meant an entire town could have blabbed Daria's identity on any one of the hundreds of online true crime forums. "Does anyone else visit Daria regularly? Relatives? Family friends? Daria's old friends?"

"I wouldn't know."

This was getting me nowhere. "What can you tell me about Daria's romantic life?"

"Romantic life?" Her mother practically snorted. "Daria stopped that after what happened. We thought it'd be best."

"I wasn't aware dating was decided by committee."

"Excuse me?"

One of these days, I'd learn to hold my tongue. "Was Daria seeing anyone before she was attacked?"

"Several people." Based on her tone, Mrs. Waylon didn't approve.

"Do you remember their names?"

"Why does it matter?"

"I'm not sure it does. But stalkers often feel they have an

intimate bond with the person they target. That could be true of a rejected suitor."

"That was six years ago. Why would someone like that come around now? Daria doesn't even live in the same city. How would they have found her?"

"Humor me, please, ma'am." She struck me as the type who would find the term respectful rather than insulting.

"You'd have better luck asking Daria about it. She always kept a diary. She probably has everyone's name written down in a little black book. Guys, girls, and everyone in between. I could never keep them straight." She laughed at her little joke. "I thought it was an art school thing. Maybe it was just part of the lifestyle. But no one ever made Daria happy. Art was her first love. Her only love. I doubt any of them would have felt a strong enough connection like the one you mentioned. Frankly, this is a waste of your time. Andrew Holland is the cause of my daughter's anguish. No one else."

FIVE

Lucien Cross's office door was closed. I leaned against his assistant's desk, waiting for Justin to look up. When he did, I could see the warning bells go off in his brain as if asking, *now what do you want?* "Can I help you with something, Ms. Parker?"

"Is the boss around?"

"He doesn't have much time."

"This won't take long." I stared at the nameplate on his door. "I'm surprised Cross is even here."

"You and me both." He pressed a button on the intercom. "Lucien, Ms. Parker would like a word with you."

Justin and I stared at the intercom, waiting for a response. Instead, Justin's cell phone buzzed. He flipped it over and read the screen.

"What's that about?" I nodded at the phone. "You already said he was inside, and we're too high up for Cross to jump out the window to avoid me. Why the secrecy?"

"Maybe he's giving the window a try. I wouldn't put it past him to sneak out," Justin teased. He came around the desk and opened the door. "Let me make sure he's still here. Hang on one second." He and Cross exchanged a look. "Do you want me to reschedule, boss? You could leave later tonight."

"That's not necessary," Cross said. He peered past his assistant. "I don't have all day, Alex. What's going on?"

Justin retreated from the doorway. I stepped inside, surprised Cross wasn't seated behind his desk, like he usually was. Instead, he was lying on the couch with several pillows propped up behind him. The skin beneath his newly grown beard was tinged a yellowish-green from where the bruise had yet to completely fade. He made no move to sit up. Instead, he turned off the screen on the tablet and placed it on his thighs.

"Shouldn't you be at home recuperating?" I asked. "It's only been a few weeks since someone tried to kill you."

"Is that why you wanted to speak to me?"

"No." I took a seat in the chair across from him. "Agent Lucca asked me to look into something for him."

"An FBI case?"

"Not exactly. A victim in one of Lucca's old cases claims she's being stalked. The police have nothing, and the man she says is stalking her is dead."

"Are they sure about that?"

"Funny, that's the first thing I asked too. But I'm positive he's in the ground."

Cross ran a hand through his hair. "I'm not surprised the authorities have no interest in this. What have you found so far?"

"A whole lot of nothing." I summarized the situation and the research I'd done.

Carefully, he sat up, keeping one hand on his side while he reached for his coffee. He took a sip and put the cup down. "I've seen this movie before. It's the one with the guy who tattoos everything on his body so he doesn't forget, right? Oh wait, it could be that other one, where the guy has to get the girl to fall in love with him every single day."

"It's neither." I narrowed my eyes. "But I never pegged you for a rom-com guy."

"I'm not."

"Your previous statement suggests otherwise."

"I don't have time for this. Get to the point. What do you want?"

"Amir can't put a rush on my requests without your approval."

"Fine." He reached for his cell phone and sent a text. That explained why he hadn't responded to Justin via the intercom. "Anything else?"

"Until I figure out what's going on, I'd like to assign a team to keep an eye out. Do you have any security personnel you can spare?"

Cross got up and went behind his desk. Leaning over, he clicked a few keys. "Farzen's team is available until Tuesday. After that, we'll have to figure something else out." He hit the intercom button and told Justin to let the team know they had a new assignment. "Alex will brief them. She's running point."

"Yes, sir," Justin said.

Cross eyed me. "Is there any chance Daria Waylon wants to sign a contract with Cross Security?"

"I don't know." I hadn't even considered asking.

"Find out. Less than a decade ago, she was on the rise. Then she faded into obscurity." He clicked a few keys on the computer. "Is she planning a comeback? I've heard rumors she has plans for something major, something the art world has been anxiously awaiting."

"I don't know anything about it."

He frowned at the screen. "The value of her art has greatly diminished. According to this, she works mainly on commission now. She's practically a commercial artist. She even has an online store with items she can make and customize." He shook his head and closed the window. "Did you notice if she was working on any new projects?"

"Is this about your bottom line and signing more A-list clients? Because I didn't take this job for the money. I'm paying back Lucca by returning a favor. I'm not making a dime on this."

"I know." He narrowed his eyes. "The reason I ask is because a comeback would be motive for someone to keep tabs on Daria and the progress she's making. Have you looked into her fans and competitors? Fiber art has its own niche. It's not as common as painting and photography. I bet there are people who've been keeping tabs on Daria and her progress since she fell off the radar."

"I didn't find anything."

"Look harder."

"Thanks for the tip." I gave him another look. "Are you okay?"

He cleared his throat, one of the things he often did when he was annoyed or buying time. "We've already been over this. You don't have to thank me for surviving. And you need not worry. I have no intention of dropping dead anytime soon. I'm fine. Just a bit sore." He cocked an eyebrow and shrugged. "I have plenty of other things to focus on. From the sound of it, so do you. Brief Farzen on the situation and give him Daria's address. He'll handle the team assignments. She'll be protected."

Taking the hint, I headed for the door. "Thanks."

"Hey, Alex," he stopped me before I could leave, "where's James?"

"Martin?"

"Who else?"

"L.A." I didn't like my boss's obsession with my beloved. "For how long?"

"He'll be there through next week, possibly longer." I tried not to scowl but gave up when I realized it was a losing battle. "Why?"

"Tell him I'll be seeing him."

Before I could ask another question, Justin interrupted over the intercom. "Lucien, your car's here."

Cross pressed the button. "I'll be down in a minute." He turned off his computer and slipped into his jacket. "Walk me out. I'll introduce you to Farzen before I leave."

"Why do you care where Martin is?" I asked as we headed out the door.

"Just curious."

"That's not an answer."

"It's the only one I have."

"What are you doing, Lucien? Does this have anything to do with your scrapped partnership?"

"Let's just say I'm hoping he'll reconsider. Now that I've been cleared of those pesky murder charges, I'd like to get back to business as usual."

"You can't seriously want to go back into business with him. Your partnership was dissolved only weeks ago. Martin Technologies is still dealing with the fallout. Martin's across the country, scrambling to come up with an alternative solution." I clamped my mouth shut, regretting telling my boss any of this.

"Think about it this way," Cross said. "If I can swing the optics and get Martin Technologies back on board, James won't have to keep making these trips to California."

"You're too late."

Cross raised an intrigued eyebrow. "We'll see."

I let out a displeased sigh, loud enough for Cross to hear, but as usual, he remained unfazed by my dramatics. He punched the button on the elevator, and we went down one level. When the doors opened, he strode toward one of the offices. Joe Farzen practically jumped to attention when Cross entered.

"Relax, Joe. This isn't the military," Cross said.

"No, sir, Mr. Cross."

Cross chuckled, gesturing toward me. "This is Alex Parker. Until that protection assignment I gave you begins, you and your team will follow her instructions. Tuesday, you'll start your assignment for me. Are we clear?"

"Yes, sir," Farzen said.

"Alex?" Cross glanced at me.

"Aye, aye, captain."

Cross shook his head and headed out the door, calling over his shoulder, "And Joe, don't put up with too much of her bullshit."

Farzen grinned, his posture relaxing ever so slightly. "Ma'am." He gestured to the seat in front of his desk.

"First, don't call me ma'am. Bad memories." I sat down, hoping he'd relax.

"All right, Alex. Then it's only fair you call me Joe."

"Great."

He retook his seat. "How can my team be of assistance?"

"I have a client who thinks she's being stalked. We don't have any proof, but she has provided a general description of her stalker." I filled him in on the times, dates, and locations where she'd seen him. "I'm not sure how serious the threat may be, but I'd like round-the-clock protection. When she leaves her house, I'd like someone to follow her and someone to remain behind, in case he shows up."

Joe wrote down a few notes. "We can do a two-man rotation. Twelve on, twelve off. That should cover all our bases and ensure my team is well-rested and paying attention."

"Excellent." I gave him Daria's address. "She's shy around new people and has some trouble remembering things." I told him about her brush with death. "I'll introduce you, but it'd probably be best to keep your distance, if possible."

"We'll set up outside. Since we're keeping an eye out for a stalker, we don't need to provide protection inside her home. When she's out, we'll stay close, but we won't be that close. What do you want us to do if we spot the guy?"

"Call the authorities and notify me. The more information you can get on him, the better."

"Photo surveillance?" he asked.

"That'd be great. Even a license plate number would work wonders. I just want to figure out who he is and stop him from terrorizing her. She's suffered enough."

Joe entered something into the computer. "When do you want us to get started?"

"As soon as possible."

He checked the screen. "I'm the only one in the office right now. But everyone else is on the way. I'll brief them as soon as they arrive. We'll divide up the duty assignments and devise a schedule. We should be geared up and ready to go within two hours."

I looked at my watch. "Okay, drop by my office first, and we'll head over there together. Daria will need a familiar face to introduce you."

"Very well."

SIX

Joe Farzen and one of his teammates remained on the sidewalk while I stood on Daria's porch, waiting for her to answer the door. She cracked the door open only a few inches. She looked at me before narrowing her eyes at the two men standing in front of the three identical silver sedans, courtesy of Cross Security.

"May I help you?" Daria asked. She didn't remember me.

"Hi, Daria." I offered her a reassuring smile. "We met earlier today. I'm Eddie Lucca's friend. I work security. He asked me to help you out."

She studied my face before pulling out her phone. "Alex, right. Sorry." The woman was smart. She made sure to verify what I told her. "I wasn't expecting to see you again so soon." She gave the men behind me another uneasy look.

"That's Joe and Miles." I pointed to each of the men, who nodded and waved. "They're going to keep an eye out to make sure you're safe, if that's okay with you."

She stepped away from the door. "Can we speak privately?"

"Sure." I followed Daria inside.

She closed and locked the door before leading me back to the main room. She stood in the center, spinning as she surveyed her surroundings. At first, I thought she had lost her train of thought, but instead, she found a blue notebook and picked it up.

"Daria, what's going on?" I asked.

She narrowed her eyes, as if straining to hear something in the distance. I opened my mouth to ask another question, but she pressed her finger to her lips and scribbled something on the blank sheet of paper. She held the notebook out for me to read. *Listen.*

I concentrated, wondering if she was in the midst of some sort of episode. After thirty seconds of silence, I moved closer to the back door. The sun had set an hour ago, so it wasn't completely dark yet. And that's when I heard a thump.

I spun around, nodding to let her know I heard it. She backed into the corner of the room, like a frightened animal. "It's okay," I said. "You're safe. I won't let anything happen to you."

"What is it?" she asked.

"I don't know." I couldn't even tell where it was coming from. "When did you first hear it?"

She looked at her phone. "Twelve minutes ago. I texted Eddie. I didn't think to contact you. I'm sorry."

"Don't be sorry."

"Do you think someone's outside? Do you think he's trying to get in?"

"I don't see anyone. Let me text the team. They can search outside. They're good at their jobs. You can trust them."

"Okay."

I shot a text to Joe, asking him to sweep the area. But I didn't think the sound had come from outside. "I'll check the house. Where were you when you first heard it?"

"In here." She pointed to something on her desk. "I was working on this. At first, I thought something fell off the table, but I don't think that's it."

"Stay here." I glanced in the kitchen and dining room before stepping back into the main room. If someone had been in the living room, I would have noticed when I entered.

Palming my gun, I moved down the hallway. Two steps in, I heard three thumps in rapid succession. They sounded like heavy footsteps.

Forcing my mind not to wander to worst case scenarios, I peered into the guest room, making sure it was empty before moving on. The washer and dryer were turned off, so that couldn't be the source of the sound. Again, I heard another faint thump. The noise seemed to come from everywhere and nowhere at the same time.

Turning on the light, I stepped into Daria's bedroom. The saints hadn't moved. Since they weren't upside down or bleeding from their eyes, I took that as a good sign. *Parker, this isn't a horror movie.* With my left hand, I pulled open her closet door and shifted the hangers from one side to another to make sure no one was hiding. A hand touched my shoulder, and I spun, a surprised scream escaping from my lips.

Daria jumped back, trembling. "I'm sorry. I didn't mean to."

"No, it's okay." I laughed. "Are you okay? I didn't mean to scare you."

She nodded, staring at my gun.

I lowered it, holding it down at my thigh as I made my way across the room and into her bathroom. She stayed on my heels, and I realized she'd been too afraid to wait in the main room by herself. At least I didn't shoot her. Lucca would never forgive me if I had.

Just as I pulled the shower curtain back, the thump sounded again. It was much closer. Daria pressed against my back. I could feel her trembling.

"It's him," she whispered. "He's trying to get in."

I turned, cocking my head as the thump sounded again. The curtain further blocked my view of the backyard. Since it was dark outside and light inside, I couldn't see out. Blindly reaching for the switch, I fumbled around until I turned off the bathroom light. Then I approached the window.

Whatever had caused the sound had come from outside.

Now that the light was out, I'd be able to see what it was. Yanking the curtain open, I pressed my face close to the glass. A figure popped up in front of me. Daria screamed and fled into the bedroom. My heart hammered in my chest.

"Daria, stay hidden," I ordered, racing out of the bedroom. Narrowly opening the back door, I crouched down, using it as cover as I visually swept the backyard. "Freeze."

The figure raised his hands. "Take it easy, Parker. Joe sent me around back to check on the noise."

"Miles?" I lowered my gun as soon as he stepped into the light. "Did you see anyone?"

"No."

"Shit." I hadn't checked upstairs yet. Before I could run back inside, he stopped me.

"Is this what you heard?" He reached for the air conditioner cover and gave it a gentle tap. It thudded. From out here, the sound was more metallic, but it was close enough.

"Why's it doing that?" I asked.

"Two of the screws must have fallen out. It's not closed right. When I came back here, I heard it bang. I was checking it out when you turned off the light." He pointed to the bathroom window. "I didn't mean to scare you."

"Add air conditioner repairman to your CV." I exhaled a breath and holstered my gun. "Just to be on the safe side, I'm going to clear the rest of the house. Keep an eye out, just in case we're wrong."

"Yes, ma'am."

I opened my mouth to ask him not to call me that, decided now wasn't the time, and headed back inside. "Daria?" I called. But she didn't answer. "Daria?"

Again, I cleared the first level. But I didn't spot Daria, so I went upstairs. "Daria?" She wouldn't have run outside. If she had, Joe or Miles would have texted me. She had to be here. Ignoring the worst case scenarios that played through my head, I flipped on light after light, checking the two rooms and bathroom, but she wasn't here. "Daria?"

I moved closer to the window, hearing the faintest

squeak. Now what? Shaking it off as just another odd air conditioner noise, I went back down the stairs. Daria must have taken my instructions to stay hidden to heart.

"Daria, it's Alex. It's okay. The man outside is Miles. He works with Joe. He found the source of the sound. It's safe. You can come out now."

"Okay," she said. A moment later, she slid out from beneath the bed. I hadn't thought to check under there. Next time, that would be one of the first places I looked. Sweat coated her skin, and she wiped her brow with the back of her hand. "I called Eddie," she said. "I didn't know what else to do. I wasn't sure you were going to make it back."

"That's good." I pulled out my phone, just as it started ringing. "Speak of the devil."

She laughed, releasing some of the nervous energy.

I answered, updated Lucca on the situation, and promised I had it under control. Then I tucked the phone away. "Your air conditioner cover came loose. We think that's what's causing the thumping. Have you ever heard that before?"

"I don't know." Now that the situation was handled, she looked embarrassed. "I bet you're regretting getting roped into this."

"Not at all. It's okay to be scared. To be honest, I was pretty freaked out too."

"But you went after the guy. You didn't hide under the bed."

"I have a gun. If I didn't, confronting him would have been stupid. Plus, I knew I had backup nearby."

"The two men you brought with you?"

"Yes. They'll keep you safe, and I'm pretty sure one of them has already replaced the missing screws."

She rubbed her face. "God." She glanced up at the religious figures. "Sorry, guys."

We left her bedroom and headed back to the main room. Admittedly, we were both a little shaky. "Have you considered having a safe room installed?" I asked.

"Um..."

"That's okay. I was just curious." I looked at the piles of

notebooks and art supplies on her desk as she led the way into the kitchen.

"Does Cross Security install stuff like that?" she asked.

"Sometimes. Most of the security systems and safe rooms we recommend are contracted out."

She filled a pot with water and put it on the stove. "Would you like some tea? It's chamomile. It soothes my nerves and helps me wind down."

"Sure."

She pulled out a second mug and put a tea bag in each. Then she put a honey bear down beside it and took a seat at the table. "Why did you stop by tonight?"

"I wanted to introduce you to the security team. Joe and Miles are only half of the team. The other half will be here tomorrow morning. Would you like Joe to introduce them to you?"

"That's not necessary." She reached for her phone. "They drive silver cars, just like yours?"

"Yes. Those are Cross Security vehicles."

She jotted down a note. "I'm sorry," she said, "is there anything else you told me earlier? In the commotion, a lot gets jumbled in my brain."

"That was pretty much it. I just wanted to ask for your permission to have them watch the house."

"That's fine," she said distractedly.

"Since I'm here, do you mind if I ask you a few more questions?"

"Go ahead."

"I spoke to your mother earlier."

"Do I even want to know what she said to you?"

"She didn't say much. She's just worried about you living alone."

"Uh-huh." Daria rolled her eyes.

"Anyway," I sensed it was best to avoid this subject, "she said you aren't dating anyone. Eddie didn't mention anything to me about it, so I'm guessing he didn't explore the possibility."

"What do you mean explore it?"

"We're trying to figure out who's stalking you. You said someone's been watching you and following you. I wanted to make sure it wasn't a jilted lover or rejected suitor."

"I bet my mom had loads to say about this." She got up to fill the cups with water before putting them on the table. She squeezed some honey into her cup before offering me the bear. "I can't remember the last time I went on a date."

"That's okay. I was never one for awkward socialization, if I could avoid it."

She smiled. "I used to date a lot. When I was in school, someone always took me to parties or out to dinner. It was fun. I liked it. I'm just not comfortable around people, especially strangers. Maybe one of these days I'll get back out there."

"Did you have any bad break-ups? Did anyone obsess over you?"

"Not that I recall. I had a few intense relationships, but we just kind of fizzled. Ever since the attack, everyone started acting differently around me. Once I moved, I lost touch with most of my friends. Eddie's one of the few people who stuck by me through everything."

"Eddie's a good guy. Did the two of you ever have anything going?"

Daria nearly spit out her tea. "No."

"But you like him?" I asked.

"He saved my life. He listens to me. He doesn't make me feel stupid or crazy, like everyone else. I appreciate that. But we're just friends. I like him as a friend."

"Do you have many other friends?"

"A few." She leaned back, suddenly wary of my questions or possibly of me. "Why are you asking about them?"

"I'm just trying to figure out who's been watching you."

"I already told you what he looks like." She pointed to the descriptions on her fridge. "Light brown hair, red sneakers, dark, scary eyes. His clothes change, but those eyes and shoes never do. None of my friends look like that or dress like that. I know my memory is wonky and my eyesight's not always the best, but I would recognize one of my friends if they were following me or loitering in my backyard. The person following me is the Lightning Killer. That's all there is to it."

"But Daria, he's dead."

"Then it's someone who looks a hell of a lot like him." She finished her tea. "Let me ask you a question." She nodded toward the window over the sink. "You said the thumping we heard was from the air conditioner cover."

"That's correct. Miles said it was missing a few screws, and the breeze was making it bang."

"How do you think those screws went missing?"

"They might have rusted or broken off due to exposure to the elements."

"Or someone removed them. We both know I don't have my air conditioner installed in that window. Without the cover, there'd be a giant hole in my wall."

"Do you think someone removed the screws in an attempt to get inside?"

She shivered. "He used the fire escape last time. But this isn't an apartment. It's a townhouse. The doors are always locked, so he has to find another way in."

SEVEN

After leaving Joe Farzen and Miles Bridger to keep an eye out, I returned to the office. Lucca was waiting for me in the lobby. He stood up the moment he saw me.

"How did it go? Is everything okay?" he asked.

"It's fine."

"It didn't sound fine. Daria called me, frantic. Was it really just the air conditioner cover?"

"I think so."

"You think?"

"I cleared her townhouse. The Cross Security team searched every inch outside. The missing screws are the only thing we found. When Miles moved the cover, it banged against the wall. That had to be it." But I hadn't been able to shake Daria's question. How did the screws end up missing?

"How was she when you left? What did she say? Was she on board with having a couple of bodyguards parked outside?"

"She's okay. We had some tea, and she calmed down. She's happy to have two guys keeping watch outside." I pressed the button for the elevator.

"I'll bet. Have you come up with anything?"

"Nothing solid yet, but it's only been a day. What about the websites and message boards I asked you to look into?"

The elevator doors opened, and we stepped inside. "The stuff you asked me to look into didn't result in anything. Like I told you last night, I already checked into all of that."

I turned to him, glad we had the elevator to ourselves. "Since Daria first noticed someone stalking her the day after her parents left, I looked into them."

"They're clean," Lucca said.

"Appearances can be deceiving, so I called her mom."

Lucca rubbed a hand down his face. "How did that go?" His response was on par with Daria's.

"I've had worse conversations. Mrs. Waylon answered my questions, but she made it clear she doesn't want Daria living alone or remaining in the city. She wants her daughter to move back home. I'm guessing she always wanted that. Apparently, she never approved of Daria's dating life either." I squinted at Lucca. "Anything to that?"

"Moms always hate who their kids date. You should meet my mother and mother-in-law. The only thing they agree on is that Kelly and I should have never gotten together. But now we better stay together for Grace's sake."

"Too much unrelated information, boy scout."

"What's your point, Parker? You think Daria's mom hired someone to scare her kid into moving back home? Because that's just crazy."

"No." Admittedly, that thought had come to mind, but I didn't have any proof to back it up. At least, not yet. "I was wondering if someone from Daria's past could be behind this. A scorned lover or rejected suitor, perhaps." The elevator opened, and I led him down the hall to my office. "According to Daria's mom, Daria dated a lot and had no gender preference. But her mother couldn't give me any names. Daria might have had diaries or journals from back then. At least, that's what I was told. But when I asked her about her dating history, she got a little defensive. I didn't ask her if I could see the journals. It didn't seem like the right time. If I'd asked, she might have told me to fuck off." I exhaled. "She's still wary of me. When I first rang her bell, she didn't even remember me from earlier this afternoon."

"Give her time. It's not like you're particularly memorable."

"That means my hands are tied while I wait for her to get used to me. Once she's comfortable, I'm hoping she'll be more forthcoming."

"Wow, tactful. That's a first."

I glared at him. "I dug through old news articles and searched Daria's social media accounts, but I didn't come up with much. I have a few names of people who attended gallery openings and art events with her, but they might have just been friends. It's hard to tell from photos, unless someone had his or her hand up Daria's dress, and I didn't see any pictures like that."

"That was years ago. I'd think if one of those people wanted to stalk her, they would have done so before now," Lucca said.

"What about more recent dating interests?"

"As far as I know, she's not seeing anyone. She hasn't since the attack. None of the friends I spoke to mentioned anyone of concern."

"Who did you speak to?"

"I'll make you a list."

I rolled my eyes. "You could have done this sooner before I bumbled around and got myself into trouble."

"You like trouble."

"No, I don't."

"Shocking, since you have a hell of a time causing it."

"Lucca, stop busting my chops." I had a rough night. I didn't need him to pile on.

"I'll try, but this is what I miss most about you."

"Zip it." I regretted agreeing to this for every single reason imaginable.

"In all seriousness, I appreciate you going easy on Daria. She's had it tough, but if you think you're on to something, you should pursue it, regardless of how uncomfortable it makes her or you. Better safe than sorry, right?"

"I know, and when I drove over there, I planned to ask to see her diary, but when I showed up on her doorstep, she was so freaked out. And then one of Cross's guys scared the crap out of her. When I finally found her, she was hiding under the bed. After that, I didn't want to push, not with the way her mind is. I'm not sure how she functions. I barely know what I'm doing half the time, and I was never in a coma."

"She's a survivor. She learned to cope."

"Yeah."

"Don't beat yourself up. Not pushing was the right call. She'll get used to you eventually. Just be patient, and give her some time."

"That's what I figured. Unfortunately, it won't get my questions answered, and you just said I should pursue this."

"I'll call her tomorrow and ask for a list of names. Will that help?"

"Why not do it now?"

"Given what you told me, she's had quite the day. When she's tired, it's harder for her to focus and concentrate. We'll have better results tomorrow. Is there anything else you want to know?"

"A million things. What can you tell me about her condition and her doctors?"

"Why?" he asked, suspecting this might be a trap. "Are you doubting her claims?"

"I'm not sure what I think. She's insistent that the person she's seeing is the Lightning Killer, but we know that's not possible. I'm just looking at the facts. Officers found no trace of a stranger's presence. No footprints. Nothing. I read the police reports. The officers canvassed the neighborhood. No one saw anyone lurking in the bushes. And I didn't see anything amiss when I looked around outside." Except the missing screws, but I was blaming mother nature for those.

"That doesn't mean someone wasn't there," Lucca said. "But you're probably right. More than likely, this is all in her head. Still, we can't be too careful."

"I know." A thought came to mind, and I opened the FBI file Lucca had given me, finding the printed stills eerily familiar.

"Spit it out, Parker. What are you thinking?"

"I'm not sure." I spread the photos out on my desk. "Daria said she saw him outside her bedroom window. She was already in bed, nearly asleep, when she heard noises last night. Her hearing aid was out, and she didn't have on her glasses or contacts. How could she have heard anything?"

"Her hearing and vision are only partially impaired. She's not blind or deaf. She could have heard something."

"What about the other times when she was in bed and saw him outside her window? She doesn't sleep with her glasses on."

"She could still make out shapes in the darkness. Perhaps she went to look and saw someone outside. Maybe she didn't get a good look at the guy, so her mind filled in the blanks with a description of the Lightning Killer."

"It would have been dark. Maybe she thought she saw a shape, but it could have been nothing but shadows or a blowing branch. That would explain the tapping she heard last night, which I'm not even sure she'd hear if she was lying on the same side as her good ear."

"Maybe it was loud enough or at just the right pitch. It was probably the air conditioner cover knocking against the building." He gave me a sideways glance. "You don't think the noise she heard last night was someone unscrewing it, do you?"

"I don't know." I grabbed another folder from my drawer and removed the copies of her notes. I found the sheet with the unsub's description. "She went into extreme detail on how the unsub was dressed every time she spotted him." I placed Daria's notes on the desk beside the surveillance photos Lucca had given me. "Don't these descriptions sound familiar?"

Lucca picked up Daria's notes, reading each one from each of her encounters with the unsub. He reorganized the surveillance photos of Holland, placing them in the same order. "She's remembering him from before the attack."

"Has she seen these photos before?" I asked.

Lucca picked up each one, reading the location, time, and date on the back. "I don't think so." He flipped them over. "These were taken in the month leading up to his attack on Daria. The descriptions she gave us match her fleeting encounters with Holland before anyone realized he was a threat. Maybe she isn't seeing anything. Maybe she's remembering."

"How do we fix that?"

"I'll call Dr. Chen in the morning and run this by her. But if that's the case, this is out of our hands. The mind tries to protect itself from trauma. The things she's seeing could be repressed memories resurfacing."

"Like hallucinations?"

"Stranger things have happened."

"Do you know if she's experienced this before? Her mom said she has, but I haven't spoken to her doctors or gotten a look at her medical records yet to verify it."

"Not exactly. When she was still recovering, she exhibited a lot of symptoms of post-traumatic stress. Most were in the form of nightmares. She couldn't access the memories from the event. She saw plenty of neurologists and shrinks. They hoped to figure out a way to help her, but the memories were locked away or erased from her mind. They tried all kinds of therapeutic techniques. But her memory of that night was gone, and given how long her brain had been deprived of oxygen, they thought it might have been permanently damaged, like corrupted files."

"Do you have access to her medical records?" I asked.

"No. The hospital gave me a breakdown of her injuries but nothing privileged. Daria's mom and dad would fill me in on her progress every time I checked up on her."

"Did you ever see her brain scans?"

"No."

"Do you think Daria would consent to letting me speak to her doctors?"

"She's weird about that. She won't even give me consent, but her therapist asked me to join them for a session once. That's how I know Dr. Chen. It's how I know she'll listen to my concerns and approach the subject delicately the next time she sees Daria."

"Will the good doctor divulge anything to you?"

"Chen won't breach doctor-patient privilege." Lucca narrowed his eyes. "What are you hoping you'll find?"

"I'll know it when I see it. But asking Daria for access will only make her more skeptical of me. I'll have to go about this another way."

"Are you planning on violating HIPAA?"

"It's probably better if I don't answer that."

"You're probably right."

I pushed a legal pad and pen toward him. "Write down whatever you know about Daria's condition and any improvements or setbacks she might have had."

"I don't know much."

"You checked in after the attack. You kept tabs. If you hadn't, we wouldn't be here now. You probably noticed things about her recovery because you were there for part of it." I jerked my chin at the paper. "Get cracking."

While he did that, I grabbed two cups of coffee from the break room, texted my request to Amir, and grabbed a couple of leftover pastries from the morning meeting. By now, they were stale, but I hadn't eaten, and Lucca wouldn't mind.

I put the plate and cups down on the glass coffee table and sat on the couch, wondering if Lucca would make himself comfy behind my desk. Instead, he joined me, taking a seat in the chair across from me and handing over the legal pad before picking up an apple Danish and taking a bite.

I skimmed the page, chuckling at his neat and precise handwriting. He always had to be perfect. But his notes didn't tell me anything I didn't already know or suspect. I'd have to wait for Amir to dig up everything he could on Daria before I'd know more.

"Oh, hang on." He reached for the pad, tugging it out of my hands. "You wanted to know about her friends. She only has one she frequently talks to, and a few others she sees a couple of times a month. I already looked into them. They're clean," he turned to a blank page and wrote down their names and numbers, "but maybe she confided in one of them. Perhaps they know something about this situation that she's forgotten to mention."

"Did you ask if any of them spotted this mysterious figure following Daria?"

"Give me some credit, Parker. I'm a federal agent. I know how to work an investigation."

"Then why do you want me to question them again?"

"If Daria's remembering things from the past, she might have told one of them. Plus, you know how witnesses are. They forget things and remember other things. It's been a couple of weeks since I spoke to them. Something might have changed."

I let out an exasperated grunt. Lucca had brought me this case, but he'd already put in most of the work. The cops had done the same. "Fine."

He bit into the Danish. "You have my permission to do whatever needs to be done."

"I didn't realize I needed your permission. Does that extend to breaking the law?"

He stared at me for a long time. "It does, as long as you don't get caught and you don't tell me about it."

"Stop acting so squeamish. You threw the rulebook out the window when Jablonsky got shot." Which is how I ended up owing Eddie Lucca my life.

"This is different."

"Are you sure? It seems like you might have crossed a few lines when it comes to Daria."

He drew air into his lungs and put his plate down. "I told you last night, nothing's going on between us. We're friends. I know it's weird. I know we shouldn't remain in touch with victims beyond the scope of an investigation and subsequent prosecution, but she lost so much. I just wanted to make sure she had someone she could depend on. Someone who made her feel safe again." He brushed a few crumbs off his slacks and stood up. "I'm sure you understand that better than most. In fact, wasn't your fiancé originally a victim?"

"More like my boss."

"Glass houses, Parker." He pointed to the clock. "It's getting late. I'm gonna get out of here. I'll bring you a list of Daria's former lovers once I get it."

"Make sure you get everyone, not just the people she saw several times, but the one-night stands, coffee dates, and stand-ups too."

He tapped his brow with his pointer finger. "Will do, but I don't imagine there will be many names on the list."

"We'll see."

EIGHT

If anyone knew what was going on with Daria, it'd be her best friend. When I phoned Brin Tatlik, she seemed confused why I was calling. "Who are you again?" she asked.

"Alexis Parker. I'm a private investigator."

"What does that have to do with Daria? You said she hired you for something."

From her tone, I feared Brin might hang up on me, so I spoke quickly. "Special Agent Eddie Lucca said he spoke to you a few weeks ago. I'm following up."

"On what? He asked about my whereabouts, as if I were some kind of criminal. What is this about?"

"That's all he said?" I could strangle Lucca. He told me he'd done his job.

"More or less. He didn't give me many details. He was vague. He wanted to make sure Daria wasn't in danger."

I exhaled slowly. "I'm sorry, Brin. You aren't in any trouble. This has nothing to do with you." I glanced at Daria's phone records, which indicated the two spoke or texted every day. "This is about your friend Daria."

"Is she okay?" Brin asked. "She made me her emergency contact since I'm the closest thing she has to family in the city. What's going on? I texted her earlier, but we didn't speak. Did something happen?"

"She's fine," I said. "She's safe."

"Thank god." She paused. "What is this about? Agent Lucca thought some guy might be threatening her."

"Are you aware of Daria's past?" The last thing I wanted to do was reveal some hidden secret. That wasn't my place.

"You mean what happened to her in D.C.? Yeah, I know about that."

"Have you noticed if Daria's been acting anxious or fearful lately?"

"She always does to some extent. It's just how she is. When we met for lunch last Friday, she kept looking out the window. I asked her why, and she said she thought someone was following her."

"Did you see anyone?"

"No."

"Is that the only time Daria's mentioned this to you?"

"She's been talking about this for a month or two. At first, she just complained that she kept losing stuff, misplacing it. I figured she probably just forgot. Her memory's not really there. But it drove her crazy. She swore to me that wasn't the case. She even showed me her journal with every minute detail. I just thought she forgot to write something down. That happens on occasion."

"Do you remember what she lost?" I asked.

"The first time was her hairbrush. I don't remember what it was after that. More recently, it was a pack of colored yarn she'd gotten for a project."

"Do you know if she ever found these missing items?"

"The yarn turned up two days later. I think most of the other stuff did too, but she had to buy a new hairbrush. Who knows where that went? I told her it probably got knocked into the trash without her noticing. But it was weird. How does someone lose a hairbrush?"

"Could it have fallen out of her purse?"

"She never took it anywhere. She has a specific spot where she keeps it. Actually, she has specific places where she keeps almost everything. The only things that move around are her art supplies and her notebooks. Like I said, I thought it was weird."

"Did Daria mention anything else weird happening?"

"Besides the guy she insists is stalking her?"

"Did she say anything else about him?"

"She told me she thinks a dead guy is following her around. I know you must think she's a nutjob. Frankly, I think that's crazy. But she has her reasons. When that psycho attacked her a few years ago, she said it started with stuff disappearing. I'm not sure if that's true, but that's what she remembers."

"Yeah, it happened," I said. "The Lightning Killer stole things from each of his victims' homes prior to attacking them."

"So this kind of thing has happened before. No wonder she's been so freaked out lately. She says she's seen him following her. That he's been waiting for her when she gets home. He likes to show up outside her house a lot. But he takes off before she can do anything about it. By the time the cops arrive, he's long gone."

"Do you believe her?"

"I'm not sure. Daria's seen things before that weren't there. It always freaks me out when that happens. But she normally snaps out of it pretty quickly. This thing with the dead killer following her, it hasn't gone away. I don't really believe in ghosts or the supernatural, but I don't know. This is the kind of shit they make those scary movies about. Maybe there's a reason."

Truth was usually scarier than fiction. "Have you ever seen anyone suspicious loitering around?"

"Not really." But her words held little conviction.

"Humor me for a second," I said. "Think back. You and Daria hang out regularly. You've been to her place. I'm guessing she's probably been to yours."

"Yeah, all the time. We like to get dinner and have movie nights. Girls' nights."

"Has anyone ever shown up at more than one of the restaurants or bars you've been to?"

"I don't know. I've never paid much attention. Daria's never pointed anyone out."

"That's okay. What about around your place? Has there been any suspicious activity in your neighborhood, particularly when you and Daria are together?"

"You don't think this is Daria imagining things or that she's in the midst of some sort of PTS flare, do you?"

"I don't know. But I was asked to look into it, so that's what I'm doing. Do you remember anyone or anything? Please, I could use your help. Daria could use your help."

"A few times, I noticed an old, green Charger parked across from my apartment when Daria's been here. He always pulls out just as she's leaving. The engine is so loud, it's hard to miss."

"Did you get a look at the driver? Or a plate number?"

"I never paid much attention. I know it's a guy driving, but that's all I can tell you."

"That's good. That gives me something to dig into." I pulled up her home address and checked to see what kinds of surveillance cameras covered the area. "Okay, it's time for the bonus round."

"What?" she asked, clearly confused.

"Sorry, that was my attempt at levity. I just have a few more questions. What can you tell me about Daria's love life?"

"Shouldn't you ask her about that?"

"I should, but I have you on the phone. You're her best friend. She'd confide in you before she'd confide in anyone."

Brin sighed heavily. "What do you want to know?"

"Has she gone on any dates lately?"

"She was seeing one guy she met through her agent. He's another artist. Her agent represents him too. They went out once or twice, but now they are strictly platonic."

"His choice or hers?"

"Daria's, I think. She has trust issues, especially around men. She doesn't like being alone with them. She told me he made her feel trapped, helpless."

"Did this guy do something to her?"

"If he had, she wouldn't hang out with him anymore."

"What do they do together," I asked, "that doesn't make her feel trapped or helpless?"

"They go to see some art stuff, always out in public with plenty of other people around. She has a lot of fun with him, but he's just friend material. He fills that art void that I don't understand. She'll randomly go off on some art theory tangent or stop in the middle of the sidewalk to stare at a leaf hanging from a branch. This guy gets it. Apparently, it's an art thing. I thought it was just a Daria thing. But he'll be clicking photos of the leaf or whatever before she even points it out. Frankly, they'd probably make the perfect pair, but she's not interested in him like that. The attack left her uninterested in pursuing a physical relationship, or so she says."

"Have you met him?"

"Just once."

"When was this?"

"Um...three or four months ago."

"Did you get his name?"

"Reagan something. He's some kind of bigshot art guy, but I never heard of him and neither had Daria."

"Do you remember what he looks like?"

"The night we met was at an exhibit opening at the art museum. He was dressed all in black. No tie. And he hadn't bothered to button his shirt. He just had it tucked in. I think he thought it made him look like a rock star. It made him look like an idiot. He was kind of tall. He wasn't in bad shape, but he wasn't in good enough shape to be parading around a party with his shirt opened to his naval. Frankly, no one should do that. Ever."

I chuckled. "Agreed."

"His hair's brownish-black, so are his eyes. He kinda reminded me of a pirate. He had earrings and gold chains and stuff. Oh, and eyeliner. He just needed a hat and a parrot, and he'd be set."

"What kind of shoes did he have on?"

Brin laughed. "I'd say you were crazy for asking, but he had on sneakers. White with red."

Shit. "Do you know anything else about him? How I might be able to get in touch with him?"

"Daria probably has his number. But I don't know much. I try not to ask her a lot of questions. It frustrates her when she doesn't remember things, and I don't like doing that to her."

"You said they met through an agent?"

"Yeah, Daria's agent."

"Artist agents are rare."

"Celeste started out that way, but she owns her own gallery now. But Daria still calls her her agent."

"And she represents this Reagan guy's art too?"

"That's what I was told."

I had a million questions, but I didn't think Brin would be able to answer most of them. Instead, I tried to rein in my thoughts. "You said Celeste is Daria's agent. I didn't realize Daria was still making art."

"Um...she isn't, really."

"But you said she bought yarn for a project."

"She makes small, personalized items. Tapestries, rugs, little figurines, stuff like that. Cutesy stuff people buy on the internet. A few serious art collectors have approached her over the years. She had a giant life-size scene in the works, but that had gotten derailed when she was attacked. Celeste has been trying to convince her to go back to work on it, but Daria's been hesitant. She thinks the project's cursed."

I wasn't sure if the project was cursed, but Daria might be. At least, I had an actual potential lead. Lucca hadn't checked into Reagan the rock star wannabe. He'd barely asked Brin any questions. I'd give him hell about that tomorrow, but I didn't want to waste time doing it now.

Instead, I phoned the techs upstairs, hoping they'd be able to track down the green Charger. It would take days for them to gain access and parse through the footage, but it was something. I wondered if the same green Charger had been parked outside Daria's place, so I called Joe and told him to keep an eye out for it.

One quick call to Daria and I had Reagan's full name and the name of her agent. If only everything could be that easy. Before hanging up, I asked her what she thought of Reagan. She seemed uncertain. But without seeing her face, I wasn't sure if her discomfort had to do with him or me.

NINE

Reagan LaRoche had committed a few minor offenses as a youth. He'd gotten into a couple of bar fights but nothing of any major consequence. He had no other history of violence. As far as I could tell, he'd never tortured animals or abused his girlfriends. But he had an apartment in the warehouse district and drove a 1978 frost green Charger.

The hairs at the back of my neck prickled. Maybe Daria wasn't hallucinating or remembering previous trauma. Maybe someone was following her. Brin's insight might just put Daria's mind at ease. I pulled the DMV records, copying down the VIN and plate. Then I phoned the techs upstairs and told them to scrub the footage. More than likely, this was the same green Charger Brin had seen peeling away.

Since I couldn't get a look at Reagan LaRoche's internet history without access to his computer or service provider's records, I searched social media. LaRoche's photos were plastered all over the place. He had a profile on every platform known to man. But his posts were usually photos, art, or selfies taken with his buddies at art events. He always had the same smirky grin. I didn't like it.

Copying his e-mail address, I searched to see what types

G.K. Parks

of websites he frequented. He wasn't a registered user on any of the true crime websites I'd previously explored. That didn't mean he didn't go to these places, but until I got a look at his computer, I'd have no way of knowing for sure.

Just like Andrew Holland, Reagan LaRoche was an artist. But he didn't physically resemble the Lightning Killer. For starters, his hair was too dark and his build too lanky. But from a distance, could Daria have gotten them confused?

Aside from the physical differences, the two men shared some similar traits. For starters, they were both photographers. According to Brin, Reagan wore outlandishly colored high-top sneakers and had a fascination with Daria.

But unlike Holland, Reagan had become successful at his chosen profession. He'd gone on to sell his photos, first to stock photo sites and later directly to media outlets. From there, he'd been pursued by a marketing agency. Eventually, he was hired and became head of their art department.

I looked into the agency, but they were on the level. I'd have to contact their HR department in the morning and see if I could learn anything else about Reagan. But he held down the same, steady job for the last four years.

I wanted to believe stalkers couldn't function in normal society without someone getting suspicious, but I knew better than that. As far as I could tell, no one had ever filed a complaint against him. That didn't necessarily mean he was clean. It just meant he was careful.

After sending Reagan's photo to the security detail outside Daria's house, I headed to his address to see what was what. By the time I arrived, it was too late to knock. Instead, I circled a few times until I found the green car parked in a nearby garage.

I'd driven past it three times before I noticed it. Reagan had covered it with a beige car cover. The metallic green paint beneath reflected the dim garage lights. There was just one thing missing, or rather four. The car was on blocks. The tires had been removed, but given its condition and upkeep, I didn't think someone had stolen them. I uncovered the car and took a few photos, wondering when Reagan had driven it last.

Coincidences didn't exist. Old cars like this weren't commonly seen on the streets. I doubted Daria's unknown stalker just happened to drive the same color and make of car as her friend Reagan. The probability of such an occurrence was extremely slim. Sure, Reagan might have been in Brin's neighborhood for some other reason, but I doubted it.

Reagan didn't have any other vehicles registered in his name, but that didn't mean he didn't have an active rideshare account or utilize public transportation. Everyone knew one of the easiest ways to avoid detection in the city was to walk. Even Daria claimed the man stalking her would walk away before she got too close. Reagan had to be the cause of her anxiety, and if he wasn't, the similarities between him and the Lightning Killer might have been close enough to trigger some repressed memories and ignite her fears.

After circling for another twenty minutes, I found a place to park that allowed me to keep an eye on Reagan's apartment. From the street, I could see lights on inside, but I wasn't sure those were his windows. I hadn't bothered to look at the building blueprints before I headed out, so I didn't know how the warehouse had been sectioned off into apartments. But based on his address, he had to be somewhere on the second level.

Just to make sure I wasn't wasting my time, I called the tech department again. By now, they were probably planning on having one of the security teams eliminate me after all the requests I'd made in the last twenty-four hours. But they pinged Reagan's phone and told me he was home.

While I remained outside, watching and waiting for something to happen, I thought about all the things in his background that I found similar to the serial killer. Was Reagan emulating Holland? Or was I reading too much into this? At this late hour, I couldn't count on rational thought to prevail over nonsense theories, but my gut said I was on to something.

If I was picking up on these things, Daria might be too. The sightings and her anxiety correlated perfectly to when she and Reagan started hanging out. While I sat alone in the dark, I made a list of questions to ask Daria about Reagan. But since it was well past midnight, they'd have to wait until the morning.

A part of me wanted to knock on his door right now and get this over with, but something told me to wait. I didn't want to tip him off yet. We had no proof. No evidence. We'd need something if we wanted stalking charges to stick. And with Daria's unreliable memory, whatever evidence I found would have to be rock solid.

At two a.m., the lights went out in what I assumed was Reagan's apartment. I waited forty-five minutes, but there was no movement. Everyone was asleep. It was about time I took the hint. The last thing Daria needed was a hallucinating private investigator.

But as I headed home, my mind raced. Detouring, I returned to the office, unable to shake the one question from my mind. *Why didn't Lucca find this?* The only reason I could think of was he hadn't questioned Brin to the appropriate degree, or she hadn't thought to mention any of this to him.

When I entered the building which housed Cross Security, the guards on duty let me upstairs. They were used to seeing me enter at all hours of the night. I looked through Daria's phone logs again. She and Reagan spoke once or twice a week and texted every few days. On the surface, it looked innocent enough. Maybe that's why Lucca hadn't bothered digging deeper.

Chalking it up to agent prerogative, I reminded myself Lucca might be able to quote the rulebook backwards and forwards, but that didn't mean he was perfect. He was human, like the rest of us. Even if he screwed up or crossed a line, he was my friend. I'd have his back. I owed him that much.

*   *   *

"Sleeping on the job, again?" Kellen Dey asked, pushing

open my office door.

"Bite me," I mumbled, shifting on the couch and pressing my forehead against the backrest. From where I was lying, I couldn't see Kellan, but from the sound of his approaching footsteps, he hadn't taken the hint.

"I'd rather not." He put a steaming paper cup on the glass table. "How many times have you slept at work this week? Three? Four?"

Giving up on going back to sleep, I rolled over and sat up, brushing the tangles out of my hair with my fingers. I nodded at the cappuccino. "Thanks."

"You're welcome." He looked at the pile of papers and the dark screen of my open laptop. "What are you working on?"

"I'm not sure." I rubbed my eyes and reached for the coffee. Holding it close, I inhaled deeply, savoring the rich aroma before taking that first sip. Heaven.

"You've been burning the midnight oil a lot for someone who's not sure what she's doing."

"Story of my life."

"C'mon, tell me, what's Cross assigned you this time?"

"It's not for him. I'm working a personal case involving a possible stalker. It's too soon to say. But I might have a suspect." I grabbed my phone and checked my messages. Joe messaged me to say it had been a quiet night. The techs hadn't found anything on the car yet, but they were making progress on pulling Daria's medical records. There was no word from Lucca. "Do you think I have time to shower before the morning meeting?"

"There is no morning meeting."

"What are you talking about? Cross loves his morning meetings." I looked at the calendar, hoping it wasn't already Saturday. Martin would be pissed if I missed my flight. But it was only Wednesday.

"Cross isn't here. Justin's handling the administrative stuff in his absence, but that's why the boss loaded us up with casework yesterday and scheduled a bunch of follow-ups with our current clients. Weren't you paying attention during yesterday's morning meeting?"

"I make it a rule not to."

"Obviously." Kellan shook his head. "Go take a shower. You've got plenty of time. No one around here wants you stinking up the place."

"Thanks."

"Anytime, baby doll."

"Baby doll?"

"What? You don't like it?"

"Say it again, and I'll shoot you." I took another sip from the cup. "On second thought, I rather enjoy our current arrangement, so maybe I'll reconsider. Just no more cutesy names, please."

"Y'know, I'm not entirely sure I want to be your friend."

"No problem. Most people don't." But things ran smoother when we were friendly.

Kellan rolled his eyes, letting me know he didn't find my remark funny. "What's the deal with you sleeping at the office? Did you and Mr. Tall, Dark, and Handsome have a fight? I'm sensing trouble in paradise."

"No trouble."

"So why have you turned the couch into your bed? Did he kick you out?"

"Quite the contrary. I can go home if I want. I've just been busy."

"Whatever you say. But we're all investigators around here. You're not fooling anyone." Kellan strode across the hall and opened his office door. It was time to start another day.

I grabbed my overnight bag from the closet and went to the locker room to shower and change. After washing up, I braided my wet hair and went to grab some breakfast before going back to researching Daria's case.

Bennett Renner, former homicide detective turned private eye, looked up when I entered the break room. He pushed the pink box toward me. "The everything and sesame bagels are already gone, but there are a few blueberry and cinnamon raisin left." The toaster popped, and he grabbed the breakfast pastry and put it on his plate. "If you're looking for something with a bit more substance, check the fridge, just don't tell anyone what's in there. I'm hoping to save those for lunch."

"Any idea why Cross isn't here today?" A platter of breakfast sandwiches and fresh fruit took up two shelves. I popped open the clear plastic top, removing an egg and cheese croissant before grabbing a fruit cup with fresh kiwi.

"You're his favorite. Didn't he tell you?" Renner asked.

"I'm not his favorite."

"You saved his life. If you weren't before, you definitely are now." Renner handed me a plate from the cupboard and a fork.

"So he didn't mention it to you?"

Renner shook his head. "He said he had business to take care of." He took a bite from the toaster pastry, burning his tongue on the filling and gulping down some orange juice to cool the sting. "My guess would be Cross is finally taking time off to recuperate. He's been in and out of the office these last few weeks. He doesn't seem to understand the harder he pushes himself, the longer it'll take to fully recover." Renner tapped his hip. "I would know."

"On the bright side, I don't have to worry about being late for the morning meeting or getting assigned a ton of busy work." I sat down beside him. "Do you remember the Lightning Killer?"

"Vaguely. The Feebs put us on alert, but nothing ever crossed my desk."

"Homicide wasn't briefed?"

Renner shook his head. "Didn't they catch the guy?"

"Yeah, in D.C."

"Did he ever kill anyone here?"

"I don't think so." I frowned, realizing I had no idea when or why Daria moved to the city. She'd emerged on the art scene in D.C. How did she end up here? How would she have known to contact Lucca for help? When he came to the rescue the first time, they were both in D.C. Now they were both here. I was getting really sick and tired of all these supposed coincidences.

"Is something wrong?" Renner asked.

"Maybe."

He opened his mouth to ask a question, but my phone buzzed. I picked it up and read the display. The files I requested were ready. Perhaps now I'd get some answers. I stuffed the rest of my breakfast sandwich in my mouth and put the fruit back in the fridge. Waving goodbye to Renner, I headed back to my office to see if I could finally get some answers.

The computer experts had performed a deep dive on Daria Waylon. They sent me digital copies of her medical records, everything from her birth certificate to her latest brain scan. Instead of starting at the beginning, I started with the question currently on my mind.

TEN

Lucca wasn't at his desk. I should have called first before heading straight to the federal building, but we needed to get on the same page when it came to the Daria situation. I considered leaving him a note, but if I had to resort to that, I might as well just call him instead. No, we needed to talk face to face.

I knocked on SSA Mark Jablonsky's open door. "You got a minute?"

He looked up from his computer screen. "What are you doing here? Weren't you banned from the federal building?"

"It's nice to see you, Alex. How are you today?" I said, making a point.

"I don't have time for this. What do you want?"

"Where's Lucca?"

Mark leaned forward in order to peer out the open slats of the blinds and into the bullpen. "Out."

"You're our fearless leader. Shouldn't you know a little more than that?"

"I'm not your fearless leader. You handed that privilege over to Lucien Cross, or have you forgotten?" He snickered. "Correction, you're probably just hoping to forget."

I entered and pulled the door shut behind me. I closed

the blinds and took a seat on the tiny sofa which was wedged against the side wall. "Lucca and I went to dinner a couple of nights ago."

"I heard."

"Lucca told you?"

"No, Marty did."

I sighed dramatically. Even in my own life, I was always the last to know anything. "Did Lucca tell you why it was imperative we get together?" I narrowed my eyes. "Or maybe Martin filled you in."

"Lucca said it had something to do with an old case, but he didn't get into the meat of the matter. And Marty probably would have told me what was going on, except you didn't tell him." Mark leaned back in his chair and folded his hands over his stomach. "But I'm sure I'm gonna hear all about it. Go on. What's the problem?"

"Lucca's a good agent, right? That's why he got tasked with investigating our unit and why he helped out when we needed him."

"I'm already convinced." An amused glint shone in Mark's eyes. "He's the best agent I've got."

"Great."

"But I've seen better."

"Be that as it may," derailing this walk down memory lane would save us all some time and heartache, "no one's perfect. Me. You. Lucca." I exhaled. "I think he did something he shouldn't have. I'm just not sure what."

"Is this something that's going to jam him up?" Mark asked.

"I don't think so, but I'm not sure. It'd be best if we speak only in hypotheticals."

"I'm pretty sure that's the only way you know how to speak."

I stuck my tongue out at him.

"But your nonverbal communication is astonishing." He grinned. "I guess that makes up for it."

"You're in a playful mood. Did you get lucky last night?"

"Do you really want to know?"

"Actually, that's one of those things I'd prefer you tell Martin about."

"I already did." He jerked his chin up. "Let's get back to Lucca. Hypothetically, what do you think he did?"

I briefed Mark on Lucca's involvement in stopping the Lightning Killer and how that connected him to Daria Waylon. "I went through her phone records. He's remained in contact with her since the incident. She was one of the first people he called when his transfer request to remain at the OIO was approved. Before that, they hadn't spoken since he transferred back to D.C. But within two weeks of him contacting her, she started calling him. And she never stopped."

"Do you think they're having an affair?"

"He said they aren't."

Mark blinked a few times, considering the possibility. "You know the stats on law enforcement officials. Hell, I've been divorced three times. I could never get it right."

"But you didn't cheat."

"No, but my last ex-wife did." He shrugged. "OPR might have a different outlook on things, but we aren't the scarlet letter brigade. What two consenting adults do is not our business. Since when do you care about this stuff? You usually don't judge people that harshly."

"It's not that. I mean, if he is having an affair that would explain some things, but I've asked him and he denies it. He handed me the case because he doesn't believe a threat exists. Hell, I didn't think one did either. I even told him that. He's supposed to be checking with Daria's therapist about the possibility these recent sightings are repressed memories resurfacing."

"Okay. I'm not seeing the problem. The two of you agree for once."

"But then I looked a little harder, and I found something. I don't see how he missed this." I told Mark about my conversation with Brin, Daria's phone records, and how both led me to Reagan LaRoche.

"He's not you."

"But this is basic investigation 101 stuff."

The look on Mark's face told me he agreed. "Are you sure Brin didn't change her story?"

"I don't know. But I'd imagine he asked Daria about her

friends. He said he spoke to them. He even gave me a list, but Reagan wasn't on it."

"Daria has memory problems. Maybe she forgot. Or maybe she intentionally failed to mention him to Lucca. She might like Lucca or this Reagan guy, and figured telling one about the other wasn't a good idea."

"True, but Daria gave me Reagan's contact info."

"You aren't Lucca."

"Do you think that makes a difference?"

"I have no idea. This is all hypothetical. How the hell should I know?"

I thought about Lucca's familiarity with Daria's kitchen and habits, but that could be explained away easily enough. After all, Brin said Daria had no interest in pursuing a physical relationship, so maybe she and Lucca were just friends. Perhaps, she forgot to mention Reagan and Lucca had too much on his plate to double-check the information she gave him.

"What do you really want to ask? I know you didn't come all the way down here to confront Lucca about an extramarital affair, especially since you've already done as much. You've established he and Daria are friends, which explains why he contacted her when he found out his transfer request was approved."

"I don't think they're good enough friends for that to be the case." I stared at the back of Mark's monitor. "Can you find out how many times Daria has called the FBI to report she's being stalked?"

Mark tapped the button on his mouse and slid his keyboard closer. "Give me a sec." He hummed while he typed, something I'd never heard him do before. "In the last three months, she's phoned this office on six separate occasions. Before that, she contacted the D.C. field office five times. I'm guessing she was looking for Lucca. That would explain why Lucca called her once he received his transfer."

"Did she ever speak to any other agents?" I asked.

"Her call was redirected here those five times she tried calling D.C., so I guess Lucca's the only one she wanted to talk to. Agents advised her to contact the local authorities."

"Someone must have told Lucca she was looking for him, so he reached out to her. What about less recently?"

Mark brought up the records and angled his screen so I could see. I slid to the edge of my seat and leaned over, counting the number of times Daria had called in the last six years. It was no wonder the police didn't believe her. She'd been reporting the same thing several times a year ever since she was nearly killed. But she wasn't doing it for attention. She believed it.

"Looks like we got a frequent flyer," Mark said.

"Lucca mentioned this has happened before. I just didn't realize how frequently. I guess I should have looked at her phone records more carefully too." I scanned the dates on the screen. "There must be a pattern of behavior that's triggering these episodes, unless she's just remembering, and each time she does, she starts seeing him again." But I already suspected what had triggered her this time. I just had to prove it. "Can you print that for me?"

"You want access to official FBI phone logs?"

"I already have Daria's phone records, but this will save me time from having to parse through all the calls she's made in the last six years."

"So I'm doing you a favor," Mark said.

"Yes."

"Good. I just wanted to make sure you were clear on that."

"Technically, I'm doing a favor for Lucca, so by helping me to help him, he's actually the one you're doing the favor for."

"Nope." Mark printed the records for me. "That's not how this works. You owe me. End of story." He grabbed the sheet off the printer and held it out of my reach. "Agreed?"

"Seriously, Jablonsky, you're scaring me. I've never seen you like this." I gestured at him. "I don't even know what to call it. Giddy? Manic? Ecstatic? What gives?"

"Ask Marty. He knows."

* * *

The first thing I wanted to do was compare Daria's dating life to the calls she placed to the FBI. But I still didn't have her diary. Lucca was on his way to deliver it, so while I waited, I reviewed Daria's history. When she called the FBI, she only ever asked to speak to Lucca. He'd make a note of the call in the log, but she never asked him to open an investigation until now.

From what I'd gathered, Lucca checked in with her on a regular basis. His presence must have reinforced in her mind that she was safe. But when his calls became less frequent, she started to panic. That's when she started phoning him. At first, it had been an occasional call to the FBI field office. He probably talked her through it, possibly sent some local law enforcement to her place to check things out, and that was it. Satisfied, she'd go back to living her life until something else triggered her anxiety.

Her mom had alluded to this, but without going into specifics, I had no idea what she had been talking about. Each of these freakouts resulted in more brain scans and therapy sessions. I didn't know if that was Daria's idea or her mother's, but if her memory was returning, it'd make sense why she had the need for additional tests and doctor's visits.

However, she hadn't seen her neurologist in the last four months. And she hadn't scheduled any additional therapy sessions in addition to her standing appointments. I couldn't figure out what was different this time for Daria to have phoned the FBI offices here and in D.C. at least ten times before Lucca reached out. She'd never been that persistent before. She even phoned the police several times. But something about this was definitely different.

Thoughts of the missing screws came to mind. Paired with the green Charger Brin saw loitering in her neighborhood on the nights she and Daria had plans, I couldn't help but think my original impression had been wrong. Still, the descriptions Daria wrote down of each of these alleged sightings were an exact match to the security cam footage the FBI pulled after they stopped the Lightning Killer and retraced his footsteps. None of that information had ever gone public. Only law enforcement had access to those files. If Reagan LaRoche or someone else was stalking Daria and recreating the events leading up to the attack, how would he have known what to wear?

The intercom buzzed. As I pressed the button on my desk, someone barged into my office.

"Here." Lucca tossed one of Daria's journals at me. "That should be everything you wanted to see. Those are all the guys she's gone out with in the last five years."

"Great." I flipped it open, running my finger down the page until I found a date. I reached over and scanned the FBI call logs before checking Daria's phone records. But they didn't line up. They weren't even in the same ballpark. I moved quickly through the short list, but none of the others coordinated with Daria calling Lucca for help, except this last one. "Prior to a couple of months ago, when Daria called the FBI for help, what was she calling to report?"

"What are you talking about?"

"I've seen her phone records. I even paid Jablonsky a visit. I know how many times she's called you in the past. That's in addition to the number of times you've called her."

"She gets confused and freaks out. Talking to me helps calm her down. It's not a big deal. I told her to call whenever she feels panicked or overwhelmed. She isn't causing any harm. It's a few phone calls. After everything that happened to her, giving her a few minutes of my time is the least I can do. We've already been over this."

"This time is different."

"You might be right. Dr. Chen thinks these latest sightings could be repressed memories resurfacing. By now, Daria's brain has probably rewired itself in terms of how it works. Maybe it's found a way to access the details that had previously been inaccessible."

"Daria's not a computer, Lucca. She's a person."

"I know that. I'm just telling you what the doc said. After all, you're the one who pointed it out to me."

I made a face. "Actually, I'm rethinking that." I filled him in on my conversation with Brin and the workup I'd performed on Reagan. "When you first brought this to me, you said this time is different. Let's go over it again. How is it different from Daria's other freakouts?"

"In the past, when Daria's been afraid, she'd glimpse a shadowy figure. But she never saw him well enough to give me a description. It was more a feeling she had than an actual person. She might have heard noises. And she'd occasionally misplace some things, but they always turned up. She still hasn't found her hairbrush. It's weird, unexplainable things like that, which made me give her claims more credence."

"There's more to it."

He took a seat across from me. "She's never been this afraid. When she called me last night, she was hyperventilating. I thought she was dying."

"That was my fault. One of the Cross Security guards popped up outside her window at the most inopportune time."

"Regardless, I've seen Daria scared and lonely and struggling. This feels different." He patted his chest. "I know it in here. Every other time, she didn't truly believe someone was out to get her. She knew it was just her fear returning. This time, it's more than that. Whether those are her memories returning or someone terrorizing her, I don't know. The one thing I know for sure is we have no physical proof someone is doing this to her."

"What about the items she can't find? Or the missing screws?"

"Really, Parker, do you hear yourself?"

"Aren't we on the same side?"

"Yes, but you have to approach this rationally. Going along with her delusions won't help matters."

"Is that what Daria's therapist said?"

"More or less."

"Well, coming from someone who blacked out and lost an entire night, one of the scariest things is not knowing what's real and what isn't. Do you know what helped? People who believed me, who told me I wasn't crazy." Martin.

"This is different. This isn't alcohol induced."

"I know that."

"It sounds like you're projecting. This isn't about you. It's about Daria."

"I know that too. I'm just saying maybe Dr. Chen is wrong. Maybe we all are. Maybe Daria isn't remembering. Maybe someone's recreating this to fuck with her."

"Who?"

"Reagan LaRoche."

"How would he know what went down the first time? No one does. I was there and I barely know the lengths this psycho went to in order to hunt and torment his victims. Knowing what he wore or what he took from them isn't in any public document. It's filed away."

"You gave me access. Maybe someone else saw the records too. Did you or another agent leak the information at some point?"

"After everything we've been through, don't you trust me?"

"That's not what I meant. I'm just saying it wouldn't hurt to verify these details aren't circulating. You were on the Lightning Killer taskforce. Call up your old teammates and ask them about it."

"They're good agents."

"It won't hurt to check."

"You have trust issues like I've never seen. No wonder your boyfriend's in California." He eyed me. "Are you planning a trip to see him just to make sure he's actually there?"

"As a matter of fact, I am."

"Jesus." He rubbed a hand down his face.

I picked up Daria's journal and skimmed the pages, hoping to find a few entries on Reagan LaRoche to reinforce my point. He was near the back of the book. In fact, there were no entries after his.

I kept reading. The entry provided a basic description of the man, which read a lot nicer than the way Brin had described him. After meeting a couple of times at art events, Daria made it clear she was only interested in a platonic relationship. After that, she and Reagan appeared to have a standing afternoon meet-up every Saturday. Unfortunately, she hadn't mentioned what he wore or drove in any of her journal entries.

"Daria never mentioned Reagan to you?" I asked Lucca.

"I don't think so."

I turned Daria's journal back a few pages and slid it over to him. "Brin didn't tell you about him either?" I narrowed my eyes, recalling the lack of questions it seemed he had asked.

"I didn't ask if Daria was dating anyone. I just asked if she had trouble with anyone recently."

"And?"

"Brin didn't mention this guy. She said Daria had been creeped out that someone was watching her. They even left a restaurant because of it."

"Did she tell you about the green Charger?"

"Yes, but without a plate or description of the driver, it was worthless." Lucca almost smiled. "You found the car, didn't you?"

"I don't know yet. But I have a theory. It's a little rough. I'm still figuring some things out."

"All right. Let's hear it."

ELEVEN

After going over the situation with Lucca, I found myself outside Reagan LaRoche's apartment. As of this moment, I had no proof Reagan was stalking Daria. Honestly, I wasn't even certain if that was true. But Brin didn't care for him. And best friends usually had a good sense of the situation, or so I hoped. My friend, Kate, always had a sixth sense about the guys who came sniffing around me. She even encouraged me to give Martin a second glance at a time when I thought he was utterly insufferable. I decided it'd be best to defer to Brin on this matter and investigate further.

Lucca cautioned me to tread lightly. Stalking was hard to prove. Illegal trespass and breaking and entering were easier. But at the moment, we didn't know enough about Reagan. All we knew was his car was currently on blocks. I stuck one of Cross Security's tracking devices beneath the rear bumper, wondering if he would notice it when he put new tires on the vehicle. I hoped he wouldn't, but even if he did, the tracker wouldn't lead him to Daria.

My research showed he had moved to the city soon after Daria. Since they connected through their shared agent, they had spoken on the phone, text messaged, and e-mailed back and forth. If anyone was stalking Daria, my money was on Reagan. Even if he wasn't stalking her, I was nearly certain his presence was enough to trigger these nightmarish memories which had her convinced the Lightning Killer was back.

Taking a breath, I knocked on his door.

"Just a sec," he called.

A moment later, the knob twisted. He stood before me with his shirt unbuttoned to his naval and various beaded chains hanging from his neck. His highlighted brown hair was swept back with two strands falling forward over his forehead and practically into his eyes. He brushed them backward with one hand. He wore a thick leather cuff on his wrist and had various rings on each of his fingers. Artists.

"Mr. LaRoche?" I asked, even though he resembled a messier version of the photos he'd posted online.

"Damn straight." He held out his hand in such a way that I wondered if he wanted me to shake it or kiss it. "Are you my model for the night?"

"I'm a private investigator." Since I had no idea where that hand had been, I decided to play it safe by ignoring the gesture altogether. I peered into his apartment. "May I come in?"

"Sure." He leaned back against the door, using his already outstretched arm to wave me inside. "A private investigator, huh? I wasn't sure that was a real thing. I've never met a private eye before. What can I do for you?"

I hadn't decided how I wanted to play this. Lucca and I discussed the pros and cons of potentially spooking Reagan, but I thought it might be best to gather additional information before making unsubstantiated allegations. So I made up something on the fly. "It's about your art. My client would like to remain anonymous, but she's expressed an interest in acquiring a few of your pieces. She saw your water photos at the gallery a few weeks ago. Unfortunately, she wasn't able to buy any of them before they sold, so she hoped I could hunt you down and find out if you have any other pieces planned along the same lines."

"That depends." He gave me an odd look. "Why didn't

she have an art dealer approach me?"

"I used to work for an art gallery. Several, actually. She's an old friend. When I changed careers, she said there was no reason why I couldn't track down artists just as easily as cheating husbands. I couldn't exactly argue with that kind of logic, now could I?"

He laughed. "Is that what you do all day?"

"More than I'd like. But truthfully, most days, I just sit behind a desk and drink coffee."

"That sounds like my day job." He eyed me up and down. "Are you sure you aren't a model? I'd love to shoot you."

"Excuse me?" My hand slid inside my jacket, closer to my shoulder holster.

He pointed to the backdrop and camera equipment he had set up at one end of the room. A box of props sat beside the table. "You're very beautiful, not at all grizzled or burly."

"Thanks, I think. But I'm not particularly photogenic."

"I don't believe that."

"Doesn't matter. I don't like having my picture taken."

"But my photos aren't about the person. They're about what your presence signifies. The deeper meaning. The grit. The raw determination. Figuring out the mystery and how that feeds into the overarching mystery of life. That's why shooting a private eye would be incredible. Think about the symbolism. You investigate mysteries, which are just a small part of the human experience. I'd love to see you in action." He stared at me, seeing something with his mind's eye. "I could pay homage to the noir films. Picture this. Female detective in the classic trench coat and oversized hat, printed in black and white, or maybe sepia tones, with just the right pop of color. The blue of your eyes, perhaps. Or something red. A rose or," he blinked a few times, his mind a million miles away, "a single drop of blood. Or a flash of gold. Stolen jewels or coins. Something classic but with a modern flair. You make the old new again. Forget the trench coat. Your leather jacket would be perfect. With the right lighting, it would create the perfect contrast. We could even do something with rain. How do you feel about shooting outside?"

"A bystander might be struck."

"I'm not sure if you're taking that literally or if you're just having fun with the play on words." He quirked his head. "I find you fascinating. I can imagine a whole series of prints. What can I do to convince you to change your mind? We could work something out in trade. I'll let you know about the art you wanted if you pose for me."

"I'm not a commodity in this deal."

"What about the exploration of the mystery? Isn't that what drives you?" He cocked his head to the side. "What drew you to this line of work? I'd love to figure out what makes you tick."

"Let's work on one mystery at a time, okay?" I glanced around the apartment. The kitchen island partitioned off the cooking area from the rest of the room. The two doors at the other end must have been the closet and bathroom, but there was nothing more to the apartment than this one room. Yet, given the size and location, the rent must have been astronomical. Several framed photos hung on the wall. Most of the colors muted, except for a pop of just one.

Near the bed, Reagan had hung a photo of Daria in the midst of creating a small fiber sculpture. Most of her features were obscured since her back was turned to the camera, but I recognized her. She was manipulating yarn around a frame. "Did you take these?" I asked.

"Of course." He took a seat on top of the leopard print comforter which covered the black satin sheets beneath. "Do you like what you see? I'd create something even more incredible with you." He stretched back, exposing more of his abdomen. I wasn't impressed. He patted a place beside him on the bed. "Why don't you sit down? We can talk about whatever you want. I'm sure you have tons of questions. Which piece was your client's favorite? I have several waterfalls that haven't been shown to the public yet with the water droplets catching the lens. They're gorgeous."

"I bet she'd love something like that. How much?"

"They'll be unveiled two weeks from now. I have a flyer for the show somewhere, unless you want to work this off in trade."

I ignored him. "When does the bidding start?" I asked, wondering how I could breach the real reason for my visit.

"Contact the gallery owner, Celeste Nash. She'll have all the details. She brokers my deals."

"Celeste Nash, isn't she Daria Waylon's agent too?"

"You know Daria?"

"Yes," I said, "we've done business before." I pointed to the photo of her hanging on his wall. "It looks like the two of you are friends."

He grinned. "Yeah."

"How did she feel about you photographing her?"

"She didn't mind. Honestly, I'm not sure she noticed."

"Don't your subjects have to sign waivers?" I asked.

"Only for commercial use. Anything that's part of my private collection is precisely that."

"When's the last time you saw Daria?"

"Last week. We met for coffee and walked around the sculpture gardens."

"And before that?"

"The week before. We went to an art opening, and she stopped by here for a bit. That's when I took that photo."

"That's cool." But the photo on the wall looked like it was taken in the main room in Daria's townhouse. "She's been inside this very apartment?"

"Does that impress you?"

I narrowed my eyes at the photo. "You're lying. That wasn't taken here. It doesn't match anything in this room."

He glanced at it. "Sorry, I was thinking of a different print. That was taken at her place."

"Oh, so you've been there?"

"Once or twice."

"I didn't think she liked having houseguests."

"I'm the exception."

"Are you dating?"

"We're not monogamous, if that's what you're asking."

It wasn't. "How long have the two of you been together?"

"Why the sudden interest?"

"If you want me to pose for you, I'd like to talk to a few

of your other subjects."

"Well, if you must know, Daria and I have been going out for a few months. I practically had to twist Celeste's arm to introduce us. But it's rather hush-hush. Daria's a very private person. She doesn't share her relationship information with just anyone. And it's not like we're a regular thing. We mostly talk about art, but sometimes the passion just ignites when we get excited about a particular piece or project."

"You're friends with benefits?"

"I don't like labels. That doesn't describe the soulful connection we have. If you must label it, I'd say we're ships in the night."

It was the same thing, but his verbiage sounded more poetic. "Do you know of any other ships Daria's seeing?"

"I don't think she's seeing anyone else." He narrowed his eyes. "What does this have to do with anything?"

"I'm sorry. It's just a hazard of the job. Being naturally inquisitive is what got me fired from the gallery. I asked my clients too many personal questions." I bit my lip, wondering where to go from here. "I heard Daria's not making much art these days. But you said she was so enthralled in her work that she might not have noticed you taking the photo. Is she making a comeback?"

Some of the color left his face. "I don't know much about that. She talks a lot about wanting to finish this life-sized jungle thing she started before the coma, but she's not working on that in the photo. She makes these little desktop figurines she sells online. Frankly, it does nothing but devalue the rest of her art. It's too commercialized for a fine artist of her caliber. I'd know, since I deal with commercial art and marketing all damn day. But hey, it pays the bills."

"The coma?"

"Yeah," he nervously ran both hands through his hair, tucking the long strands behind his ears, "she nearly drowned. That's why she stopped working and fell into obscurity."

"Has she shown you any of her other projects?"

"I haven't seen any of her serious work. But if she ever

finishes that project she started years ago, I'm sure it'll be amazing. She showed me the sketches she made. Those blew me away."

"It's a shame what happened to her." I squinted at him. "Do you know about her past?"

"Everyone in the art world does. That psycho, the Lightning Killer, murdered a lot of great artists. To find one who survived is extraordinary." He stared at her photo. "She's amazing. I have yet to capture her true essence on film. But I will."

I didn't like the way he said it. "That shot looks pretty amazing to me."

"Thank you."

"How many other photos of her do you have?"

"Just that, and a few candids I took when we were hanging out."

"May I see them?"

"They'd bore you."

Sensing he wouldn't budge, I tried a different tactic. "From what I know about Daria, she's skittish around people. You must have really wooed her."

"Animal magnetism." He winked. "I don't know. We just click. Most intense hookups burn brightly and quickly. It's the afterglow that's allowed us to cultivate a lasting friendship and connection."

He sounded delusional enough to be dangerous. "Afterglow, huh?" I wondered what would happen if I poked the bear. "So the hot and heavy part is over?"

His eyebrows drew together, surprised I'd asked such a thing. "No, we're just getting started. The girl's got an itch that needs scratching."

"They sell devices and ointments for that."

"Are you always this abrasive? Is that how the stereotype for cynical, hard-boiled detectives came about?"

"I'm not sure. Find another one and ask him."

He glanced longingly at his camera and box of props. "Don't be like that. It won't take me long. Everything's set up already. Just let me shoot you."

"Most people who try to shoot me end up dead. I like you too much to allow that to happen."

"You like me?" He tucked the strand of hair that had fallen in front of his eyes back behind his ear, making the two hoop earrings he wore jangle. I had noticed the same thing happen when Daria brushed the hair behind her ear. "What?" he asked as I continued to stare.

"You have the same earrings as Daria." Hoops weren't uncommon, but these had tiny etchings in the metal. I wondered if hers had recently gone missing.

He climbed off the bed, growing increasingly uncomfortable by my questions. "Since you won't let me photograph you, would you mind cutting to the chase? I have projects to work on. Is there anything else your client wants to know?"

"Why did you move here?"

"What?"

"Did you move to the city for Daria?"

"Okay, lady, I'm not buying it. What is this about? I don't believe a private eye came all this way because someone wanted to buy a piece of art."

I held up my palms. "I'm just here to do my client's bidding. I can see myself out."

He stared at me, a predatory look in his eyes. As I made my way to the door, I wondered if he'd try to stop me. But he didn't move from where he sat atop his bed. As I opened the door, he called out, "In case you change your mind about letting me photograph you, I'm sure you can figure out how to find me. But seriously, you should think about it. Refusing is doing a disservice to the world."

"I guess the world will have to get over it."

TWELVE

The moment I got back to my car, I called Lucca and updated him on the situation. Everything about Reagan set my radar buzzing, from his attitude toward Daria to her photo on his wall to the earrings hanging from his left lobe. I'd even caught him in a lie. And if he lied about one thing, he probably lied about other things too.

"I'm heading over to Daria's now," I said. "I need to ask her a few questions."

"In the meantime, I'll see what I can find on Reagan."

"He doesn't have much of a record. I already checked."

"I'll take it a few steps further. If you need anything, let me know."

"Will do." I hung up, gave Reagan's apartment one final look, and pulled away. He only had the one car. The tracker would alert me if he moved it, but given its condition, I didn't think it'd be going anywhere fast.

It took almost forty minutes to get from Reagan's apartment to Daria's. The other two men from Joe Farzen's security team were monitoring the area. One man was parked out front. The other on the side street so he could monitor the back of the townhouse. Neither had seen anyone suspicious. I couldn't say the same.

After knocking, I wiped my feet on the welcome mat. Daria peeked out the side window before opening the door. "Alex," she said. From her expression, I was almost positive she remembered me.

"Hi, Daria. How are you?"

"I'm okay." She stepped back. "Eddie said you had a few more questions. Is this about my journal?"

"In a way." I stepped inside and locked the door behind me. Daria led me into the large room at the end of the hallway. She took a seat behind her desk and gestured to the sofa along the back wall. "I'd like to ask you a few questions about Reagan LaRoche. Are you seeing him?"

"We aren't dating, but we hang out a lot. We go to museums and stuff on the weekends, nothing romantic."

"How do you feel around him? Do you feel safe?"

"We meet in public. I don't worry as much when I'm alone with someone when there are other people around."

"Does he make you uncomfortable?"

"Most men make me uncomfortable. Eddie's the exception."

"Have you ever been to Reagan's apartment?"

"Once. We were going to an art opening. He said he forgot something at home, but his place was on the way." She reached for one of her journals and flipped back a few pages. Her forehead glistened as she read. She swallowed, the color draining from her cheeks. "I didn't like being there. It scared me. I don't know why, but my chest got tight and I couldn't breathe. I ran out of there. I just couldn't..." She sucked in a breath, slowly blowing it out. "I'm not always good in new places or with new people."

"That's okay." I waited for her to calm down. Even the memory of being inside his apartment made her anxious. "Do you know what made you so uncomfortable?"

"I don't know. I talked to Dr. Chen, my therapist, about it. But we haven't pinpointed the cause yet. She thinks it's something subconscious. Maybe his aftershave or the shape of his face or something that reminds me of Andrew Holland."

"She might be right. I've noticed several similarities between the two."

"Like what?"

"They both like photography."

Daria chewed on her bottom lip while she mulled it over. "That could be it."

"Has Reagan ever been to your place?"

"No. Only people I absolutely trust are allowed here."

"You're sure he hasn't been inside?"

She scrunched up her brow while she searched her memory. Then she scoured through the top few journals, reading each entry carefully, before consulting her phone. "No. I make it a point to meet him at a coffee shop. We always take public transit or walk wherever we're going. And after it's over, we leave separately."

"How did you end up at his place that one time?"

"We were walking from the coffee shop to the gallery. We had to pass his place, and he invited me up." She held out the journal for me to read, but I believed her. "I don't invite people here. My parents and Brin are the only people I allow in my house. And Eddie, of course."

"And me," I said.

"Well, Eddie vouched for you. Since he trusts you, I trust you." She laughed softly. "I have a different set of rules for law enforcement and first responders. Anyone who puts his or her life on the line to save mine is welcome inside my home."

"What can you tell me about Brin?"

"I love Brin. She's the best. She puts up with all my flaws and impediments. I don't know where I'd be without her." Her eyebrows knit together. "Brin doesn't like Reagan. She never did. She told me he gives her bad vibes. Do you think there's something to that?"

"Actually, that's why I wanted to look into him." I looked around the room. "Were you working on a small fiber art angel recently?"

She opened a cardboard box beside her desk. "Like this?"

It looked like the finished version of the sculpture she'd been making in the photo Reagan had taken. "When did you complete that?"

She looked up at the calendar. "Four days ago. Someone

ordered it from my website." She went into an in-depth explanation on how she chose the yarn and flax fibers, forged them into fiber paper, molded the paper around a form, removed the form to create each part of the angel, and combined the pieces into the finished sculpture.

"That's beautiful. How often do you make these?"

"It depends. They're big sellers around Christmas and First Communion. But right now is an off season. This one is a birthday gift. Why do you ask?"

"Does anyone watch you work?"

"Only if I'm sharing a studio with other artists, which hasn't happened in a very long time."

I assessed the room. Given the angle of the photo, it could have been taken from outside the back window. Daria had been turned away from the window. The wall behind her desk was blank, making the perfect backdrop. She'd been right about one thing. Someone had been in her backyard.

"Why do you look like that?" she asked. "What's wrong?"

Lucca warned me that telling her would send her into a tailspin, so I withheld the information. "I was just curious. Reagan seems interested in all things art. I thought he might have asked to watch you create."

"He did, but I said no."

Some men needed to learn what that word meant. Reagan was one of them. If I ran into him again, I'd be sure to impress the point upon him.

"Why do you still look uncertain?" she asked.

"No reason. I tend to be overly cautious."

She gave me an odd look. "Me too."

"I'd strongly suggest you avoid Reagan for a while, until I finish investigating."

"Why? What does he have to do with the Lightning Killer?"

"I'm not sure yet." I decided to risk it and asked, "Could he be the guy you keep seeing? The one who's been following you?"

She looked into the kitchen, where the descriptions of the man she saw were stuck to the fridge. "I'd recognize him if it were Reagan. It's not. I'm sure of it."

I wasn't, but I didn't see any reason to argue. "I still think it might be best to take a few extra precautions until we figure this thing out."

"Okay," she picked up her phone and typed out a text, "I'll cancel our plans for Saturday. Honestly, I'd much rather stay in and get some work done." She sent the text and put down her phone. She picked up a hair tie and pulled her hair into a ponytail.

I zeroed in on her visible earlobe. "The other day you had two tiny gold hoops in your ear, but you're not wearing them now."

Her fingers brushed against her earlobe, finding two studs instead. Again, consternation etched her features. "They're in my jewelry box. I had four of them. Two for each ear, but I haven't been able to find the other two. And since I wanted to match today, I couldn't wear them."

"How long have the hoops been missing?"

Again, she reached for her journal, but when she couldn't find the details, she put it down and picked up her day planner instead. "The first time I noticed them missing was eight days ago. They are just one of many things that have disappeared lately. Someone's gotta be moving my stuff around and taking my things, or I'm losing my mind."

"I don't think you're losing your mind."

"Unfortunately, that doesn't make me feel better."

I made a list of the other items Daria noticed were missing or had been moved, but I wasn't certain if I'd seen any of them at Reagan's apartment. The photo proved he'd been lurking outside her place. The earrings might be enough to prove he broke in, except they weren't custom-made or engraved, so that could be a coincidence. No judge would sign a search warrant on such flimsy evidence like that. The photo was another story, but if Reagan repeated the lie he told me, that Daria invited him over, I wasn't sure who the police would believe. I had to dig deeper. I had to get proof beyond a reasonable doubt. Reagan said he had other photos of Daria. I had to find them.

After doing my best to reassure her, I went outside and briefed the guards to keep an eye out. I told them what I found and suspected. They knew to be wary of any green sedans or anyone matching Reagan's description. However, I warned them it was too soon to narrow their focus. Anyone they spotted in the area who didn't belong could be terrorizing Daria.

* * *

I spent most of the night digging up everything I could on Reagan LaRoche and figuring out the best time to break into his apartment. The techs upstairs had checked his phone logs and financial statements. Lucca didn't necessarily need to know about that, especially since the information didn't result in much of anything. Reagan didn't act particularly suspicious, at least on paper. In person was another story.

Daria didn't remember where she bought the gold hoop earrings, so I couldn't see if Reagan had made a similar purchase. But my gut said the ones he wore were the same pair she couldn't find. "Don't jump to conclusions, Parker," I warned. But that was easier said than done.

Around lunchtime, I phoned the marketing agency where Reagan worked and tried to set up an appointment under a fictitious name. "I'm sorry, ma'am," his assistant said. "Mr. LaRoche is booked solid today. He has an opening Friday at 2:30."

"How late does he usually work?"

"The office closes at five."

"Thanks." I hung up before she could put anything on the books.

With at least four hours to spare, I grabbed my lock picks, changed into something more casual, and headed over to his place. Daria had lost more than a pair of earrings. If Reagan were terrorizing her, those items had to be here. Somewhere. And since he hadn't offered to let me search his apartment last night, I'd have to do it now that I had the place to myself.

My previous trip prepared me for what to expect. Reagan didn't have a doorbell camera, and the few security cams in the hallways didn't pose much of a challenge to my hooded jacket and sunglasses. Since the area was bohemian, his neighbors didn't work nine to fives. But the two or three I passed on the stairs and in the hallway didn't pay me much attention.

Hoping that wouldn't change, I knocked gently on the door while glancing around. "Reagan?" I called.

When the woman in the peasant skirt disappeared into the stairwell, I leaned into the doorjamb, took out my lock picks, and set to work. The single cylinder deadbolt took a little more time than I would have liked, but the coast remained clear.

Easing the door open, I slipped inside. Before removing my sunglasses or hood, I scanned the area, but I didn't see any security devices. No cameras. No alarms. It was time to get to work.

Tucking my sunglasses into the neck of my shirt, I went straight to the photos hanging on the wall and snapped shots of each of them. Determining the precise location where the photo was taken would give me something to work with. The other prints were likely of no consequence, but most stalkers didn't just target one victim. There were usually others in their past. Any one of the subjects in these photos could have been people Reagan fixated on. If all else failed, I'd dig into them.

Turning, I examined the rest of the room, wondering where to begin. At Quantico, we were taught to work methodically. We were also taught to prioritize. Who knew what kinds of secrets the bathroom might contain?

I slipped inside and turned on the light. The shower and toilet tank didn't conceal anything sinister. The medicine cabinet contained the usual assortment one would expect to find. The bathroom drawer was another story.

Reagan LaRoche had four different kinds of eyeliner. That was three more than what I owned. He also had plenty of other makeup items. Given his penchant for dressing like a '90s vampire or flamboyant pirate, I didn't think any of the makeup belonged to Daria. She hadn't said any had gone missing, but I snapped photos of it just in case.

He also had two different hairbrushes and three combs.

Daria's missing brush was black and purple. So was the one staring at me from Reagan's drawer. But I resisted the urge to take it with me. That was evidence the authorities would need to legally obtain. Instead, I pulled out a pair of tweezers and an evidence bag, removed a few strands of hair that looked to be too long and dark for Reagan, and slipped them into the bag. The lab would have to determine if this was Daria's brush.

My stomach clenched. He must have been inside her house. I wondered how many times. Was she home when he entered? Or had he waited for her to leave before sneaking in?

As soon as I finished in the bathroom, I checked the door beside it. Initially, I thought this was a closet, but it was practically the size of a small storage room. Martin would love if his walk-in was this big.

Reagan kept everything in here: clothes, towels, sheets, boxes of props, and photo equipment. I could spend an entire day sorting through it, but I didn't have that kind of time. I did a quick search of the boxes, but I didn't find any incriminating evidence or severed heads. He probably kept those elsewhere.

Leaving the closet the way I found it, I returned to the main room. I dug through his work area. Several memory cards sat beside his computer. After bypassing the log-in screen with a trick I'd recently picked up at Cross Security, I checked the files on his computer, but he didn't store much on the hard drive.

However, the memory cards were filled with photos. I copied each of them onto a thumb drive and put them back where I found them. I'd view the photos once I was back at the office. For now, this would have to suffice.

I checked the time. I'd already spent over two hours in the apartment. I didn't want to risk getting caught, so the faster I got out of here, the better.

His dresser and nightstand didn't reveal much. He was a boxer guy, who probably went commando frequently, given the limited amount of underwear he owned. Unless he didn't change them often. Shaking away the thought, I moved my search to his bed.

He'd pulled the comforter up but hadn't made the bed. As I suspected, I didn't find anything between the sheets. In the drawers built into the bedframe, I found his porn stash.

Not surprisingly, his tastes ran a tad on the voyeuristic side. That didn't bode well, but given his passion for photography and stalking, I expected as much. I snapped a few photos and pushed the drawer closed.

The only items of interest in his kitchen were the flyers for art exhibits and gallery events. I spread them out on the counter, photographed each of them, and returned the stack to the drawer, hoping I'd kept them in the same order. I wasn't sure how persnickety Reagan was about his belongings. Something told me he wouldn't notice if things had been moved or went missing, but I wasn't sure. And I didn't want to spook him yet. However, a part of me wanted to screw with him the same way he screwed with Daria. I would have loved to take his camera or something he'd be sure to miss just so he'd know how it felt to not feel safe at home.

Instead, I did one final check and carefully let myself out. Luckily, the hallway was clear. I didn't bother to manipulate the dead bolt with a piece of tape in order to lock it behind me. But I locked the bottom lock. If he noticed the top was open, maybe that'd be enough to freak him out. Right now, the only thing I wanted was to get under his skin. But I knew better. We couldn't rattle him until we had the evidence we needed.

The earrings, the brush, and the photo on the wall should be enough to determine who'd been terrorizing Daria. Now I just had to make sure my assumptions were correct.

THIRTEEN

After leaving Reagan's, I stopped by Daria's. The photo of her working had been taken from outside her back window. I snapped a few shots with my phone in order to compare the angle, but it looked right. Then I collected a DNA sample and dropped everything off at the office.

Amir said he'd do what he could, but the DNA comparison would take time. Twenty-four hours at the very least, but that was unlikely. Forty-eight or seventy-two hours was a more likely estimate.

While I waited for that analysis to complete, I showed the photos to the techs. They agreed with my assessment. The print hanging on Reagan's wall had been taken from outside Daria's house. The photographer had worked some magic to minimize the window glare, but the techs were able to enhance it, proving it was taken from outside, most likely without Daria's knowledge. Unfortunately, the photographer's reflection wasn't visible. It wasn't a smoking gun, but it was damn close.

Reagan LaRoche had been in Daria's backyard, but my search had come up empty, just like when the police checked. Could Reagan have removed the screws from her air conditioner cover? I didn't know. More importantly, I didn't know why he would, but I'd worry about that later. All I knew was he hadn't left any evidence of his presence behind. But since I had no idea when that photo was taken, any evidence, if there had been evidence, could have blown away in a storm or washed away in the rain.

Plugging a copy of the thumb drive into my computer, I scanned the thousands of photos in thumbnail size, but nothing stuck out. Too hyped up to sit behind my desk and move frame by frame through every photo Reagan had taken, I handed that off to the techs and told them what to look for. Then I called Lucca.

"This is out of my jurisdiction," he said. "It's not federal, so I can't put a surveillance team on LaRoche. Even if I did, anything we uncover would be inadmissible."

"I know, which is why I'm on my way to the precinct."

"Do you think your friends in major crimes can swing something?"

"I'm hoping." But we both knew what I had was flimsy. Daria never reported a break-in, so saying LaRoche was in possession of stolen property wouldn't fly. The photo might be enough to prove stalking or, at the very least, get a search warrant. "I'm guessing, if he is our guy, which I think he is, he's probably done this before. I'll see if the police know anything about him. No charges were ever filed against him, but maybe someone made a complaint and changed her mind. If nothing else, there are those bar fights he got in. Maybe there's something to that."

"That was years ago. More than a decade. I don't see that going anywhere." Lucca paused. "I can't believe I missed this."

"It happens. Daria didn't mention him. She told you she wasn't dating. Everyone said the same thing. No one bothered to tell you her new friend started out as a failed date."

"But they told you."

"That's because people like me better than you."

"That'll be the day." He waited a beat before asking, "What are you planning on doing while you wait for the DNA analysis to come back on the hairs in that brush?"

"I'll keep my eye on him and make sure he doesn't try

anything else." I feared even if the DNA matched, which I was sure it would, Reagan would say Daria borrowed his brush. A defense attorney would come up with a logical explanation, and given Daria's memory lapses, it'd be hard to prove otherwise. "Worst case, even if we can't build a case against him, there are other ways to convince him to back off."

"Does Cross keep heavies on the payroll?"

"Cross Security would never resort to intimidation tactics." Actually, I didn't know, and I didn't want to. "However, I can be pretty damn scary."

"Yeah, I've seen. Just don't do anything until we see what the police have to say. We don't know how LaRoche will react to threats. He might back off or charge full speed ahead. Nothing in his record indicates he's dangerous, but we know he's been spying on Daria. If he's broken into her house, who knows what else he's capable of doing?"

"The photo should be enough to get a warrant." Or so I hoped.

"Run it by the PD and see what they say. I'm guessing they're going to have to see it for themselves before they can do anything about it."

"Reagan doesn't have it posted on any of his social media accounts and has made no mention of it online. I contacted Celeste Nash, but she doesn't know anything about it. Reagan told me last night he doesn't need consent if a photo is not available for commercial use."

"See if you can track down his friends or anyone who's been to his apartment in the last three or four months. Someone he's invited inside must have seen the photo on the wall. Once we get corroboration, that should be enough for the police to get a search warrant."

"Thanks for the tip," I said sarcastically.

"Sorry," Lucca said. "I just don't want either of us to miss anything else."

"I get it. I'll see what I can do. Reagan's on a few dating sites. Surely, he's taken at least one person home who remembers the photo."

We hung up just as I pulled into a visitor space at the precinct. If I hurried, I'd make it upstairs right at shift change. That would double my chances of finding a friendly face who'd be willing to hear me out.

"Shit," Detective Derek Heathcliff cursed as I made my way toward his desk, "I forgot to call you."

"Why? What's wrong?"

He stared at me, as if trying to determine if I was serious. "It's Thursday." He glanced around, lowering his voice a little. "We have plans."

"Don't worry about that. I'm in the middle of something. I can't make it tonight."

His eyes narrowed, and he pointed a finger in my face. "No. You skipped Monday's session because you had dinner with Lucca. You're not skipping again."

"Heathcliff, you coming?" Detective Jacobs called from the stairwell.

"Two seconds." Heathcliff stared at me. "You promised."

"This isn't about that. I'm working on a case. Actually, that's why I'm here. I need a favor."

"That'll have to wait." Heathcliff gave me a look. "You should go to a meeting, Alex. You need to take care of yourself."

"I'm okay." I lowered my voice. "Grief counseling can wait. I have something far more pressing to take care of, and it looks like you do too. We'll go next week. No harm, no foul." I jerked my head toward the door, nodding at Jacobs. "Get going, Detective. Crime doesn't wait."

Heathcliff muttered something under his breath, covering his words with his hand as he rubbed his mouth. After a moment of searching the bullpen, he waved down Detective Nick O'Connell who was on his way out of Lt. Moretti's office. "O'Connell, Parker needs a favor. Afterward, take her to her meeting. Ignore her excuses. She comes up with something new every week, but I'm not buying it. And you shouldn't either." He brushed past me before I could object. "You and me, next week," he called as he jogged toward the stairwell. "Don't forget."

I rolled my eyes and took a second to put a smile on my face before spinning around to face O'Connell. "Hey, Nick. How's my favorite detective?"

O'Connell appeared utterly confused. "What's Heathcliff

talking about?"

"Who knows? Anyway, are you busy? I need to run something by you. I caught a case, and I'm hoping you might be able to get a search warrant."

He grabbed a folding chair and placed it beside his desk. "Since when does Cross Security worry about search warrants?"

"They don't. I do. A victim from one of Lucca's old cases has a problem. She's being stalked. She's placed several calls to 9-1-1, filed a few reports, but the responding officers never found anything."

"That's not surprising. Does she have a protection order against the guy?"

"Not yet. I'm still building a case against him, which is where you come in."

"I'm off duty."

"You're a major crimes detective. There is no off duty."

"I'm sure Jenny would agree with you."

"You should listen to your wife."

He pulled a blank legal pad out of his drawer and grabbed a pen. "All right. Fill me in."

I told him everything I knew about the situation, leaving out the parts I deemed irrelevant or harmful. Daria's medical condition was of no consequence when Reagan had a photo of her hanging in his apartment which she had not consented to him taking.

"But you aren't sure he stole her hairbrush or her earrings?"

"I'm sure they're hers. I just can't prove it yet."

"Did she ID them?"

"Not yet."

"How are you planning to prove they belong to her?"

"Forensic science. I'll have the results in one to three days."

O'Connell snickered. "That's how long DNA analysis takes. I take it you've already collected some evidence."

"Nothing we can use against him in court."

"Do you think this guy's dangerous?"

I shrugged.

"What's his name?"

"Reagan LaRoche." I spelled it while Nick typed it into the computer.

"I'm guessing you already ran him." He narrowed his eyes, reading the results. "One charge of misdemeanor assault. He pled and served no jail time."

"Anything else?"

He glanced at me. "You mean to tell me you didn't already look? I'm shocked."

"I looked. I just didn't find anything else."

He scanned the page. "I don't see anything either."

"Have any complaints been filed against him? Has he ever been a person of interest or a witness to a crime?"

"Has anyone ever told you you ask a lot of questions?"

"All the damn time, but it's why I get paid the big bucks."

"I'll have to remember that." He expanded the search parameters. "Why would you think he might be a witness to a crime?"

"He's a photographer. According to Daria's friend, Reagan's always noticing things. He probably takes that damn camera everywhere he goes. That would explain the thousands of photos on his memory cards."

"Photos?"

I shook my head. "Don't worry about that."

"I'm not seeing anything here. Can you prove he took the photo of your client without her knowledge?"

"He told me he took it, but he never said she didn't know about it."

"How can you be certain she didn't?"

"The angle of the shot proves it was taken from outside her window by someone looking in. Her back's to the camera. You can tell it's still her based on the side of her face, but there's no way she saw the person taking the photo. And she's never invited him to her home. That reads stalking to me."

"Was the photo on one of these memory cards?" he asked.

"No, it's hanging on his damn wall."

"I'll run it by Moretti, but I don't think it's enough. Everything you have is circumstantial at best."

"But this information is coming from a reliable source." I waved my hand down my body. "Me."

"Sit tight. I'll be right back."

I slid into his chair and tried a few searches of my own. The police had an open file on Daria's case. But they had no suspects, no leads, and no witnesses. My intel fell into line with the open case, but O'Connell was right. I didn't have anything yet. Sure, I'd given the police my word that I'd seen a suspicious photo hanging in Reagan's apartment, but he and Daria were friends. Even if she swore she hadn't allowed him to take the photo, he could deny being the photographer. Yet, I doubted his ego would allow him to say such a thing.

Maybe Brin could help. I ran a quick check on her. Lucca had assured me she didn't have an arrest record, but I found something a little unsettling. Brin Yatlik had been the victim of domestic abuse. Her ex-boyfriend had nearly beaten her to death.

I texted Lucca, asking if he knew about this.

That's how she and Daria met and bonded. They're both patients of Dr. Chen.

The police report was dated fifteen years ago. Brin had been nineteen at the time. Based on our brief conversation, she'd made leaps and bounds in her recovery. She didn't exhibit any of the behaviors most women in her situation did. A decade and a half of continued therapy had a positive benefit. I could practically hear Heathcliff's snide remark in my head. Luckily, he wasn't around to point to this as a reason why I shouldn't skip another group therapy session.

However, I couldn't help but wonder if the authorities would use Brin's history against us when trying to obtain a search warrant. I didn't see how the two were related, but I'd run up against several narrow-minded judges in my day. Their preconceived notions often made obtaining search warrants next to impossible. Still, the photo was proof.

O'Connell returned to his desk a few minutes later. "Moretti said if you have reason to believe Reagan LaRoche is dangerous and poses a threat to Daria or the public at large, we can put a unit on him. Once we get eyes on him, if he does anything shady, we might have cause to get a search warrant."

"Lucca's afraid what will happen if we spook him."

"What do you think?"

"My priority is making my client feel safe. But in this particular situation, it's a little more complicated than that. I don't want to scare Reagan away until I'm certain he's the guy who's been making her life a living hell."

"A patrol car's out." O'Connell cocked his head to the side. "You still haven't answered my question."

"I don't know if he's dangerous. His history suggests otherwise, but maybe he's never been caught."

"Are you looking into his past? All the predators I know are repeat offenders."

"I'm working on it."

"Okay." O'Connell glanced toward the LT's office. "We can put a car outside Daria's house."

"I already have a team on that."

"So she's safe," O'Connell said.

"For now." The DNA results would be back before Tuesday. Hopefully, once we had those, we'd be able to take official action against Reagan. If not, I'd have to speak to Cross about assigning another team to take over. If I dangled the possibility that Daria might be interested in signing with Cross Security because of the phenomenal job we were doing, my boss would be more likely to agree. I rubbed my eyes. "There's got to be some way to get this guy. I gotta find something."

O'Connell tugged his jacket free from his chair, forcing me to get up. "How about we get some dinner and I'll take you to that meeting Heathcliff was talking about?"

"I have a better idea."

"Heathcliff warned me about this. You heard him. No excuses."

"I thought you didn't know what he was talking about."

O'Connell held out his phone. "He texted me the details while I was talking to the LT."

"Meetings are supposed to be anonymous."

"Yeah, but I already knew. Remember, you talked to Jen

about it."

"Forget what I said before. You should never listen to your wife."

"Come on, Parker, it won't be that bad. They have snacks. Coffee and cookies. Maybe some donuts."

"I will buy you whatever snacks you want, Nick. But I don't have the time or energy to spend on a meeting. Not when I feel like I'm this close to something. You know me. Even if we go, my focus will be elsewhere."

"What do you want to do instead?"

"Are you up for conducting a little surveillance?"

FOURTEEN

"I still don't get it." O'Connell reached into the brown paper sack and pulled out another taco. He unwrapped it, holding the paper beneath his chin while he took a big bite. "Who puts his car on blocks?"

"Do you think someone stole his tires?"

"If they did, they should have stripped it."

"Do you think it's worth anything?" I picked up my soda and took a swig. The fizz from the cherry cola tickled my nose.

"The car?" He considered my question while he finished his taco and scooped the fallen toppings off the paper with a spork and shoveled them into his mouth. "It didn't look like it was in very good shape."

"Missing tires can do that."

"True." He peered into the bag, but we'd exhausted our supply of tacos. Instead, he grabbed another bag from the floor. "Would you like a churro or nachos?"

"Churro, please."

He held out the fried, cinnamon-sugar coated stick. "Just remember, if Jen asks, you know nothing about this."

"And the same goes for Heathcliff." I bit into one end, chewing thoughtfully while I watched Reagan LaRoche through his apartment window. Reagan had gotten home a few minutes before we arrived. I wasn't sure how he got home. He could have walked from the bus stop or taken a rideshare or taxi. Figuring out his preferred method of transport would make tailing him easier, but O'Connell had been in desperate need of sustenance. And since I promised I'd buy him dinner and whatever junk food he wanted, it was a necessary delay.

"What normally goes on at those survivor meetings?" O'Connell asked.

"Someone shares a sad story. People cry. It's not a pleasant experience."

"How are the cookies and coffee?"

"Stale and cold."

"That sucks." He glanced at me from the corner of his eye while he popped the top off the container of loaded nachos. "Is it helping?"

"I wouldn't be torturing myself if it wasn't."

"Isn't the self-torture the reason you're going to these meetings?"

I snorted, nearly choking on the churro. "I never considered that. I wonder if I've replaced one method of self-loathing and torture with something equally painful. Maybe if I share this epiphany with Martin and Heathcliff, they'll get off my back about me going to every single meeting."

"But it's helping."

"I guess."

"Do you speak at these meetings? It's group therapy, so that's the point. That's how it works, right?"

"I don't know how it works. All I know is I'm sleeping better, which means I have a firmer grip on reality."

"That's good." He seemed fascinated. "Does everyone sit in a circle and take a turn?"

"Do you think I'd go if they did?"

"Probably not."

"There's your answer." I balled up the greasy napkin and tossed it into the bag. "I spoke once. I don't plan on doing it again."

"What do you normally do? Just sit there?"

"Why the interrogation? If you're that curious, go to a meeting. I think AA meets in the same room after we do. And they have some kind of sex addict recovery group some other day during the week. Ooh, I even think they have an overeater's anonymous meeting you could attend." I jerked my chin toward the half-eaten nachos in his lap. "I'm starting to think someone needs to drag you to that one. What gives?"

He held up his palms. "First off, I'm not interrogating you. I'm genuinely curious. You might be a giant pain in the ass, but you're family. I've told you that a million times. After what happened to Cooper, you had everyone worried about you. I'm glad something's helping."

"Yeah, me too." Just hearing his name brought horrific images to mind.

"We could create our own little therapy session here in the car. What do you think?"

"At most meetings, I cry. Do you really want to deal with that?"

"Hell no. I hate it when you cry."

"I hate crying, so we're even." I watched him inhale the rest of the nachos. "What kind of health kick has Jen forced upon you this time?"

O'Connell wiped his mouth. "Some thirty day whole foods thing. No dairy. No sugar. One of the doctors she works with swears by it. He says he feels twenty years younger. She figures with all the running around we do, it'd be nice to feel like teenagers again."

"How many days into it are you?"

"Thirteen."

"Does this mean you have to start over from the beginning?"

"Why would it? She wants me to feel like a teenager, so I'm eating like a teenager." He pointed a finger at me. "Just remember, what happens inside a Cross Security vehicle is confidential. Not a word of this to anyone, or I'll tell Heathcliff you tricked me into letting you skip tonight's meeting."

"Extortion's illegal, Detective."

"It's not extortion." He winked. "Not to mention, it was

your idea. You bribed me, an officer of the law, in order to convince me to come with you. Need I remind you that is illegal?"

"But you took the bribe. That's entrapment."

"Don't worry. I devoured the evidence."

I smiled. "That's why we didn't take your car. You didn't want Jen to smell the fast food." I looked at him. "If she finds out, she's going to kill me. And since she's an ER nurse, she'll get away with it."

"If it makes you feel any better, Heathcliff's a homicide detective. They won't even find my remains."

"I guess that means we have to nail this guy in order to make our detour from my usual Thursday night meeting worthwhile."

"Guess so."

O'Connell and I chitchatted for the better part of the next two hours. However, Reagan remained in front of his computer. Every once in a while, he'd get up to get something from the fridge or use the bathroom. Then he'd return to his seat. The man never even thought to pull his curtains or invest in blinds, which made my job easier.

"Look," O'Connell pointed, "he's taking off his shirt."

"How many buttons did he have left to open? Two?"

"Three."

"Do you think he goes to work like that?"

"Most places have a dress code, so he'd have to abide by it. We didn't see him when he came home, but I thought when we first arrived, he was buttoned up to mid-chest. As he's been working, he's been dropping buttons. Does he do the same thing with his pants?"

"I only met him once, but they seemed securely fastened," I said.

"Did he assault your client?"

"I don't think so, but I can't be sure."

"She didn't tell you?"

"She wouldn't necessarily remember."

"Do you think he drugged her? Or did they drink to excess?"

"Neither." It was time to let the cat out of the bag. Against my better judgment, I told him about Daria's condition. "She freaked out the one time they were alone in his apartment. Every other time they meet, they always do it in public. She's afraid to be alone with him, which makes me think he might have done something that made her uncomfortable, but it's also possible he didn't do anything except drop a few buttons."

"What kind of vibes does this guy give you?" O'Connell leaned forward and peered out the windshield, trying to get a better look at Reagan. "He strikes me as a fraud. Like one of those Vegas magicians."

"That's the perfect comparison. I was going with vampire or pirate. But you're right. He dresses like an illusionist." That meant everything he did was a misdirect to hide something else. "He's supposed to be a serious artist, but he works a corporate gig to pay the bills."

"Maybe he dresses like that to convince everyone he really is one of these artsy people and not a corporate sellout."

"Yeah, maybe."

While I mulled it over, Reagan put on a black silk robe. Then he picked up his camera and adjusted a few lights. He moved a stool in front of the white fabric backdrop. He grabbed another stool from the kitchen and moved it to the center. He placed a fruit bowl on top and rearranged the apples. While he was polishing a granny smith, my phone rang.

"Hello?"

At first, the only thing I heard on the other end of the line were a few frantic gasps. And then Daria squeaked out, "He's here."

Before I could say a word, the call disconnected. "Shit." I tried calling her back, but it went straight to voicemail.

"What's wrong?" O'Connell tugged on his seatbelt as I started the engine.

I gave Reagan's apartment a final look. "She said he's there."

"It can't be Reagan."

"No kidding." I tried calling her back again, but her phone was off or broken. I dialed Joe Farzen and peeled away from the curb. "Joe, this is Alex. What's going on over there?"

"Nothing."

"Daria just phoned. She said he's there."

"We're outside. We haven't seen anyone enter."

"I don't care. Get inside. Now." I tossed my phone to O'Connell. "Call Lucca. Tell him Daria's in trouble and to meet us there."

"Do you want me to call this in?" O'Connell asked as he found Lucca's number. "I can get patrol units over there."

"Not yet. Not until I know what's going on." Daria had already called in too many false reports. I zipped through traffic, which at this hour was pretty light.

"Parker, I hate to point this out."

"Then don't."

"We had eyes on Reagan LaRoche all night. We're his alibi."

"That doesn't mean anything. Not yet."

"But—"

"Don't, Nick." The only thing on my mind was getting to Daria. She sounded terrified. I glanced at my phone, which Nick had put in the cupholder after speaking to Lucca. Why hadn't the Cross Security team called me back with an update? Were they under fire? "How could they have missed this? Two men in two cars were watching her place. How could someone get past them?"

"Maybe this guy took out one of Cross's guys."

"Maybe." I stomped down harder on the gas pedal.

Four minutes later, I parked haphazardly in front of Daria's townhouse. Her front door remained open. I ran toward it with O'Connell at my heels. As I entered, I unholstered my gun, slowing as I checked the living room for hostiles.

"Police," O'Connell announced, moving ahead of me toward the main room, "is anyone here?"

"Take it easy. I'm with Cross Security." Joe Farzen raised his hands to shoulder height. "I'm armed, but I have a permit."

"It's okay, Nick. That's Joe."

Nick nodded to him, and Joe slowly lowered his hands.

"Where's your number two?" I asked.

"Miles is checking the perimeter for signs of a breach."
Joe pointed to the back hallway. "Daria took one look at us
and started screaming. I called the mobile medical team.
They're on the way."

"Is she hurt?" I didn't wait for an answer as I made my
way down the hallway. O'Connell followed at my heels,
checking each room as we passed. "Daria?" I called.
"Daria? It's Alex. I'm here to help."

Her bedroom door was cracked open. Cautiously, I
pushed it slowly, holding up a hand to stop O'Connell from
taking point. I didn't want to know how terrified she'd be if
she saw another unfamiliar face enter her room with a
pointed gun. The woman was already traumatized. And the
men I sent in to help had only made it worse.

"Hang back a sec."

"Parker," O'Connell warned, "he could be inside."

"Security would have seen him. Just give me a minute."

"Thirty seconds."

Nodding, I stepped into the bedroom. "Daria?" Frantic,
pained gasps came from the other side of her bed. I glanced
at the saints and religious icons. *You guys were supposed
to protect her.* "It's me. It's Alex. Eddie's on his way. I
brought a police detective with me. His name's Nick. He
wants to help too. Are you okay?" I glanced into the
attached bathroom as I made my way around the bed. The
bathroom light was on. Blood drops and pieces of broken
glass made a trail from the bathroom to the side of the bed.
"Daria?"

She reached a bloody hand out. I holstered my weapon
and helped her slide out from beneath the bed. The upper
right side of her forehead was bleeding. Based on the
injury, I'd guess it was from blunt force trauma.

Once she was out from under the bed, she hugged me
hard. Her entire body trembled. "Shh," I soothed. "It'll be
okay." I heard O'Connell's footsteps behind me. Daria
tensed. "That's Detective Nick O'Connell. You told me
police were always welcome inside your house,
remember?"

She nodded, struggling to find her voice in between
sobs. After a few more seconds, she pulled away, and I

helped her sit on the bed. Her head was still bleeding, but I didn't see any other injuries on her.

"In there," she managed, pointing at the bathroom door.

O'Connell held out a hand, stopping me from entering. "I'm calling this in. Don't touch anything." He pulled out his phone, requesting patrol units, forensics, and an ambulance to our location.

I kept one eye on Daria while I peered into the bathroom. The mirror was broken. The center was cracked. The glass spiderwebbed around the point of impact, which happened to be at eye level. The attacker must have slammed Daria's head into the mirror.

Red streaks ran down the broken glass, leaving a few faint droplets on the silver faucet. A bloody hand had grabbed the edge of the vanity. Most likely, Daria's. More handprints showed a path out of the bathroom and back to the bed. She'd crawled away.

The bathroom window was closed. The shower curtain didn't appear disturbed. I angled around, avoiding the broken bits of glass on the floor while I tried to see what other evidence Daria's attacker might have left behind. In red on the wall next to the door was written, *I'm still here.*

Snapping a few quick shots, I tucked my phone away. "Can you tell me what happened?" I asked her. "Who did this to you?"

"He did."

"He who?"

Her face scrunched up as she tried very hard to stop crying. "I didn't see his face. But I saw his shoes. I heard his voice. It was him. Did you see the wall? He's not dead. He's here."

"Breathe." I knelt in front of her, giving the gash on her forehead a closer look. Pieces of the mirror were embedded in her face and the palms of her hands. "Walk me through it. Everything you remember."

"I just finished working upstairs, so I went to wash my hands and get ready for bed. When I looked up from the sink, he was behind me. I didn't even have time to scream before he grabbed the back of my head and slammed me into the mirror. He threw me down on the floor. I thought," she squeezed her eyes closed and bit her lip to stop herself from hyperventilating, "I thought he was going to fill the tub and drown me. But he didn't. He just trapped me in there. His shoes squeaked. I remember the crunch of glass. At one point, he slid. The glass scratched the tile, like nails on a chalkboard. After that, things get hazy. But as soon as he left, I grabbed my phone and called you."

"Where did he go?"

"Out the door." She pointed to her bedroom door as tears streamed down her cheeks. "I know what I saw. He had the same soulless brown eyes. And those damn red sneakers. It's him, Alex. The Lightning Killer's back."

FIFTEEN

Daria sat in the back of an ambulance while Lucca stood at the rear of the rig, talking to her and keeping an eye on things. I paced back and forth, flummoxed as to how this could have happened. O'Connell had already spoken to Joe Farzen and Miles Bridger, the two Cross Security bodyguards. Neither of them had seen anyone enter or exit.

"Are you sure, Joe?" I asked.

"Yes, ma'am."

"Don't ma'am me. You saw Daria. Someone attacked her. You can't deny that. So what happened? I get it. Stakeouts suck. Maybe you had to take a leak or got distracted by a call. It happens. Just tell me now."

"Nothing happened. We weren't distracted. We installed dash cams in our cars, which we had aimed at the front and rear of the townhouse. No one entered or left. I checked the footage. Your detective pal checked the footage. We didn't screw up."

"Sorry." I walked away before I said anything else I'd regret. Cross hired professionals, but we weren't the best of the best. We were the rejects and broken toys. I wasn't sure what Joe had done in his previous life to screw up and end up at Cross Security, but he must have done something.

However, he hadn't lied about the recordings. The footage didn't show anyone approaching Daria's front door or any of the windows.

"How do you think he got inside?" I asked O'Connell when I found him walking away from the patrol officers he'd sent to canvass the neighborhood.

"No idea. Your guys should have seen something. But they didn't. I didn't find anything on the footage either. The first time anyone entered that house today was when the Cross Security team breached the front door."

"Do you think they could have done this?"

O'Connell raised a surprised eyebrow. "You put them on the house. Don't you trust them?"

"I don't know. I don't know anything right now."

"The timestamp on the footage shows they didn't enter the house until after you called them. I don't think it's been altered or tampered with. They already gave me complete access, so I can have the lab double-check, if you want."

I stared at the increasing number of porch lights coming on as officers continued to knock on doors and ask Daria's neighbors if they'd heard or seen anything. "That's not necessary."

"What did she say to you?"

"Not much."

O'Connell clicked his pen a few times. "Did she describe her attacker?"

"Brown eyes. Brown hair. Red and white sneakers."

He wrote it down. "Anything else?"

"Nope."

"Detective, you need to see this," one of the crime technicians called from the open doorway.

I followed O'Connell, catching Lucca's eye on my way back inside the house. The tech led us to Daria's bedroom. They had lifted up her mattress. Stitched into the padding was a large pentagram-like symbol. It wasn't quite a pentagram. Frankly, I wasn't sure what it was. But I'd seen the same thing sewn into the rugs and on the few hanging tapestries.

"Jesus, Mary, and Joseph." O'Connell glanced up at the row of saints. "Take a few photos. Once she gets checked out, I'll ask her about it." He patted the tech on the shoulder. "Good work."

"What's going on?" Lucca asked, meeting us in the hallway outside her bedroom.

"Daria has some weird symbols stitched into the bottom of her mattress," I said. "She has them on the rugs and those decorative drape things she has hanging from the walls."

Lucca peered into the room. "So what? It's not related. It's nothing to worry about."

"It doesn't look like nothing," O'Connell said. "She's got Orthodox icons, Catholic saints, and some kind of Hoodoo or paganistic symbolism going on under the covers. I might have seen a Star of David and some Hebrew writing mixed in. I'd say there's a whole lot of something going on in that bedroom."

"What are you thinking, Nick?" I asked.

"I don't know." He eyed Lucca. "Why don't you tell me?"

"Daria's religious. Spiritual. Whatever you want to call it. There's nothing wrong with that."

"Never said there was." O'Connell patted the pendant tucked beneath his collar. "I got my St. Michael right here. But that doesn't explain the hodgepodge in her bedroom." He stared at Lucca. "Why are you so adamant that it's not related to tonight's attack?"

"Why would it be?"

They stared at one another for what felt like an eternity before O'Connell nodded. "Okay."

"Did you find anything else?" Lucca asked. "Anything of actual relevance?"

"Not yet," O'Connell said. "Cross Security didn't see anyone enter or leave. None of the doors or windows appears to have been tampered with. But we have no way of knowing for sure since Mr. Farzen bumped the locks in order to gain entry."

"Could the unsub have already been inside the house before Farzen and Bridger arrived for shift change?" I wondered aloud. O'Connell and I had cleared the main level during our search for Daria. Nothing struck me as odd, but I looked again, maneuvering around the CSU guys as I went from room to room. "Daria said she just finished working and went to wash up and get ready for bed."

"Daria gets ready for bed at ten," Lucca said.

"She didn't call me until," I checked my call log, "11:27."

"That's an hour and a half later." O'Connell narrowed his eyes at something. "Are you sure she goes to bed at ten, Lucca? She said she was working. What exactly does she do?"

"She makes fiber art," Lucca said. "She does most of her work upstairs."

We headed up the narrow staircase. An officer stood at the top of the stairs, keeping watch, while a man with a CSU windbreaker dusted each of the window sills for prints. At least the cops were being thorough. Having a major crimes detective calling the shots and an FBI agent hanging out on the sidelines might have had something to do with it. And if that wasn't enough, the Cross Security name carried some weight on account of Lucien's connection to the police commissioner. Or so I suspected, even if my boss would disagree.

"Find anything?" O'Connell asked.

"No, sir. Not even a smudge. I doubt these windows have ever been opened," the tech said.

I glanced into the upstairs bathroom, but the mirror remained intact and no haunting messages had been written on the wall in what I assumed to be blood. The spare room, where Daria worked on more of her elaborate projects, looked nothing like it had the previous day.

A large rectangular folding table took up most of the room. Various colors of threads had been woven together in specific patterns to mimic the fur of a leopard. The end had been rolled around a form, where it appeared to be drying. It was about as thick as a firefighter's hose.

"Do you know what she's working on?" I asked Lucca.

"She didn't say, but she always keeps her projects a secret, unless she's fulfilling orders. That she doesn't care about." Lucca opened a box, which was filled to the brim with various yarns and threads in every imaginable shade of green. We searched the rest of the upstairs. But we didn't find anything. "While she was working up here, someone could have entered and waited for her downstairs. Anyone familiar with her routine would know when she'd stop working. He could have planned the attack. Daria is a creature of habit, by necessity more than choice."

We left the townhouse, leaving the techs to finish collecting prints and evidence. While we waited, O'Connell took Daria's statement. She didn't tell him anything she hadn't already told me. Lucca stood beside me, close enough so she could see him.

"We covered all our bases," he said. "She should have been safe. Where's that asshole LaRoche? We need to find him and put an end to this."

"He didn't do this," I said.

"Are you sure?"

"Nick and I were staking out his place, making sure he didn't do anything stupid. We had a clear view of his apartment. He came home, worked on his computer, took off his shirt, and played with his lenses." I showed Lucca a few of the surveillance photos I'd taken when I'd gotten bored. They were a bit blurry on account of the angle and dirty windows, but they'd suffice.

"This doesn't make any sense."

"I know." In light of what just happened, I couldn't help but think I pointed the finger at the wrong guy. But how could that be when Reagan had a photo of Daria hanging on his wall, along with the rest of the stuff I'd found? "Eddie, what's up with the weird symbols in Daria's room?"

He whispered so no one would overhear us. "Daria's mom has some unconventional views on things. She thinks her daughter died and came back to life. She's afraid Andrew Holland's essence might have tried to come back with Daria. Unfinished business and all that."

"Her mom thinks she's possessed?"

"More like she wants to make sure Daria isn't being haunted." Lucca shook his head. "Once the cops hear about that, I'm sure they'll be a little less gung-ho about working this case."

"O'Connell's not like that. You've worked with him before. You know that's not how he operates. Daria's mom can think whatever she likes, but whoever did this is a corporeal asshole with a violent streak. O'Connell knows that. He won't stop looking."

The ambulance driver climbed out of the back of the rig. "We think it'd be best to take her to the hospital to get checked out."

Lucca leaned into the back as O'Connell stepped down. "I'll meet you at the hospital, Dar. You're okay. These guys will take good care of you. I'll see you in a few minutes. Okay?"

"Eddie," she stared at him for a moment, "can you get my phone?"

"I'll see what I can do. Don't worry. Everything's going to be okay. I promise."

The three of us watched the ambulance drive away before Lucca palmed his keys. "Has her phone been taken into evidence?"

"I doubt it." O'Connell called to one of the techs, but aside from a few items they found in the bathroom and near the bed, CSU had left most of Daria's house untouched. Her phone was on her desk in the main room. After a quick scan of her recent calls and texts, O'Connell handed it to Lucca. "You better get going. I'll have more questions for you in the morning regarding her history. Give me a call first thing tomorrow."

"You got it." Lucca turned to me. "I'll call you with an update as soon as I know something. But she's not sleeping here tonight. I'll stay with her and keep watch. We'll figure out our next step tomorrow."

I watched him go, wondering if Lucca had changed his mind about my competence and ability to help in this particular situation.

O'Connell tapped me on the shoulder to get my attention. "I heard her tell you the Lightning Killer is back, and he attacked her tonight. Care to elaborate?"

"Not particularly, but you'll find out anyway." So I told him everything I knew.

"What's Lucca's connection to her?"

"He worked the case. He was there when they pulled her out of the tub."

O'Connell's quirked eyebrow told me he believed there was more to the story than that. "That doesn't explain how he knows her bedtime routine."

"Lucca's a good agent. He's thorough and pays attention to detail."

"Bullshit. You notice more unimportant details than anyone I've ever met. And you didn't even know what time she went to bed." He glanced around to make sure we were alone. "Did they have something going on at one point?"

"No."

"You're sure?"

"Almost completely."

O'Connell mulled a few things over. He knew everything I did about the situation, Daria's history with the Lightning Killer, and whatever mess we walked into tonight. A few uniformed officers were headed in our direction. "Let's hope the canvass turned up something."

Just as the officers reached us, my phone rang. The display said *Martin*.

O'Connell glanced at it. "Go ahead and take that. I'll see what's what."

"We're in the middle of something."

"Yeah, but aren't you supposed to be getting on a plane tomorrow?"

"Not anymore."

O'Connell jerked his chin at the phone. "Which is why you need to answer that."

SIXTEEN

Martin wasn't surprised by the sudden change of plans, but he was definitely annoyed. "I take it you didn't make it to your meeting tonight, either." From his tone, he already knew the answer.

"Is that why you called? Did Heathcliff contact you?"

"No, sweetheart. But at least we know your paranoia is alive and well."

The last thing I needed right now was to fight with him. "I'm not paranoid. Don't twist this around on me. You and Derek conspired to force me to go to these meetings in the first place. You manipulated me into sharing, promised you'd support me however I needed, and then you left. I'm doing the best I can. But something more urgent came up."

"It always does."

"Martin, it's work. You wouldn't be on the other side of the country if you didn't understand how important that is."

"You're important too."

"What am I supposed to do with that?" I exhaled. "Never mind. Ignore me. Tonight's been a headache and a half. O'Connell and I are in the midst of it. I really should go. I'm sorry I can't fly out tomorrow. As soon as we come up with a new plan, I'll reschedule my trip. Maybe we can do it next weekend."

"Wait a sec," Martin said. But my words stung. I could hear it in his voice. "I didn't mean to drop the ball. I never meant to abandon you." He paused awkwardly, as if distracted by something. "I didn't abandon you, Alexis. I'm here, even if I can't be there with you."

"I know." But once he said it, I realized that's how I felt. I hated how he knew me better than I knew myself.

"This was supposed to be a short trip, a week, maybe two. Now it's been a month with no end in sight."

"That's life. Shit happens."

His tone was softer. "Are you okay? You said it's been a rough night. How rough? Any broken bones or bullet wounds I should know about?"

"I'm fine. Can we talk about this tomorrow?"

"Absolutely. I'm coming home."

"What? When?" I stared at the flashing police lights on the parked cruisers as I leaned against the passenger's side door of the company sedan. "If you're doing that just so we can fight in person, that's not necessary."

He laughed. "The only way make-up sex works is in person."

I smiled, despite the chaos around me. "Is that why you're flying home?"

"Sex with you is the only reason I need, but I have a few other things on the agenda besides that, if there's time. I planned on telling you to cancel your flight, but somehow, I got derailed."

"You're not back for good?"

"Not yet, but I'll see you tomorrow night. I love you."

I tucked the phone into my pocket and watched the red and blue illuminate the townhouses. Martin shouldn't have to fly home because he felt guilty or because I couldn't get away, but ever since he left, there had been an unexplainable friction between us, and not the good kind. He felt it too. That's why he was making the trip when I couldn't.

Shaking it off, I tucked those thoughts aside and focused on the scene before me. We had no idea how the bastard got inside Daria's house, but the better question was when did he leave? The surveillance cameras never saw anyone go in or out. As far as I knew, only ghosts could walk through walls. But I'd already dismissed that possibility. How did he enter and escape undetected?

I searched the entire property, hoping to come up with a feasible explanation. The dash cams covered the doors. The attacker must have found another way inside, and given all the weird occurrences and sightings Daria previously reported, he must have found an unknown entry point and exploited it.

The maple tree in the backyard didn't look easy to climb. The bottom branches were too high to reach, but maybe he used a ladder or stool. With my flashlight in hand, I checked for disturbed earth. The ground was hard from the lack of rain. I didn't spot any fresh footprints or indentions, but I didn't think I would.

Daria's backyard consisted of a patio, a postage-sized patch of grass, and that one big tree. She hadn't put any effort or money into landscaping. I didn't think she ever used her patio, since the weeds and leaves had overrun the concrete. Even in broad daylight, it was impossible to tell where the grass ended and the pavement began.

After tugging on a glove, I ran my hand over each board of the privacy fence. None of them were loose or rotted. They didn't give way as I ran my fingertips from the top of every plank to the bottom. Maybe the unsub accessed Daria's home through the back of her neighbor's unit. That was the only way I could imagine he wouldn't be caught by the surveillance cameras.

I went around the tree and searched her next door neighbor's yard. But I didn't find even the slightest hint anyone had been back there. I checked the next neighbor's yard and the next until I reached the end of the building.

From this end, Joe and Miles might not have been able to see who was coming and going. Miles had parked on a side street, angling the camera so it covered the side of the townhouse. It didn't actually show Daria's back door on account of the privacy fences separating the units, but it showed the side and rear. If anyone had entered the opening at the back of the fence, we would have seen it on the footage.

Since no one had gained entry from this side of the townhouse or from the rear, maybe they'd hopped the fence on the other side. However, I hadn't found any evidence to reinforce my theory. And Miles would have noticed someone leaping over the fence or jumping down from the tree, or so I hoped.

It was after two a.m. when the police released the scene. They'd photographed and dusted everything. But they hadn't found any evidence of the intruder. I called Cross Security and requested our mobile crime lab go over everything one more time. The boss said I could use whatever resources I needed. Hopefully, he wouldn't change his mind once word got back to him about this.

No matter how hard I tried, I couldn't wrap my mind around any of this. If O'Connell and I hadn't been outside Reagan's apartment, I would have sworn he was to blame. But he couldn't have been in two places at once.

Tapping my fingers against my thighs, I itched to confront him. Even though he didn't sneak into Daria's house and attack her, he'd done plenty of sneaking around. Once the DNA results came back, I'd prove it. As soon as Reagan was inside an interrogation room, O'Connell would persuade him to tell us how one would go about breaking into Daria's house in exchange for a deal, and if that failed, I'd take a crack at him.

"Find anything?" O'Connell asked as he joined me near the car. He waved to the last remaining patrol officer as he pulled away.

"No. What did CSU turn up?"

"They found one set of prints they couldn't eliminate. They aren't in the system, but we know someone else was in the house at some point in the last few weeks. When I speak to Daria tomorrow, I'll ask. Do you know who's been inside lately?"

"Me and Lucca."

"Anyone else?"

"Her parents came to visit a little over two months ago."

"It's possible the print could belong to one of them, but

the techs thought it looked more recent."

"Where did they find it?"

"On the light switch in the dining room. Daria's prints were above them, but CSU pulled the partial from underneath."

"What about closer to the scene? Did they find anything in the bathroom?"

"No other prints and nothing we didn't already see."

"What about the bloody message on the wall? Was that written in Daria's blood?"

"Nope."

"Let's run DNA."

"We can't, Parker."

"Why not?"

"It wasn't blood. It was fire engine red lipstick. They found a tube of it in the vanity. The tip was pretty ragged. The lab will verify it, but I'm sure that's how the message ended up on the wall."

"What about handwriting analysis?"

"It's not an exact science. We'd need to have someone in mind in order to conduct a comparison. And right now, we have no suspects."

"I hate this. I could have sworn Reagan was stalking her, but he didn't attack her. At least not tonight." I chewed on my lip as I climbed behind the wheel. "I wonder what that bastard is up to right now." Even though it was after two a.m., I asked, "Do you mind if we make a quick stop before I drop you off at the precinct?"

"That's fine."

I headed back to Reagan's apartment, hoping with a little bit of luck whoever attacked Daria would be hiding at Reagan's. Instead, Reagan's apartment was pitch black. Digging out the high-tech toys Cross paid for, I set the binoculars to infrared and stared up at Reagan's apartment. I only spotted one heat signature flat on the bed. "Dammit."

"There's one other possibility we haven't discussed," O'Connell said.

"What?"

He watched me carefully as I drove back to the precinct.

"We both know, for whatever the reason, Lucca's compromised on this."

"So? He's not responsible."

"The thought never crossed my mind."

"Okay, so what's the problem? He's not calling the shots. He didn't put the security team on Daria. He didn't let this happen."

"Neither did you."

"Regardless, she's my client. This is my case."

"Be that as it may," O'Connell said, "I'm sure you're seeing this as plainly as I am. We checked every door and window. None of the neighbors saw anyone out of the ordinary in the vicinity. Three of the neighbors across the street have doorbell cameras. They didn't pick up anyone entering or leaving, just like the Cross Security dash cams. It doesn't appear that anything was stolen."

"What's your point?"

"Daria's prints were the only ones in the bathroom. They were on the vanity, the mirror, the wall, and the lipstick." He paused. "Do you think Daria hurt herself?"

"Why would she?"

"I don't know. But you know how it looks. I looked up the symbols in her bedroom. Do you know what they are?"

"Unrelated."

"Possibly."

I turned to look at O'Connell. "What are they? What do they mean?"

"They each mean different things. Some are meant to ward off evil spirits. The big one stitched into her mattress is meant to prevent possession."

"You think she's possessed?"

"No, but she must fear the possibility or she wouldn't have it on her mattress."

"Lucca said that was her mother's doing. Daria might not know it's there."

O'Connell pulled out his notepad. "I'll need her mother's contact info. If she thinks her daughter is under the influence of someone or something else, she must have reasons to think that. Maybe there's a pattern of odd behavior. Have you spoken to Daria's doctors? We could be looking at something like DID or fugue states."

I parked beside O'Connell's car. "She didn't hurt herself."

"Given everything she's been through, her mind might have fractured to protect her from the trauma. Another identity might be at the helm some of the time. That identity could have gotten angry and taken it out on Daria."

"The next time you accuse me of having a crazy theory, I'm going to remind you of this very moment."

"I never say your theories are crazy."

"Then you'd be the only one." I gave him a look, contemplating the message left on Daria's wall. *I'm still here.* "You could be right about this. But I didn't see any mention of it in her medical records."

"What about her psych evals?"

"Her shrink doesn't take a lot of notes or perform that many tests."

"Or she doesn't record her observations in order to avoid turning them over. I've seen a lot of that going on lately. What's her name? I'll have a chat with her in the morning."

I gave him the info. "I don't know. I still think the stalking and attack have something to do with Reagan LaRoche. Too many odd coincidences surround him."

"This whole situation stinks." O'Connell opened the door. "Let me know as soon as you get that DNA analysis back on the hairbrush. In the meantime, I'll do what I can." He glanced at the door to the police station. "Lt. Moretti won't be happy when he hears his off duty detective took lead on a case that has nothing to do with major crimes."

"Tell him it was for Agent Lucca. Hopefully, that'll keep you out of the doghouse."

"Speaking of, it sounded like you and Martin had some words. Is everything okay?"

"I don't know. It's been hard ever since he left for California. I'm used to him being away on business trips, but this time's different."

"How come?"

"I'm not sure."

"Maybe it's the ring around your neck."

I ignored the comment. "It's because he's stuck in limbo. He said he'll be working from the L.A. office indefinitely until this gets straightened out. He's supposed to come home for the weekend since I can't get away, but how's this going to work long-term?"

"You've been through worse."

"A lot worse." I shook it off. "This is stupid. I'm being stupid."

"You miss him."

"Whatever you do, don't tell him that. I'll never hear the end of it."

"I'm sure he already knows. I'm guessing you've probably told him as much."

"It's different when I admit it to someone else. It makes it real."

"This isn't permanent. I'm sure he knows what he's doing and has a plan to get things back to normal."

"I hope so."

SEVENTEEN

After leaving O'Connell, I returned to Daria's townhouse and watched the Cross Security lab techs as they repeated the same search the police had just finished. While they worked, I replayed everything that happened, sketching out a timeline on a blank sheet of paper. One tiny detail irked me. How did Daria's cell phone end up in the main room when she called me from the bedroom suite?

She carried that phone with her everywhere. It alerted her to everything. There was no way she hadn't had it with her when she was attacked. If for some reason she had left it in the main room, why did the Cross Security team find her cowering in the bedroom after she called me?

According to Joe and Miles, they'd found Daria huddled on the floor between the wall and her bed. When she saw them, she started screaming. Miles checked the bathroom while Joe tried to calm her, but she'd gotten even more agitated and crawled beneath the bed. That's when Miles cleared the rest of the house and Joe called for a medical team.

Eventually, Joe left her alone, afraid his presence would do more harm than good. When Nick and I arrived, we found him in the main room. But he didn't have Daria's cell phone in his hand. I called to make sure he hadn't picked it up during the commotion, but he swore to me he never touched it. The police dusted it for prints, finding only Daria's.

Was Joe wearing gloves? I didn't think his hands were covered. After calling the precinct, I spoke to one of the crime techs who worked the scene and asked for the list of names of people whose prints they eliminated as scene contamination. Joe Farzen's and Miles Bridger's names were both on the list, along with Lucca's, O'Connell's, Daria's, and mine. That meant the security team hadn't worn gloves.

The phone didn't just walk out of Daria's bedroom by itself. Someone moved it. The security team swore they hadn't touched it, and the cops said the same thing. Whoever attacked Daria must have taken her phone, but that meant her attacker took it after she called me. Maybe he panicked when the security team broke in, left the phone, and ran. But where did he go?

"Dammit." I slammed my palm against the steering wheel. I knew what the evidence indicated. No one left Daria's house. Given the timeline, her attacker would have had less than two minutes to get from the bedroom to one of the exits. Since the security team came through the front, the only way out was through the back or a window. And we'd checked them all.

I went back inside and stared at the writing on the bathroom wall. *I'm still here.* Was that Daria's handwriting? I couldn't tell.

I went into her kitchen, grabbed the whiteboard off the fridge, and returned to the bathroom. Holding it up beside the wall, I tried to see if the letters looked the same. Maybe. Maybe not.

Initially, O'Connell's theory seemed far flung, even by my standards, but he might be the only one seeing things clearly. Lucca was biased, and his bias made me biased. This was a mess.

When the Cross Security team finished searching the house, I followed them back to the office. It was late or early, depending on one's perspective. Sleep would help clear my mind.

But even after I settled onto the sofa, I couldn't turn off my brain. Too many questions needed answering, so I got up to do some research into dissociative identity disorder and fugue states.

I'd researched them before when I thought I was losing my mind. One of the first things Daria had said was that she feared she was crazy. With both dissociated personalities and fugue states, one had no recollection of the actions she took. That could explain the misplaced and moved items in her house. It might even explain why Mrs. Waylon feared her daughter was under the influence of someone else's spirit.

Trauma could cause the mind to do all kinds of things, including dissociating one's identity to the point of creating additional personalities. Or something could have triggered Daria and caused her to enter a fugue state in which she wasn't conscious of her own behavior. Given her brush with death at the hands of a serial killer and the resulting coma and brain damage, mental issues would be a common side effect.

I skimmed a few medical sites, trying to better understand the concept. While I knew I didn't comprehend all the intricacies and implications, what I read sounded pretty unsettling. The hour and twenty-seven minutes it took for her to call could have been due to her no longer being the conscious identity. When I asked her what happened, she said she saw him in the mirror, and then things got hazy. According to Lucca, she had trouble forming new memories, but maybe that was just half the story or a symptom of another underlying issue.

None of Daria's doctors mentioned episodes like this in her medical records. Perhaps Daria exhibited this type of behavior while she was recovering, and that's how her mother got it in her head Daria was possessed. I considered calling to ask, but calls this early in the morning never bode well. I didn't want to put the Waylons through that, especially if I was wrong. O'Connell would handle it at a decent hour.

Returning to the couch, I sprawled out and stared at the

ceiling. What was I going to tell Lucca? Did he know Daria had episodes like this? He knew about the religious symbols in Daria's bedroom. What else hadn't he shared?

We need to talk, I texted him. But he didn't reply. He'd probably fallen asleep, or he'd turned off his phone out of an abundance of caution for the hospital equipment. Still, OIO agents didn't just turn off their phones. I didn't like it.

I stared at the screen for another minute before deciding it could wait until the morning.

* * *

O'Connell looked up when I entered the bullpen. He rubbed a hand over his face and jerked his thumb at a nearby chair. "Don't steal Thompson's seat. He went to get coffee. He'll be back in a second."

I dragged a chair beside his desk and sat down. "You look like shit."

"So do you."

"It must have been the fast food we ate."

"Must have." Nick laughed. "What have you got for me?"

I handed him the envelope containing the DNA analysis Cross Security ran on the strands of hair pulled from the brush in Reagan LaRoche's apartment. "99.9% match."

He read the report, scratching his head. "You realize this isn't admissible. A defense attorney would have a field day with you stealing evidence."

"This proves LaRoche has been inside Daria's house and he's stolen from her. That goes along with her reports of an unidentified stalker. Is this enough to get you a search warrant?"

"It is, but we both know LaRoche didn't attack her last night."

"I don't care. He has something to do with this. I know it. If nothing else, his actions are triggering her. We have to stop him."

O'Connell eyed the report again. "You said you saw a photo hanging on the wall and her earrings hanging from his left lobe. I'm guessing that means you also happened to notice the hairbrush in his bathroom when you used the facilities."

"Sure, that sounds about right."

The detective knew how to take a creative license to the facts in order to get the brass on board. "But you said she's been to his place."

"Just once."

"That's a problem."

"Can we work around it?"

"We'll try." He put the paper down. "At the risk of sounding like a broken record, we know LaRoche didn't attack her last night. Are you sure you want to keep after this guy? If he realizes you tipped us, he's not going to like it."

"That doesn't matter. If Reagan makes a move on me, it'll solidify our case against him. But I don't think the magician wannabe has the balls to do something when he's been running and hiding every time Daria spots him following her."

"Are you sure he's the one she's been seeing?"

"No," I jabbed my finger at the DNA analysis, "but I am certain he's been inside her house uninvited. I want to know how he got in and out undetected. Let's squeeze him until he tells us."

"I thought magicians never reveal their tricks."

"Good thing he's not really a magician."

O'Connell narrowed his eyes. "You spoke to Daria about LaRoche."

"Yes."

"If the guy's a creeper, why does she meet him every week? That's ass-backward. If someone gives you the creeps, you stay the hell away from him, especially when you've already been targeted once by a crazed psycho."

"I think that's why she hangs out with him."

O'Connell stared at me as if I suddenly started speaking a foreign language. "Come again?"

"A part of her doesn't believe it'll happen again, or she needs to test the waters to prove it won't happen again. It's about learning to feel safe. She isn't comfortable enough to be alone with him in private, so they meet in public. Again, so she'll be safe."

"Given her recent string of 9-1-1 calls and whatever the hell happened last night, I don't think it's working."

"Actually, I'm pretty sure it's backfiring. Reagan shares a few similar traits with the Lightning Killer. I think those are triggering memories for Daria and causing a lot of her fears and anxieties. They might even be triggering some hallucinations."

While O'Connell mulled that over, Thompson returned with two mugs. He put one down on Nick's desk before taking his seat. "Parker," he said, more like an observation than a greeting.

"Thompson." I jerked my chin at the steaming mug in his hands. "Is that for me?"

"No." He pointed to the pot in the corner. "By all means, help yourself. It's a little extra burnt today."

Wondering just how long I could run on fumes, I decided it wasn't worth risking a total shutdown and got up to pour myself a cup. It didn't taste burnt exactly, more like battery acid. But I drank it anyway.

O'Connell slid the DNA analysis over to his partner. "What do you think?"

"You're sure this guy has an alibi?" Thompson asked.

"Pretty sure, unless he has an identical twin we don't know about."

"And your timeline is sound?" Thompson asked.

O'Connell looked at me. "What do you think, Parker?"

"Even if we're off, it could only be by an hour or two. Daria was still bleeding when we found her. She couldn't have been attacked much earlier than that or she would have clotted or scabbed." I remembered the sticky, wet blood on her hands.

Thompson sipped his coffee, making a face before putting it down. "Woman gets attacked in her house. The police are notified that a man has a photo of said woman in his apartment, along with her missing hairbrush and earrings. We should follow up on that."

I smiled at Thompson. "Wow, keep that up and you'll be in the running for top spot as my favorite detective."

"I've seen the shit that comes with the title. All the crap you dump on Nick and Heathcliff." Thompson shook his head. "I don't want to have anything to do with it."

"But there's a trophy," I insisted.

"Keep it," Thompson said.

"I've never seen a trophy. I'm guessing it's because you're getting it polished and engraved with my name." O'Connell tucked the envelope into his pocket and palmed his keys. "Let's go have a chat with Mr. LaRoche. If he doesn't want to cooperate, we'll tell him what we know and bluff a bit." O'Connell eyed me. "Have you spoken to Lucca yet?"

"Briefly. He's at work. Daria's still in the hospital. Her doctor wanted another set of scans, and her psychiatrist is hoping to hold her over the weekend for observation. Her shrink said it'd be best to make sure this recent incident didn't trigger anything, but Lucca's pretty sure the real reason they want to hold Daria for the next couple of days is to make sure she doesn't pose a danger to herself."

"That gives us time to figure this out," O'Connell said. "Hospital security is keeping an eye on her. Visitors have to sign in and out, so if someone is stalking her, we'll at least get a name and description from the security cams."

"What about posting a uniform at her door?"

"I couldn't swing it, not with such flimsy evidence. All I got is an unknown partial in the dining room."

"Fine. Let's go." I gulped down the rest of the coffee and got up.

"Not you," O'Connell said. He pointed to Thompson. "You and me are taking a ride. Parker is going to the hospital to have a chat with some doctors and see what she can wheedle out of them."

"I am?" I asked.

"You are."

"How did I get stuck doing that?"

"You've already confronted LaRoche. He doesn't need to know you're the reason I'm knocking on his door, especially if he realizes he is under no obligation to answer our questions. Plus, I started my day by speaking to Daria's doctors. Without a warrant, they won't tell me jack shit. But you're an expert at fudging details, so maybe they'll talk to you."

"Daria won't consent?" I asked.

"She made it clear she doesn't want them talking to me. Take from that what you will." He brushed past me with Thompson at his heels.

Daria hadn't given Lucca access to her medical records either. But I'd seen them and hadn't found anything damaging to her allegations of a stalker turned attacker. Regardless, people valued their privacy. Maybe that's all this was. At least, that's what I reminded myself as I made the drive across town. But the voice in the back of my head didn't believe it.

EIGHTEEN

I hated hospitals. Just being here reminded me of far too many tragedies and close calls. Forcing my mind away from the bad memories, I found Daria's room on the fourth floor. They had her in a special wing. I had to sign in at the nurse's station before they'd even buzz me into the unit.

A bored security guard sat in a chair near the corner, watching me as he balanced the chair on two legs. He reminded me of an Old West sheriff with the way he leaned back against the wall. All he needed was a cowboy hat dipped low over his brow.

"She's right through there," the nurse said. "Is she expecting you?"

"I'm not sure."

She led me to the room and knocked gently on the door. "Daria, you have a visitor. Is that okay?"

Daria looked up from where she'd been playing a game on her phone. Her brow crinkled.

"Hi, Daria. It's Alex. Eddie's friend," I said, wondering if she remembered who I was.

"That's right. I called you."

The nurse smiled pleasantly. "I'll give you some privacy. If you need anything, just press the call button."

Daria watched her leave.

"How are you feeling?" I asked.

"Better." She looked around the small room. Unlike most people I'd seen in hospitals, she didn't have any tubes running to or from her body. She wore a t-shirt and sweatpants rather than a hospital gown and sat on top of the covers with her legs crossed over one another. The only indication of her injury was the bandage covering her forehead. "Thanks for coming to help last night."

"Do you remember that?"

"Bits and pieces. I was so scared. If it hadn't been for you, I'd probably still be under the bed."

"Do you mind if I ask you a few questions?"

"Go ahead. Everyone else has asked me a million things."

I asked her to recall what she could about the previous day leading up to the attack. As far as she remembered, it was a typical day. No one had come to visit. The Cross Security team stayed outside. She checked the notes on her phone in order to tell me the exact time the second team arrived.

"Did anyone else show up at your house yesterday?"

"No."

"You didn't receive any deliveries?"

"I had leftovers, so I didn't order food. I spoke to Celeste after lunch," she continued scrolling, "and then I spent the rest of the day working."

"What are you working on?"

"A sculpture. A big one."

"I didn't see any supplies in the main room. Where were you working on your project?"

"Upstairs. There are fewer distractions up there. It helps the creative juices flow."

"Did you notice anything odd while you were up there? Did you hear anyone downstairs?"

She shook her head, the color in her cheeks diminishing. "How long was he down there waiting for me?"

"I don't know. No one saw him enter or leave your townhouse. I checked the security footage, but I didn't see anything. Neither did your neighbors."

"How is that possible?"

"I don't know. I'm still trying to figure it out. I thought you might have heard or saw something."

She stared at the wall, puffing out her cheeks as she exhaled through her mouth. "I don't remember. But I'm sure if I had, I would have called Lucca or you. Someone."

"Where was your phone?"

"In my pocket. It's always in my pocket when I'm not using it."

"And you're sure you had it with you upstairs?"

"Yes." But the look on her face told me she wasn't positive, but that was human nature to doubt and second-guess. "The alarm goes off at ten to tell me it's bedtime. If it doesn't, I'm liable to get wrapped up in a project and work all night."

"Do you ever ignore the alarm or stay up later?"

"Sometimes. But I'll reset the alarm just so I don't completely lose myself in it. I find it's hard to function when I don't get enough rest."

"Tell me about it." I held out my hand. "Do you mind if I look at your phone?"

She handed it to me. The police checked it before they gave Lucca the okay to return it, but they weren't interested in things like alarms and schedule reminders. However, it didn't store enough information for me to tell if Daria had reset her alarm the previous night.

"Would you mind walking me through everything that happened from the time your alarm sounded until I found you under the bed?"

"I really don't want to think about it."

"I know, but it's important. We have to find him and stop him." I handed her back the phone.

She held it against her chest, hugging herself. "At ten o'clock, I went downstairs to wash up and start my bedtime routine."

"Did you stop in the kitchen or make a note in your journal?"

"I don't know. I can't remember."

"That's okay. Just tell me whatever comes to mind."

"I had glue on my hands, so I went to wash it off before I got out my pajamas. I went into my bathroom, turned on the light, and started scrubbing. The adhesive I use to make my fiber paper washes off my skin just fine, but it always sticks to my nails." She put her phone down and held out her hand, which shook slightly. A tacky residue with a few green threads clung to the side of her nail. "I was too focused on this to notice anything else."

"You had the water running full blast?"

"I must have. That would explain why I didn't hear him sneak up behind me."

"Do you know where he came from? Do you think he was waiting inside the bathroom for you?" I'd been inside her bathroom. The vanity was to the side of the doorway. He'd written the message on the side wall, which wasn't visible from the doorway or reflected in the mirror.

She swallowed, grabbing a piece of the blanket and crushing it between her fingers. "He was there when I looked up, but I didn't notice him when I entered. I think he was hiding behind the shower curtain."

"You don't think he followed you into the bathroom?"

"No, he was there. He wanted to fill the tub. He wanted to drown me again." She gasped, a frightened scream squeaking past her lips.

I held up my palms. "Easy, Daria. Easy. You're safe. It's okay."

"No, it's not. He came back to finish what he started." She stared right into my eyes. "I saw him."

"The Lightning Killer?"

She nodded, a sheen of sweat coating her pale skin.

"Daria, he's dead."

"No, he's not. I saw him." She shuddered, the bed rattling beneath her. "I swear to you. It was him. God, those eyes. They were so angry. That's what I saw in the mirror right before he hit me."

"What did he do after that?"

"He dragged me into the tub and held my head under the water. I couldn't breathe. I tried to fight back, but he was too strong. I couldn't get free. I just kept sliding. My arms, my legs, they just kept sliding. It hurt. Every time I slipped, it hurt. But I didn't care. I didn't notice." She held out her trembling arms, examining her wrists and forearms. "I had bruises from..."

"Daria—"

She exhaled, tears welling in her eyes. "Where are the bruises?"

"None of that happened last night."

"It didn't?" She sounded so lost.

"No."

She curled into the fetal position while the tears streamed down her face. She hugged her knees and stared at the floor. "I never knew what happened. I never remembered. I...I don't want to remember. I want it gone. I want him gone. I don't want to see him anymore. I don't want him in my head. I want him out." She slapped her palms against the sides of her head. "Get out. Get out."

I grabbed her hands as gently as possible. "Daria, stop." I sat on the edge of the bed and stroked her back while she sobbed. But she was inconsolable. Her wails increased in volume and frequency.

When Daria let out an earsplitting cry, the security guard outside rocked forward and lumbered to the door. He peered into the window just as one of the floor nurses pushed her way into the room.

"What happened?" the nurse asked.

"We were talking about the attack last night," I said. "She got confused. I think she's remembering what happened to her six years ago."

"What happened to her?" the nurse asked.

I didn't know what details were in Daria's file. "Someone tried to drown her."

"Sweetie," the nurse sat on the bed, reaching for Daria's wrist while she counted beats and checked her watch, "you're okay. Just take a few deep breaths for me. We don't want you to hyperventilate." The nurse pressed the call button, and a second woman in pink scrubs appeared in the doorway. "Cheryl, page whoever's on call."

"Sure thing." Cheryl gave me a look before heading toward the nurse's station.

"Daria," I said, but the nurse shook her head.

"It'd be best if you let her rest."

"Is that okay, Daria?" I asked.

She squeezed her eyes shut, giving me a tight nod. Holding up my palms, I backed out of the room.

The security guard cornered me in the hallway. "What happened in there? What did you do to her?"

"Nothing."

"It doesn't sound like nothing."

Slowly, I reached into my jacket and removed a Cross Security business card. "Detective O'Connell's working her case as a favor to me. His wife, Jen, is an ER nurse in case you need someone to verify my identity. But I'm here to help, not hurt."

Satisfied with my answer, he gave a gruff nod and returned to his chair. Security was a joke. If I wanted to harm Daria, I would have walked into the room and done just that before anyone was the wiser. The woman needed better security. But after what just happened, the danger might only exist inside her head.

I hung around for a few minutes, hoping she'd calm down. While I paced outside her room, a weasely man in a brown suit with a plaid blue shirt entered the unit. His identification hung from his shirt pocket, but I didn't get a look at his name before he entered Daria's room. I only caught a couple of words before the nurse stepped out and closed the door.

"Dr. Mulroney wants to speak to you when he finishes with Daria," she said.

"Why?" Even if I hadn't seen his name tag, I could spot a therapist a mile away.

She pointed to a few chairs near the nurse's station. "You can wait there."

While I waited, I called O'Connell. When he didn't answer, I assumed it was because he was busy with Reagan. I tried Lucca. He answered on the second ring.

"Any progress on figuring out what happened last night?" he asked.

"You were with Daria all night. Did you talk to her? Did she say anything useful?"

"She was pretty rattled. She just kept talking about his

eyes. She believes Andrew Holland attacked her. I reassured her he's dead, but when she gets like that, there's no reasoning with her. It's all instincts and emotion. That's something I'm sure you can relate to."

"Did she go into the logistics of the attack?"

"She told me the same thing she told you. He shoved her head into the glass. After that, she doesn't remember a lot of details. But something spooked him, and he left. Once he was gone, she crawled out of the bathroom and called you. Then the security detail entered, and she freaked out and hid until you showed up."

"Does that make any sense to you?"

"Not really, but she was scared. In the heat of the moment, she probably didn't remember that you introduced her to Joe and Miles."

"No, not that. I mean the attack. We know Holland isn't back for revenge. That's the only thing we know for certain. And in case we had any doubts about his spirit coming back to haunt her, her room is full of warding off symbols."

"I don't believe in ghosts, Parker. I didn't think you did either."

"Only the ones that haunt me."

He didn't speak, no doubt contemplating my sanity.

"Relax, boy scout. I didn't mean it literally."

"Okay, so I'm not seeing the problem."

"For argument's sake, let's say an unsub attacked Daria in the bathroom. He knocked her into the glass. Why? What's his endgame? Why attack her and run away?"

"He got interrupted."

"By whom?"

"Okay, so maybe she surprised him. He knocks her out and runs before she can identify him."

"How did she surprise him? We're assuming whoever attacked her is the same person who's been stalking her. Wouldn't he know her routine?"

"Maybe he tried to knock her out, she didn't lose consciousness, and he panicked."

"Did she lose consciousness?" I asked.

"She must have. That would explain why it took her over an hour to call for help."

"There's a million reasons why it took her that long. What I'm trying to figure out is how her phone ended up in a different room."

"A different room?"

"It was in the main room, not her bedroom."

"Do you really think someone was there last night? Evidence says otherwise."

"Just humor me. I have no idea what happened. That's why we're having this conversation. So you're suggesting her attacker knocked her out cold. If he did, why did he panic and run?"

"Maybe he thought he killed her and fled the scene."

"That would mean he didn't intend to kill her."

"In this hypothetical, I don't think he did," Lucca said. "The attack wasn't brutal. Daria doesn't have enemies. We've both explored that possibility. Everyone loves her. No one has any reason to want to harm her."

Except for the freaks who idolized Andrew Holland, but I didn't bother voicing it. "But in this scenario, we're saying someone attacked her. Obviously, that person has a motive. We know far too many stalking cases end in sexual assault or murder. Sometimes, murder-suicide. When I found her under the bed, nothing about the scene indicated he intended to rape her, but I didn't ask. Did you?"

"The nurse in the ER did," Lucca said. "Daria said she didn't think it happened. They performed a physical, but she didn't have any bruising or defensive wounds. The only obvious sign she was attacked is where her head collided with the mirror. They didn't find any other contusions or lacerations unrelated to the broken glass."

"That's it? No signs of being held down or restrained?"

"Nothing. Her hands and arms were clean, except for a few glass shards they pulled out of her palms from where she crawled out of the bathroom." Lucca sighed. "I know what you're thinking, Parker, but no one attacked her. She hit her head on the glass. I don't think she did it on purpose. I've never known her to want to hurt herself. The impact probably knocked her out. I'm sure the blood scared her."

"How do you explain the message on her wall? Do you

think Daria wrote it?" She never mentioned her attacker scrawling the message with her lipstick. In fact, the police found the lipstick in the drawer in her vanity, which I imagined was where she always kept it.

"Why would she?" Lucca asked.

"I don't know. That and her phone make me question everything. The message on the wall said *I'm still here.* Does that mean anything? Was that relevant to Holland in any way?"

"No." Lucca thought for a moment. "Maybe she wrote it as an affirmation. Like *I survived* or *I'm alive.*"

"Did you ask her about it?"

"She didn't remember it at all."

I wondered if the experts at Cross Security would be able to match the writing on the wall to a sample of Daria's handwriting. They had taken photos of each, but I hadn't heard anything yet.

"Could she have written it while in an altered mental state?" I asked.

"Altered mental state?"

"Y'know, from being knocked out, possibly concussed, or at the very least one hundred percent panicked."

Lucca paused. "C'mon, Parker, put me out of my misery here. Is this what you're thinking?"

"That's more or less what O'Connell thinks."

"What do you think? I brought this to you because I value your opinion."

"I think you should have picked someone else. Jablonsky would be better at this than I am."

"Unfortunately, he's busy running ops at the OIO. You're the only person I know with a bunch of free time."

I ignored the crack. Dr. Mulroney exited the room and stopped a few feet away to speak to the nurse. She pointed to me. Time was almost up. "I'll do a bit more digging. I don't see how anyone could have attacked her last night without getting spotted. But I won't know for certain until I question Reagan LaRoche. He might have pushed her anxiety over the edge and triggered some nasty memories by terrorizing her. But the bastard stole her hairbrush, which means he knows how to get in and out of her house undetected. If someone entered Daria's home last night and attacked her, LaRoche will know how he did it."

NINETEEN

The doctor had a million questions for me. But since I didn't know what was going on, I didn't have much to say.

"Have you spoken to Daria's therapist?" I asked. "Her name's Dr. Chen."

"She's on her way," Dr. Mulroney said. The longer we spoke, the more he reminded me of a weasel, with his pointy nose and long, gray whiskers. "Daria Waylon was admitted early this morning for head trauma and now she's in the midst of a breakdown. I've ordered more scans, but if her mental state is due to an injury, the sooner we figure that out, the better off she'll be. That's why it's imperative you tell me what you were doing right before Daria became upset?"

"We were talking."

"About?"

"About what happened last night." I glanced at the nurse, knowing she'd already told him everything I said. "Daria might be recalling another traumatic event in her life."

"Has she been treated for post-traumatic stress?"

"I don't know."

"How long have you known Daria?"

"A few days."

He stared with his mouth open for a moment longer than any professional in a position of authority should. "You barely know her. How do you know any of this?"

"A little bird told me."

"Miss, we take hospital security and patient privacy seriously."

"I can tell by the buzzer at the door. This might not be the psych ward, but you go through a lot of trouble to make sure your patients don't wander off. I'd hate to see how you treat the people you actually think are crazy."

"The people on this level are suffering from neurological disorders. On occasion, they may get disoriented or wander off. Furthermore, they may become agitated by interlopers." He glared when he said it. "I'll ask you again, how do you know Daria?"

"I'm a private investigator."

"What business do you have with my patient?"

"That's private."

"Does it have anything to do with the injury she sustained last night?"

"Winner, winner, chicken dinner."

"Do you know what happened to her? I've received conflicting reports."

"I'm still investigating. I was asking her to walk me through it when she freaked out. Like I said, it brought up some old memories she didn't want to think about. That wasn't my intention. I never meant to hurt her. I'm sure her regular therapist and neurologist will be able to sort this out." I sidestepped and walked away.

I felt bad enough that my questions had ripped open old wounds Daria might have never even realized she had. I didn't need some doctor who was unfamiliar with her case to confront me about it. Confidentiality was just as important in my line of work as it was in his.

Since Daria had gone to great lengths to keep her situation quiet, I didn't want to spread rumors. The last thing I wanted was to have her bumped to the psych ward or forced into a mandatory hold while the guys in lab coats conducted an evaluation. I couldn't think of anything more frightening or worse than that. And since Lucca believed that was the hospital's intent all along, I didn't want to play a part in it when I didn't know what happened or if she intentionally hurt herself the previous night.

On my way out of the building, I pulled up Dr. Chen's office number and left her a voicemail explaining who I was and the situation. Now that the mess was made, the least I could do was help clean it up.

"Hey," an angry voice yelled from a few feet away. I tucked the phone into my pocket, turning to see the cause of the commotion. Reagan LaRoche stormed toward me. I almost didn't recognize him with his chest completely covered. "I thought that was you."

"Me?" I glanced around, shifting into a more defensive stance.

"Don't play innocent. Are you really a private eye? Or are you an undercover cop?"

"You need to calm down. I told you who I am."

"Calm down?" He shoved me into the wall next to the hospital entrance. "How do you expect me to be calm when cops just accused me of attacking Daria?"

I noticed several people eyeing us from where they were clustered on a bench near the pick-up and drop-off area. "I suggest you back off."

"Bitch, you're the one who needs to back off. Did you tell them I hurt Daria? Is that what she told you?"

"What are you talking about?"

"No." He pointed a finger at me. "Don't do that. You knocked on my door asking about my art. Then you asked about her. I called around. No one's heard of you. You never worked for an art gallery. Who are you? What do you want?"

"Right now, I want you to get out of my face."

"Too damn bad." Spit flew from his lips. On the other side of the automatic doors, a uniformed cop who'd been in the lobby keyed his radio. "Tell me what happened to Daria. Is she okay?"

"How would I know?"

"You're here." Sparks practically shot from his eyes. "What did you tell the cops I did to her?"

"I didn't say you did anything to her."

"Lie to me again and you'll see what happens."

I fought to keep the sick smile off my face. This would be interesting. "Did you do something to her? Is that why she's inside?"

"No," he shouted. "I'd never harm her." His voice cracked, his eyes wild. "You told them about the photo. They wanted to know where it was taken. They didn't believe Daria invited me to her house. But we're friends. You know that. You know we hang out every week. I told you all of that. Why did you lie to them about me?"

"I didn't lie." I watched as the officer inside spoke to a few members of hospital security.

"Don't play with me."

"You're the one playing some kind of sick, twisted game. You took that photo outside Daria's house. I recognized the angle. You were in her backyard, which makes me think she had no idea you were there. How many times have you gone to her place? Were you there last night?" I knew he wasn't, but I wasn't about to admit I'd been staking out his place while Daria's head was colliding with a mirror.

"She's my friend. I watch out for her."

"You're delusional." I wondered just how far to push.

"What happened to her?" he screamed.

"What did you do to her?" I retorted.

"Nothing." He grabbed my shoulders, yanking me forward before shoving me back into the wall.

Normally, this is when I'd introduce my knee to his groin, but given the growing audience, I went with the slightly more painful alternative. "She doesn't trust you. You scare her. She'd never invite you inside her house. That's why you had to sneak around and take her photo. How often do you follow her around and spy on her? Every day? Every week? The only reason she agrees to hang out with you on Saturdays is because she pities you. She figures it's the only way to stop you from acting like a total creeper. But it just makes you want her more. You'll never have her. You're just another wannabe loser. You're not even a real artist."

"You have no fucking clue. Daria loves me."

"Daria barely tolerates you. Why do you think she freaked out when you invited her to your place? That's not love. That's fear."

"Shut up," he screeched.

I stared up at him, defiance in my eyes. "Is the truth that hard to hear?"

"Is this the shit you told the cops?"

"I told the cops everything."

He slapped me. That's all it took for the cop inside to intervene.

"Sir, back away from the woman." The officer kept his hand near his weapon while he held out his other hand.

Fire burned in Reagan's eyes. "You set me up."

I rubbed my cheek. "Don't hurt me. Please. I didn't do anything to you. I barely even know you."

"I'm gonna kill you," Reagan swore, pulling his arm back to hit me again.

The cop grabbed Reagan's shoulder, yanking him away from me. "Sir, step back." When Reagan failed to comply, the cop shoved him into the wall a few feet from where I stood and patted him down. "Ma'am, are you okay? What's going on here? Can you tell me what happened?"

"He assaulted me," I said. "Arrest him. I want to press charges."

*   *   *

"I thought you were going to handle Reagan LaRoche," I said.

O'Connell rubbed the bridge of his nose. "He didn't want to cooperate, and I didn't feel like getting smacked in the face."

Thompson snorted. "At least Parker was willing to take one for the team."

"What was he even doing at the hospital?" I asked.

"After we told him Daria was attacked, he decided to go see her. I checked his phone records. He called her, but she didn't answer. Clearly, that wasn't enough to deter him."

"Why didn't you intervene sooner?" I asked.

"How? We didn't have enough to arrest him. When we

spoke to him, he wasn't wearing the earrings and didn't consent to allowing us to search his apartment," O'Connell said. "But now that he's been arrested, the judge granted us a court order. Unfortunately, his call log doesn't further our theory that he's stalking her."

"Are you sure? Did you find anything else in his phone records?"

"We're still looking. He calls Daria a couple of times a week. They talk for a few minutes. The frequency and duration aren't what we typically see in stalking cases."

"That doesn't mean anything. There are no established parameters for what constitutes unwanted and repeated contact."

"Did you tell Daria not to answer when he called her today?"

"I had warned her to keep her distance from him, but that's not why she didn't answer."

"Why didn't she answer?" Thompson asked.

I reached for LaRoche's phone records. "By the time he called, Dr. Weasel had Daria sedated."

"Dr. Weasel?" Thompson looked at O'Connell. "Is that really his name?"

"I'm sure Parker's taking a creative license. At least, I hope so." O'Connell eyed me. "Was that his name?"

"It should have been, but it's Mulroney."

O'Connell tapped the complaint I made. "Are you certain this is what went down between you and LaRoche outside the hospital?"

"A uniformed cop and several hospital security guards saw the whole thing."

"But they couldn't hear what was being said. They only heard Reagan yelling at you, calling you names, and threatening to kill you. It backs your story, but I want to make sure I'm not missing anything."

"Nope, that's it. Most of it is even verbatim."

O'Connell read each line carefully. I'd included all the things Reagan had said. "When you confronted him about the stalking, he didn't admit it to you."

"He said she loves him. That's not normal."

"And you're sure they aren't having an affair? Her brush

was at his apartment. Her photo's on his wall. They have matching gold hoop earrings. That sounds like relationship stuff to me."

"That's probably what Reagan thinks too. But their love affair is only going on in his head. You can ask Daria. She denies having any romantic feelings for the guy."

"Are you sure she isn't lying?" O'Connell asked. "Or that she'd remember?"

"Let me put it this way. Her best friend doesn't believe they're a couple. And Daria made no mention of having warm gooey feelings or of doing any of the steamy, gross things that go along with such feelings in any of her journals," I said.

"Still, Reagan LaRoche could twist it around on her. Given her memory lapses, a judge might not give much credence to your statement, especially since it's hearsay," Thompson said.

"So ask Reagan about it," I suggested.

"He's likely to clam up," O'Connell said. "I'm not sure arresting him has done anything other than make this situation messier."

"But you have a search warrant," I said. "There must be something in his apartment that proves he's stalking her besides what I've already told you about."

But I wasn't sure. I hadn't found anything else, but I'd been rushed. Maybe Reagan had more clandestine photos of Daria. I shot a text to the Cross Security techs, asking if they ever finished analyzing the memory cards. They had found several photos of Daria, taken at various other venues. She never looked at the camera, which might have meant she didn't know she was being photographed. I asked them to e-mail the photos to me. I opened the message and enlarged the images on my tiny screen. I couldn't tell where they were taken, which meant these might be proof Reagan was stalking her. But I wasn't sure, so I held off on sharing them with O'Connell.

"All right." O'Connell climbed out of his chair. "Now that the ink's dry, I'll see what I can dig up."

"Ooh," I waved my arm in the air like an over-eager five-year-old, "take me with you."

"That's not happening," O'Connell said. "An hour ago, this guy attacked you. You're not exactly unbiased."

"But I wanted him to hit me. If he hadn't, you wouldn't have the search warrant. I earned the right to go with you."

"No."

"But Nick—"

"Right now, the only thing we know for certain is LaRoche didn't harm Daria last night. No matter what I find inside his apartment, it's not going to change that fact."

"I know, but if you can prove Reagan's broken into Daria's townhouse, we'll be able to figure out if anyone else has."

"That sounds pretty damn convoluted," Thompson said. "Are you sure you didn't hit your head too?"

I stuck my tongue out at him.

"Play nice, Parker," O'Connell chided. "Unless LaRoche broke into Daria's apartment while surveillance teams were sitting on the place, I doubt anything he says will be that useful."

O'Connell was right. Unfortunately, if Reagan didn't have a magic trick up his sleeve that allowed him to disappear and reappear inside Daria's apartment without tampering with the doors or windows and avoid being spotted from the front and side of the building, then that meant Daria hurt herself. In which case, there was nothing I could do to help her.

TWENTY

Lucca stood beside me. He'd left work as soon as possible. Given that it was just a few minutes past five, he must have violated several traffic laws to get to the precinct.

"Any word on Daria's condition?" I asked.

He stared straight ahead, sizing up Reagan LaRoche from the other side of the glass. "They're keeping her under observation for the next few days while Dr. Chen assesses her condition and figures out the best way to proceed."

"Can Daria refuse?"

Lucca shook his head. "Dr. Chen can't dismiss the possibility Daria is a danger to herself. The mandatory seventy-two hour psych hold is in her best interest."

"I hoped we could avoid that."

"It's for the best, Parker."

"I didn't mean to break her."

"It's not your fault. At least now, she can get the help she needs."

I didn't believe it, not when I was sure the man in handcuffs on the other side of the glass was to blame. He was the one who should be locked up, not Daria. Instead, she'd been targeted by a killer and retargeted by a lunatic, and now she had to suffer even more because of what this asshole did to her. "Reagan said she loves him. He has her hairbrush. Her photo. He could have all kinds of things at work or in his car that he took from her. I don't know what else he stashed away."

"Daria gave me a list of things that have gone missing since she met Reagan. The police recovered a few items in his apartment. We'll figure out where he put the rest of them." Lucca squared his shoulders. "Brin's on her way here. She can shed some additional light on this situation." But Lucca didn't move from his spot beside me. "You know what the worst part about this is?"

"So many things."

"Reagan did this by triggering her, but that's not a crime. He didn't go to her house last night. He didn't attack her, so even if we nail him on the stalking charges, the damage is already done." He brushed past me. "Thanks for trying, Parker. I appreciate it. I should have come to you sooner."

"You tried, Eddie."

He turned in the doorway, gave me a forlorn look, and went into the interrogation room. I watched him and Nick grill Reagan for over an hour. Reagan didn't say much, but when Lucca started talking about Daria's condition and the damage he caused, Reagan finally cracked.

He insisted everything he did was for Daria's benefit. They shared a passion for art. Taking her to galleries and museums inspired both of them. Without him, Daria wouldn't have gotten back to creating. She would have remained a has-been, but it was his pushing, his nurturing, his love for her that got her back to work.

"And what about the rest?" Lucca asked. "Daria has a history with men like you. You invaded her life. You took away her privacy, her sense of safety and security. You stole from her." Lucca slid the evidence bag containing what the police believed to be Daria's missing hairbrush toward him. "She's been frantic. You made her think she was losing her mind. What kind of sick fuck recreates the worst experience in another person's life?"

"Did you get off on that?" O'Connell asked. "Do you like

torturing people?"

"I'd never hurt her. I protected her. I helped her. Aren't you listening?"

"How is stealing a woman's hairbrush helpful?" O'Connell asked.

Reagan seemed to snap out of it. "I don't know how that ended up in my apartment. Are you even sure that's Daria's?"

"DNA will prove it." O'Connell shoved another evidence bag toward him containing the framed photo of Daria. "You can't tell me that's not her. You want to know what CSU told me? They said," he pointed to a faint reflection from the window pane, "she had no idea she was being photographed. She probably didn't even know you were there."

"You're wrong. Daria knows about that photo. I told her I wanted to shoot her while she worked. Ask her. She'll tell you." Reagan blinked a few times. "Actually, she might not remember. She has memory problems. Sometimes she gets confused."

"You're confused," Lucca muttered.

"How is she?" Reagan asked. "You said she had a breakdown? Is she okay? When can I see her?"

Lucca looked ready to kill. "You gotta be kidding me."

O'Connell took over. "We don't know. Has Daria ever talked to you about what happened to her?"

"Celeste told me before she introduced us."

"Celeste Nash, your agent?"

"She's a gallery owner. She always showcases my photographs. She gives me a new show every other month. She has several of Daria's pieces on display as well. Celeste told me about Daria's history. The first time we hung out, I asked Dar about it."

"Is that when you got the idea to stalk her?" Lucca asked.

"I'm not stalking her. Daria loves me. She wants me around. She needs me to protect her," Reagan insisted, his volume increasing. "How many times do I have to say that?"

"Do you love her?" O'Connell asked.

"She's sweet and not bad on the eyes. We have so much in common. But I'm not sure I'd say I'm in love with her," Reagan said.

"Her affection isn't reciprocated?" O'Connell asked.

"What affection?" Lucca blurted out.

O'Connell glared at him before giving the two-way mirror a desperate glance. Knowing what he wanted, I left the observation room and knocked on the door. Lucca stepped into the hallway, and I pushed the door closed.

"I know," he said, "O'Connell's building a rapport, hoping to get Reagan to open up, and I'm screwing it up."

"Yeah."

"I need to get out of my own way." He glared at the closed steel door for another moment. "Daria has this intensity when she talks to someone. She makes them feel like they are the center of the universe. She gives whoever she's speaking to her entire focus. She asks questions. She shows actual interest. No one does that nowadays. It's easy to mistake that for more than it is." He looked at me. "You know why she does that, right?" Lucca didn't wait for me to respond before supplying the answer. "It's because she's so desperate to form a new memory. She wants to hold on to as much information as she can so she can scribble it down in one of her books."

"I read what you gave me. She didn't have much to say about Reagan. She made it clear early on she had no interest in him. I don't think he got confused. He saw something that wasn't there because he wanted it to be there."

"Reagan's a narcissist. And like most narcissists, deep down, he's insecure. It's not about Daria. It's about the way she makes him feel."

"How did she make you feel, boy scout?"

He let out a breath, fighting to keep his face neutral. But I saw several microexpressions that he couldn't control. "Like it wasn't my fault this happened to her."

Before Lucca could go back inside the interrogation room, O'Connell came out. He shook his head. "That guy's crazy."

"Did Reagan tell you how he got inside Daria's house?" I

asked.

"He says Daria left him a key, but he didn't steal her things. He's not sure how they got inside his apartment. He says he didn't put them there." O'Connell signaled to a uniformed officer. "Escort Mr. LaRoche to a holding cell."

"Daria didn't give him a key," Lucca said.

"No kidding." O'Connell led us back to the bullpen. "After some wheedling, LaRoche said he found it underneath the welcome mat. He's under the impression she left it there for him."

"Talk about delusional," I said.

"I'm thinking most of this is an act. It's how LaRoche plans to get away with it, figuring Daria's memory will work against her when it comes to prosecuting him. Her testimony would fall under all kinds of scrutiny. He probably figures he won't face any real charges. It's petty theft."

"But you have him for B&E and stalking," Lucca said. "He deserves to be locked up."

"He's getting moved to central booking. We're charging him. I just don't know how much will stick."

"Brin said she saw a green Charger outside her apartment on the days Daria came to visit. That's your witness," I said.

"I'll speak to her too." O'Connell reached for a form and grabbed a pen.

"He's probably done this before," I said. "I barely scratched the surface, but I can keep digging."

"No need. It looks like we have enough to substantiate Daria's claims." But the unsaid implication hung heavily in the air. "I'll take over from here. This is a police matter now," O'Connell said.

Lucca held out his hand, and the two men shook. "Let me know if I can be of any assistance."

"Will do." O'Connell glanced at me. "I have your statement. If I need anything else, I'll be in touch."

"You're kicking me out?"

"You can stay if you want, but I thought you had plans this evening." He pointed the end of his pen at the clock. "If you rather hang around here and watch me do paperwork, by all means."

Lucca tugged on my elbow. "C'mon, Parker, you've done enough."

I gave O'Connell a final look before letting Lucca lead me out of the precinct. We stopped at the top of the stairs, watching people move along on the sidewalk. "This doesn't feel right," I said.

"Parker—"

"Does this feel right to you?"

"You identified Daria's stalker."

"But she was attacked. She's in the hospital. She thinks she's losing her mind."

"Reagan LaRoche didn't assault her last night."

"But he's responsible." I sucked in a shaky breath. "The worst part is he's going to get away with it."

"O'Connell has proof. Reagan practically admitted to it."

I fought to keep the scowl off my face. "He did that so he can twist the narrative. Assuming the DA's office agrees to prosecute, defense counsel will turn everything around. They'll make him look like some kind of white knight protecting the damsel in distress. They'll sell his lies, and they'll use her handicap against her. The fact that she's been forced to stay in the hospital on a mandatory hold because of some kind of suicide watch will make it that much harder to prove Reagan's the scum who put her there."

Lucca grabbed my arm, a sad smile on his face. "She got you too."

"What?"

"Daria. You kept asking me why I couldn't let it go, why I stayed in contact, why I kept trying to help her. She sucked you in too."

"It's not her. It's the situation. It's the injustice."

"I know."

I sat down on the step and put my head in my hands. Lucca took a seat beside me. "This isn't fair."

He stared at the traffic. "If I'd looked into LaRoche earlier and figured out what was going on, Daria wouldn't be in so much pain right now. But Dr. Chen said the memories were bound to resurface sometime. LaRoche triggered them, but if it hadn't been him, it would have been someone or something else."

"This sucks."

"At least we can tell her someone was following her, watching her, sneaking into her house, and taking her things. She didn't imagine it. That's gotta count for something."

A few cops were making their way up the steps, so I stood, moving out of the way so they could pass. "Why do you think he did it?"

"I don't know. But you heard O'Connell. LaRoche is crazy."

But something told me it went deeper than that.

Lucca and I parted ways. He planned to stop by the hospital and see if he could convince the doctors to let him speak to Daria. He wanted her to know she hadn't imagined everything. I headed back to the office. Even though my job was done, it didn't feel done.

The first thing I did was phone Celeste Nash. The gallery owner told me she introduced Reagan to Daria at a gallery event. When Reagan had shown an obvious interest in Daria, Celeste had arranged for them to meet privately. She thought the two would hit it off.

"Daria's creativity had stagnated. She was surviving, but not thriving. I thought Reagan would inspire her," Celeste said. "He sees the world in such vibrant colors. Have you seen his photos?"

"A few."

"Well, then you know what I mean. The way he captures the perfect shot. He sees the true essence of things. Daria's art used to reflect that same wonder and passion, but her more recent things are drab and gray."

"Don't you think there's a reason for that?" I asked.

"Oh, you mean because of what happened. That's ancient history. It's time she moves on."

I gripped the handset so tightly, I thought it might break. "So you sent a predator after her."

"Excuse me?" Surprise and offense competed for control of her vocal cords.

"You heard me. Reagan LaRoche is a predator. I'm sure

Daria isn't his first victim."

"Oh my god. I had no idea. Is she okay?"

"I don't know. Reagan said you told him about her history. What else did you tell him?"

"No-nothing."

"Did you give him her phone number or address?"

"I did. I didn't mean to. I mean, yes, I gave him her phone number. I thought he should call her. I thought they'd be a good match."

"I didn't realize your gallery is also a dating service."

"It isn't. But I've known Daria a long time. She needed a muse. I thought Reagan's joie de vivre would ignite her passion. If that meant they also got together, well, good for them. I had no idea he was dangerous. He never seemed that way to me. I should have never..."

"Never what?"

"A couple of weeks after I gave him her number, he called me and said they had plans to meet up before a gallery event. He was supposed to pick her up at her house, but she'd forgotten to give him her address. He said he didn't want to call her and ask for it because he thought that'd be insensitive."

"So you gave it to him?"

"Yes."

That explained a few things. Since Daria stuck to such a strict schedule, he'd know what days she would be hanging out with Brin. He probably found the key under the mat.

"Ms. Parker," Celeste said, "what happened to Daria?"

"I don't think sharing her personal details is a good idea." And I hung up.

I wanted to scream. Frustrated, angry, and sad, I grabbed the phone off my desk and asked the techs upstairs to pull every bit of dirt they could on Reagan LaRoche. I wanted to know every woman he'd ever looked at twice. Regardless of what O'Connell and Lucca thought, Reagan would walk unless I could prove he'd done this before to someone whose testimony couldn't be as easily ripped apart on the stand.

TWENTY-ONE

My phone beeped, notifying me of an incoming text. *I'm home. It's your move.*

Sighing, I knew it was time to call it quits for the night. Martin had dropped a pin, letting me know he was at our apartment, which meant I didn't have to make the drive back to his estate. He must have figured I'd be working late at the office. This would save time on the commute. Our apartment was also closer to the Martin Technologies building and the airport. It made sense why he'd chosen to spend the weekend there instead of at his house.

By the time I got home, I'd run myself into the ground trying to figure out exactly what I thought about the last few days. I let myself hope that Reagan would be able to tell us how he snuck in and out of Daria's apartment undetected and that would prove someone else had been there the previous night and attacked her. But that hadn't been the case.

Reagan said he had a key. He must have entered and exited in broad daylight, as if he were meant to be there. He probably behaved the way I did whenever I committed a B&E. That's why no one ever reported it or even noticed. I was sure O'Connell would question Daria's neighbors again and get some corroboration or proof, but that didn't help Daria any. The truth of the matter was she hurt herself. It'd be up to the professionals to figure out why and how it happened. I failed her and Lucca.

Pushing open the door, I immediately spotted Martin. He was on the balcony with a drink in one hand and his phone in the other. He wasn't pacing, but he kept moving from side to side, shifting his weight and stretching his legs. It must have been a long flight.

I closed and locked the front door, watching him through the sliding glass door. He put the phone away, swallowed the remainder of his drink in one gulp, and turned to come back inside. Our eyes met, and a smile tugged at his lips.

"Hey, beautiful," he pulled the balcony door closed behind him and put the glass on the coffee table, "I figured you'd be working late."

Butterflies filled my insides. "I missed you."

He gave me a sexy grin. "Not enough to come see me."

"I'm sorry."

"No." He moved toward me with a sudden urgency. Gripping my face in his hands, he kissed me hard on the mouth, stealing my breath away. My knees shook. He lifted me off the ground, and I wrapped my legs around his middle while he backed me against a wall, his lips never leaving mine. My fingers found their way into his hair. All I wanted was to lose myself in him and forget about these last few days. When the need for oxygen became too great, he backed up just an inch, his chest heaving. "I'm sorry. We never talked about any of this."

"I don't want to talk." I tugged his face closer to mine, my lips latching on to his.

He laughed against my mouth, gently pulling away. "Hold that thought. Have you had dinner?"

"I don't want dinner, unless you do."

"I'm okay, but the fridge is empty."

"We'll worry about it later."

"Everything will be closed later. I don't want you to starve."

"I won't, and I don't understand why we're having this

conversation. Are you hungry?"

His eyes twinkled. "Absolutely ravenous."

"Then shut up and kiss me."

He carried me into the bedroom and dropped me onto the bed. After pulling the t-shirt over his head, he paused, his brilliant green eyes finding mine. In that moment, he saw the toll the last few days had taken, but I tugged on his belt, pulling him closer before he could ask what was wrong. I didn't want to talk about it. In fact, I didn't want to think about Daria or Reagan or any of it. And for the rest of the night, Martin made sure I didn't.

*　　*　　*

The next morning, I woke up before Martin. That was something that rarely happened. The jetlag and time difference must have taken a toll. As quietly as possible, I slipped out from beneath the covers and grabbed the t-shirt Martin had worn the night before. I tied the bottom, letting the knot hang just above my naval as I went into the kitchen to make coffee.

While it brewed, I checked my phone for any messages. Nothing. I put the phone down, unsure what to do. The case was over, but it didn't feel resolved.

My stomach growled. I'd stashed a few boxes of marshmallow cereal in the back of the cupboard. Finding one, I pulled it out and filled my bowl. I opened the fridge, but aside from a few condiments and several bottles of water, there was nothing inside. Returning to the cupboard, I stood on my tiptoes and felt around until I found a couple of chocolate milk boxes.

Popping the straw through the tiny hole, I squeezed the first box into my bowl of cereal and topped it off with a portion of the second milk box. While I was reaching into the cupboard to see if there was anything else of any interest, Martin came into the kitchen.

"Damn, if that's not the sexiest thing I've seen in two weeks."

I turned, finding him studying my bare legs and torso. "I doubt that. You're renting a beach house in Malibu. The place is lousy with aspiring models, actresses, and porn stars. Throw a rock and you'll hit a bombshell."

"Or an entertainment lawyer. The place is crawling with them too, and they are damn litigious."

"Oh, so you've tried the rock trick?"

He laughed, snaking his arms around my waist. His thumbs brushed against the hem of his t-shirt. "You know I usually hate it when you tie knots in my shirts. It stretches them out."

"Do you want me to take it off?"

He nibbled on my earlobe, making me giggle. "After breakfast."

I ran my hands along his chest, feeling the definition of his muscles beneath my fingertips. He took my hands in his and kissed my knuckles. "Are you heading to the office?" I asked.

"Are you?" he countered.

"No. O'Connell made an arrest. I'm done."

Martin cocked his head to the side, studying me. I didn't like it when he did that, so I pulled away and filled two cups with coffee. "So you could have flown out to see me for this weekend."

"I didn't know that at the time." I handed him one of the cups and sat down, picking up my spoon and shoveling the cereal into my mouth. "I already told you I'd reschedule my trip. You didn't have to fly home just because our weekend plans got derailed."

"I wanted to see you, and I didn't see any reason why I couldn't have what I wanted." He examined my breakfast. "How about we try again for the weekend after next?"

"That works for me."

"Good." He pulled out his phone. "I'll reserve a plane ticket for you. How does Friday at four sound?"

"Martin, I can get my own ticket."

He hit the screen a few more times. "Too late. I already booked it."

"You didn't have to. I would have done it."

The look on his face said he doubted it. "I'm just asking for a weekend. I want to show you the house. The beach, the waves, the sunsets. I'm pretty close to Santa Monica.

We can go to the pier and the Farmers Market. We'll do the whole tourist thing. How do you feel about celebrity bus tours?"

"Martin—"

"Fine, we'll skip that." He winked "Maybe." I let out a displeased grunt. "You can spare one weekend to visit me and have some fun," he insisted.

"Do you think you'll be able to tear yourself away from work long enough to do all those things you have planned?"

"I'll try, if you will."

I put my spoon down and reached for my coffee cup. "Okay."

He snagged the lip of my bowl and moved it closer. Grabbing my spoon, he ate a few bites. "Where did you get the chocolate milk?"

"It was in this little box."

"Amazing." He picked up the box and sucked on the straw. "I used to love these as a kid. It never occurred to me to put it in my cereal."

"I picked up that trick more recently. I didn't grow up getting to eat this stuff."

"We really should go grocery shopping." Martin slid the bowl toward me. "Have you eaten anything that hasn't come in a box with a cartoon character on it since the last time I saw you?"

"Cross keeps the break room stocked. He has breakfast and lunch covered."

Martin ran a hand through his hair, making the brown strands stick straight up. "I never know whether I should thank that guy or kill him."

"Probably neither." I rinsed the bowl and put it in the dishwasher. "He said something strange to me the other day."

"He wants back in on the project."

"You know?"

"Yeah, I saw him yesterday."

"What time did you get in? I thought you came straight here from the airport."

"I did." He searched my eyes for a moment. "Cross

didn't tell you?"

"Tell me what?"

"He's been in L.A. these last few days."

"What?"

"He had other business and made an appointment to see me. We met for lunch before I hopped on the plane."

"What do you think of his proposal?"

Martin eyed me, his hands finding their way back to my midriff. His fingers traced the outline of my ribs, making me squirm. "It's something to consider. Do you think it's a good idea?"

"I can't answer that."

"But you have an opinion. I'd like to hear it."

"You really wouldn't."

"Humor me, Alexis."

I pulled away from him, needing space. "You already know what I think. I never wanted you to partner up with him. He played you. That's why he hired me. That's why he introduced you to Jade. It's why he's done every single thing he's done."

"You give him too much credit."

"You don't give him enough."

Martin exhaled. "Regardless, the man makes a valid point. He wants to make sure his people are outfitted with the best protections available. I want that too."

"It sounds like you already made a decision."

"I'm meeting with Luc Guillot for drinks later to discuss the implications before I present it to the other members of the Board." He stared at me. "But you've made it clear I should stay away from Cross. Tell me why."

"Scandal follows you around. Partnering with Cross again will only compound the problem. He's not clean. He does a lot of illegal things. You've always been on the up and up. He'll drag you down, Martin. And it'll be my fault because my job is dangerous and you want to do everything you can to protect me from it." We'd fought about that time and time again. I couldn't fault him for having that attitude, only for acting upon it. But I remembered what Cross said to me, and I laughed cynically.

"What?"

"Cross asked me to convince you to draw up a new contract. He says once you do, you won't have any reason to stay in L.A., which means you'll come home."

"I guess that means we should discuss the elephant in the room."

"What elephant?" I looked around. "I don't see an elephant."

"Alex, please, as soon as I told you the original backer fell through and I had to go back to L.A., you tried to cut and run. You haven't called me once. You come up with excuses not to see me. You're pissed that I left."

"No, I'm not."

His green eyes were laser focused on me, staring into my very soul. "I'm not abandoning you. This is only temporary."

"I know."

"Do you?"

I looked away, unable to take the intensity of his gaze. He moved closer, grasping my chin between his thumb and forefinger and forcing me to look at him. "Why don't you call me?"

"Don't you think we talk enough? You call almost every day."

"Would you call if I didn't?" He waited, but I didn't answer. "Dammit, I wouldn't have flown across the country to see you if I didn't want to. You're my everything. None of this other stuff matters without you." He swore. "I won't hurt you. You don't have to put up these walls and insulate yourself. I'm not going to drop a bomb on you."

"I know."

"You don't act like it. Do you even want me here?"

"More than anything." I didn't like showing my vulnerability, but I swallowed the lump in my throat and soldiered on. "But this isn't one of your normal business trips. You don't know when you're coming home, or even if you're coming home. I see the writing on the wall." I snorted, thinking of the message in Daria's bathroom. "Quite literally, in fact."

He blinked, realizing that was the problem. "Shit." He pressed his forehead against mine. "I love you. We'll figure this out. We didn't talk about it before, but we will now. I'm sure we can find some solution to make the long-distance thing work. So far, we haven't spent more than two weeks apart. I think that means we're on the right track."

"I don't know, Martin. I'm confused. You just bought me a plane ticket for two weeks from now, but you're meeting with Luc in a few hours to figure out your next move. If you're thinking of getting Cross back on board, why won't you be sticking around?"

"It's complicated. I have a few other things in the works."

"This isn't just about your R&D into biotextiles?"

"It's all interconnected. A million little things have to line up. It's business. As soon as I know more, I'll tell you. But let's not jump to any conclusions."

"What kinds of conclusions? When do you think things will get back to normal?"

The expression on his face nearly broke my heart. "I'm not sure. It might be a few months."

I exhaled, resigned to whatever had to be done. He'd put up with my lengthy assignments. I owed him the same. "Okay."

He rubbed his thumb across my cheek. "I want you to do two things for me."

"What?"

"First, stop living out of your office."

"But it's weird being here without you, especially at night."

"Then call me. We've always been good at the late night phone calls. We can even have a *Sleepless in Seattle* moment, if you think it'll help."

"Fine."

His fingers moved to the knot on my shirt. "Now, take this off."

TWENTY-TWO

"Are you sure you don't want to join us? Luc can bring Vivi, and we'll make a night out of it."

"Some night. You'll be discussing business the entire time."

"But we'd be together. I thought you missed me."

"Not enough to watch you and Luc go over spreadsheets and next quarter's projections while I'm forced to make uncomfortable small talk with Luc's wife. Go to work, handsome. I have a few things to take care of, anyway."

Martin gave me one last kiss and slid his laptop into a messenger bag. "I won't be gone that long. Two hours. Three tops. I'll bring dinner home. What are you in the mood for?"

"Whatever you want."

"I'll remind you of that later."

"I'm sure you will."

Once he was gone, I printed a few photos of Reagan LaRoche and his car and headed over to Daria's townhouse. It was late enough that most of her neighbors would be home by now, but early enough that it hadn't gotten dark yet. The daylight made knocking on doors and asking questions less intrusive, or so I hoped.

Daria's townhouse was situated at the front of the cul-de-sac. The street contained five buildings. Two on either side and one at the end. With five townhouses per unit, there were plenty of potential witnesses.

The police had thoroughly canvassed the neighborhood the night of the alleged attack, but they hadn't asked the right questions. Detective O'Connell would be back at some point to ask if anyone had ever seen Reagan LaRoche or his vehicle in the area, but I couldn't wait. I had to make sure O'Connell wouldn't run into any surprises. From the way Reagan reacted to the interrogation, I feared he might have a trick or two up his sleeve.

I parked outside Daria's house and started with the townhouses directly across the street from hers. I knocked on all five doors, but none of her neighbors recalled seeing Reagan LaRoche or the green car in the area. That didn't mean he hadn't been here, but it wouldn't help O'Connell's case either.

I asked if I could check the recorded doorbell cam footage. One neighbor was nice enough to bring out a tablet and let me see it, but with a limited field of view, the only way I'd see Reagan or his car was if he'd veered onto the sidewalk. "Thanks, anyway," I said.

Trudging to the next unit, I repeated the process while I slowly made my way around the horseshoe and back to Daria's townhouse. No one noticed anything, but most of Daria's neighbors admitted they never paid much attention. It was a safe neighborhood. They had no reason to be extra vigilant.

I rang the doorbell on the end unit, but no one answered. It was Saturday. Some people had lives and plans. Or maybe the guy was stuck at the office. Either way, I moved on to the next doorstep.

A woman opened the door, giving me a bewildered look. "May I help you?"

"I hope so. I'm a private investigator. I'm working with the police. I have a few questions about your neighbor, Daria Waylon."

She narrowed her eyes while she wiped her hands on her apron. "Is this about the other night? I heard her screaming. I called 9-1-1, but they said someone had already alerted them. The police never told me what happened. Is Daria okay?"

"I hope so." I held out the photo. "Have you seen this man?"

"I don't think so. Wait just one second." She stepped backward. "Hey, Tom, can you take a look at this?"

A man with gray hair and glasses joined her at the door. "What do you want, Uma?"

"This nice lady's looking into what happened next door. Do you remember seeing this guy?"

He took the photo from her, holding it close to his nose and frowning. "Can't say that I do." He handed it back to his wife while sizing me up. "No one bothered to tell us what happened. Was it a break-in?"

"The police are still investigating."

Tom didn't like that answer. "Who is this guy?"

"Reagan LaRoche." I showed him the photo of the car. "Maybe you saw his car."

"That I remember, but it hasn't come around here in some time."

"Did you ever get a look at the driver?"

Tom shook his head, turning to his wife. "Don't you remember, you bitched about the noise."

Uma rolled her eyes. "Well, it sounded like a plane was about to land."

"Excuse me?" I wasn't following.

Tom made a face at his wife. "His muffler was loose. You know how it makes that humming, sputtering noise. She thought that racket was a plane heading straight for the house."

"That's just how it sounded," Uma said. "The whole place shook."

"You're always hearing weird things, waking me up in the middle of the night. It's the damn squirrels, woman."

"I don't like them up there," Uma said.

"You have squirrels?" I asked.

"A ton," Tom said. "They feast on the bird feeder we have out back. They're nothing but bushy-tailed rats."

"Have you ever noticed anything weird in your

backyard? Footprints or anyone loitering around?" I asked, but they both shook their heads. "How often do you remember hearing the car?"

"We'd hear it every time it cruised by. I don't remember it ever coming down the cul-de-sac. It usually turned before getting to us. But since we're right on the corner, we'd always hear it, especially when it shifted gears," Tom said.

"How often was this?"

Tom blew through his lips, imitating a horse. "I have no idea."

"Maybe once or twice a week," Uma said. "Every once in a while, that car would drive by on Saturday afternoons. I remember hearing it while weeding my garden. But it was usually in the middle of the week, around dinnertime."

"Do you remember what time on Saturday?" I asked.

"Mid-afternoon. Sometime before I'd start on dinner. Around two or three." Uma glanced back at Tom. "Speaking of, will you make sure the soup doesn't boil over?"

"Fine." Tom lumbered away.

"What else can you tell me about Thursday night? You said you heard Daria screaming and you called 9-1-1. Does anything else stick out in your mind from that day?"

"Not really." She went through the detailed list of everything she did, including what time she got up and what she ate at every meal. The one glaringly obvious detail she failed to mention were the two Cross Security sedans parked nearby. Since she didn't notice those, I assumed she wouldn't have noticed Reagan hanging around either. "I knocked on Daria's door today, but she didn't answer. Is she okay?"

"She's in the hospital. They're taking good care of her." I hoped that was true.

"It's such a shame. She's such a nice girl."

"Are you close?"

"We say hello if we see each other outside. Daria always gets her mail around the same time I do. We run into each other a lot then. We exchange pleasantries. That's about it."

"Have you ever seen her with anyone or noticed when she has company over?"

"Her parents visit often. Other than that, I can't really tell you what goes on over there. Have you tried asking the Gardners? They live across the street. They're both retired. The wife, Mary, likes to sit on the front porch. She might have seen something."

"I spoke to them already."

Uma nodded a few times, stepping closer to the edge of the porch while she looked around. "What about the Finkels? Or the Ortizes?"

"I'll make sure to check with everyone."

Uma waved to a man who was walking down the sidewalk. "Hey, Kevin, do you have a minute?"

"Sure, what's up? Does Tom need help with the sink again?" Kevin stepped up beside us. He had a baby face and glasses. He looked like a kid, dressing up in his father's clothes with the way the navy sports coat hung from his shoulders. The elbows had brown patches, and he carried a backpack over one shoulder, reminding me of an academic.

"No, he finally got that fixed, thanks to you. I swear, if you hadn't been around, we'd have a swimming pool in our kitchen." Uma turned to me. "This is Kevin Danziger. He lives one door down." Before I could introduce myself, Uma did it for me. "This young lady's helping the police. She's showing us photos."

"Photos?" Kevin cocked his head, waiting for me to hand him the prints. "Is this the guy who attacked Daria?"

"The police are still investigating."

Kevin studied the image carefully. "But he's in custody, right? That's why you have his picture and stuff."

"I'm not actually with the police. I'm a private investigator, assisting on the case."

"I see." Kevin handed me back the prints. "I don't think I've seen him before."

"What about his car?"

"Possibly, but I can't be sure."

"Does anything stick out in your mind from the night of the incident or anytime during the prior two months?"

"A lot of police cars have been showing up lately," he

said. "They always go to Daria's house." He narrowed his eyes at the photo in my hand. "I kind of thought it might have been a domestic thing."

"Really?" Uma asked. "Why?"

"I don't know. But every time the police got called, they'd knock on my door," Kevin said, "and ask if I'd seen or heard anything. They always asked if I'd seen anyone strange in the area. I just figured maybe our neighbor had boyfriend troubles."

"Did you ever see Daria with any men?" I asked.

"I saw her out with an older guy a few times." He described the man, and I jotted down the description.

"That's her dad," Uma said.

Kevin laughed, holding up his palms. "Oops."

"Anyone else?"

"Recently, someone's been visiting her. He drives a black SUV with government plates. I noticed because he always takes my spot. I've seen him drop by a few times." He described Eddie Lucca. "That's the only men I've ever seen her with. But I figured someone so pretty must have a partner. I just never saw him."

"Maybe it's a her," Uma suggested.

"Could be," Kevin said. "Daria does have a friend over sometimes." He described Brin. "But that's the extent of her houseguests. Daria's pretty shy. She keeps to herself a lot. She never comes to any of the block parties or barbecues. Since she doesn't want to mingle, I figured she must have a pretty busy life." He looked at me. "What does she do for a living?"

"She works from home," I said. "What do you do for a living, Mr. Danziger?"

"I'm a research assistant." He reached into his pocket and pulled out a card. "I should get going. But if I can help in any way, let me know." He looked around, shifty-eyed. "Rumor is Daria's townhouse was broken into and she was attacked. Should the rest of us be worried?"

"Take precautions, but this appears to be an isolated incident," I said.

"What does that mean?" Uma asked.

"It means Daria was targeted for some reason, which is

good for us but bad for her." Kevin nodded to me. "I hope she's okay."

"Me too," Uma said. "When you speak to her, tell her we said hello."

After I finished questioning the rest of Daria's neighbors, I checked the time and stopped by the office. Detective O'Connell had his work cut out for him. Aside from Uma and Tom Berry, none of Daria's other neighbors remembered seeing Reagan LaRoche in the area. On the bright side, they didn't remember Daria inviting him into her house either.

Uma had been as helpful as she could be, pointing out the car and establishing a possible timeline. Since Reagan and Daria met Saturday afternoons for coffee before touring art exhibits, he must have backtracked to her house after she left. I assumed he also dropped by when she was at Brin's. Reagan was careful. He made sure not to get caught.

The techs upstairs had pulled additional traffic cam footage from the streets nearest to Brin's apartment. They finally located the frost green car. The angle only allowed for a partial plate, but they had gotten a close up of the driver. It was Reagan.

"Send me a copy of the photo," I said. Once it hit my inbox, I forwarded it to O'Connell. The deep dive into LaRoche's background had yet to turn up anything hinky, but Amir had started building a list of LaRoche's recent paramours based on his dating profile.

"No one's launched any complaints against him," Amir said. "At least not officially."

"What about during his university days?"

"Sensitive matters like this often require a more personal touch."

"I'm not going to Rhode Island to visit his alma mater."

"Maybe Agent Lucca knows someone in the local FBI field office who could help."

"I'm sure he does." But in the meantime, I'd explore every local avenue available. "Has facial rec been able to spit out any names to go with the photos from Reagan's memory cards?"

"Only a few. It's slow going. Reagan took so many photos, and they aren't exactly at the best angles for the software to process them efficiently. Each one requires a lot of manipulation and extrapolation."

"I have faith in you."

"Now you sound like Mr. Cross," Amir said.

"Don't say that."

He laughed. "I'll text you when I have more. Right now, this is everything we have."

Deciding a short list was better than no list, I collected my things and headed home. My three hours were up, but something told me Martin would be working overtime too.

TWENTY-THREE

Martin was pulling plates from the cupboard when I walked in. He carried them out to the balcony while I locked the front door and took off my shoulder holster.

"I thought we'd eat outside tonight," he said.

"What about the pigeons?"

"Sweetheart, there are no pigeons." He kissed me gently on the cheek. "Grab that box. I'll get the wine."

"With pizza?"

"What was I thinking?" He slapped his forehead. "Let's go straight for the champagne."

"Martin," I wasn't sure if he was drunk, but he was definitely happy, "it's pizza."

"Which is why we need something bubbly."

"Most people would have soda or beer."

"In case you haven't noticed, we're not most people." He opened the fridge and grabbed a bottle of Dom which hadn't been there this morning.

"You went shopping?"

"I stopped at the liquor store on my way home. My case of Macallan came in, and since Marcal is in another time zone, I figured I better pick it up before they sell it to someone else. Also, the bar cart needed restocking, and I thought since we're together this weekend, that's more than enough reason to celebrate."

"Did you and Luc figure things out?"

Martin shrugged, busying himself with filling the ice bucket. "What were you doing while I was gone?"

"Working."

He eyed the files I'd left on the chair near the door. "Didn't you say you closed your case yesterday?"

"I didn't exactly close it. I handed it off."

"But it's finished."

"O'Connell's taken over. He made an arrest. I thought I should help him gather evidence."

"Is he stopping by to pick up those files?"

"No, those are for research purposes."

Worry shone in his eyes, but he forced the smile back on his face. "Take this outside." He handed me the ice bucket. "I have to grab one thing. I'll meet you out there."

When I stepped onto the balcony, I found that Martin had laid a white linen tablecloth over the table and had lit two long, elegant tapers. The table was carefully set. It was beautiful.

I put the pizza box and ice bucket down. One of those did not belong. I took a seat, wondering why he went to this much trouble. Pizza was best served straight out of the box.

He joined me on the balcony with a large gift-wrapped box in hand. "Surprise."

"What's this?"

"Open it."

Even the box was elegant. It was wrapped in silver paper with a pale pink ribbon tied in a perfect bow. I felt bad untying the ribbon and tearing through the paper. Martin watched excitedly, like a kid at Christmas. "Lingerie?" I asked.

"You'll see."

Hesitantly, I removed the lid while Martin grabbed the discarded wrapping and tossed it back into our apartment. I pulled the leather jacket out of the box and held it up.

"Do you like it?" he asked.

"It's gorgeous." He'd bought me other leather jackets in

the past. Each one was stunning and unique. This one was a racing jacket in dark silver with accents in various pink hues. The bright pink satin lining felt soft and smooth against my skin. I slipped it on, leaving the buckle at the collar undone. "When did you have time to go shopping?"

"While being stuck in L.A. traffic." He opened the pizza box and put a slice on each of our plates. "We were at a standstill a few blocks from the MT building. And I spotted this boutique. The jacket was on display in the front window. When I saw it, I thought of you. So I got out of the car and bought it. They have tons of styles and designs. I'll take you there when you visit, so you can pick out something else."

I nibbled on the pizza, careful not to get any grease on my new jacket. "So this is a bribe?"

"It's added incentive." He grabbed another slice of pizza, chewing thoughtfully.

"What did Luc say?" I asked after we'd both finished our third slice.

"We ran the numbers a dozen different ways. The preliminary research is promising. Even lowballing the estimates, my original project idea will be extremely lucrative. But we have to complete the research and figure out how to streamline production. The earliest we can move on this is eighteen months, but that's only if we get the financial backing we need."

"Your investors pulled out when Cross got arrested."

"They figured the project would nosedive. They didn't understand that his project and mine are separate."

"How is partnering up with Cross going to solve the money problem? Is he personally investing in this?"

"He says he has clients who want to finance his project. And by doing so, he'd use some of their money to finance my research." Martin shook his head. "Luc doesn't want to risk it." He gave me a lopsided smile. "You're right, you know, about scandal and Cross. I don't need this. My company can't take another hit. My reputation is already hanging by a thread."

"What's the alternative?"

"I find investors, anyone willing to fund the project

without requiring access to MT's research or proprietary secrets. Luc and I came up with a few incentives in addition to the usual profit sharing and dividend disbursements." Martin blotted his lips with the napkin. "It looks promising."

"Why can't you woo these investors from here?"

"I could, but that's only part of the problem."

"What haven't you told me? When you returned from L.A. the first time, that was supposed to be the end of this. But then the following week, something changed. You had to go back, and you had no idea when your business there would conclude."

He ran a hand through his hair. "I should have realized you'd pick up on that."

"I do plenty of stupid things, but I'm not an idiot."

"That's why you've been distant."

"You started it."

"I..." He inhaled, resisting the urge to argue. "That wasn't my intention."

"Tell me what's going on?"

"A few other internal matters have surfaced that need my attention. I'll spare you the details, but dissolving my partnership with Cross was the straw that broke the camel's back. We've been seeing decreasing profits in the last year. The Board doesn't want to take on more expensive projects, even though they'll make us money in the long run. They want to cut the fat. That's why they are hesitant to approve my project without additional financial backing and why they want to shut down the least profitable branches. The L.A. office is at the top of their list, since it's one of our biggest spenders. But that's only because the Board is narrowminded enough to only see things in dollars and cents. They don't realize how important the relationships we have with suppliers and tech moguls are and how advancing our R&D will lead to more lucrative developments." He leaned back. "Not to mention the hundreds of people who'd be out of work if they start shutting down our offices. I won't let that happen. I'm not my father. He would have shut down the office without a second thought. But I won't do that."

"How bad is it? Can the Board overrule you?" When we first met, Martin had been afraid of being removed from his own company. That fear had diminished. After all, he was majority owner, but the Board still exuded a lot of power.

"I'll turn it around. They can't touch me. I haven't violated any of the clauses, even though they looked long and hard at a few of the moral and ethical ones when Cross was arrested."

"That was him, not you."

"But I brought him on board. I partnered with him."

"That shouldn't matter."

"It's perception," he said. "Though, I have half a mind to sign him just to piss them off."

"I understand the impulse, but it's not a great idea."

Martin shrugged. "We'll see."

"I still don't understand why any of this means you have to work from California? Are you planning to chain yourself to the office building so they can't shut it down?"

"Nothing quite that dramatic. I want to put the West Coast branch in charge of the R&D and subsequent production line. That's why I'm working from there. This is my project, so it requires my signature and oversight. Once everything gets going, they won't need me anymore, and I can come home."

"Why didn't you mention any of this before?"

"I thought I could hold them off, but when everything fell through with Lucien, the Board pushed back. Hard."

"That's why you've been scrambling."

"Yeah."

"Okay." The pizza felt like a brick in the pit of my stomach. "That means we have to figure out our schedules. Should we shoot for seeing one another every other weekend?"

"I'd like to see you more than twice a month."

"Same here, but we have to be realistic. We both work a lot."

"What about when you're in between cases? You could stay for a week or two."

"I'd love to, handsome, but I've already used all my

personal days. Cross doesn't have a cap on sick days, but I've used so many, I can't just ask for more. And even when I'm not on a case, he expects me to show up. This was easier when I worked for myself. I could spend weeks at a time with you and it didn't matter. Now, it does."

"Once I find an investor for the project, I can cut down to four day work weeks and fly home every weekend, but I need to know we have the money first."

"So two weeks," I said. "We'll alternate, unless something comes up. Agreed?"

"Are you okay with this arrangement?"

"I have to be."

"Alex, you are my priority. If this is too much, I'll find another solution."

But this was business. And I always said work came first. Martin changed the rules on that, but I stuck to the basic tenet. He bent over backward trying to accept all the terrible things that came with my career. I could accept this. "It's okay. You don't have to. We'll make it work."

TWENTY-FOUR

Sunday night, I drove Martin to the airport. It was the first time I'd ever done it. Martin usually had his driver take him or he'd call a car, but since it meant we got an extra hour together, it was worth battling the kamikaze taxi drivers zipping around the loading and unloading area.

"Call me when you land," I said.

"I will." He kissed me like he'd never see me again.

I blinked a few times, refusing to get emotional. This was an airport, not a cemetery. Why did people always cry here? I wouldn't be one of them. "I'll see you in two weeks."

"I already booked your ticket." He ran his thumb across my cheek, wiping away what must have been a random raindrop. "Try not to cancel again."

"I don't plan to." I stole another kiss. "But no guarantees."

He gestured at the driver behind us who felt it necessary to lean into his horn. "He wants you to move."

"He can kiss my ass."

Martin snorted. "Go, sweetheart. I'll see you soon."

"I love you."

He smiled. "Good, maybe that means you'll actually call me one of these days."

"Don't push it."

"I wouldn't dream of it." He leaned in close. "But I plan on dreaming of plenty of other things." He whispered a few inappropriate suggestions in my ear before giving me a final, longing kiss. "Two weeks. I'll make it worth your while." With a wink, he grabbed his bag and walked away. I watched him make his way along the crowded sidewalk to the entrance. He turned at the door, pressed two fingers to his lips, and held them out in my direction.

Letting out an exhale, I shifted into drive, flipped off the impatient asshole behind me, and headed away from the insanity. No wonder I hated flying. The flight itself was nerve-wracking enough without the added airport drama. But plenty of trips were in my future. Martin better be worth it.

Even though I promised him I'd go home, I went back to the office. He wasn't set to land for another seven hours, and until I heard from him, I wouldn't be able to sleep. I might as well use that time to get some work done.

Over the weekend, the Cross Security team had identified more women from Reagan LaRoche's past and added several more names to the list of people he'd photographed. I dug into them with gusto, deciding I should use my emotional turmoil to my advantage.

In less than an hour I'd spoken to fifteen women, all of whom had gone out with Reagan at some point in the last six months. He hadn't been the ideal date, but he hadn't crossed any lines either. As far as they were concerned, he was nice enough, but a bit full of himself. He talked about nothing but art. The only creepy thing he did was ask to photograph them. A few of the women had been flattered. Those were usually the ones he went out with several times.

When the casual dates fizzled, Reagan didn't beg or plead with them for another chance. In fact, in most cases, he was the one who suggested they shouldn't continue seeing each other. He'd taken more than half of his dates back to his apartment. Several of them had spent the night. The more recent ones had seen Daria's photo on the wall. Reagan had been very proud and boasted about the angle and natural lighting involved in the shot. From what I gathered, it had only been hanging there for about a month.

Reagan hadn't kept the photo a secret. I marked every woman on the list who recalled seeing it, figuring O'Connell would want to speak to them. None of Reagan's dates ever met Daria, but Reagan had talked about her and her art when he was showing off the print. From the way it sounded, he was obsessed with her. But none of the women caught on to it.

Reagan never said he was dating Daria or that she was in love with him. Those were the details he had shared with me and O'Connell while inside an interrogation room, but not with his dates. On the surface, it made sense. But if he was as obsessed with Daria as he appeared, it should have leaked out while he was having other conversations, especially with women who were on the lookout for red flags before sleeping with the guy.

As I made call after call, I thought about the drawer full of makeup in Reagan's apartment. I asked several of the women if they'd left anything behind, but they didn't think so. If they had, it wasn't important enough for them to remember. The makeup probably wasn't theirs, but a part of me wondered if Reagan kept trophies of his conquests.

I just dialed O'Connell on my office phone when my cell phone rang. It was too early for Martin to have landed. Ignoring the cold chill that traveled through me as my mind went straight to plane crashes and terrorist takeovers, I hung up my desk phone and answered my cell.

"Parker," I said.

"I'm thinking of going out on a limb. Will you come with me?" Lucca asked.

"Are you drunk?"

"What? No. But the hospital won't release Daria."

"Why not? Is she that bad off?"

"I don't think so. She's kind of tired and lethargic. They have her on medication, which might be causing it, but I'm not sure." An emotional or psychological breakdown was physically taxing, but I didn't bother to mention it. "They won't release her unless someone signs her out. Her parents were supposed to arrive, but they got delayed. They won't be here for another week or two. She can't wait that long. She wants to go home. I can sign her out, but that'll make me responsible for her. Someone has to stay with her 24/7 to make sure she's okay."

"You want me to do it?"

"We can work in shifts. Cross Security has nurses and medics on staff. You had them look after Jablonsky when he was shot and moved to a secure location."

Given the problems Cross caused Martin, I felt entitled to use the resources my position afforded me. "I'll try to swing it."

"Okay. I'll take her home tonight and get her settled. Can you meet me at Daria's in the morning?"

"You're staying the night?"

"Don't say it like that."

Thoughts of Daria trembling and screaming came to mind. "I can stay with her."

"Are you sure? She might be more comfortable with me."

"Because I'm the one who broke her?"

"You didn't," Lucca insisted. "Just come by tomorrow. It'll give me a chance to touch base and see if she remembers you."

"Trust me, she remembers. I made quite the impression."

"I'll see you at oh seven hundred."

"Is that military time for nine thirty?"

"7 a.m."

"How about nine?"

"Nine works if Jablonsky okays me being late."

"Deal." My phone beeped, alerting me to an incoming call. "I'll see you at nine. Maybe I'll even bring you breakfast." I hung up before he could tell me he'd been joking about the nine a.m. thing. I switched phones and hit answer. "Hello?"

"Did you call me and hang up?" O'Connell asked.

"Yes."

"Are you in trouble?"

"No."

"Then why the prank call?"

"It wasn't a prank. Lucca called me while I was in the process of calling you. Daria's getting released from the hospital tonight."

"That's good. I spoke to her earlier today. She didn't remember me or much about the night we thought she was attacked. However, she apologized for placing the 9-1-1 calls and wasting our time with her complaints about a stalker."

"Didn't you tell her she's being stalked?"

"I did, but I'm not sure she understood. Talking to her was like talking to a robot. Things just didn't compute. Everything she said sounded hollow. Rehearsed."

"She memorizes things as a way to ensure recall."

"How can she memorize it if she can't form new memories?" O'Connell asked.

"She can, but it takes time and repetition. I don't understand it either, but I'm not a neuroscientist. The only thing I know about the human brain is how it looks when it's no longer inside someone's skull. And quite frankly, I wish I could forget that."

"You and me both," he muttered.

"Lucca said they have her doped up on something. Maybe that has something to do with it."

"Very possible. A lot of sedatives and mood stabilizers have side effects like that. But without her cooperation, I'm not sure I can make a case against Reagan LaRoche. As it stands, I'm not entirely sure I have sufficient evidence."

"Hopefully, the drugs will wear off soon. That's actually the reason I was calling you." I told him everything I'd learned so far from Daria's neighbors and Reagan's dates. "Do you have a copy of the items inventoried during the search?"

"You really think we make a list? You watch way too many cop shows."

But I knew he was only teasing. "Do you mind forwarding that to me?"

"I will as soon as we write one up. What are you hoping to find?"

"I'm not sure, but Reagan has a lot of makeup in his

bathroom. I'm thinking he might keep trophies."

"Come to think of it, we came across something a little odd. I'm not sure what to make of it. It's probably some kind of freaky coinky-dink."

"I thought you didn't believe in those either."

"Not usually. Tell me what you think of this." He must have found the inventory list. "Reagan has several concealers and foundations in various shades, along with palettes of eye shadow, different eyeliners, blushes, lipsticks, et cetera."

"I know he wears some of them. I've seen him with eyeliner on."

"Sure, but warm hazelnut foundation just isn't his shade," O'Connell said. "Thompson kicked around the idea that it's makeup LaRoche keeps on hand for his models."

"Probably, but it could also be items he's taken from his overnight guests. Did the makeup get dusted for prints?"

"Yes, Reagan's was on all of them, but we pulled several unidentified partials as well. That would be indicative of either theory."

"Did you find Daria's prints on anything inside his house? What about the hairbrush?"

"CSU pulled a smudge. It had two points in common with Daria, but it won't hold up in court."

"Two points doesn't mean shit."

"Yeah, I know. But back to what I was saying. I found a lipstick in his drawer. It's the same brand and shade as Daria's. Fire engine red."

"Is it hers?"

"The lab's testing it for DNA. But the results haven't come back yet. Her prints weren't on the tube. Only his. It's odd that we find the same stuff in his drawer that was used to write a message on her bathroom wall."

I ran through several possibilities. "More than likely, Reagan took the lipstick from Daria, and when it went missing, she replaced it with another tube."

"Are we sure he didn't write the message on her wall some time earlier that day?"

"No, we're not," I said. "But Daria was home all day. Cross Security was keeping watch. I explored every possibility. I don't see how he could have gained access to her house without someone noticing, especially when she was inside."

"Maybe the message had been there for days or weeks and Daria never noticed."

"It wasn't. I checked every inch of her townhouse twice. I would have seen it."

"I guess it is just one of those weird, random coincidences."

"I guess." But I wasn't sure I believed it.

TWENTY-FIVE

Lucca looked at his watch. "We said nine a.m. You're ten hours too early."

"Jablonsky won't give you the morning off. Sorry." I pushed past Lucca, nearly knocking him over as I lugged my overnight bag in through the narrow doorway. "Where's Daria?"

"She's in her room, probably asleep."

I glanced down the hallway that led to her bedroom. The door was closed. "How is she?"

Lucca rubbed his eyes and led me into the kitchen. He tossed me a pill bottle. "They have her on a low dose tranquilizer to keep her calm. Dr. Chen wants her in therapy four times a week."

"But how is she?" I asked. "Is she freaked out to be back in her house?"

"Oddly, she finds it comforting. It's familiar."

"That's because everyone keeps reassuring her it's safe and it's all in her head."

Lucca gave me a stern look. "I don't like that tone."

"What if we're wrong?"

"No, Parker. You are not mentioning a word of that nonsense to her. I don't care if Reagan LaRoche has the same lipstick in his drawer that was used to leave a message on her wall. He didn't write it. You know he didn't."

"Then why does he have it?"

"I don't know. Maybe he gets his rocks off dressing in drag. Or he chose such a bold color because it pops better in photos or because he saw Daria wearing it and wants to emulate her, like with the earrings."

"I bet those are her earrings, just like it's her hairbrush."

"He probably took her lipstick too. She could have had more than one, or she bought another one to replace the one he stole."

"That's the consensus."

"There you go." Lucca watched me tuck my overnight bag in the corner of the dining room. "Did O'Connell tell you the prints he found on the light switch belonged to Brin? We have zero evidence suggesting anyone else was inside Daria's house the night she was allegedly attacked, unless you or I did it. Which is also impossible since you have an alibi, and I know I didn't do it."

"Good thing I have an alibi," I said sarcastically.

"Yeah, good thing." He took a seat at the table while I paced in front of the fridge, eyeing the notes she made. When I couldn't read them again, I opened and closed the cabinets, hoping to find something.

"Parker, sit down. You're making me anxious. We agreed this is over. A hearing will be set. LaRoche will go before the grand jury. Hopefully, O'Connell will have found sufficient evidence by then so the bastard can stand trial. That's all we can do."

"It's not enough. I've been where she is."

"Don't. You've never been there. You don't have the deficits she does. You don't have the repressed memories. You aren't certifiable."

"Neither is she. She's not crazy. That fucking psychopath made her feel like she was. But she isn't."

"All we can do is tell her that."

I slumped into the chair across from him. He was right. I'd been spinning out over this since walking out of the precinct on Friday. I just couldn't figure out why.

Lucca nodded toward the bag I'd left in the dining room. "I take it this means you're staying the night."

"Yep."

"You don't have to."

"I don't have anywhere else to be. Martin left. Going back to an empty apartment doesn't hold much appeal. It's either here or the office, and I've already called every woman Reagan's dated. The techs upstairs told me the handwriting analysis was inconclusive, so that was a bust. I'm running out of things to do. And breathing down their necks while I wait for facial rec to identify everyone Reagan's ever photographed will probably lead to my untimely demise, so you're stuck with me."

Lucca stretched. "I called the Rhode Island field office. Tomorrow, an agent will speak to the dean of admissions at Reagan's alma mater and see if Reagan has a history of stalking."

"He must."

"Has O'Connell found anything to indicate that? Because I haven't. And you haven't either." Lucca tapped his fingertips against the tabletop. "Everything I've seen indicates this is the first time Reagan's fixated on anyone."

"But he's in his thirties. Behavior like that usually manifests earlier in life."

"Daria's special."

"There has to be more to it." The need to act was overwhelming, so I filled a glass with water for something to do. "What about Celeste Nash?"

"The gallery owner?"

"She introduced them. She gave Reagan Daria's phone number and address. Could she have encouraged this? When I spoke to her on the phone, she sounded repentant, but that could have been an act."

"Why would she want to harm one of her artists?"

"She gets a commission every time she sells one of Daria's pieces. According to Cross, the value of Daria's work has diminished in recent years."

"Because of the commercial pieces she sells from her online store," Lucca said. "The sheer quantity of Daria Waylon creations available made the value of all of her pieces decrease."

"Right, because she's not creating as many original pieces. She's mass producing a few smaller pieces that everyone loves."

"I wouldn't call it mass producing," Lucca said. "But go on."

"I've worked with art crimes enough times to know the value of an artist's work usually increases after her death."

Lucca looked uncomfortable, possibly constipated. "You think Celeste wanted to drive Daria over the edge so she'd commit suicide?"

"I don't know."

"Do you have anything solid to back that? Or is this pure speculation?"

"I'm working to connect the pieces we have in front of us. As far as I'm concerned, Reagan's voyeuristic pursuits are the perfect prerequisite for stalking, but you don't think he's done it before."

"I didn't say that. You did. We should know more tomorrow."

"Let's say he has no history."

"He doesn't have any priors."

But we both knew that didn't necessarily mean anything in instances of stalking. "If he's not a Peeping Tom or some kind of clepto, someone must have put him up to this. The only person I can think of with something to gain if Daria was no longer in the picture is Celeste."

"You're wrong," Lucca said. "Daria's estate would go to her parents. I've seen the paperwork. If she dies, they get everything."

"Celeste still gets a commission, and art collectors would be in a mad rush to buy up every last thing they could if Daria was no longer creating."

"What about other artists in her field?"

"I don't think so. Everyone I spoke to in the art world said it doesn't work like that. Either you're talented and good or you're not."

"Still, someone could be looking to dethrone Daria and take her place."

"I hate to break it to you, Lucca, but she hasn't sat on

that throne since the Lightning Killer attacked her."

Lucca decided he should also get a glass of water. "What about that new project she just started? Could Reagan triggering her be an attempt to stop her from working on it?"

"That seems counterintuitive."

"We don't know anything about it, but it looks like it'll be massive. Some kind of garden scene maybe."

"I think it's the jungle scene she started years ago. Maybe we're looking at this wrong, and Reagan thought by triggering Daria's memories, he'd help her move past the trauma so she could pick up where she left off. That's why Celeste encouraged them to hang out." But even as I said it, I didn't believe it. Reagan didn't strike me as altruistic enough for that. "You don't think Daria would have asked him to do this, do you?"

"Whoa, timeout." Lucca formed a capital T with his hands. "You're jumping from one insane theory to another without even taking a breath. Where are you getting any of this?"

"I'm just trying to figure out why Reagan did what he did. Our evidence is flimsy, so determining motive will help."

Lucca pointed to the clock. "Look, Parker, I appreciate what you're trying to do here. I really do. I don't want to believe it either, but this is over."

"He shouldn't get away with it."

"The man who did this to her didn't." Lucca finished his water and put the glass in the sink. "But Reagan LaRoche didn't do this. Andrew Holland did." He peered into the main room. "I'll take the couch in here. In case Daria gets up in the middle of the night, she'll be less panicked if she spots me asleep in her house than you."

"Do you expect me to sleep in the car?"

"You can go home."

"Not a chance."

"Then take the couch in the living room. It's bigger. You'll probably be more comfortable out there, anyway."

"Is this what you do when you and your wife are in the middle of an argument and you don't want to fight anymore?"

Lucca chuckled. "You were a damn good agent, Parker. But I'm glad you're no longer my work-wife."

"That's why you transferred back to D.C. You know, you could have saved on the paperwork by asking me for a divorce. Jablonsky might have granted it." But we both knew his transfer had nothing to do with me or our partnership.

"I'm going to sleep," he said. "You're exhausting. Just do me a favor, and tone down the speculation in front of Daria. She's dealing with far too much. She can't handle any more."

I nodded. "Night, Lucca."

"Good night." He settled onto the couch in the main room, covering himself with a throw. Within twenty minutes, he was out like a light.

I crept into the room and picked up Daria's most recent journal and returned to the kitchen. Taking a seat on the counter beside the stove, I turned on the small light and read. She wrote entries every few hours. They included basic information like what she ate or what she did. She'd given me a few of her other journals to read, but not this one. This was the meat and potatoes of her day, from the clothes she wore to the work she performed to the TV shows she watched.

I don't know what I hoped to find, but it wasn't contained in the pages. After carefully replacing the journal on the top of the stack, I went into the living room to wait for Martin to call. According to the app on my phone, he should have landed ten minutes ago. I put my phone on vibrate and settled onto the couch.

My eyes closed, and I started to drift. A sound jolted me upright. I checked my phone, but that wasn't it. Reaching for my purse, I removed my gun and listened. *Thump.*

What the hell was that? Quietly, I moved closer to Daria's front door. *Thump.*

As swiftly and silently as possible, I unlocked the door. Opening it, I bit back a scream. A figure loomed directly in front of me. The door opening surprised him as much as it surprised me, and he stepped back, falling off the porch and landing on his back.

I rushed outside with my gun aimed. "Don't move," I said.

Lucca heard the commotion and raced outside, flipping on the porch light.

"I didn't mean to scare you. I didn't know anyone was here." Tom Berry held up his palms.

"What are you doing outside Daria's front door?"

Lucca tucked his gun away, urging me to do the same. "Sir, what's going on here? Who are you?"

"Tom Berry. I live next door." He struggled to get up, making a grunting noise. "Uma said she heard something outside. She thought someone might be trying to break-in again. I told her she was crazy, so she sent me out here to check it out." Lucca and I got off the porch to help Tom up. He used the baseball bat like a cane to hoist himself off the ground and rubbed his back. "While I was looking around, I thought I saw a light on in Daria's. I thought she was still in the hospital," Tom said. "I thought I should get a peek inside before calling the cops."

"She's home," Lucca said.

"Good to know." Tom gave us both a look. "You I remember," he said. "You're with the police."

"I'm a private investigator," I corrected, "who happens to be working with the police."

"Who are you?" he asked Lucca.

Lucca removed his credentials from his pocket. I didn't know any agents who slept with their badges, but that's what made Lucca a boy scout. "Special Agent Eddie Lucca, FBI."

"OIO," I mumbled.

Tom gave me a sideways glance. "Is this a stakeout or something?"

"Something like that," Lucca said.

"Alrighty. I'll tell the missus she can stop worrying since we got a special agent keeping an eye on things." Tom rubbed his back again, making a face. He walked with a limp as he headed home.

"You're a light sleeper," I said.

"Thanks to Grace. When you have a baby, you learn to

listen for signs of trouble." Lucca rubbed his eyes, looking up and down the street. "Did you hear anything?"

"I heard thumping."

"It was probably Tom," Lucca climbed the porch steps. "You coming?"

"In a minute." Turning my cell phone into a flashlight, I circled the townhouse, but no one else was outside. Lucca waited for me at the front door. "Clear." I followed him back inside, making sure the door was locked. Lucca checked the rest of the doors and windows before settling back on the couch.

It was going to be a long night.

TWENTY-SIX

A few minutes after I settled in the living room, Martin called. We didn't speak long, but he wasn't happy I broke my promise. But it wasn't my fault. I blamed Lucca. After that, I decided it'd be best to get some sleep, but every creak and groan made me jump. At one point, I thought I heard footsteps overhead, but when I went upstairs to check it out, no one was there.

Deciding I must be losing my mind, I tried to go back to sleep, but all I managed to do was twist and turn the rest of the night. Once the sun came up, I relaxed. Bad things shouldn't happen in broad daylight. Lucca was awake, which meant he could keep an eye out while I slept, except that's when the scurrying and chirping started.

Lucca came into the living room. "Parker, are you awake?" he whispered.

"No."

"Okay, well, I just wanted to tell you Daria's up. I'll get breakfast started, update her on what's going on, and head out."

"Give me ten minutes."

The ten minutes turned into something closer to forty-five, but when I heard Daria and Lucca conversing in the kitchen, I knew it was time I got up. I said good morning to Daria, relieved when she recognized me and didn't appear startled by my appearance. Lucca must have told her I was here. After washing up in the guest bathroom and changing my clothes, I went into the kitchen. A steaming cup was waiting for me.

"More coffee?" Daria asked when I drained the cup.

"Please." I held out my mug for her to refill. She finished pouring and put the pot down on the table. "How are you feeling?"

"I'm okay."

Lucca smiled at her. "You look better today. More alert. How did you sleep?"

"Like a brick." She shook her head. "I feel less fuzzy, more like myself."

"That's good. That's really good." Lucca glanced at the time. He had to get going, but he didn't want to rush her.

"Would you go already, Eddie?" Daria finally said. "I know you have more important things to do than babysit me."

"I'm not babysitting you," Lucca said.

"Sure, you are. That's why you had to sign all the forms at the hospital, taking responsibility for whatever happens to me. But Eddie, I'm okay. Really. You worry too much."

"He never listens," I said.

Daria looked at me and smiled. "I'm thinking he's not the only one."

I held up my palms. "Hey, you're doing me a favor by letting me hang out with you. My boss is out of the office. My boyfriend is across the country. And Detective O'Connell and the rest of the police department are tired of me nagging them. If I go to the precinct, they'll arrest me for being a pain in the ass."

"They'd call it interfering in a police investigation," Lucca said in that know-it-all tone that always grated on my nerves. But hearing him use it now made me realize he was teasing. He winked at Daria. "And then Alex will call me to bail her out, and it'll be a big mess. But if you don't want to put up with her antics, I totally understand that too. We can make other arrangements."

"No," Daria said, "it's fine. She can stay." She made a shoo gesture with her hands. "But you have to go."

"How about I bring you ladies dinner when I get off work?" Lucca asked.

"I never turn down a free meal, but I have an appointment this evening." I glanced at Daria, wondering if she was aware of why we were being so weird.

"Good, more for us," Lucca said. "What would you like, Dar?"

"Fried chicken sandwich with pickles."

"You got it."

I walked him to the door, but Daria followed so we didn't say anything else. On the porch beside the door was a small potted plant with a get well card. Lucca picked it up and examined the card before handing it to me. It was from Uma and Tom. After he drove away, I handed Daria the plant. "Did we make too much noise last night?"

"I didn't hear anything. Those stupid pills knocked me for a loop."

"It's okay. You needed to rest."

She stared at the floor. "I'm sorry."

"For what?"

"Everything that happened. I don't remember a lot of it, but so many doctors repeated it to me over and over. I just...I'm really embarrassed. I can't believe I'd do something like that. I swear, I saw someone behind me. I saw him." She took a few uneasy breaths. "At least I thought I did. I guess in my panic I must have turned too fast or something. I don't know. But that must have been how I hit my head. Still," she bit her lip, fighting to control her breathing and anxiety, "I felt his hands on me. Between my shoulder blades and on the back of my head, shoving me forward. I can't explain that, but I felt it or thought I did. Memories are weird."

"Yeah."

She looked at me, having heard something in my voice.

Lucca warned me not to compare. I had no intention of diminishing what she was experiencing. I just wanted to show her some empathy. "I've been through some traumatic things. The memories don't always resurface at the most opportune times."

"What happened? You had a nightmare?"

"Actually, yeah. And I tore open a wound on my side, bled all over the place, and convinced myself I had killed the love of my life. When he found me curled up in a ball on the bathroom rug, I was terrified to let him anywhere near me. I don't remember too much from that night, but he said it took him two hours to convince me to even let him get close enough to touch me."

Daria looked shocked. "You're serious?"

"Yeah."

She seemed to relax, forgetting her own issues. "Then what happened?"

"We spent the night on the bathroom floor. I wouldn't let him take me to the emergency room. There was blood everywhere. He had to get new carpeting installed in the bedroom. The next day, he took me to work with him because he was afraid to leave me at home by myself."

"You get it, more or less. That's why you aren't hovering or rushing to do things for me, the way Eddie does."

"If you want me to, I can. I don't mind. But I didn't think that's what you wanted."

"It's not." She swept her hair back. "I just want to get on with my life."

"Then let's do that. I have some work to do. After I finish my coffee, I'll set up in the living room and stay out of your way, but if you need me for anything, I'm here."

"That sounds good." She nodded a few times, examining the plant in her hands. She put it on the table near the window. "Why do you think Uma and Tom gave me a plant? Do they know what happened?"

"They think someone broke in. They thought you were hurt in the attack. No one's told them otherwise. Tom thought he heard something outside last night, saw the light on in here, and thought the guy came back. I startled him, and he fell off the porch."

"Oh my gosh, is he okay?" Daria asked. "Maybe I should give him the plant."

"I'm sure he's fine."

She frowned. "Too bad. This thing is really ugly."

While Daria made notes in her journal, I made a few phone calls to the office. Cross wouldn't be pleased I wasn't there, but since he wasn't there either, he wouldn't notice my absence. The first thing I did was check on the progress facial rec had made. After that, I spoke to the medics and made sure someone was on standby. In the event I had to step out, a medic might be less intimidating than members of the security detail, especially if Daria had another episode.

Once that was taken care of, I powered on my laptop and checked my dropbox. The techs had e-mailed me whatever names the facial recognition software had spit out. I started at the top of the list. After a quick background check and internet search, I made call after call.

About a third of Reagan LaRoche's subjects had posed for him. They'd been hired for the photoshoot. From what I gathered, the models were part of Reagan's day job. Custom photoshoots guaranteed the marketing firm had new and different images to use instead of tired, old stock photos. But that only accounted for a portion of the photos Reagan had taken.

Several people I phoned had never heard of Reagan LaRoche or had any idea they'd been photographed. A few thought I was running a scam. And the ones who didn't thought I was mistaken or wondered why it mattered if someone took their photo. People were allowed to take pictures in public. One woman even cited the statistics on the number of times a person is caught on camera during the course of the day.

I was nearing the bottom of the list when I found a familiar name. Brin Tatlik. Daria's friend. Instead of phoning Brin, I scrolled through the copy of the images I'd saved to my computer until I found it.

I'd performed enough surveillance in my day to know those photos had been taken with a telescopic lens from a distance. Given the height and angle, I'd say Reagan had been parked across the street from Brin's apartment when he took these. I suspected he had taken them one of the times Daria had been visiting. After all, that's when Brin saw the frost green car parked outside.

I didn't care what the evidence suggested or what O'Connell could prove. Reagan had been stalking Daria. That photo proved it. Too bad a judge might see it differently.

"Hey, Daria," I said, joining her in the main room. She let out a yelp and jumped in her seat. I held up my palms. "Sorry."

She clutched her chest dramatically with one hand while she narrowed her eyes at me. "Alex?"

"Yes." I waited, unsure if I should remind her I was in the other room or wait for her to ask why I was inside her house.

She reached for the hearing aid she'd removed and put it back in her ear. "I didn't hear you."

"I didn't mean to be so loud."

"Loud?"

"I was on the phone."

"Oh, right." But the look on her face told me she hadn't remembered that.

"I wanted to ask you a question."

"Go ahead."

"Photographers take tons of photos in public spaces of all kinds of things, people, architecture, flowers, animals, whatever. Sometimes the subjects are unaware."

"That's not a question."

"No, it isn't." Lucca's warning echoed in my head. "The rules are different when it comes to private property, particularly in regards to a person's right to privacy. Reagan LaRoche had a photo of you which he took from outside that window." I pointed to the window that overlooked her backyard. "Did you ever agree to let him shoot you?"

"No."

"You're sure?"

"Not really, but I know I wouldn't have invited him to hang around outside my house to do it." Automatically, she reached for one of her journals, but she didn't open it. "I never invited him here. I don't invite people over. You're the exception, not the rule. And to be fair, I didn't invite you. I invited Eddie."

"What about Brin?"

She leafed through the book, searching for a specific page. "Brin's been here a few times. We mostly go to her place."

"Did Reagan know that?"

"Alex," she looked anxious and more than a little confused, "why are you asking these things?"

I took a seat on the sofa, leaning forward and resting my forearms on my thighs. "Daria, Reagan's been stalking you."

"Why?"

"I don't know."

She shook her head as if refusing to believe it. "No, that doesn't make sense. The times I saw someone, those were just memories. That wasn't Reagan. I know what he looks like."

"Maybe he wore a disguise. You said the guy you kept seeing never let you get that close to him. Wouldn't Reagan want to keep his distance so you wouldn't recognize him?"

"That's how they do things, isn't it? They keep their distance at first, so you don't notice them until it's too late."

"Daria?"

She shivered.

"Hey, look at me. I'm here. You're safe."

"I don't feel safe. I'm not sure what I feel, but it's definitely not safe." She rubbed her eyes, rocking back and forth in her desk chair. Finally, she put her feet on the seat and hugged her knees into her chest. She rested her cheek on top of them and stared at the open planner on the desk in front of her. "Dr. Chen said there is no danger. That these are just old memories. The police detective," she squinted, but she couldn't recall his name, "said no one attacked me, but he believes someone had been following me."

"Reagan LaRoche."

"That's what he said. That's what you said too." She rocked forward, lifting the planner and holding it open in my direction. "I have it written right here." In red, she'd crossed out her Saturday plans and had written a note saying why she canceled them. "Do you have any idea how fucking confusing this is?"

"I didn't mean to make this complicated."

"I don't care," she snapped. "I just don't. Okay? I was told Reagan didn't attack me. I hurt myself. I don't think I meant to. I don't even remember it happening, not like that, but what I remember doesn't fit. It's wrong. It's a memory from before, not now. I don't know if I believe it. I don't know what to believe or think, but that's what I was told. I have to figure that out. I can't figure out the Reagan stuff too." She dropped the planner back on the desk. "I just can't."

"You don't have to figure it out. I will."

We sat in silence for a long time. I didn't want to just walk away, but Daria was angry. Some of that was directed toward me, but I deserved it. Lucca told me not to touch this. Finally, she spoke. "You never asked your question."

"It's not important."

"Just ask. I doubt I'll be able to answer anyway."

Resisting the urge to argue or offer words of encouragement she didn't want to hear, I asked, "Would you mind looking at a few photos and telling me whatever you can about them?"

She sighed. "Fine."

I grabbed my laptop from the other room, blew up the photos I'd found of Brin, and handed Daria my laptop.

"That's Brin," she said. "Where did you get these?"

"They were found on a memory card inside Reagan's apartment."

She moved the cursor, pointing to a blurry silver tea set. "That's Brin's dining room. Do you know when it was taken?"

I checked the metadata, leaving it up on the screen.

Daria grabbed her planner and flipped back a few pages. "I was there. That was two movie nights ago. We watched *Jaws*." She tapped the page with the end of her pen. "Reagan wasn't there. How does he have this photo? Do you think I took it?"

"No, Daria," I said, unsure I wanted to cut deeper into this already open can of worms, "Reagan took them from outside without her permission, just like he took the photo of you."

"Why?"

"I have no idea, but I'll find out."

TWENTY-SEVEN

O'Connell sat behind his desk, typing a report. I took a seat and waited. He didn't even bother to look in my direction.

"Now what?" he asked.

"Reagan's stalking Daria."

"Again? I didn't realize they let him out on bail yet."

"They let him out this morning," Thompson said. "Didn't you get the notice?"

O'Connell blindly picked up a stack of papers. "I'm sure I did." He dropped the papers and went back to typing. "She needs a TRO. Once she gets it, we'll pick him up for violating the protection order."

"That's not what I meant." But O'Connell didn't ask me to elaborate. "I take it you're busy," I said.

"Yes, so let's not play twenty questions." O'Connell had yet to stop typing. "Tell me why you're here."

I looked at Thompson, who appeared to have plenty of free time on his hands. "Why is your partner so grumpy? Did you guys get stuck working a double?"

"Nah. He's not grumpy," Thompson said. "He's hangry. Jenny found a napkin from that taco place where you guys ate. She's been packing his lunch ever since."

"That's terrible." But I didn't buy it. I glanced at

O'Connell who punched the keys with renewed aggression.

"It's worse when you're stuck riding around with him all day. The man won't let anyone else eat since he isn't allowed." Thompson crinkled his nose, his eyes glued to his partner.

O'Connell stopped typing. "I asked you not to bring the bagel in the car. You could eat it, just don't bring it in the car. But you wouldn't listen, so I don't want to hear it. This is your fault."

"My fault? I didn't roll down the window and chuck the bag."

"Boys, what am I missing here?" I didn't want to know, but since I needed O'Connell's help, I had to hear him out.

O'Connell looked at me. "It doesn't matter. What do you want?"

"It sure as hell matters," Thompson said. "The reason we're stuck with all this extra paperwork is because you hit the deputy mayor's car."

"You were in an accident?" I asked.

"No." O'Connell glared at Thompson. The only other time I'd seen that look was when O'Connell wanted to kill me. "I hit his car with the bagel."

"It's bread. How much damage could it have done?" I asked.

"Don't ask." O'Connell gave Thompson a final warning look, silently urging him to shut up. "I'm sure that's not why you're here."

"I spent the day going through the photos I found on Reagan's memory cards. In addition to the photos of Daria, I found a few shots he took of Brin. Daria said the shots are of Brin's apartment, and the metadata indicates they were taken when Daria was there. It proves he's stalking her."

"How did you get access to the photos and metadata?" Thompson asked.

It was my turn to glare at him. Frankly, it was better if he didn't know.

"That's more evidence we can use against him." O'Connell jotted down a note and stuck it to his monitor. "Anything else I should know?"

"Unfortunately, Reagan doesn't have a history of

stalking. An FBI agent spoke to the dean of admissions at the university he attended, but no one ever reported Reagan for any inappropriate conduct."

"That doesn't mean he didn't do it," Thompson said.

"No, it doesn't, which is why I've spoken to every woman he's dated in the last six months and conducted every web search known to man. If he's done this before, no one ever caught on."

"What about the other photos he's taken?" O'Connell asked. "Maybe another one of his victims is in the footage."

"That's a hard sell too. I spoke to everyone facial rec IDed, but half of them didn't believe me and the other half didn't care. None of them even knew Reagan's name." I told him about my conversation with Daria, but O'Connell wasn't surprised.

"I told you she didn't care when I told her she was being stalked," O'Connell said.

"She cares, but she's just so lost and confused right now."

"Does she even want to press charges?" Thompson asked. "If the victim won't cooperate, we might as well drop this now."

"Give her time. She'll come around," I said.

"Where is she now?" O'Connell asked.

"At home. Lucca's with her. They're having dinner."

"And you weren't invited?" Thompson asked.

"You normally don't talk this much. Maybe you should stop now," I said.

"I know when I'm not wanted." Thompson climbed out of his chair. "Are you going to finish the rest of that paperwork, Nick? Or do you need me to stick around?"

"I got it. Go have your chili dog or whatever it was you wouldn't shut up about." O'Connell waved off his partner.

"Later." Thompson smoothed the back of his jacket and headed out the door.

"I can give you the names of several couples counselors. None of them were very good, but you might have better luck than Martin and me."

"Jenny and I don't need couples counseling. We're fine."

"Not you and your wife. You and your partner."

O'Connell rolled his eyes. "You seriously drove all the way here to tell me you found more evidence proving Reagan's been following Daria. You could have done that over the phone."

"Heathcliff and I have a meeting tonight. I had to stop by anyway. But I wanted to run an idea past you. Since Reagan also photographed Brin, couldn't she press charges?"

"Have her come in and fill out a report."

"Is that enough for you to build a case against Reagan in the event Daria decides not to pursue this?"

"Brin can file a complaint, but most of the evidence we collected proves he's stalking Daria, unless you can establish a pattern of behavior, proving he also stalked Brin, the most we can charge him with is a misdemeanor under the Peeping Tom laws."

"He's more than that."

"That's why Daria has to pursue this. If she doesn't, the DA will drop it."

"She's spinning, Nick. She's confused. I told her I'd figure it out for her, that she wouldn't have to."

"Legally, I'm not sure how that'll work. Everything we built the case on is aimed towards proving Reagan stalked Daria. We'd need more evidence that he was following another woman too, more than just a photo or two."

"Keep looking, okay? Maybe have a chat with Celeste Nash. She gave Reagan Daria's address and phone number. From the way it sounded, she put him up to asking Daria out in the hopes of getting her creative juices flowing again."

"I'll do that." He nodded towards Heathcliff's desk. "Now get going. You have places to be, and I have to figure out how to get myself out of hot water on this car thing." He blinked a few times. "Stupid cream cheese. Jen warned me dairy was the devil."

"If there's anything I can do, let me know."

"If it comes to that, I'm screwed."

As I approached Heathcliff's desk, he looked up and smiled. "Wonders never cease, unless you're here with an excuse."

I dropped into an empty chair and stared at the gold nameplate. *Det. D. Heathcliff.* "Actually, I could use a meeting."

"Is everything okay?" He gave O'Connell a sideways glance. "Is something going on I should know about?"

"Nick's great. That's not it." I shook my head before he could ask anything else. "I'll tell you on the way."

By the time we arrived at the church, I'd spilled my guts on Martin's absence and Daria's case. Heathcliff hadn't said a word, but the muscles in his shoulders appeared tighter than they were before. Apparently, I'd stressed him out.

"Cal has some experience with stalkers and how they operate. After the meeting, you might want to pick his brain about it," Heathcliff suggested.

"How is our grief counselor supposed to help? I'm not even convinced Reagan is a stalker. Sure, he stalked Daria, but I stalk people for a living."

"You think he got paid to do this?" Heathcliff asked.

"I'm not sure what kind of incentive he had, but he isn't a stalker. I'd say he has voyeuristic tendencies, but most of the time, his fascination ends as soon as he snaps a photo. It isn't about the subject so much as the meaning of the moment. At least, that's what he said when he asked to shoot me."

Heathcliff opened the side door and led the way down the steps. "Why would anyone want to trigger Daria's memory from the night she almost died?"

"That's what I keep asking myself. According to her doctor, the repressed memories would have resurfaced at some point on their own. But Reagan sped up the process."

"Did he dress the part? Or were those just her memories resurfacing?"

"I'm not sure. But I found red sneakers in his closet, like the ones the Lightning Killer wore." As usual, self-preservation kicked in the moment we reached the meeting room. I found myself backing away from the door. Heathcliff waited, keeping a watchful eye on me in case I bolted. I wasn't much different than Daria. When confronted with devastating memories, I wanted nothing more than to hide under the bed.

"Good evening," Cal said, bounding down the steps behind me. "Are you joining us tonight? We missed you last week." He held out his fist for Heathcliff to bump. "Are you okay, Alex?"

"If I was, I wouldn't be here."

Cal gave me a wry smile. "Sure, I understand that. But you're here now. Don't you want to come inside? We don't bite."

I resisted the urge to say no. Instead, I followed Cal into the room and found a seat near the wall, per my usual. Heathcliff sat beside me. After Cal welcomed everyone and started the meeting off with his usual introduction, I zoned out, my thoughts finding their way back to the situation with Daria.

At some point, Heathcliff nudged me. I looked up, realizing the meeting was nearly over. I blinked a few times. "Are you okay?" he asked.

"Yep."

"We have a couple more minutes. Does anyone else have anything they want to share?" Cal asked. No one spoke. "Okay, I guess that's it. Help yourselves to the coffee and cookies in the back."

A few people clustered together in small groups, talking while drinking stale, lukewarm coffee. Heathcliff reached into his pocket for his keys. "I can wait in the car."

"Please don't."

He gave me a shy smile. "Okay."

It didn't take long for Cal to make the rounds and find us still huddled together in our seats. Ever since I started coming to these meetings, he'd taken a special interest in me, which only made me more uncomfortable. Cal was like a cat. The less attention I gave him, the more he craved it. But the people who always participated and fawned over him, he ignored. "What's troubling you tonight, Alex?"

I fought to keep the scowl off my face. I didn't like the prying, but that was the purpose of this group. "I'm working a case." I gave him the fundamentals about the situation. "Nothing fits. I'm just wondering why someone may want to trigger her repressed memories?"

"Are you sure that's what it is?" he asked.

"I don't know."

"Do you know why she hurt herself?"

"She doesn't remember. She was sure someone else attacked her. Could she have multiple personalities?" That had been O'Connell's theory.

"Without knowing her or her history, I can't say for certain. Disorders like that are uncommon but not unheard of. In rare instances, one personality will exhibit violent tendencies toward the other personalities, but unless you've interacted with another personality, there's no way to know for sure."

"I thought hitting her head was an accident," Heathcliff said.

"It might have been, but the message on her wall wasn't."

"What did it say?" Cal asked.

"I'm still here."

Cal glanced around the room, looking uneasy for the first time since I met him, which was saying something since he routinely caused an entire room of hardened first responders to cry like babies without batting an eye. "That's unsettling."

"Any other thoughts?"

"Watch yourself," Cal said. "If this is a dissociated identity, it could mean a non-dominant personality is emerging and vying for control. He or she could lash out again at Daria or anyone perceived as a threat."

"I thought these personalities were the mind's way of protecting a person."

"A person yes, but not necessarily a personality. A lot remains unknown. Studies are still being done, but these situations are so individualized it's hard to predict what's going on."

"But you think Daria has multiple personalities based on the message?"

"You should defer to her psychiatrist. She'd know better than anyone. But whoever left that message isn't going away. So be careful."

TWENTY-EIGHT

Over the next few days, Daria fell into a new routine, and so did I. She'd work on her commissioned projects in the morning after breakfast. After lunch, I dropped her off at her therapist's office before heading to Cross Security. Lucien Cross still hadn't returned. His assistant, Justin, said the boss was on vacation, but I didn't believe it.

After picking up whatever tasks I'd been assigned, mostly performing background checks and security assessments, I'd retrieve Daria from her session with Dr. Chen. She didn't tell me anything about the sessions. Once we returned to her house, she'd hide away in her bedroom to decompress, and I'd spend the afternoon working.

Whenever Lucca finished up at the OIO, he'd return to Daria's. At that point, I'd go home, which kept Martin happy and gave me time to work out, shower, change clothes, and eat before going back to work. I hated assignments like this. Every time I took one, I swore it would be the last, and yet, here I was again.

Friday night, I returned to Daria's after my brief reprieve. She was upstairs working, and Lucca was in the living room. He stared up at the light fixture.

"What are you looking at?" I asked.

"The lights were flickering earlier. I thought the bulb needed changing, but it's happening throughout the house."

"It's been happening a lot lately. I don't know if it has to do with the security cameras I installed or if it's something else."

"It could be the wiring. Did you check the circuit breaker?" Lucca asked.

"No."

He looked at me as if to say *why the hell not?* "Anything else I should know about?"

"You're not a handyman or the super," I said. "But since you've decided you want to be Mr. Fix-It, ask Daria."

"How's she doing? She was quiet at dinner again."

I shrugged. "Life's hard. It kicked her in the teeth, and even though she's down, it keeps on kicking. I don't know how to fix that. O'Connell's still working on the case, but every time I bring it up to Daria, she shuts down. I don't think she'll testify, and without that, the DA might drop the charges."

"Have you spotted Reagan or his car?"

"No."

"You don't have a Cross Security team stationed outside. Are you sure you didn't miss something?"

"I can't be, but the cameras I installed at the front and back doors haven't picked up anything."

"Good." Lucca glanced toward the stairs. "She hates that we're hanging around all the time."

"You, mostly," I teased. "I stay out of her way. Actually, I just stay in here as much as possible. The help's supposed to be invisible, so I'm perfecting that skill."

"In that case, I'll take a page out of your book and head out. Daria won't remember if I said goodbye, and I don't want to disturb her. She's working on that secret project again, which means she doesn't want anyone anywhere near her studio." I walked him to the door. "I meant to ask, how are you holding up? When we talked about it, I thought you were going to spend the day with her and have someone else keep watch at night. But you're here all the time. Do you need a break? It's the weekend. I have some time off," he offered.

"I don't want to interrupt her routine again. We only have a few more days until her parents get here. I can hold out until then." I wanted my life back, but I told Daria I'd figure this out. And I hadn't. If anything, I'd made matters worse. But grief counseling had taught me one thing; I couldn't control Reagan LaRoche or the things he'd done. All I could do was my best to stop him from doing it again, except I wasn't sure how to do that without Daria's help.

After Lucca left, I settled onto the sofa and checked the time. Figuring Martin might have knocked off early for the weekend, I called him. "Hey, handsome, guess who?"

He snickered. "I'm amazed."

"I aim to please."

"Where are you?"

"Daria's. Lucca just left, and she's upstairs working, so I had a few minutes."

"That's all I have. I'm meeting with the head of the research department. We might have come up with a compromise that will make everyone happy."

"Including me?"

He made a contented sound. "I never imagined the day you'd be the clingy one in our relationship. It feels pretty damn good. But to be fair, you never stood a chance. Being deprived of my irresistible good looks and godlike stamina has made you yearn for me."

"I'm not yearning."

"Yes, you are."

"I'm yawning from all that modesty and self-deprecation you constantly exhibit."

"I just call it like I see it." He laughed. "Yearning."

"You poor bastard, all that sunlight has made you delusional. Drink some water. It might help."

"Refresh my memory. What were some of those clingwrap jokes you used to make? I think I might have use for them."

"This is why I don't call you."

"But I like it when you call."

"Wouldn't that make you the clingy one?"

"Touché." He exhaled. "I hate to say it, beautiful, but I

have to jump off here."

"I hope you're not standing on a bridge or the edge of a cliff."

"Smartass." He paused. "I love you. We'll talk tomorrow. I'll call you."

I smiled. "Maybe I'll even answer."

"You better."

Putting down the phone, I picked up the file on Reagan LaRoche and skimmed the evidence we'd collected. Reagan had never stalked anyone before, but he'd done an excellent job following and terrorizing Daria without her ever realizing it was him. That couldn't be beginner's luck.

Reagan knew intimate details regarding the Lightning Killer's attack on Daria, but as far as I knew, he'd never been to any of those true crime websites and had no connection to Andrew Holland or anyone involved in the investigation. I wasn't sure if Reagan had worn the same clothing as Holland when he stalked Daria, but the red sneakers were enough. Still, it wouldn't hurt to get a few photos of his wardrobe for comparison.

I hadn't thought to pay that much attention when I searched Reagan's apartment. Neither had the police when they executed the search warrant. They'd been looking for the items I'd pointed out, nothing more.

"Hey, Nick," I said when O'Connell answered, "is there any chance someone paid attention to the shirts and slacks hanging in LaRoche's closet?"

"Did you finally get Daria on board?" he asked, ignoring my question.

"Not yet, but I was just thinking about the sightings she reported. The descriptions she gave of her stalker coordinate exactly with the surveillance photos the FBI later pulled once Andrew Holland was identified. I don't know if what Daria saw is accurate, but if it is, someone fed Reagan this information."

"Why didn't we think about this sooner?"

Daria's unreliable memory and impaired vision had something to do with it, but I didn't want to say it when she'd be down the stairs at any moment. The lights overhead flickered again. I looked up at the bulb. Like they say, when it rains, it pours. "It must have been because you were so preoccupied with the bagel."

"Ugh. Don't remind me."

"Have you made any progress on the case that you might have forgotten to mention?"

"I haven't had much time to look at it. I've been a little busy." O'Connell didn't have to say it. This wasn't a priority. The only reason he got involved was as a favor to me. "I'll see what I can do about looking into Reagan's wardrobe, but I need copies of the Lightning Killer files and the descriptions Daria provided so I know what I'm looking for."

"I'll send them to you tonight." But I'd left them in the company car, which was parked outside my apartment since I'd driven my car here. "Are you still at work?"

"No, but if you tell the desk sergeant they're for me, I'll get them in the morning."

I checked the time again. "All right."

It'd probably take me an hour to get them, drop them off at the precinct, and get back here. I didn't want to ask Lucca to come back, but springing a stranger on Daria this late at night wasn't a good idea either.

When Daria came down the stairs, little pieces of green and brown fuzz were stuck to her arms and hands. But she looked happy. It was one of the few times I'd actually seen her like that.

After washing up, she told me good night and went to bed. I waited a few minutes and called Lucca. We agreed Daria should be fine by herself for an hour. But just in case, I wrote her a note and put it on top of her journals, telling her I had to step out for a minute and would be right back.

Since traffic was light, I made the entire trip in fifty-three minutes. I parked my car in a different spot than when I'd left and silently headed back inside. The small lamp in the living room remained on, but the rest of the house was dark. Out of an abundance of caution, I crept down the hall and peered into Daria's bedroom. She was sound asleep.

Given the progress she'd been making, I doubted she needed someone watching her twenty-four hours a day.

How long was this supposed to last? The woman couldn't be on suicide watch for the rest of her life. In fact, she didn't exhibit the usual signs of someone who wished to harm herself. Again, thoughts of O'Connell's theory and Cal's words repeated in my head. But I'd been with her day in and day out and hadn't noticed any odd behavior.

After taking off my shoes and stowing my gun in my bag, I sprawled out on the sofa. Thoughts of the symbols stitched into the bottom of Daria's mattress came to mind. Supposedly, that was her mother's doing, but I wasn't sure if that was the woman's crazy ideas or if she'd seen something unsettling come over her daughter that caused her to take protective measures.

I reached for a pen to make a note to call Christina Waylon in the morning and find out more about her beliefs and exactly why such a worried parent hadn't dropped everything to come to her kid's rescue. Before I even sat up, the power went out, plunging the house into total darkness. I went to the window and peered outside, but the rest of the neighborhood still had lights.

A moment later, Daria screamed. Blindly grabbing my bag, I hurried down the hall, familiar enough with the layout not to bump into anything on the way. "Daria?"

"I can't see," she said.

"I know." I fumbled inside my bag for a flashlight or my phone, only to remember I left it on the coffee table. "The power went out." I edged deeper into the room. "Are you hurt?"

"What?"

"Are you hurt?" I repeated.

"No, I'm okay."

Realizing she probably didn't have her hearing aid in or glasses on, I spoke loudly. "I'm going to check the circuit breaker." Lucca would ridicule me mercilessly for this one. "Stay here."

Returning to the living room, I grabbed my cell phone and used the screen's light to guide me. But the glow wasn't strong enough, so I relied on my other senses as I made my way up the stairs.

As I ascended, a cold breeze brushed against my skin.

This is why it didn't pay to watch horror movies. Shaking off the insane thoughts and the tiny voice in the back of my head that screamed these were signs of paranormal activity, I felt along the railing until I reached the wall. The utility closet was somewhere on my left.

Did something move? I pressed my back against the wall. But I didn't see anything, just the glow from my phone screen. "Parker, you're crazy," I muttered. But that didn't stop the hairs at the nape of my neck from prickling. Again, cool air blew against my skin, and goosebumps erupted on my arms.

Hurrying to the utility closet, I opened the door and fumbled around to open the cover on the circuit breaker. The steps creaked. I glanced in that direction. Daria must have come to help. I turned back to the circuit breaker, blindly flipping switches, but nothing happened. How many of these things were there?

"Hey, Dar," I said, "where's the reset switch? Is it at the top or bottom?"

The floorboards creaked again. This time much closer. I turned at the noise, but it was pitch black. I couldn't see anything, but I felt a presence.

My mouth went dry, and a sudden chill went through me. "Daria?" But I knew it wasn't her. I stepped backward, edging further down the hallway. I caught only a glimpse of a long, thin, rectangular object. Before I could react, it sliced into my side.

That one hit put me on the ground. I screamed, wondering if I'd been cut open by a machete. I couldn't move and could barely think. Rushed footsteps hurried away from me. Something squeaked, followed by more creaking. The light from my dropped cell phone didn't allow me to glimpse any of it.

A moment later, the creaking stopped. I inched forward, grabbed my phone, and dialed O'Connell.

TWENTY-NINE

A minute after I hung up, a shaky voice called to me from the abyss. "Alex, is he gone?"

Whoever attacked me had come at me fast and hard. At first, I thought it was Daria, but when that object struck me, I didn't think Daria had been wielding it. She didn't possess the strength, but now I wasn't so sure. "I think so." I listened. "I don't hear anything. Did he go past you? Did you see anyone?"

"No, I can't see," she said. "It's dark. Too dark. Everything's dark."

"Stay where you are. Help's on the way." The first thing I had to do was get the lights back on. Struggling to pull myself up, I bit back a curse. How deep had I been cut?

Bringing my phone close to my side, I was relieved when I didn't see much of anything. My shirt had been torn, the edges bloody, but that was the extent of it. Before I could attempt to get off the ground a second time, the power came back.

Daria was huddled in the corner of the loft behind the couch. She rocked back and forth, clearly terrified. Carefully, I touched my side. Fire shot through me, but when I pulled my fingers away, there wasn't much blood. It

G.K. Parks

hurt to breathe, so I did my best not to.

I scanned the area. Propped against the railing beside Daria was a cricket bat. Blood droplets clung to the edge. My blood. Luckily, it wasn't a machete, like I originally thought, or I'd be sliced open like a Christmas ham.

Slowly, I lifted off the ground, exhaling as stars exploded behind my eyelids. Daria cringed at the sounds I made, but she didn't offer to help.

"Are you okay?" I asked.

She didn't answer.

I shifted into a seated position, careful not to press my left side against the wall. Nausea came in waves, so I took some shallow breaths through my mouth until it passed. When I could, I climbed to my feet, using the closet doorknob for support.

I wasn't sure why the power returned or what caused it to go out in the first place. The chill remained in the air, but I no longer felt a breeze. Had one of the windows been open? I reached for my shoulder holster, remembering my gun was in the bag which I'd left downstairs.

"Stupid," I muttered. Slowly, I cleared the upstairs, knowing if someone else was up here, I'd have no chance of taking him down. But I had to know if Daria attacked me or if someone else had.

The power had gone out while I was in the living room. If anyone had entered the house, I would have heard him, unless he came in after I went upstairs. But I couldn't imagine that had been the case. What was going on here?

"Are you okay?" I asked again, keeping my distance. Cal's warning came to mind. Did another personality attack me?

"I think so."

"What happened?"

"I didn't see anything." Tears ran down her cheeks. "But I heard you scream. I thought he was coming for me next."

"Why did you come up the stairs?"

"I didn't want to stay down there by myself."

"So you were right behind me?" Growing dizzy, I slid back to the floor, wondering if I'd pass out or vomit first.

"Not right behind you, but close. If I'd been closer, he

would have gotten us both."

If Daria was to be believed, that meant the assailant hadn't snuck up behind me. "Did he follow you up the steps?" I asked.

"He was already here." Her voice shook as more tremors wracked her body.

"Try to breathe slow and deep. Whoever was here is gone now," I said. "I don't want you to pass out. I might, which means you can't."

"Please don't." She cried, her shoulders shuddering to a rhythm separate from her trembling.

"I'll do my best." I felt along my side, finding a giant knot over my ribcage. That's why it hurt so much. O'Connell would be here soon, but I didn't want Daria hospitalized or committed when I wasn't sure what happened. Against my better judgment, I didn't call Lucca since I wasn't sure whose side he'd be on.

A loud banging sounded beneath us. Daria practically dove under the couch. "He's back."

"Parker?" O'Connell yelled from the floor below.

"Upstairs," I called. "Those are the police. They're here to rescuc us." From what, I still wasn't sure.

O'Connell took the steps two at a time, the barrel of his gun leading the way. The first thing he saw was Daria tucked against the corner of the couch. She froze, a silent scream etching her face.

He held out his badge in his left hand. "Police," he said. "Are you hurt?"

"He came back," Daria gasped. "He attacked Alex. Then he came for me."

"Who?" O'Connell kept one eye on her while he checked each room.

"Put the gun down, Nick." My voice came out strained. "We're clear. No one else is up here. I already checked."

He holstered his weapon, crouching beside me. "Easy, Parker. What happened?" He cringed as he examined the visible flesh through the tear in my shirt. "That looks like it hurts."

"You have no idea." I nodded toward the cricket bat as he peeled the hem of my shirt away. "I'd say that's what caused it. Someone swung for the fences."

"Someone?" The look on his face told me the wound didn't look good.

"The power went out right before it happened."

"He was waiting for her," Daria insisted. "He turned off the lights. It was a trap. He set a fucking trap." Her breathing became frenzied. "He's going to kill us. He's here. He won't stop. He just won't, not until I'm dead."

"Who?" O'Connell asked.

"Andrew Holland."

O'Connell met my eyes.

"It wasn't him," I said.

"Well, whoever it was had a hell of a swing. Have you pissed off any pro cricket players lately?" O'Connell asked.

"Not that I know of."

He reached for his phone. "Cross's medics are taking too long. I don't like the looks of this. Let me get some guys here to check you out." He glanced back at Daria. "Are you injured?"

She shook her head.

"She's in shock, Nick. But no one touched her."

Again, he gave me a look. I knew he was thinking Daria attacked me. In a twisted way, it made the most sense. But watching her cower and hide, I couldn't imagine she'd been behind the attack. "That's a good thing, right?" he asked.

I ignored the pointed look and lowered my voice, hoping she wouldn't hear it. "Cross's team is familiar with her history. They'll be able to assess the situation better than we can. We need to wait for Cross's people to get here."

"Can you even breathe?" He frowned as I panted like a dog.

"Breathing's overrated."

But he ignored me, like so many people often did.

A few minutes later, flashing lights illuminated the white slats of the closed blinds. Doors slammed. Daria let out a wail.

"It's okay," O'Connell said. "They're here to help."

"I want this kept in-house," I insisted.

"And I want to win the lottery. We'll see what happens."

*　　*　　*

Since the scene was already secure, O'Connell sent officers to knock on a few doors and find out if anyone saw or heard anything. By now, Daria's neighbors were probably circulating a petition to force her out. Cross's mental health expert, Francine Miller, had taken Daria downstairs to assess her.

"Did she do this?" O'Connell asked.

"I don't know."

"You don't know, or you won't say?" He moved closer to the cricket bat.

"Don't touch that. I want it printed."

He slipped a glove on and picked it up from the flat rectangular end, carefully examining the handle. "Why does Daria have a cricket bat?"

"Are you sure it's hers?"

"Don't tell me the unknown assailant brought the bat with him and tried to frame her for the attack by intentionally leaving it behind."

"I don't know what happened. But you should check the windows. When I came up here, I felt a breeze."

"I'll do that while you get checked out. I don't want you bleeding to death or suffocating on my watch." He looked at the medic who'd been checking my vitals. "Make sure that doesn't happen."

"I'll do my best," the medic said.

"Nick," I warned.

"Alex." He used the same tone I had.

The paramedic fought to hide his amusement as he pressed the stethoscope against the left side of my chest. "Deep breath."

"Easier said than done." I sucked the air in slowly, stopping when it became too excruciating.

The medic repositioned the cold metal on the other side of my chest. "Again."

I did as he asked, my head swimming.

"Even breath sounds. From the looks of it, you're lucky your lung didn't collapse. Your O2 is low, probably on account of your shallow breathing. Let me give you something for the pain. That should help you breathe easier, and then I'll take some x-rays."

"No meds. I can't be impaired."

"You already are," he said.

"You know what I mean."

Several members of Cross Security were recovering addicts, so the medical team was used to having their hands tied on such matters. "Fine, I'll take the x-rays and give you something localized. How's that?"

"Perfect."

"Should I get the stretcher?"

"I can walk." I tried to push off the floor, immediately regretting that decision.

O'Connell returned from the window check and ducked beneath my good arm. "I got you." He lifted me to my feet and walked me slowly down the stairs. "I didn't find any indication any of the windows had recently been opened."

"I'll get Cross's forensic guys in here to check everything out."

"You know, that's what the police department's for."

"Only in the event of a crime. I'm not filing a report or giving you an official statement until I figure out exactly what happened. So no crime."

"We both know that's not true," O'Connell said. "You were assaulted."

Outside, the officers spoke to Uma and Tom, who had heard our screams. Tom spotted me, his expression sullen. His eyes said it all. The neighborhood was supposed to be safe because I was here, but I failed.

Shaking it off, I allowed O'Connell to hand me off to the medic who helped me get on top of the gurney. The medic cut off my tattered shirt. "It looks like you took one hell of a hit. How big was the guy who did this?"

"I didn't get a look at him. The power went out."

The medic repositioned me on the gurney and set up the portable x-ray machine. He pushed O'Connell out of the van while he took my picture. After that was done, he carefully cleaned the laceration, put a bandage over it, and shook one of the instant ice packs before pressing it against me. I inhaled sharply, biting back a whimper. "Hold that there while I get you something for the pain." He unlocked one of the glass cabinets as O'Connell stepped back inside. He gave me a shot of something. "That'll take the edge off." He spun to check the computer. "Are you sure you don't want anything stronger? You don't have an issue with narcotics."

"I don't want to develop one either."

The medic grabbed a bottle of prescription strength pain relievers from the cabinet. "These shouldn't impair you too badly, but don't operate heavy machinery."

I read the label, popped one in my mouth, and dry swallowed it. "I'll try not to."

The computer processed the data from the x-ray. "The good news is nothing's broken."

"And the bad news?"

The medic removed the ice pack, gingerly running his fingers against my skin to track the shape of my ribs.

"If you're going to keep that up, knock me out before you continue with your diagnosis."

He retracted his fingers. "More than likely, it's an intercostal muscle tear. The edge of that bat hit you between two ribs." He replaced the ice pack. "But given your history, it could also be a costochondral separation. We won't know for sure without more sophisticated imaging."

"What's that?" O'Connell asked.

"Dislocated rib," I said. "Been there, done that. Really don't want to do that again."

"It's on the same side, but it's not the same rib. We shouldn't jump to conclusions."

"It doesn't feel the same. Last time, there was a pop and lots of pain. This time, it feels like someone knifed me." I waited for the medic to secure the ice pack in place with an elastic bandage before I sat up. "But since there's nothing you can do about it either way, I'm going back to work."

"Ms. Parker, you need more scans and to get some rest."

"I will, when I'm done here." I pocketed the pill bottle, slipped into one of the extra t-shirts the mobile medical unit kept in the back, and headed toward the house.

O'Connell fell into step beside me. "Are you sure you're

okay? You weren't breathing so good when I found you."

"The shot helped. The ice and pills will too."

"Don't pass out on me. If you do, I'm calling actual paramedics who will take you to a real hospital."

"It's a couple of bruised ribs. You and I have had much worse."

"Like the time I had a collapsed lung?" He stopped me before I made it to the porch. "You don't want that."

"I'm fine. I promise."

"Hey," Kevin Danziger called out from his doorstep where one of the officers was taking his statement. "I thought you were staking out the place. What happened? Didn't you say the other night was an isolated incident?"

The officer blocked Kevin from approaching us. "Calm down, sir."

"I am calm." Kevin let out a frustrated grunt. "I thought we had no reason to worry, but cops are knocking on my door again. Won't somebody tell me what's really going on?"

"Who are you?" O'Connell nodded to the officer to let Kevin off the porch.

"I'm Daria's neighbor. Who are you?"

O'Connell identified himself and showed Kevin his badge. "Did you notice anything out of the ordinary tonight?"

"Before all the flashing lights arrived, I thought I heard something. Like a loud bang. Maybe a car door. I can't say for sure." Kevin glanced at Daria's open front door. "Is she okay?"

"She's shaken but fine," I said.

The other officer was still speaking to Uma and Tom, who were gesturing toward the upper level of the townhouse. Since Kevin lived on the other side of them, he probably hadn't heard my scream or Daria's.

"What were you doing around midnight?" O'Connell asked him.

Kevin's lip quirked in the corner, as if he'd been insulted. "I was watching TV."

"What time did you hear the car door?"

"I'm not sure it was a car door. It might have been. I

guess that was maybe 12:20."

"Did you look out your window?" O'Connell asked.

"I caught a glimpse of some taillights."

"What kind of vehicle was it?" O'Connell asked.

"I can't be sure. I think it was a car."

"Did you see the color?" I asked.

"It was blue, I think, or teal. Something like that."

"How about green?"

Kevin shrugged. "Possibly, but I wasn't paying attention. I didn't go to the window to look. It just happened to catch my eye. I didn't think anything of it until the cops knocked on my door. Again." He let out a grunt. "Seriously, I'm about ready to move. I've lost track of how many times this has happened lately."

"I'm sorry we've inconvenienced you," O'Connell said.

"Just do us all a favor and catch this guy. I'm tired of being questioned, and I'm sure everyone else is too." Kevin looked at me. "Didn't you say someone had been arrested? What happened with that? Was he released?"

"We're still investigating," O'Connell said. "If you remember anything—"

"I'll call you," Kevin said.

THIRTY

By the time forensics finished searching for clues, Daria had fallen asleep. Unlike the last incident, Daria's memory didn't get fuzzy. She remembered waking up in total darkness. She heard noises, got scared, and screamed. That's when I told her to stay put, but she'd been too afraid to remain alone, so she came to find me. She'd just made it up the stairs when she saw a figure attacking me. The figure rushed toward her, but he disappeared in the darkness. She hid between the couch and the wall, figuring he wouldn't find her there.

"Do you think she could have multiple personalities?" I asked.

Francine Miller, Cross's expert, shook her head. "Daria's story is cohesive. She didn't have a blackout or time lapse. She knew where she was and how she got there."

"Is it odd she remembered that?" O'Connell asked.

"It was an ongoing event. When I spoke to her, she hadn't had time to forget. If you question her again tomorrow, you might get a different answer," Francine said.

"Forensics didn't pull any prints from the bat," O'Connell said. "Given what you know, do you think it's possible Daria attacked Parker?"

"I can't say for certain, but considering her core personality traits, I highly doubt it. When she has a flight or fight response, she goes straight into flight mode."

O'Connell bit his lip, eyeing the living room. "People can surprise you."

"True. Do you need me to stay?" Francine asked.

"No," I said, "I'll keep an eye on her."

"She needs to discuss the trauma further. All these events keep building up. The stress will cause more damage. If left untreated, the anxiety will kill her eventually," Francine said.

"Daria has a session with Dr. Chen tomorrow afternoon."

"Good. If you need me for anything else or you'd like to talk, you know where to find me."

But I was more concerned whoever attacked me might make another pass at Daria and whoever stood in his way.

"How does he keep getting inside?" I spun, but besides the front door, all other entry points were secure.

"Did you watch the security footage?" O'Connell asked, even though he knew the answer.

"We can't say for certain what happened after the power went out. We lose visuals. Someone could have gained entry after the cameras were disabled. I should have requested another security detail remain outside. Then we'd know for sure what happened."

"Maybe not," O'Connell said. "Last time, they didn't see anyone, assuming there was anyone to see."

"She didn't do this."

"Are you a hundred percent sure?"

The two patrol officers finished their canvass and knocked on the open front door.

"What do we have?" O'Connell asked.

"Not much, I'm afraid. Uma and Tom, the next door neighbors, heard a scream. But they didn't think they should report it since they were told law enforcement was staking out the place." The officer stared at me when he said it.

"What about the neighbor on the other side?" O'Connell

asked. "Did she hear anything?"

"No one's home. She left for a month-long cruise a few days ago."

"What about the two end units?"

"You heard what Kevin Danziger said. But the neighbor on the other end didn't see or hear anything at all."

"Did Uma and Tom hear a car door or anything slamming?" I asked.

The other officer consulted his notepad. "They didn't mention it. According to Tom, he looked outside after they heard the scream but didn't see anything."

"The neighbors are giving us conflicting accounts," the other officer said. "What do you want us to do about that, Detective?"

"Nothing to do," O'Connell said. "Write it up and stick it in the file. Ask dispatch to up the patrols in the neighborhood."

"Copy that." The officer nodded to us before he and his partner strode out the door and back to their patrol car.

"What do you think?" I asked.

"We got nothing, just like all the other times. The unsub must be the Invisible Man because that's the only way he got in and out of the house without anyone noticing."

"You're wrong. He killed the lights. He came at me. I got the knot on my side to prove it."

"Alex, look at the evidence. You said it yourself. When you first heard footsteps behind you, you thought it was Daria. That means you didn't hear anyone else enter the house."

"He could have been quiet."

"Or Daria got freaked out like she said, picked up the bat, and followed you up the stairs. She didn't have her glasses on, and it was dark. All she would have seen was the glow from your phone and your general shape. She could have gotten confused, thought you had come to hurt her, hit you once, heard you scream, realized her mistake, and ran away. Doesn't that seem possible?"

"It's possible, but I doubt she could hit that hard."

"She didn't hit you that hard. She just hit you in the one spot where you couldn't afford to get hit."

I narrowed my eyes at the bat, picking it up from where forensics had left it on the table in the foyer. "You said they didn't find any prints on it."

"None."

"Not even Daria's?"

O'Connell frowned at the lack of telltale black smudges from the fingerprint powder. "Nope."

"Explain that."

"She had her sleeves pulled down over her hands."

"She wore short sleeves."

"Okay, so she wiped it."

"Do you really think in her panicked state she thought to wipe the handle? She could barely get a sentence out. She didn't have the wherewithal to cover her tracks. If the bat had been in her hand, her prints should be all over it. And since you're so sure it's her bat, why aren't her prints on it from previous use?"

"I don't know. She could have cleaned it or polished it prior to tonight's events."

"Did she also use some sort of magic to make the lights go out?"

"Parker—"

"The lack of prints makes no sense, unless Daria planned to lure me upstairs and attack me."

"Are you sure she didn't? Daria said he set a trap. Why would she jump to that conclusion, unless she had thought to do it? Think about it. The power goes out. You go upstairs to check the circuit breaker and bam."

Daria wasn't crazy. She was the only one seeing this for what it was. "How does this guy keep getting inside?"

"Whoa, back up the crazy train." O'Connell held up his palms. "How many of those pain pills have you taken?"

"Not enough. But you just laid it all out. Those are distraction tactics. Divide and conquer. By knocking out the power, he knocked out the security cameras and blinded me, which evened the playing field. He got me alone, or tried to, and figured he'd take me out and then go after Daria. He wanted to eliminate me first because I posed the greatest threat."

"Slow your roll. That's crazy talk."

But it wasn't. "It makes as much sense as you telling me some voice in Daria's head took control and told her to do this." I shivered. "He's still here."

O'Connell pointed a finger in my face. "Don't say that."

"But what if he is?"

"We've searched every inch of this place. No one's here."

"That's what I thought too." The last time something weird happened, that was the message that had been left on the wall. Cal told me whoever wrote that wasn't going away. After tonight, I believed it. "Did you check the air conditioner cover?"

"Yes. Everything's been checked and double-checked." O'Connell glanced down the hall. "Since we're throwing out insane theories, I have one. Poltergeist."

"Don't make me laugh. My side can't take it." But the flickering lights, scary messages, and invisible attacker freaked me out. I'd never admit it, but a teeny tiny part of me wondered if something otherworldly could be happening here. Plenty of my colleagues had responded to calls where they'd seen or heard things they hadn't been able to explain. I never put much stock into those outrageous tales. There was a logical explanation. I just wasn't sure what it was.

O'Connell stayed the rest of the night. He slept in the chair while I struggled to find a position that didn't make me want to stop breathing. Surely, oxygen wasn't nearly as important as people said. I could survive on less of it. But when that theory proved inaccurate, I popped a few more pills, refreshed the ice pack, and passed out on the couch.

Vibrations moved through me. At first, I thought I was dreaming. But the shaking only got stronger. Earthquake. I bolted upright to find Lucca standing at the end of the sofa.

"Ouch." I lifted my shirt to check the bandage beneath the melted ice pack. The baseball sized knot had shrunk to the size of a golf ball. "What'd you do that for?" I glanced at the chair where O'Connell had slept, but it was empty.

"Why didn't you call me?" Lucca put his hands on his hips, waiting for an answer.

"Where's Daria?"

"I just took her to her appointment."

"What time is it?"

"Twelve."

"Shit." I rubbed my eyes. "Where's Nick?"

"He left hours ago. He briefed me on the situation, which is something you should have done. He told me to let you sleep, that you needed to rest. But you slept enough. I want to know what's going on."

"Stop busting my chops," I said.

"Oh, I haven't even started."

I jerked my chin at the cricket bat. "You might as well use that. Go ahead. Take a swing. It'll make you feel better. I deserve it."

"Don't start that shit. I'm not in the mood for Alex Parker's woe is me crap. Not today." He strutted back and forth, his hands still on his hips. "Daria attacked you, Alex. Whatever's going on with her is so far beyond something we can handle on our own. She needs professional help. The kind we aren't equipped to provide."

"She didn't do it."

"That's not what O'Connell thinks."

"He's wrong." I climbed off the couch and grabbed Lucca by the elbow and dragged him to the bat. "Forensics dusted this last night. What do you see?"

He stared down at it. "Nothing."

"That's right. Daria wasn't wearing gloves last night. In fact, she was freaking out and panicked. Her hands were clammy. She would have left all kinds of prints and residue behind. Where is it? Huh, boy scout?"

"I don't know, but no one else was here."

"You're wrong. He was here. He was fucking here. Danziger thought he heard a door slam. Maybe a car. That could have been the assailant escaping. The power went out. Who knows what happened in the dark?" I grabbed my phone to check the tracker I'd placed on Reagan LaRoche's car, but it hadn't moved.

"Fine. Then why don't you tell me exactly what happened?"

So I did.

"No one entered through either door. The police checked, and when O'Connell arrived, the front door was locked tight. How does this bastard keep getting inside?" Lucca asked.

"I felt a breeze." Without waiting, I moved down the hall to Daria's room. Under normal conditions, I wouldn't barge into a client's bedroom and search through her personal belongings, but this was a special case.

I didn't find anything damning in Daria's bedroom suite. The air conditioner cover remained firmly in place. The newly replaced screws were fastened tightly.

"If he's not coming in through the bottom, he must have a way in through the top." I headed up the steps, turning on the lights as I went. Unlike last night, this time I was armed, and I had Lucca for backup. Closing my eyes, I took a few steps, letting my memory guide me. "This is where I first felt it." I opened my eyes and looked around, but there were no vents or nearby windows. Unsure what I expected to find, I ran my fingers against the wall and checked behind every mirror, painting, and photograph, but I didn't find any holes. "A short didn't cause the power outage. The circuit breaker was never tripped. That's why I couldn't reset it."

"Do you think he was hiding in the utility closet?" Lucca opened the door and peered in. The circuit breaker, water heater, and a few other essentials filled the small space. "Someone could fit behind the support beam."

"He didn't jump out at me." I turned to look back at the staircase. "He came from behind." I shuffled along the floor, listening for the creaking floorboards I heard the previous night. They were near the railing. Easing onto my hands and knees, I examined the carpeting, finding some of the fibers had been disturbed. It wasn't deep enough to cause an obvious indention, but something had briefly occupied the space, causing the fibers to fold in on themselves.

None of the nearby furniture had legs that wide. I looked up, noticing the rectangular hatch which led to the attic. "Help me up," I said. Lucca offered me a hand, and I hissed like a balloon as I got back on my feet. "Can you get that open?"

Lucca gestured for me to step backward. I moved to a

cover position on the other side of the railing and aimed at the ceiling. Lucca grabbed a chair from Daria's studio and placed it beneath the hatch. After feeling along the seams, he slid the panel open and reached for his flashlight.

THIRTY-ONE

"Federal agent," he announced. "Is anyone up here?"

"What do you see?" I asked.

Lucca turned on the chair, scanning the immediate vicinity. "Not much." He hoisted himself up through the hole. I moved closer, waiting to see what would happen. "Clear," he called, "but you're going to want to see this. Move the chair out of the way. I found a ladder."

I tucked my gun back in my holster and moved the chair. The attic ladder descended from the hatch. The rungs matched the patches of disturbed carpet I'd observed. This was how the bastard got the jump on me.

I stopped on the top rung, pulling the flashlight from my keychain. I swept the light around the attic. Lucca moved in a crouch. The low-sloping ceiling made it impossible to stand. "Watch your head," he warned, shining his flashlight in my direction.

Bits of insulation littered the unfinished floor, combining with other debris and cobwebs. Dust particles hung in the air, dancing in a pinprick of light. Crawling toward it, I realized a small hole had been drilled in the floor which looked directly into Daria's art studio.

"He's been watching her," I said. "She wasn't

hallucinating or remembering."

"It looks like he's been at it a while." Lucca pointed to several snack food wrappers and a few uneaten granola bars, beef jerky sticks, and several bottles of water. Beside them was a tube of lipstick and one of Daria's journals.

"How long do you think he's been hiding up here?" I asked. "And where did he go?"

"The better questions are who is he and how did he get in here."

I examined the dirt patterns on the floor. The layer of pink insulation dust grew thicker the closer I got to the wall. The brown paper wrapper was torn in the middle and held in place by two clips. Lucca unhooked the clip, and the paper rolled to the side, revealing a hollowed out path leading to a section of demolished wall which led into the next unit's attic.

Without waiting for Lucca, I made my way through the opening. The owner of this townhouse had stowed enough boxes to hide the hole in the wall. Shoving them to the side, I felt an unpleasant stabbing in my ribs. After a few shallow breaths, I moved deeper into the attic and checked to see if there was another opening on the other side. But there wasn't.

"Parker," Lucca hissed from Daria's attic, "I'm calling this in. You're trespassing right now."

"The hell I am. Whoever lives here could be in danger." Or the source of the danger. Sliding the hatch open, I pushed the attic ladder forward and descended into the neighbor's townhouse. Briefly, I wondered if they were gun owners. I'd find out when they realized they had an intruder in their home.

The townhouse was laid out identically to Daria's. It was another middle unit with windows at the front and back. A quick glance outside showed I wasn't in Tom and Uma's house, which meant I was in the other neighbor's house.

"Hello?" I called, remembering what the police officers had said the night before. "Is anyone here?"

I moved as swiftly as possible, checking each room as I went. Lucca must have thrown the rulebook out the window since he followed after me. "What are you doing?"

I asked.

"He could be inside. You need backup."

We moved in tandem, checking each room before regrouping at the front door. The security system on the wall showed it was active. Without the code, it couldn't be disarmed.

Lucca pulled out his phone, notifying the police of this new development, while I used a pen to flip through the large pile of mail on the kitchen table. All the letters and flyers were addressed to Ginger Kendrick. I didn't know anything about Ginger, but I was pretty sure she hadn't attacked me last night.

The envelopes at the bottom of the stack were postmarked almost two months ago. I scanned the pile again, but I didn't find a single bill. The framed photos on the wall featured an attractive blonde-haired woman in her late twenties taken at exotic locales. In one photo, she was hiking a snowy mountain. In another, she was near a waterfall. In another, she was seated on the ground with several small children in what might have been an African village. On a separate wall, near her computer, was a framed plaque with her name engraved in the center.

"She's a travel writer," I said.

"And activist." Lucca pointed to a certificate she'd gotten for her contributions and volunteer work with an international relief organization. "I don't think she's stalking Daria."

I opened the fridge and peered inside, but it was empty. The freezer had a few TV dinners which were a few months away from expiring, but that was it. "She's on a month-long cruise. At least, that's what the neighbor next door said. But according to him, she only left a few days ago."

Ignoring Lucca's protest, I searched the rest of her desk. But she hadn't written down her travel plans. On her coffee table was a pile of magazines, presumably the one she wrote for. I flipped through the most recent issue, finding her article. It didn't provide any helpful details as to her current whereabouts, but the photo credits included a name I shouldn't have been surprised to see. Reagan LaRoche.

"They know each other," I insisted, as Lucca dragged me up the stairs and out of Ginger Kendrick's townhouse. "He took her photo for the article. That bastard. The neighbor said he heard a door slam and thought he saw a car leaving around the time of the attack. It must have been Reagan. I have to get to the garage and see if his car's still there. The tracker says it hasn't moved, but it could have fallen off or he found it."

"Or he used a different car," Lucca said.

As soon as we were safely back inside Daria's townhouse, I phoned O'Connell with the news while Lucca scouted around outside Ginger's place. A patrol car was on the way to secure the scene while we waited for forensics to arrive and check out the attic.

"I'll put in for a court order," O'Connell said. "Since this involves someone else's house, we have to tread carefully."

"What about Reagan?"

"I'll have someone sit on him until we put everything together. Right now, the only thing we know for certain is he professionally photographed Daria's neighbor. As soon as I get a chance, I'll head over to the magazine and see what they can tell me. I'll check in with the marketing firm where Reagan works and find out if they know anything about this. I don't want him to slip away again, especially when we're already on such thin ice. But we can't be sure it's him."

"I know, but he has to be involved somehow."

"Stay away from him, Parker. I mean it," O'Connell warned.

"Yeah, okay."

"Promise me."

"What is up with everyone expecting me to make promises? Isn't my word good for anything anymore?"

"It's just an added precaution. If you prefer, I can assign a unit to keep an eye on you or have a patrolman handcuff you to something immovable."

"I'll behave."

"Good. I'll call you when I know something."

Lucca came back inside. "Why didn't we check the attic sooner? Daria's been hearing strange things. I never thought to look up."

"She never said he was above her. She always said she saw him watching her from the backyard." I stared out the front door, desperate to make sense out of the one thing that still didn't make sense. "The night she was attacked, I had two cars watching the place. One was out front, and the other was parked on the side street. They didn't see anyone enter or leave."

"That's because he never left. He must have already been inside Ginger's townhouse. He gained access to Daria's through the hole in the attic and when she freaked him out, he retreated back through the hole he climbed out of, like the rat he is."

"But we had eyes on Reagan that entire night. He was home. He couldn't have attacked Daria."

"He's working with someone." Lucca checked the time, just as a patrol car pulled up. "Daria's session with Dr. Chen is almost over. Can you pick her up while I stay here and brief these guys?"

"No problem." I bent down for my bag, letting out a squeak as I tried to straighten.

Lucca scooped the strap out of my hand and hefted my overnight bag over his shoulder. "I'll put this in your car." He watched as I slipped the pill bottle into my pocket. "Are you sure you can drive after taking those?"

"I haven't taken any today." But after all that crawling around and lifting, I was reconsidering my stubborn stance.

"Okay." He gave me a cockeyed look. "And you're okay to drive?"

"It's my side, not my leg. We'll be fine."

"I hope so." He opened my car door and waited for me to slide in. "You didn't drive the company car yesterday?"

"No."

A funny look came over Lucca, but he didn't say anything. "While the police are tearing the place apart, it might be best if Daria's not around to see it."

"I'll take her back to the office with me. I have plenty of work to do on this."

"I'll meet you there as soon as I can."

*   *   *

"Are you all right?" Lucien Cross asked.

I looked up from my computer screen. "What are you doing here? Shouldn't you be on a beach in Malibu?"

"I asked first."

"I'm fine. Your turn."

He leaned against the doorjamb, tucking his hands into his pockets. "I work here. It's called Cross Security for a reason."

"You sound like Martin." I narrowed my eyes. "Have you seen him lately?"

Cross ducked his head, chuckling. "I take it he mentioned we had lunch and drinks."

"Lucien, I'm in the middle of something. Get to the point or get out."

He peered around the doorjamb. "Where's Ms. Waylon? I'd love to meet her."

"She's taking a nap in Renner's office. He said he didn't mind."

As soon as he heard that, Cross strode into my office and closed the door. "I heard what happened last night. What can I do to help? I can have updated security systems and motion sensors installed. They'll have a stored power supply, so they'll remain active in the event of another power failure."

"You'll have to ask Daria if that's what she wants."

"What do you want?" he asked.

"A safe house until the person responsible is apprehended."

"Done."

That was easy. Too easy. "What do you want in return?"

"Besides an introduction, not a thing." He cocked his head to the side. "You know, I spent a hell of a lot of money on the medical equipment upstairs. You should take it for a spin."

"I'm fine."

"Suit yourself." He circled around the back of my desk, reading over my shoulder. "Ginger Kendrick's passport records show she's been traveling a lot recently. In the last ninety days, she's only spent four of them in her house."

"Which four?"

Cross smiled. "See, I said all you had to do was ask." He reached for my mouse. "May I?"

Raising my hands in surrender, I slid out of my chair and let Lucien work. The smug look on his face annoyed me, but at the moment, everything annoyed me. "You usually don't grant wishes. Why the sudden change of heart?"

"I gained a new perspective while on vacation."

"Vacation? I thought you took time off to stalk Martin."

"Funny." His eyes flicked to mine before returning to the screen. "California is lovely. Warm weather. Nice beaches. You'd enjoy it."

"I'd enjoy figuring out who Reagan LaRoche is working with." I took a seat in my client chair and stared up at the ceiling. At least this place didn't have any trapdoors, but I wasn't sure about hidden surveillance devices. Cross always knew more than he should about everything.

The printer whirred, and Cross handed me the sheet. "That's Ginger Kendrick's entire travel itinerary for the year. It has times, dates, and locations."

"How did you get this?" It included hotel listings, phone numbers where she could be reached, and any travel guides or assistants she hired.

"The owner of the magazine where she works is an old friend. That's everything from their internal servers. The passport records are courtesy of our tech friends upstairs. But that part you'll keep between us should your pals with badges ask how you acquired them." He leaned back in my chair. "Reagan LaRoche, the photographer?"

"Do you know him too?"

Cross cleared his throat. "No, but I can make some calls. However, it'd help if you update me on the situation first."

"You don't already know?"

"Pretend I don't." His lip twitched, and he ran a hand through his hair.

How much did he know, or was this how he bluffed? He played a lot of high stakes poker. A tell like that would have bankrupted him a long time ago. Still, I didn't see why he'd waste time if he was already up to speed, so I gave him the abbreviated version of what happened.

Nodding, he got out of my chair and opened my office door, nearly getting punched in the face by Lucca who had his fist raised mid-knock. "That would make filing harassment and brutality charges very easy, Agent Lucca."

Lucca retracted his hand. "I didn't see you."

Cross cleared his throat. "That much is clear. Carry on."

Lucca stood in the doorway, watching Cross go down the hall before stepping into my office. "What was that?"

"That was Lucien when he's in a good mood."

Lucca made a face.

"I know. It freaks me out too," I said. "But he's offering to help."

"We can use it."

"What happened?"

"The mobile crime lab dusted everything in Daria's attic. They found Reagan LaRoche's fingerprints on the empty candy wrappers and the bottles of water we found. They collected some hairs and fibers, but it'll take longer to match those. But Reagan's were the only prints up there. You and I didn't touch anything without gloves, so we didn't contaminate the scene, and Daria's never gone up there, so..."

"So we have no idea how long that hole's been there. It could have been there when she moved in."

"That's possible, but the dust and debris indicate it's probably more recent, possibly within the last few months. I spoke to the rest of Daria's neighbors in the attached townhouses. They recall Ginger having her upstairs bathroom redone at the beginning of the year."

"Hang on." I accessed the database and ran her financials. "That was a little over three months ago. Around the time Daria put Reagan in the friend zone."

"You know Jablonsky's stance on coincidences," Lucca said.

While I researched the construction team who'd worked on Ginger's bathroom and cross-referenced them with Reagan's known associates and friends, Lucca skimmed the notes I'd made on Reagan and his connection to Ginger.

"I don't think she's involved," Lucca said, "since you didn't find anything connecting them besides the photoshoot."

"Photoshoots. The marketing firm where Reagan works does a lot of advertising and promotion for the magazine. Reagan and a few other people in the art department come out quarterly to do photoshoots of the magazine writers and other contributors. Occasionally, they'll go on location to provide additional shots and filler for the travel magazine."

"But you didn't find any calls or texts between them," Lucca said.

"No, but they probably spoke when Reagan was taking photos. He must have caught on to Ginger's hectic travel schedule, figured out she was Daria's neighbor, and took advantage of the situation." I cursed at the screen. "The home improvement store responsible for redoing her bathroom contracts out the work. The crew changes all the time." I picked up the phone and dialed the contractor, pretended to be Ginger, and asked if he could tell me who worked on my project.

"I don't have that in front of me. Is there a problem?" he asked, perturbed.

"Yeah, a big one. Unless you want to be named in the lawsuit, I suggest you get me some names."

"Lawsuit?"

"Yeah, for loss and damages. My attorney suggested since this is a personal matter, it would be resolved faster without involving the entire company, but if getting their names is too difficult, I'll just list your construction company in my complaint."

"No, no, no. I can get that information. My office manager doesn't work weekends, but let me call him. He can tell me where the files are. Let me put you on hold. Five minutes. Please."

"Okay." I hit the speaker button. When the hold music kicked on, I pressed mute and put the handset back in the cradle. Too bad mute prevented anyone from hearing me instead of me from hearing the repetitive tones.

Lucca shook his head. "I thought you went to law school. Didn't they teach you that's not how this works?"

"I know that, but he doesn't." I stopped him before he could voice a protest. "This is the fastest way to find out who Reagan's accomplice is. He has to have one. And I'm absolutely certain it's not Ginger."

THIRTY-TWO

Lucca rubbed his eyes and tossed the notepad onto the table. "Maybe it's not him."

"It's him. You've seen the photos he's taken. Don't tell me Reagan LaRoche isn't stalking Daria."

"That's not what I'm saying. I agree he is or was." Lucca shifted on the couch. "But he isn't a magician. He can't be in two places at once. He wasn't responsible for the first attack."

"True, but we don't know where he was last night." I tapped my fingers impatiently on the desk. "Just because we can't connect him to anyone on the construction crew, that doesn't mean he didn't take advantage. We know Reagan's acquainted with Ginger Kendrick."

"But we can't get a hold of her either. This is ridiculous."

"The ship's out to sea. She'll be out of cell range until they dock in port, which won't be for another few days." I flopped her travel itinerary on top of the notepad.

"We spoke to everyone we could find at the magazine," Lucca said, "and all of Ginger's friends. She didn't socialize with Reagan. She barely even spoke to him at work. You heard what her best friend said. Ginger thought he was creepy."

"Everyone thinks he's creepy because he is creepy. The only people who didn't get that vibe were a few of the women he met on those dating sites, and frankly, I don't trust their judgment. You heard the things he said in the interrogation room. He's full of himself, and he's obsessed with Daria. I just can't figure out how he gained access to Ginger's townhouse."

"The locks and alarm system weren't disturbed, even the windows are sensored. Whoever entered must have had a key and the disarm code."

"What about Ginger's sister, Marlene? She stops by once a week to collect the mail and check on the place while Ginger's traveling. Maybe she let Reagan in or knows who might be hiding in the attic."

"I already checked. Her sister has no connection to Reagan either, and she was out with her boyfriend and several of their friends last night, and she has an alibi for the night of the other attack."

"I'm running out of ideas."

"Marlene said Ginger doesn't give out her house key or disarm code to anyone. I don't know how this guy is getting in. I looked into the company in charge of her home security system, but I'm pretty sure they're not involved."

"So whoever attacked Daria must have the ability to walk through walls," I said.

"If that were true, they wouldn't have had to take a sledgehammer to the dividing wall in the attic. Quite frankly, those units, even though they are connected, are meant to be separate. Those walls were solid brick. It would have taken a lot of time and made a lot of noise."

"Do you think Daria would have heard it?" I asked.

"Heard what?" She wandered into my office, looking around as if she'd never seen the place.

"Demolition in your attic," I said.

She frowned, eyeing the notepads and files on the coffee table. "I'd hope so."

"What's wrong, Dar?" Lucca asked.

"Where are we? I don't remember being here before."

"This is my office at Cross Security," I said. "The room where you took a nap, that's my associate's office. He had a late lunch meeting with a client, so we thought it'd be a quiet place for you to decompress."

"Tell him thank you," Daria said absently. Lucca cleared off a spot on the couch for her to sit. "Are we here because of what happened last night?"

"Yes." I eyed her, but she seemed to remember last night. After all, that's what the bulk of her therapy session had been about. "We figured out how he got inside your house. You were right. You were attacked. You didn't hurt yourself. Someone hurt you."

"I told you so," she exclaimed. "Everyone treats me like I'm crazy, and then I start thinking I'm actually nuts. But I'm not. It's not fair. Why won't anyone listen to me?"

"I'm listening," I said. "I've been listening."

"I know. Thank you." She turned to Lucca. "You too, Eddie." She reached for the notepad and skimmed our notes. "At least I don't have to take any more of those damn pills."

"What about the memories that resurfaced?" Lucca asked.

"I'll deal with those when my life is no longer in danger." She turned to me. "Are you okay? You were hurt last night, weren't you?"

"It's nothing an ice pack can't fix." I adjusted in the chair. "We need to discuss a gameplan. More than likely, Reagan is to blame, but he may have an accomplice or two. Until we know more, I'd prefer if you find somewhere else to stay. Cross Security has several safe houses in the city. You'll be protected there."

"For how long?" Daria asked.

"As long as it takes."

"What about my art and my business?"

"Despite the relocation, I'll make sure you have whatever you need to continue your normal routine," Lucca said.

"He won't be able to find me there?" Daria asked, turning her focus to me.

"You'll be completely safe."

"That'll be a nice change of pace." She brushed her hair back. "When do I get to see my new digs?"

"Anytime you're ready," Lucca said.

"What about my things? Do we get them now or later? I'd like to make a few notes, just in case I forget what's going on."

I handed her a blank legal pad and pen. "That's for you to use until we pick up your journals."

"I'll take you back to your house first. We'll pack whatever you need. Then we'll come back here, switch cars, and head to the safe house," Lucca said.

"Just give me a minute." She uncapped the pen and scribbled furiously. When she was satisfied that she'd detailed enough of what was about to happen, she tucked the pen behind her ear and clutched the notepad to her chest. "Okay. I'm ready."

"While you do that, I'll run down a few leads," I said.

"It's Saturday. Reagan and I would usually be hanging out right about now. Where do you think he is?" Daria asked.

"I don't know, but I'll find him."

"Be careful," she said. "I never thought he'd be violent, but I'm not so sure anymore." She frowned. "Even now, after everything, I don't remember seeing him in the bathroom mirror or following me on the street. I know it sounds crazy, but I'm telling you, someone else attacked me. Someone who looks just like Andrew Holland."

Lucca gave me a pointed look. "Alex is looking into the possibility Reagan has an accomplice. All we know for certain is Reagan isn't innocent. He's involved. We just don't know the extent of it yet. But I promise you, he'll never hurt you again."

After they left, I headed upstairs. "Do you have any idea where Reagan LaRoche is?" I asked.

Cross was hunched over a workstation beside Amir. "We pinged his phone twenty minutes ago. According to this, he's in the park. I spoke to several people at the marketing agency. Mr. LaRoche volunteered to take some photos for one of their upcoming marketing campaigns. For an art director, he's rather hands on. Then again, it is a small marketing firm. I guess everyone has to pitch in and do his part."

"What park?"

Cross gave me the address. "I'm surprised the police don't have him cornered yet."

"Until this afternoon, they didn't believe any of Daria's claims."

"But you did."

"I wasn't sure what to believe." I turned to Amir. "Can you get me nearby traffic cam footage from last night? One of Daria's neighbors thought he saw a green car driving away from the scene."

"I'll do what I can, but we didn't have much luck last time. The city hasn't installed any new cameras since. What about the tracker I gave you?"

"It never moved. I'm going to check on that first, before I see LaRoche." I nodded to each of them. "Gentlemen."

*   *   *

When I arrived in Reagan's parking garage, the first thing I noticed was the car had been moved. It was no longer on blocks but had four brand new tires and shiny spinners. Reagan had installed a light kit and had the car freshly waxed and polished. The GPS tracker I'd stuck to the bumper had been tossed on the ground, near the painted white line.

I picked it up. The small black box wasn't damaged. I looked around, but Reagan's previous spot hadn't been near any of the cameras. On the bright side, Cross couldn't deduct the cost of a broken tracker from my paycheck.

A siren let out two short whoops before pulling to a stop beside me. "What are you doing here? You promised you wouldn't go near him," O'Connell said.

"I wanted to check on his car. He found the tracker. He also got himself some new wheels. Four of them to be exact." I pointed to the vehicle parked a few spaces away.

"I told you to keep your distance."

"Relax. He isn't here."

"Do you know where he is?" O'Connell asked.

"You mean you don't?" I hated when Cross was right about things.

"His office said he's out on a photoshoot. A patrol car is stationed at his place of business. Another one is keeping an eye on his apartment, and two more are scouting the park. They have eyes on him, but we don't have an arrest warrant yet. We're waiting until we do before we take him. I just don't want to lose him."

"Don't you have enough to arrest him?"

"That's not the problem." O'Connell leaned across and pushed open the door. "Get in so we can talk."

"Am I in trouble?"

"Just get in the car."

I slid into the passenger's seat and closed the door. "Martin doesn't like it when I let other men take me for rides."

O'Connell snorted. "I'm not touching that."

"He'll be happy to hear it."

O'Connell rolled his eyes, glancing at me as he slowly circled around the garage and found a place to park near the entrance. "CSU's still investigating the demolition in Daria's attic. Given the location of the breach and last night's attack, the judge signed off on a warrant to search the neighbor's apartment. Aside from the connection her magazine has to Reagan's marketing firm, I haven't found anything else to tie the two of them together. From the look on your face, I'm guessing neither did you."

"Nothing."

"I spoke to Ginger's friends and family. None of them know Reagan. I even went so far as to contact everyone Reagan's close to. He's never mentioned Ginger to any of them either. The techs are checking the memory card to see if they can find any photos of her on it. Do you want to save me some time?"

"Cross Security looked too. They didn't find any photos of Ginger or anyone else from the magazine shoot. We're guessing those photos are elsewhere, probably at the marketing firm."

"All right. I'll let the techs know not to waste their time looking." O'Connell made the call while I stared at the garage entrance. "Reagan's prints were on the items found in Daria's attic. Unfortunately, we don't know if he was behind last night's attack. But you and I know he couldn't have shoved Daria's face into the mirror."

"I'm working under the assumption he has an accomplice. Did you ever speak to Celeste Nash?"

"She refused to talk to me. She said she's busy prepping for some art thing she's hosting tonight. Whatever questions I have would have to wait."

"And you let her get away with that?"

"I ran through the usual methods of making someone's life miserable, but she didn't cave. She told me to contact her attorney."

"Do you think she's hiding something?"

"I'm not sure, but I'll keep an eye on her. What did you find when you ran her?"

"How do you know I ran her?"

"Because I know you."

"She's clean. Everyone is. That's what makes this so insane." I shifted closer to the window, hoping to spot something useful, but no one was interested in entering the garage or checking out Reagan's car. "Why haven't you arrested him yet?"

"It's Saturday."

"So?"

"The judge is playing a round of golf. When he finishes, he'll sign the warrant."

"That's our justice system at work."

"I'm sure you remember how this goes."

"I tried to block it out." I peered out the windshield and glimpsed Reagan's apartment. Today, his curtains were drawn. "Lucca took Daria to pack her things. She's going to stay at one of Cross Security's safe houses until we figure out who's been terrorizing her and make sure he's locked up where he can't hurt her again. Even after we told her about everything we found in her attic, she insists Reagan didn't attack her."

"We know he didn't," O'Connell said. "We were looking right at him when the first attack happened. Do you think he's the one who struck you last night?"

"I don't know. I didn't see anyone. I spent all afternoon looking into Reagan, his friends, his family, and his associates. As far as the world is concerned, Reagan's never done anything like this before."

"He takes photos for a living. Someone could have hired him to photograph Daria. Did you check his financials? Has he received any suspicious money transfers lately?"

"No."

"What about payouts?"

"Nope. If we hadn't seen him with our own two eyes, I'd say he's responsible for all of it."

"Even though Daria said he's not?"

"We found the red sneakers in Reagan's closet. I'm sure he has the right clothing to impersonate the Lightning Killer. He wore those things to fool her mind into remembering past trauma and confusing the two. Given her memory difficulties, he had no reason to think she'd ever point the finger at him."

"If he wants to kill her, there are easier ways to go about it. Frankly, I don't think he's that smart. How would he have known what the Lightning Killer wore?"

"I don't know, Nick. I'm tired. I must be losing my touch. We'll get him for the terrorizing, the destruction of property, theft, and breaking and entering. Maybe you can offer him some sort of deal in exchange for giving up his accomplice or boss or whatever weird ass situation is going on here because I have no idea what it could be."

THIRTY-THREE

O'Connell's phoned buzzed. He lifted it off the dash and read the message. "Warrant's ready to be served. Patrol officers have eyes on LaRoche. He's finishing up at the park. We'll wait and take him somewhere more secure." He put his phone down. "You want to tag along?"

"Sure."

He radioed the patrol unit parked on the street and told them to keep an eye out in case LaRoche came home instead of heading back to the office. Then we drove across town to the marketing firm.

A patrol car was positioned across the street from the marketing agency. An unmarked cruiser was parked on the side street. O'Connell parked on the other side, radioing for an update.

"LaRoche is in a blue equipment van headed eastbound. He should be within visual range in three minutes," the patrol car said.

"Roger." O'Connell put the radio down. Resting one forearm over the top of the steering wheel, he allowed his other hand to rest on the door handle. I'd never seen him so anxious to make an arrest before. Then again, I rarely got to ride along when he was serving a warrant. Most of the time, he arrested people because they were shooting at us or threatening to harm someone else.

The van slowed, stopping at the light two blocks away. O'Connell tugged on the door handle, just enough so it would open but not enough for the door to swing wide. The seconds ticked by so slowly I was sure time had stopped. After what felt like hours, the light changed to green and the van continued on its path toward us. It parked half a block away in one of the reserved spaces.

Even from this distance, I could see the floppy, highlighted tendrils bouncing as the driver got out of the vehicle. He slid open the rear door, grabbed two lights, placed them on the ground, and locked the van. He slung a camera bag diagonally across his chest, picked up the lights, and walked straight toward us.

O'Connell waited until LaRoche entered the lobby before getting out of the car and darting up the steps after him. Most arrest warrants were served by the warrant squad, but O'Connell wasn't in the mood to wait for them.

"Police," O'Connell announced. "Hold it right there. You're under arrest."

"What?" The man put the lights down.

"Hands up. Turn around slowly," O'Connell said.

"Is this about climbing into the fountain because I had a permit to shoot there. I needed to move closer to get a better shot." Despite having the same hairstyle and highlights, the voice was different.

"Nick," I said, just as O'Connell grabbed one of the man's wrists and fastened his handcuff, "that's not Reagan."

O'Connell spun the guy around. "Who are you? Where's Reagan LaRoche?"

The guy laughed nervously. "You had me worried. You aren't here to arrest me?"

"Who are you?" O'Connell repeated.

"Anthony Gerhart."

"Where's Reagan?" I asked.

"I don't know. He was supposed to cover today's photoshoot. In fact, he volunteered for it. I'm his assistant. I waited for him, but he never showed up."

"But you were in the park for hours," O'Connell said. "What were you doing?"

"I did the shoot without him." Gerhart shook his bound wrists. "Am I in trouble?"

"No." O'Connell unhooked him and asked to see Gerhart's ID. When he was done, he handed it back. "When's the last time you saw Reagan?"

"Yesterday at work."

"What time was that?" I asked.

"We left a little after five."

"Have you spoken to him since?" O'Connell asked.

"No. I tried calling a few times, but he didn't pick up."

"Call him again," O'Connell instructed. Gerhart dialed, holding out the phone while we listened to it ring. The faint sound of a musical ringtone came from the bag hanging at Gerhart's hip. O'Connell reached for it, opening the bag and digging around. Inside the inner zipper, he found Reagan's phone. "How did you get this? Where's Reagan?"

"I told you I don't know," Gerhart said. "This is his bag. He keeps his camera equipment and spare memory cards in it. I took it with me to the shoot. I didn't know his phone was inside."

"You didn't hear it ringing?" O'Connell asked.

"I didn't notice."

"Do you have any idea where Reagan might be?"

"None."

"Has Reagan blown off photoshoots before?" I asked.

"Not that I know of."

"How long have you worked for him?" O'Connell asked.

"Almost two years."

O'Connell stared at the elevator banks. "Do you mind showing me his office?"

"No problem." Gerhart picked up the lights, stopping briefly to put them in the storage room, before leading us to Reagan's office. "Why do you want to arrest him? What did he do?"

O'Connell didn't answer. Instead we took turns asking Gerhart questions about Reagan's behavior, his dating habits, his friends, his interests, his hangouts, and anything else that might be relevant.

"Reagan doesn't talk about anything except photography. That's his true passion. This just pays the bills until he gets discovered and can make it as an artist. I always tease him that real artists have to starve, but Reagan's tired of starving. He's smart. A job like this will lead to contacts. He's really good friends with a local gallery owner. He's gonna become a big name, like the next Ansel Adams or Annie Leibovitz. He's a genius."

"Is that why you're dressed up like him?" I asked.

"Did Reagan put you up to that?" O'Connell asked as he searched Reagan's desk.

"This? No. He didn't ask me to do this. I just thought he had a really cool look. They say imitation is the greatest form of flattery."

O'Connell stopped dead in his tracks. "Where were you the Thursday before last at eleven p.m.?"

"Reagan asked me if I could housesit for him."

"Housesit?"

"Yeah, he said his grandma was sick. He asked if I wouldn't mind hanging out at his place until he got back."

"What time was that?" I asked.

"I went there after work."

"Have you been there before?" I asked.

"Several times. Reagan invites me over a lot to teach me new techniques. He has this huge apartment. It's like a professional photo studio. He has the backdrops and cameras to conduct shoots and all the latest software on his computer to work with the digital images. But sometimes, he likes to experiment with film. He develops the photos in his bathroom. He even showed me how to do it. It's so crazy how that works."

"Reagan wasn't home that Thursday night," I said.

"No," Gerhart said.

"How long did you stay?" O'Connell asked.

Gerhart blushed. "I got caught up working on the computer. I slept over that night. Reagan woke me up when he got home."

"What time was that?" O'Connell asked.

"It was around five." Gerhart just punched a hole in Reagan's alibi from the night of the first attack. This changed everything.

I looked at O'Connell. We hadn't been observing Reagan that night. We'd been watching Gerhart and hadn't realized the difference. For all intents and purposes, Anthony Gerhart could be Reagan LaRoche's body double. Reagan's assistant hero-worshipped him to the point of mimicking his mannerisms, trying on his clothes, and sleeping in his bed, even unbuttoning his shirt down to his naval.

I dialed the office while O'Connell asked Gerhart to log into Reagan's computer and get him Reagan's schedule for the week. We had to stop Reagan before he hurt Daria again.

"He's supposed to be attending Celeste Nash's gallery event later tonight," O'Connell said, "but that doesn't start until eight."

"I'll head over there now. Reagan might show up early."

"All right. I'll go to his apartment to see if he left anything damning behind."

I left the building, caught a cab back to my car, and called Lucca. Daria had packed her things. They were on the way back to Cross Security. My boss would make sure the transition went smoothly, but out of an abundance of caution, I called Cross and updated him on the situation.

"She'll be protected. I'll have the security team on the lookout, just in case he's installed tracking software on her phone. Under normal conditions, that'd be the first thing I'd insist she leave here."

"I know, but Daria relies on that for everything. She can't be without it."

"Good thing we're adaptable to our client's needs."

We disconnected, just as I pulled up to the gallery. Reagan's car remained in the garage which meant he could be using any mode of transportation. I kept my eyes peeled as I passed the other parked cars and pedestrians on the street. But I didn't spot him.

Entering the gallery, I was hit by an immediate blast of cold air. Several workers were rearranging the exhibits on the walls and hanging photographs. No wonder the air conditioner was working double time.

"Great, you're here," a woman said. I recognized her

from her ID photo as Celeste Nash. "You can set up along the back wall. The linens are already here."

"Excuse me?"

"Right back here, darling." She took my elbow and guided me toward a long empty table at the back of the main room.

"Is Reagan here?" I asked, assuming she had me confused with the caterer.

"Reagan?" She removed her hand from my elbow. "Oh, I'm sorry. I thought you were someone else. Reagan dropped off his photos for the show early this morning, but he won't be back until eight." She cocked her head to the side. "Are you a buyer?"

"Not exactly."

"Oh," her tone shifted, "come back tonight and bring your invitation. Formal attire is required."

"You don't understand. It's an emergency. I need to find him."

She looked me up and down. "He's not here. All I can tell you is he never misses a gallery show. He'll be here tonight. Now run along. I have a lot of work to do, and we're currently closed to the public."

I thought about telling her I was the private eye she'd spoken to on the phone, but I couldn't risk her warning Reagan. Given his erratic behavior today, he must have known we were on to him after last night's attack. His hiding place had been compromised, as had his identity.

I returned to my car and called the office. "Has Reagan made any arrangements to get out of town?"

"He hasn't charged anything on his credit card," Amir said, "since breakfast."

That didn't mean Reagan wasn't fleeing. It just meant he was smart about it, like the way he left his cell phone in his work bag. I started to dial O'Connell to ask if he had gotten access to the security cam footage from Reagan's office, but O'Connell beat me to the punch.

"Hey," I said, "did you find anything?"

"Yeah. Reagan."

THIRTY-FOUR

Patrol officers stood guard outside Reagan's apartment. They stepped aside to let me pass once O'Connell waved me through. He handed me a pair of gloves and led me to the bathroom. Reagan LaRoche's naked body was face down in the tub. An open bottle of pills sat on the edge of the tub, next to a bottle of bodywash. On the floor beside the tub were two sideways bottles, shampoo and conditioner.

I picked up the pill bottle. "These are the tranquilizers the hospital gave Daria."

"I know." O'Connell exhaled. "He took them from her house. I don't know when. Do you remember when she stopped taking them?"

"She only took them the first day back. She didn't like how they made her feel."

"Do you know what she did with the rest?"

"I'm not her nurse, Nick. She probably did what most people do with medication they don't want and put it in the medicine cabinet in case it was needed at some point in the future." I peered into the tub. No blood. No vomit. Nothing indicated this was an overdose or attack. "What do you think happened?"

"He fell asleep in the bath and drowned himself."

"Do you think it was intentional?" I shook the bottle, which remained full of pills.

"Suicide note's on his computer. He detailed everything." O'Connell closed the bathroom door, revealing the wall behind it. "Does that remind you of anything?"

In bright red lipstick was written, *I can't wait.*

The words caused a chill to travel through me. "Do we know his TOD?"

"The medical examiner should be able to narrow it for us, but the water in the tub might confuse things."

"Reagan dropped by Celeste's gallery earlier today. She said he'd be back tonight. Why would he have gone through the trouble to drop off his art if he intended to off himself?"

"Art was all that mattered to him. Maybe he thought those pieces would make him even more famous."

I stared down at the body. A moment later, the bathroom door opened and a man wearing an OCME jumpsuit entered. He nodded to O'Connell before unzipping his bag and retracting a few thermometers and other tools.

"The suicide note's open on his computer screen. Make sure you're wearing gloves before you touch anything," O'Connell instructed.

Leaving the men to do the dirty work, I exited the bathroom and looked around the large apartment. It looked exactly as it had the last time I was here. Something should have been different, but it wasn't.

I examined the items on Reagan's desk. As usual, he had camera equipment and memory cards scattered about. I moved my finger over the trackpad, causing the computer to wake up. On the screen was the letter he'd written.

Life and art merged together the day I met Daria. Celeste insisted we hook-up, that our passion would ignite my muse. That was true, but the rest was a lie.

Celeste is a selfish woman. For that, she'll be punished, if not in this world then the next. All she wants is money. That goal corrupted me and my art. Celeste told me of Daria's plight, of her encounter with that killer. She wanted me to recreate it. She said it would be shock therapy, that it would get Daria to create again. Only with my help would the art world be set right. So I did what she asked, not because I believed, but because she offered me exposure.

I'm nothing but a sellout. Not for cash, but for fame. I should have known better, but I was weak. I succumbed.

Celeste's plan worked, and Daria started creating again. Watching that was magical. The beauty of Daria's imagination taking shape humbled me. I'd never be able to capture that raw passion through my camera lens. I tried. So many times. But I failed.

Daria suffered because of what I did. She was frightened all the time. Terrified to go anywhere. Afraid to be alone with me. I hated myself for what I'd done to her, but I couldn't stop. I tried, but seeing her create was intoxicating. It became my drug of choice.

My jealousy grew each day, eating away at me and bringing evil thoughts into my head. I couldn't stop myself. Seeing Daria create made me crazy. I loved her, but I loved her passion more. I hurt her. And I'll keep hurting her. I know it. I can't stop myself. She has what I want. She is what I'll never be. The only way to protect her is to end this. I'm sorry. Tell her I'm sorry.

"It explains a lot," O'Connell said. "What do you think?"

I looked past him, at the camera and tripod set up from Reagan's last photoshoot. "Why did he drown himself?"

"He figured it'd be peaceful."

I didn't buy it. I crossed to the kitchen and opened the fridge. "He has leftovers."

"Seriously, Parker, if you're that hungry, I'll send an officer to get you a sandwich."

I glared at him. "This is from this morning. It's a breakfast burrito." I pulled the white takeout bag out of the fridge and pointed to the receipt. "He must have picked it up on his way back from meeting Celeste. According to this, he ordered two. He ate one. Why didn't he eat both?"

"He was full."

"Why save it if he had no intention of being around for dinner?"

"Habit. You're reading too much into this."

"Am I?"

O'Connell's expression told me he had doubts, but he wasn't ready to voice them. "He's out of the tub if you want to see him."

"Not particularly." But I went back into the bathroom where the ME was conducting the usual battery of tests before prepping the body for transport. "Cause of death?"

"I'd guess drowning. We won't know until we get him opened up."

"Any bruises or defensive wounds?"

"I'm not seeing anything, but it might be too soon for them to show up." He examined the rest of Reagan's body. "It's a shame. This guy had *a lot* going for him. I don't know about you, Detective, but that would be enough to keep my depression at bay."

"That explains why I'm always in such a good mood." O'Connell chuckled.

"Are you about finished?" I asked.

The ME rolled his eyes. "No offense, lady. I'm just trying to keep it light."

"I get it. Reagan was a real dick. At least we know why." I had my own wicked sense of humor and coping mechanisms for dealing with murders and suicides, but none of those involved staring at the dead guy's privates. I diverted my focus back to the message on the wall. "Why did he write that when he already left the suicide note?"

"I don't know," O'Connell said. "Unfortunately, we can't ask him."

"Officers were watching his place since this afternoon, but no one saw him come or go," I said. "How did you miss this?"

"When we knocked, he didn't answer. The receipt on his takeout bag is from an hour before anyone started watching the place. By then, we might have been too late."

"What time was that?" the ME asked, spreading the body bag out on the floor.

"Just after twelve."

"That fits with the timeline. He hasn't been dead for more than six hours." The ME called to an assistant who helped him place Reagan inside the bag. After it was zipped, they lifted him onto a gurney and wheeled him out of the bathroom. "The water in the tub is still several degrees above room temperature. You found him before he had enough time to cool off, so we'll have to use other methods of determining TOD that don't rely on body temp."

"Let me know what you find," O'Connell said. "I'd like to know the official cause of death."

"We're on it." The ME tapped his brow and followed his assistant out of the apartment.

"Did you find the lipstick he used to write that note?" I asked.

O'Connell pointed to the trash can. The tip had practically broken off. I opened Reagan's makeup drawer and looked inside, but I didn't find any other lipsticks. That was the only one.

"CSU will collect the evidence, dust everything for prints, and let me know if they find any discrepancies. But from where I'm standing, it looks like everything wraps up nice and neat. Cases usually don't do that. Take from that what you will."

"Reagan's dead. He can't name his accomplice."

"Weren't you with me when we tried to arrest Anthony Gerhart? Didn't you hear what he said about Reagan asking him to housesit the night Daria was attacked? That explains how he pulled off the attack. We weren't surveilling Reagan. We were surveilling his assistant."

"What about access to Ginger Kendrick's townhouse? We still don't know how he snuck inside there on multiple occasions. He never mentioned that in his suicide note."

"I don't know," O'Connell said. "But CSU found his prints in Daria's attic. We know he was up there."

"What about in Ginger's house? Did you find his prints there?"

"I'm not sure. They found plenty of prints, most of which aren't in the system. We have to weed through all of those in between pulling partials and running those through IAFIS in the hopes of getting a match. Reagan's prints might be somewhere in the mix. It'll just take some time to sort through it. We've only been working on this for a few hours."

"I know."

"Do you?" O'Connell asked.

"Someone attacked me last night. Assuming Reagan's the unknown assailant—"

"Which is what all the evidence suggests," O'Connell interrupted.

"Why would he decide to hurt himself? I would have been more than happy to do it for him. Last night, whoever came at me had a plan. I'm not saying it didn't go south. But there had been a plan. Reagan never struck me as much of a samurai. A vampire, pirate, magician, or even some kind of flabby, talentless boyband member, I can see. But not a samurai."

"What are you talking about?"

"Failure doesn't usually result in suicide for vampires, pirates, or magicians."

"Are you sure? Dracula got staked when he failed. Have you seen any of those pirate movies? They're all ghosts because they failed. And let's not forget Harry Houdini."

"Houdini died from a ruptured appendix. You're thinking of Gilbert Genesta, who drowned while attempting the milk can escape, which Houdini made famous."

O'Connell raised one eyebrow. "Why do you know that?" He shook his head before I could answer. "It doesn't matter. But you see the point I'm making."

"Yes, those people were murdered or died accidentally. None of them committed suicide."

"That wasn't my point."

"No, but it's mine."

O'Connell rubbed his upper lip. "According to the suicide note, Celeste Nash instructed Reagan to do this. You've spoken to her. What do you think?"

"She said she regretted pushing them together, that she felt responsible. But she's still featuring Reagan's art at her gallery. I think there's something to that."

"I'll look into it further." O'Connell looked at the screen and jotted down a few notes. By now, several members of the mobile crime lab had started photographing the scene and collecting evidence. "Until the ME says otherwise, Reagan LaRoche died under suspicious circumstances. We'll treat this like a homicide."

THIRTY-FIVE

After leaving Reagan's apartment, I called Lucca to tell him what happened. Given the news and the details included in the suicide note, he was optimistic that Daria's problems had been resolved. But he thought it'd be best to keep her somewhere safe until we determined who else might be involved.

Anthony Gerhart seemed the type who would do just about anything for his boss. If his story was to be believed, Gerhart had shown up to Reagan's apartment dressed in the same clothes and exhibited the same behaviors by unbuttoning his shirt while he worked on the computer. If I hadn't seen just how Reagan-like Gerhart had acted earlier today, I would have found this highly unlikely. But now I wasn't sure.

Celeste Nash was another name that kept popping up on my radar. She'd been representing Daria for years. They were supposedly friends, but despite the woman's contrite words the first time we spoke, she struck me as a shrewd businesswoman. Reagan's suicide note said she wanted nothing more than money. And money made people do crazy things.

At the sound of someone clearing his throat, I turned to

see Lucien loitering in my doorway. "Did you ever hear of knocking?" I asked.

He took his hand out of his pocket and banged against the doorjamb. "Daria's settled in at the safe house. Building security knows to keep watch. I also have a team set up in the lobby and another one across the hall from her apartment."

"That might not be necessary. The man we believe to have been stalking her killed himself this afternoon."

"That's convenient."

"Tell me about it. Until his death is no longer under investigation and we've ruled out potential accomplices, she'll be staying in the safe house, if that's okay."

"It is." He smirked. "We had a lovely conversation about an hour ago. Daria's fascinating. The way her mind works astounds me."

"She's a survivor."

"That much is clear."

"What's with the smile?"

"She made some notes. After she's had time to review them and think about it, we're going to meet again to discuss getting her some regular security. Of course, that will be after she finds another suitable place to live. But I suspect she'll want our recommendations while house hunting."

"So you signed another client."

"I'm not popping the champagne yet, but it looks like I will be soon enough." He nodded at me. "Well done, Alex."

I scowled at him, but he didn't notice as he strolled out of my office. He and Celeste Nash would get along wonderfully. It was always about the bottom line for them.

After performing a few additional background checks on Reagan's possible accomplices and establishing a solid timeline for events, including what time Reagan went to the gallery, picked up breakfast, and returned home, I grabbed my notes and laptop and went downstairs.

Leaving my car in the garage, I drove the company car to the safe house. I kept an eye out for a tail, but I didn't see anyone. I told the doorman who I was here to see and gave him my name. He called up to the apartment. A moment later, I was allowed upstairs.

Lucca greeted me at the door, glancing down the corridor in both directions before locking it behind me. "Remind me the next time Jablonsky has me keeping a witness company that we get Cross Security to put him up somewhere. The motels we use are a far cry from this."

"I doubt Cross would go for that."

"And Jablonsky would?"

"It depends on how large the TV is and what kind of snacks are on hand."

Lucca laughed. "Good point."

I looked around the apartment, which was large enough to put the apartment Martin and I shared to shame. Daria had taken over the kitchen table, using it to set up her latest project. Each of the six chairs had a box on it with different supplies. The master bedroom had already been redecorated with Daria's comforter and pillows.

"Did you need a moving van to get here?" I whispered to Lucca.

"Almost, but we managed. She needs certain things to feel like home. Her blankets. Her sheets. Her art."

"Did you bring the dishes too?"

"Parker," he snapped.

"I'm only teasing." I handed him the files and notes I'd made. "See what you can make of this."

"All right." He took them over to the couch and spread them out on the sofa, leaving Daria's journals and planners on the coffee table where she'd left them.

"Alex," Daria said, "when did you get here?"

"Just a minute ago." I went over to see what she was doing. "Did Eddie tell you we found Reagan?"

"Parker," Lucca warned.

But I wasn't backing down. Daria ought to know. "Detective O'Connell found him dead."

Daria covered her mouth with her hand, surprised by the news. "How did he die?"

Lucca headed toward us, prepared to clamp his hand over my mouth. "It's still under investigation," he said. "Alex brought me the files to look at."

"The ME isn't sure the exact cause of death yet, but it

looks like Reagan drowned in his bathtub," I said.

"Drowned." Daria swallowed, the color draining from her face. "The Lightning Killer's back."

"No, Dar," Lucca said, glaring daggers into my back, "he's dead. Remember?"

"Dammit, Eddie, stop saying that. I'm not a fucking moron. I heard you the first five hundred times. Everyone says it. But they're wrong. Doesn't this prove it?"

"Daria," I interrupted before Lucca could launch into an argument, "Andrew Holland is dead. Eddie made sure of it. We know he's in the ground. By now, he's nothing more than a decomposed corpse."

"Lovely visual," Lucca muttered low enough that only I could hear.

"Then Holland isn't the Lightning Killer because the killer is still out there. I've seen him. I recognize him from before. He's the face in the mirror. The man on the street." She stared into my eyes. "He drowned Reagan."

"Reagan left a suicide note," I said. "I'd like to discuss the particulars of it with you and see what you think. The police may want to do the same."

"I doubt I'll remember we even spoke about this," Daria said, "so go ahead."

Lucca threw his hands up and walked away. He thought going over this was premature and feared it'd do more harm than good. But I wanted to know if the threat was removed. The easiest way to do that was to speak to the only person who knew all the players.

I went over the details of the suicide letter. Daria didn't speak the entire time, listening carefully, as if hoping the more actively she listened, the more details she'd be able to retain.

"Celeste has always been my agent. I thought she was my friend."

"She might be," I said. "We don't know if anything Reagan said is true."

"It is. I know it is." She touched a hand to her chest. "Every time we speak, Celeste asks about this project." Daria gestured to the kitchen table. "She's been encouraging me to get back to work on it for years." She scooped up a planner and showed me. "But I just couldn't do it. It connected to before. I always feared if I started working on it again, the Lightning Killer would come back to finish the job. This jungle sculpture is my unfinished business, but I was the killer's unfinished business. They were connected," she tapped her temple, "up here."

"Why are you working on it now?"

"It's crazy. I know it's crazy. In fact, I'm pretty sure I wrote that it was crazy." She marched into the living room and picked up one of the journals, rapidly flipping pages. "Yep, I wrote it right here. *I'm seeing him again. He waits for me. Watching. He's coming to finish what he started. Time is running out, and I have so much I want to finish. It's time I start again. I pray I'm wrong, but I know I'm not.*"

I'd read that entry, but I hadn't realized it pertained to work. I thought that was just Daria's fears with a dramatic flair. "That's when you started working again."

"Who knew about that?" Lucca asked.

"I don't know. I try to keep it secret, but when I get excited, I have a tendency to blab about art and the creation process. I can't remember who I told and who I didn't."

"Reagan knew," I said.

"Celeste must too," Lucca said.

"I didn't tell her," Daria said. "She would have wanted to know when it'd be ready for showing. I would have made notes on that and marked a deadline on my calendar."

I sent that information to O'Connell, figuring when he questioned her it'd be good to have a baseline of what Celeste should and shouldn't know in order to judge the veracity of Reagan's final message. But I found myself wondering if Reagan had even written that note. Shaking it off as paranoia, I finished questioning Daria, but she remained adamant that the Lightning Killer was alive and had just killed Reagan.

"Did you ever meet Anthony Gerhart?" I asked.

Lucca held up Gerhart's ID photo.

Daria squinted, moving closer to take a better look. "He looks a lot like Reagan."

"Yes, he does," I agreed. "Did you ever meet him?"

"I don't think so." She scrolled through the contacts in her phone. "He's not in here."

"You had no reason to meet him," Lucca said. "He worked for Reagan at the marketing agency. I don't think they socialized much outside of work." Lucca had no basis for thinking that, but it caused the deep creases in Daria's brow to lessen. Making her feel like she wasn't forgetting something put her mind at ease.

"Why does it matter if I met him?" Daria asked.

"I just want to make sure no one else was responsible for the attack last night or the one last week."

"I already told you, I didn't see anyone last night in the dark. But the man who attacked me in my bathroom looked just like the photos I've seen of Andrew Holland. This guy," she pointed to Gerhart's photo, "looks like Reagan. Neither of them look like Andrew." And with that, she returned to the dining room and took out some green yarn. Settling into a chair, she grabbed the paste concoction and started placing the fibers around a form that would later be removed. The conversation was over.

* * *

By the time I made it home that night, I was exhausted and achy. Despite the terrible events of the last two days, I should have felt relieved Reagan could no longer terrorize Daria. Instead, I couldn't shake the unsettling feeling that Daria was right.

After a hot shower and a quick meal, I grabbed the ice pack from the freezer and crawled into bed. I adjusted and readjusted, finally getting comfortable. Flipping on the TV, I channel surfed, but nothing caught my eye.

Reaching for my phone, I sent Martin a text. *Are you busy?*

Are you okay? he asked.

I wondered how to answer the question. *Yes.* That was succinct but not entirely true.

Give me ten minutes.

I put the phone down and went back to channel surfing.

Eight minutes later, the tablet on the bedside table chimed. Martin was requesting a video chat. I clicked the button and propped the tablet up in its stand.

"Hey, gorgeous." His sad smile nearly broke my heart. "What's going on?"

"Not much. You didn't have to call to check up on me."

"What's wrong?" His green eyes scanned the area around me. "Your text didn't sound right."

"I'm okay, just tired."

"I'm amazed to find you at home. Does this mean you're through babysitting Daria?"

"Not yet." I narrowed my eyes. "You didn't call my phone. You sent a message to your tablet. The one you left here on your last visit. How did you know where I was?"

"A little bird told me."

"Was it a pigeon?"

He laughed. "Yes, sweetheart. One of the nonexistent balcony pigeons told me you were home."

"They aren't nonexistent. They're out there." I let out a sigh. "Was it the doorman or the concierge?"

"The doorman."

"Remind me to have a chat with him one of these days. And for the record, I don't appreciate you paying people to spy on me. I've had enough of that today."

His green eyes grew concerned. "What's going on?"

"The suspect in my case left a suicide note, saying someone paid him to spy on Daria."

"Shit." Martin reached toward the screen, his hand obscuring half of his face. "I wish I could touch you right now. Do you want to talk about it?"

"Not tonight. It's too fresh."

He retracted his hand. "I knew something was wrong."

"Nothing's wrong. I just wanted to hear your voice."

"Not to be indelicate, but if your suspect committed suicide, does this mean your case is closed?"

"I don't know. O'Connell's looking into it. Reagan might have been working with someone else. Someone we haven't identified yet."

Martin nodded, watching as I carefully pulled the blanket up higher. "Lie down, sweetheart. You don't have to sit up to talk to me."

"No?" I asked, sliding down in bed and lying on my side to face him. Martin took his phone and stretched out on the bed too, so we were both horizontal.

He grinned, a spark igniting in his eyes, even though a certain amount of forlornness remained. "I miss seeing you in my bed. Do you know what I'd do if I were there?"

"I have a pretty good idea." I gave him a playful look. "You'd take your computer and cell phone and camp out on the balcony with the pigeons."

"The first thing I'd do is take your face in my hands and kiss you until we were both breathless. Then I'd explore every inch of you with my mouth."

"Martin," my voice came out a little strangled, "I'm too spent for one of these phone calls."

"If I were there, I bet I could convince you otherwise." He blinked, sighing. "I hate this. We can't keep doing this."

"I know, but that's how it has to be."

"This week I've had a lot more free time. I haven't been able to stop thinking about you. You're always on my mind. We're good together. We work. We make sense. We don't do well apart. I don't do well being apart from you."

"Now who's clingy?" I snorted. "You'll really say anything to get some action, won't you?"

"I'm serious. I hate being away from you. We have to come up with something better. I have a few ideas."

"Not tonight." I watched him run a hand through his hair, clearly frustrated. "What would you do if you were here right now?" But it wasn't meant to be a turn-on or the opening line of a scandalous phone sex call. From my tone, Martin caught on.

"I'd tell you about my day while I played with your hair."

"I'd probably lay my head against your chest and fall asleep halfway through."

Martin smiled. "Close your eyes, Alexis. I'm right here with you."

Settling against his pillow, I asked, "What did you do today?"

THIRTY-SIX

Martin's alarm woke me, but I couldn't bother to open my eyes. "What time is it?" I swept my arm out, but I didn't find him beside me.

"Early."

"How early?"

"That depends," Martin said. "Do you want your time or mine?"

"What?" I opened my eyes, watching him lean over and turn off his alarm clock. "Wow."

"What?"

"I thought it was creepy when you watched me sleep from right beside me. It's way creepier when you do it from three thousand miles away." I stretched, wincing in pain. I'd forgotten about my bruised ribs and torn muscle. But he'd been too distracted by something off screen to notice. "This can't be our new sleeping arrangement."

"I agree." He unplugged his phone. "It's Sunday. Go back to sleep. I love you."

He hung up before I could ask why he was up at five a.m. Unfortunately, my phone rang a few minutes later. O'Connell had some updates on the case and wanted my input.

Getting out of bed required a lot more effort than I thought. My lower ribs were doing that popping thing again, so I avoided lifting heavy objects and working out. When I got the chance, I'd let Cross's medical team scan and prod me. In the meantime, an elastic bandage would suffice.

Once I was caffeinated and properly outfitted, I picked up coffee and donuts and drove to the precinct. Thompson grunted his thanks when I put a jelly donut and mocha on the desk beside him.

"Hey, Thompson, I think you're in my chair," I teased.

"Keep dreaming, Parker."

I put a vanilla latte and sprinkled donut in front of Nick's computer. That would put him in a good mood. But I'd keep my fingers crossed his wife didn't find out.

O'Connell leaned back, staring at the donut as if he'd just found a pot of gold. "Well, I'll be damned. Wishes do come true."

"You're welcome." I sipped my cappuccino before biting into a chocolate crème. "What's so urgent you had to drag me out of bed on a Sunday morning?"

"I just got the report from the ME's office. Cause of death is drowning. The ME estimates TOD was between noon and two p.m." O'Connell picked up his coffee and took a sip. "Did you ask for extra vanilla?"

"I had them sprinkle in some of that vanilla sugar stuff."

"It's good." He put the cup down.

Reagan LaRoche had been alive when the police knocked on his door. But he didn't answer. If the arrest warrant had gotten signed sooner, maybe the cops would have breached and Reagan would be alive now. I didn't want to think about things in those terms. Grief counseling advised to veer away from the what ifs, but the thought had already embedded itself in my brain.

"Did the officers outside see anyone enter or leave?" I hadn't seen anyone, but I'd been too busy checking out Reagan's car to bother looking at his apartment.

"Everyone was coming and going, but the only person we were interested in was Reagan. That might have been an oversight."

"What do you mean?"

O'Connell brought up the report, snagging his donut and scooting backward so I could get closer to the screen. Tox came back negative for drugs and alcohol. The ME checked specifically for tranquilizers, but they weren't present in his blood at the time of death or as part of his stomach contents.

"He didn't take any pills," I said.

"It doesn't look like it, but the ME is going to run the blood test again just to make sure the results are accurate." O'Connell bit into his donut.

Since no drugs were in Reagan's system, it was unlikely he had fallen asleep while taking a bath. "The Lightning Killer held his victims underneath the water until they were dead. What about trauma to the body? The shampoo and conditioner bottles were on the floor beside the tub. It could have happened during a struggle."

"True, but none of the water splashed out. If someone held Reagan beneath the water, he would have flailed. Water would have gone everywhere." O'Connell finished his donut and washed it down with another sip of coffee. "Since we found Reagan face-down, it looks like he intentionally inhaled the water in order to kill himself."

"He would have choked and coughed," I said.

"That would explain the fallen shampoo bottles," Thompson said.

"That's a hell of a way to go." I didn't want to think about how excruciating that must have been. At least asleep, he might not have realized what was happening. "I don't think he'd have the balls to do it."

O'Connell snickered. "We know that's not true."

I gave O'Connell's chair a shove. "I'm enjoying my breakfast. Don't make me think about his junk."

He held up his palms. "Forensics swept the place. The only prints on Reagan's computer belonged to Reagan. The same's true for the lipstick they found in the trash."

"What about around the tub and on the faucet?" I asked.

"Nothing indicates anyone else had recently been inside Reagan's apartment or bathroom."

"The killer could have worn gloves. The Lightning Killer

never left any forensic evidence behind. He always cleaned up after himself. That's why it took the FBI so long to identify and catch him."

"Parker," O'Connell said slowly, "he's dead. Remember?"

I felt like I was channeling Daria. "I know that."

"What are you implying? Do you think we're dealing with a copycat?"

Thompson looked up from the report he'd been reading. "Reagan LaRoche doesn't exactly fit the victimology."

"I know that too," I snapped. "I just don't understand why Reagan would have killed himself. He put new tires on his car. He had leftovers in the fridge. He brought his photos to Celeste in the hopes of selling them. Why would he have done any of that if he had no intention of making it through the day?"

"You're forgetting some things," O'Connell said. "First, the evidence suggests he attacked you inside Daria's townhouse the previous night. You fought him off and found out how he was gaining access to her house. He must have realized we'd figure out it was him, especially when he left his prints and snacks all over her attic. He was in trouble, and he knew it. Second, he ditched his cell phone at the office. Before I went home last night, I reviewed the security cam footage from his office building. Reagan swiped his key card around four a.m. that morning, and he locked up five minutes later. I'm guessing that's when he ditched his phone."

"He figured after the attack we'd track it," Thompson chimed in.

O'Connell pointed a finger at his partner. "That."

"Did you see Reagan on the building's security feeds?"

"As a matter of fact, I did." O'Connell clicked a few keys and brought it up. Reagan wore a black, long-sleeve shirt over black cargo pants. The only splash of color on him was the red on his sneakers. "He dressed like someone who'd been sneaking around in the dark."

"He hit you once, Parker," Thompson said. "It's not surprising he came back for seconds."

"And last but not least," O'Connell said, "he left a

suicide note."

"It was typed on his computer. Anyone could have done that."

O'Connell eyed me. "I thought you'd be relieved Daria is safe."

"Is she? Last night, she swore to me Reagan didn't shove her face into the mirror. She said the man who did that looks like Andrew Holland, not Reagan LaRoche. I even showed her Anthony Gerhart's photo, but she said it wasn't him either."

"Parker, I don't think Daria's crazy, but her recollection isn't reliable. You have to take everything she says with a grain of salt. It's not her fault. That sick bastard did this to her, and this sick fuck," he pointed to the image of Reagan on the screen, "wanted her to relive it. He tormented her with it in the name of art or some shit like that. It's no wonder she's confused. I'm not concerned with what happened to him, but I am concerned that he had help driving her mad. That's why I'm going to speak to Celeste Nash. If you promise not to interfere, I'll let you come with me."

"You better," I said. "I brought you a donut."

When we arrived at Celeste's condo, she didn't seem too keen on letting us inside. But O'Connell could be persistent. "Fine," she moved out of the way, "you can come in. But this better not take long. I have to get to the gallery. A few customers are scheduled to pick up the pieces they purchased last night."

"The sooner you answer my questions, the sooner we'll get out of your way," O'Connell said.

Celeste eyed me. "Do I know you?"

"I don't think so."

She stared at me for another moment before turning her attention to O'Connell. "What can I do for you?"

"Your name came up in the course of an investigation. Actually, two investigations. You represent Daria Waylon. You're her agent."

"Yes."

"What about Reagan LaRoche?"

"He's another one of the artists prominently featured at

my gallery. Would you mind cutting to the chase?"

"When's the last time you saw Mr. LaRoche?"

"Yesterday morning. It was around ten."

"How did he seem?"

Celeste cocked her head to the side. "I'm not sure what you mean by that?"

"Was he excited? Nervous? How would you describe his emotional state?"

"He seemed okay to me. He was excited for last night's opening. He couldn't wait to show me the new prints he wanted featured." She turned back to look at me. "You were at the gallery yesterday looking for him."

"Yes, ma'am."

A disconcerted look came over her face. "He didn't show up to the opening last night. Reagan never misses an opening. Did something happen to him?"

"I'm sorry to tell you this, but he's dead," O'Connell said.

Celeste stumbled backward as if she'd been punched in the gut. She grabbed for the arm of the sofa before she could fall and pulled herself backward onto the cushion. "De-de-dead?"

"Yes, ma'am." O'Connell watched her curiously. "What was the nature of your relationship?"

"We worked together. We were friends."

O'Connell glanced back at me. Her reaction seemed over the top for work friends. "Were the two of you involved in a sexual relationship?"

Celeste blinked, shaking herself from the shock of the news in order to look offended. "Why does that matter?"

"I'd like to get the complete picture, if I may."

"We slept together on occasion. Reagan was a very passionate man." She pressed her knuckles against her mouth. "I can't believe he's dead. How did it happen?"

"He killed himself," O'Connell said.

"You must be mistaken. Reagan would never do something like that. He was nothing like the other artists I've met. He wasn't tortured or struggling. He loved so many things. He was a happy person. Inquisitive." She chuckled cynically. "He was rather in love with himself.

He'd never harm himself. The guy wouldn't even smoke a joint or drink himself silly." She stared at O'Connell. "Why do you think he killed himself?"

O'Connell held out a printed copy of the suicide note. "He left this on his computer screen."

Celeste read it, the sadness on her face morphing into guilt and anger. "I didn't blackmail him. I never harmed him. No one was supposed to get hurt. Not him. Not Daria. No one."

"Is it true?" I asked.

Celeste grimaced, like she smelled something rotten. "I thought they'd be good together. Reagan and Daria. This twists everything. It makes it sound like I'm some kind of evil villain."

"Why would you set Reagan and Daria up if you were sleeping with him?" O'Connell asked.

She sighed dramatically. "Honey, Reagan was a good time. He's like a decadent dessert. Every once in a while, it's fun to indulge, but you don't want it every night."

"Still," I said, "some people get territorial when it comes to their lovers."

"I didn't mind sharing him. I sleep around. He sleeps around. It's no big deal. It's life. It's fun and it's messy and that's it. I thought Daria could use some messy fun. She had a reputation before she was attacked. What I asked Reagan to do was to bring her out of her shell and show her a good time. That didn't mean he had to sleep with her, but what two consenting adults do is fine by me. What I wanted him to do was to show her the world the way he sees it. I wanted to ignite her creative juices and get her back in the flow. Her talents have stagnated. The pieces she's been working on are uninspired and unimaginative. She's losing ground. I was trying to help."

"Help whom?" O'Connell produced a statement that he hadn't shown me. "I spoke to Mr. Isson this morning. Well, it was this afternoon for him since he's in London. He said he offered to pay eight figures for Daria's completed Jungle Prowl project. He's been interested in purchasing that sculpture, sight unseen, for the last five years, ever since he first heard about it."

"Lots of art collectors have approached me about that piece."

"But he gave you a seven figure deposit. When I spoke to him, he said that was your commission. Ten percent. He said you promised him updates on the project and photos of the progress Daria was making on completing it."

"How did you find out about this?" Celeste asked. "I haven't said a word to anyone."

"We looked into your financials," O'Connell said.

"You had no right," Celeste squawked.

"Reagan's suicide note gave us cause." He produced a copy of the court order and handed it to her. "Just tell me the truth."

"I asked Reagan to help Daria get over her past. I never told him to recreate it or whatever it is he's claiming here." She stabbed at the copy of the suicide note. "I just said it'd be such a shame if that monster deprived the world of seeing her finished project. Whatever Reagan did, that was on him." She narrowed her eyes at me. "You're the private investigator I spoke to on the phone. You said Daria was attacked. That Reagan was a predator."

"Yes."

"Reagan attacked her?" It sounded like a question, but Celeste reread the words on the page. "He hurt her. He would have kept hurting her." She shook her head. "I don't believe that. Reagan was a gentle soul."

"With an arrest record for assault," I muttered, "due to bar fights, no less." Either Reagan had changed, or Celeste didn't know very much about the man.

"Did you ask Reagan to spy on Daria?" O'Connell asked.

"I might have said it'd be nice to get a look at what she was working on. Almost dying at the hands of a serial killer made her retreat in on herself. She stays home. She keeps her work hidden. She told me once it was because she was afraid if she gained that kind of popularity again, he'd come back to finish her off. It's ludicrous. The Lightning Killer's dead. That was front page news. But no one can convince her otherwise."

"So you had Reagan spy on her?" O'Connell asked again. "Did you ask him to take photos?"

"I never asked him to spy. I asked him to take a few snapshots if he got the opportunity. He and Daria were friends. They did things on the weekend. Art related things. I figured she'd show him what she was working on. It wouldn't hurt if he shared that with me, especially when I'm working hard to make Daria a very rich woman."

"Daria doesn't care about the money," I said. "But you do."

Celeste scowled. "Daria will thank me. Her Jungle Prowl piece will make right what the universe made wrong. Once she gets back to creating, she'll remember who she was meant to be. I'm just trying to give her her life back."

"She has a life," I said.

"Unlike Reagan LaRoche," O'Connell said. "You pushed him too hard and too far."

"I never told him to do any of these things." Celeste jabbed at the paper. "That was all him. I didn't know he was unstable or had thoughts like that. He always seemed carefree and inquisitive. Not once did he have a storm cloud hanging over his head. How was I supposed to know he entertained such dark thoughts or that he'd take this way too far?" She bit her lip, her face flushed from the frantic way she'd been defending herself and justifying her actions. "I'm sorry this happened. But I couldn't have known. None of this is my fault."

O'Connell clicked his pen a few times. "Tell me who Reagan was close to. Friends? Family? Any adoring fans or burgeoning artists who hung around him?"

"Reagan always had an attractive woman hanging on his every word. Why does that matter? Isn't that just further proof he wouldn't have offed himself?"

"Did you ever notice any men hanging around?" I asked.

Celeste shook her head. "I only saw Reagan at the gallery. The only thing he ever did was talk up his photos to buyers and other artists. He never showed up at these things with anyone, unless he had a date or Daria was with him. And Reagan definitely wasn't into men."

"Did you ask anyone else to help you convince Daria to get back to work?" O'Connell asked. "Maybe you encouraged someone else to assist Reagan with his mission?"

"I didn't do anything wrong. I spoke to Reagan about Daria. That was it. Whatever he did, that's on him."

THIRTY-SEVEN

O'Connell slid back behind his desk. "You heard what she said."

"She said Reagan would never kill himself."

"She also admitted to asking him to take photos of Daria's projects. The photo Reagan has hanging on his wall of Daria working is just one example. It explains why he drilled a hole in her attic that looks directly into her studio. He did it to keep tabs on her at Celeste's request. It's just like his note says."

"How did he gain access to Ginger Kendrick's townhouse?"

"I'll call and ask as soon as she's in cell range," O'Connell said, "but I'm guessing Reagan overheard her talking to someone at work. He must have figured out where she kept her spare key or heard her mention her alarm code. The guy dressed like a magician. He probably had a trick or two up his sleeve."

"What about his assistant, Anthony Gerhart?"

Thompson whistled to get my attention. "While you two were playing good cop, not cop, I looked into Gerhart's alibi. Friday night, he was out with friends. I spoke to all of them. They even posted photos on their social media accounts."

"What about when Daria was attacked last week?" I asked.

"Gerhart told the truth. He posted selfies he took inside Reagan's apartment. I checked the metadata. The time and date match up. He was at Reagan's."

"And we know he was alone," O'Connell said. "You used those fancy infrared binoculars to check."

"Yeah, I remember."

"There you go," Thompson said. "We closed another one of your cases. How come we never get the credit?"

"I'll call the engravers and tell them to get started on the plaque."

"Make sure they spell our names right," O'Connell teased. "I'm still waiting on that favorite detective trophy you promised me."

"It's on back order."

"That explains it."

This was good news. But the familiar itch kept nagging at me. Was this too easy? "Keep digging and see what else you find on Celeste. For seven figures, I bet she'd send an entire army to encourage Daria to get back to work on her jungle sculpture."

"Will do," O'Connell said. "I'll let you know if I find anything, but I think it would have shown up by now."

Before checking in at Cross Security, I detoured to the medical examiner's office. After signing in and handing over my identification and credentials, I asked if I could see Reagan LaRoche's body. The ME's assistant gave me a look. "I'm really not supposed to do this," she said.

"I know. It's an ongoing police investigation. You can call Detective O'Connell, if you don't believe me."

"Just don't mention this to anyone, okay?"

I pantomimed zipping my lip.

She came around the desk, slid her card through the reader, and pushed open the locked door. I followed, feeling the temperature drop as we walked into the refrigerated room. She pointed to the steel table near the corner. "He's over there."

"Thanks." The Y incision hadn't been stitched closed

yet. The smell of death and industrial grade cleaning agents soaked into my clothing, hair, and skin. "I wish we didn't have to meet like this," I said.

I didn't know how long I'd been standing there, staring down at the corpse and thinking how the dead never looked like the living, when the assistant cleared her throat. Ignoring the empty, hollow void that had overcome me upon seeing the body spread out on the table like this, I reached for one of Reagan's hands, examining it for calluses or blisters. Depending on how hard he'd held onto the bat when he swung, he might have irritated his skin, but there was nothing. Not that I expected there to be.

But since I came all the way here and it'd be days before I was able to shake the smell of death or the queasy feeling that came along with facing mortality, I checked his other hand. Nothing, but I noticed a faint mark on the side of his wrist and another near his elbow.

"Excuse me." I waved the assistant over. "Did you see this?"

She reached for the light, moving it closer to get a better look. "It looks like a mild contusion."

"A bruise?"

"Yes."

"And this?" I indicated the one near his elbow.

"The same." She went to one of the drawers and found a light with a different filter. Underneath that light, the contusion looked darker and more pronounced.

"How recent are they?"

"They didn't show up during our preliminary exam. It probably happened right before he died. Bruises sometimes take time to appear after death. It's also possible this isn't from an injury but rather congestion of the cadaver, which occurs post mortem. If I had to guess, I'd say he might have banged his arm against something before he died. Given the location at the joints, I don't think these are defensive injuries." She examined the rest of his body but didn't find anything else.

"Take a few photos and send them to O'Connell," I said.

"I'll add it to the file, but I don't believe these are significant enough to mean anything. I'll have the ME look again when he gets a chance. He should be able to determine if they were pre or post mortem injuries."

"Thanks."

As I drove to Cross Security, with my windows rolled down, I couldn't help but think of what Daria said right before she flipped out. She'd thrashed, desperate to get out of the tub, which left bruises on her arms. Were the injuries on Reagan's arm caused by the same thing?

"Stop it, Parker," I screamed, causing the guy in the next car over to give me a dirty look. Lucca swore to me the Lightning Killer was dead. But Daria insisted she'd seen him. I knew that wasn't possible. Reagan had given me bad vibes from the start, but everyone I'd talked to couldn't believe he'd kill himself. And what was with the lipstick on the wall?

By the time I got to the office, I was nauseous from the constant smell of death. After showering until my skin was sore and red, I changed clothes and dried my hair. The excessive scrubbing had only made my bruised ribs worse, so I went upstairs to have the medics take a look.

After getting scanned, one of the doctors on staff felt around my side. "It's not dislocated, but the tear in the muscle is rather significant. You're probably looking at six to eight weeks for a full recovery. Stick with ice until the swelling subsides. Then you'll want to use heat to help the bruise heal quicker. But it'll take time. I'm sorry there's not much I can do to help." He unlocked the cabinet and handed me another bottle of pills. "Pain management's the most I can offer you." He counted out eight pills and put them in a separate bottle. "Take only as needed and not more than once every six hours. If you run out and need more, come back and we'll discuss other options."

In my current state, I couldn't bother arguing that I didn't want them. Instead, I took the bottle, grabbed my things, and drove the company car to the safe house. Lucca opened the door before I could knock.

"What's wrong?" he asked.

"Nothing."

"Bullshit." He stepped into the hallway. "Why do you look like you're five seconds away from a panic attack?"

"I'm fine. I stopped by the ME's office to check on something." I tugged on a strand of my hair and gave it a sniff. "The smell's making me nauseous. I showered, but it lingers."

"It does." He looked at the messenger bag hanging from my good side. "Did you discover anything new?"

"Reagan LaRoche has bruises here and here." I indicated the spots on my own arm. "Before Daria flipped out in the hospital, she remembered banging against the tub while trying to get free. Her arms and legs got bruised." I met Lucca's eyes. "You were there. Where were the bruises?"

"On the outside of her joints, where the bones protrude. Wrists, elbows, knees, and ankles."

"Are you going to tell me I'm crazy?"

"That doesn't mean someone drowned him. He could have convulsed or coughed and knocked against the side of the tub. Don't scare Daria with this, not unless you have something concrete."

"I wouldn't dream of it." I marched past him and into the safe house. Daria was at the dining room table. She was spreading various shades of brown and black fibers out in a very specific pattern. At the sound of my footsteps, she looked up. "I'll be in the living room if you need me," I said to her.

"I'll be here." She went back to work.

Lucca joined me on the couch. "She woke up before I did, made breakfast, and has been going nonstop ever since. I made her lunch, but she didn't want to take a break. I put it in the fridge in case she gets hungry later."

"I can take it from here. Go home. Be with your family."

"I'm not sure it's a good idea to leave you alone."

"I'm not alone. Cross has eight guys inside the building, and the doorman and front desk on high alert. No one knows Daria's here, and even if they did, they'd have a hell of a time getting to her." I jerked my chin at the door. "Go." I pulled my laptop out of the bag and plugged in the various cords and peripherals.

"What are you going to do?"

"Play sudoku."

"Fine. Just don't do anything stupid." Lucca muttered to himself before saying bye to Daria and reminding me to lock the door behind him.

Once he was gone, I downloaded the video files Cross Security had gotten from inside Reagan's apartment building. Even though none of the cameras covered Reagan's front door, the footage would show me who entered and left the building yesterday.

I started at midnight, which was a few minutes before he'd allegedly attacked me inside Daria's house. Several people entered and left the apartment building, but none of them looked like Reagan, his assistant, or Andrew Holland wannabes.

Around 4:40 a.m., Reagan entered the lobby. He wore the same dark cargo pants and long sleeve shirt he'd had on in the security footage O'Connell had showed me from Reagan's office. He went up the stairs and disappeared from the feed.

I fast-forwarded, waiting for the next person to appear on the feed. Around seven, a couple of people left the building. I didn't recognize them. One of them returned a little after eight. By then, several more people were leaving, and a few were coming in. I slowed the speed, paying closer attention. Around ten, Reagan left. His hair was wet, as if he'd just showered. He wore his signature dress shirt. This one was a shimmery cream color. The top three buttons were already open, exposing the upper portion of his sternum. He carried a portfolio.

A woman was entering. He smiled at her, and they exchanged pleasantries at the door. She went upstairs, and he disappeared outside. I paused the feed, noting the timestamp. Unfortunately, Cross Security hadn't been able to gain access to security footage from the garage. At least not yet. But considering the team of computer experts, a.k.a. hackers, Cross employed, I'd get the footage eventually. For now, I had to be patient.

After making a note to check the garage footage and DOT footage, I opened another file. This one was the security feed at Celeste's gallery. The place was locked up at night. The only action on the video happened after

Celeste arrived. Once she did, teams of movers, caterers, and artists came and went. A little after ten, Reagan arrived. He handed Celeste his portfolio, gestured to the walls, pointing and making big expressive gestures with his hands.

I froze the feed, but he didn't have any bumps or bruises. When I'd seen his body in the tub, he hadn't been bruised then either. It was too soon. I need not get ahead of myself. Celeste took the portfolio. He kissed her on each cheek and practically skipped out the front door.

Stopping it there, I got up to circle. My instincts said this man had no idea his life was about to end. If he had known, he wouldn't have skipped, and he probably would have done more with Celeste than kiss her on each cheek.

I switched back to the apartment feed and hit play. I was in the midst of fast-forwarding to the time when Reagan returned when a guy with a navy sports coat and brown elbow patches entered the building. He carried a backpack over one shoulder. I'd seen that outfit before.

He wore a hoodie beneath the sports coat with the hood pulled up over his head. Combined with the mirrored aviators he wore, I didn't get a clear look at his face. But I recognized the outfit. *Kevin Danziger.*

It had to be him. What was he doing at Reagan's apartment building? I watched him go up the stairs. He stopped on Reagan's floor, but the cameras lost sight of him. He could have gone into Reagan's apartment, or he could have entered any of the other units outside of camera range.

I jotted down a few notes while I kept an eye on the lobby camera. A little while later, Reagan returned. He carried the white takeout bag in one hand and an oversized cup in the other. He used his back to push open the door and enter the lobby. As he headed up the stairs, he sucked on the straw.

I continued watching the feed. Almost two hours later, Danziger reappeared. He still had his hood pulled up and his sunglasses on as he left the building. Given the time, the police surveillance unit should have seen him go. But they didn't know to look for him. And given his eclectic dress, they probably assumed he was just another one of the oddballs who lived there.

Dialing O'Connell, I circled the living room. "Nick, I found something. Kevin Danziger, Daria's neighbor, went to Reagan's apartment building yesterday. He was there during the TOD window."

"I'll look into it. Don't do anything stupid."

"Second time today I heard that."

"Then there must be a reason."

THIRTY-EIGHT

I couldn't sit on my hands and wait. I wasn't wired like that. I made Daria a promise, and I intended to keep it. After looping Lucca in to what I found on the surveillance footage, I dug into Daria's neighbors.

We hadn't thought to do it earlier, but the gaping hole in her attic probably should have clued us in. Daria's building had five units. The end unit, farthest from the cross street, belonged to Kevin Danziger. Uma and Tom were sandwiched between Danziger and Daria. Ginger Kendrick's townhouse was on the other side of Daria's, and the Trubolts had the other end unit.

No matter how I rearranged the pieces, I still couldn't figure out how the hole leading from Ginger's attic to Daria's had anything to do with Kevin Danziger. He was on the other side. But there had to be something to this.

Cross Security and the police had done a deep dive on Ginger. She appeared to be an uninvolved bystander. I pulled up her phone records and scanned the numbers, but she hadn't exchanged calls with any of the neighbors. As far as I could tell, she wasn't close with any of them.

Kevin Danziger had to be involved in stalking and terrorizing Daria. I just didn't know the extent of it, but my gut said he killed Reagan LaRoche. Unfortunately, judges and juries didn't give a shit what my gut had to say. So I dug up everything I could find on the man.

His business card said he was a research assistant at the university, a fellow in the sociology department. He studied cultures and society, assisting the dean of the department on several projects. But buried deeper in Danziger's history was the thesis he'd written on serial killer behavior and the impact it had on the populace at large.

How had we missed this giant red flag? We hadn't even looked. I phoned Cross Security, asking them to do whatever they could to get a look at Danziger's search history and anything he'd accessed while researching his thesis. Unfortunately, that had been almost four years ago. At the time, Danziger was a student at one of the universities in Chicago. That's where he'd graduated from before applying for this position and being accepted.

According to the university website, the department was currently researching matters involving prisons, reform, and rehabilitation. Danziger's paper wasn't a secret, but it wasn't easy to find either. Time and distance had that effect.

Instead, I pulled up property records and lease agreements. Danziger moved to that townhouse three and a half years ago, after Daria had already settled in. He must have moved there for her. Did he plan to observe her like some kind of addendum to his paper? Or was he as crazy as the killers he wrote about?

My phone rang, and I blindly answered. "What?"

"Kevin Danziger's girlfriend lives in Reagan's building. Her name is Ina Redmond. He dropped by to hang out with her before she had to go to work," O'Connell said.

"I don't buy it."

"I found her on his social media page. I spoke to her and asked when she saw Kevin last. That's what she said."

"She's lying."

"I don't think so."

"Did you get the exact time he arrived at her place and left?"

"She said he left an hour before she had to leave for work. She needed time to get ready."

"Where does she work?"

"At Cat Call."

"The strip joint?"

"Yeah."

"I'm not buying it. Danziger researched serial killers. He wrote a thesis on how their actions affect society. After that, he gets a position at the university and moves into the same structure where Daria lives. Don't tell me that's a coincidence."

"Shit."

"He knows what he's doing, Nick. He's done his homework. I can't find anything on him. No record, not even a freaking speeding ticket. With the amount of research he's done, I'm sure he knew about Daria and where she lived. He chose to live there for a reason. I'm not sure why, but he went to Reagan's apartment the day he died. That has nothing to do with his stripper girlfriend. In fact, I'd bet my paycheck he's only using her as a cover. Let me guess, they started dating around the same time Reagan came into Daria's life."

"Damn, I should have taken that bet," O'Connell said. "They started dating three years ago. He gave her a ring and everything. The wedding's set for October. They even booked a reception hall."

"Are they hosting it at Cat Call?"

"Surprisingly, no. But you're on to something. Let me make a few calls. You said he's from Chicago. Let me see what the cops over there have to say. It's Sunday, so I won't be able to check with the university until tomorrow. In the meantime, I'll scrub every bit of security cam footage we have from Reagan's building and any camera feed we have around Daria's place and see if I notice Danziger on the footage. If we get lucky, he'll be doing something suspicious. You sent me copies of the security footage from the cameras you set up at Daria's house, right?"

"Yes, and I also gave you the dash cam feeds from the night of the original attack."

"I'll look at them again, and I'll speak to every officer

involved in the various canvasses. Several of them spoke to Danziger over the course of the last few months. Hopefully, one of them got a funny feeling about him or remembers something not being right."

After we hung up, I scanned everything again, returning to my original research. But as far as I could tell, Kevin Danziger never frequented any of the Lightning Killer fansites or true crime websites. But he could have accessed the websites from a university computer or gained access to official records as part of his research.

Either I was seeing things that weren't there or this guy was smart. Too smart. I recalled our brief encounters. The first time we met, Uma Berry introduced us. She thought the world of Kevin, which colored the way I viewed him. The second time we met, he'd been annoyed because the police were knocking on his door again. That was a logical response, but maybe it had been a misdirect. He was the only neighbor who said he heard something slam and thought he saw a car driving away. He'd been vague enough in his description and recall for me to believe his story. But that could have been another lie.

Before doing anything else, I ran backgrounds on the rest of Daria's neighbors, starting with the Trubolts and ending with Uma and Tom Berry. Everyone else, except Ginger, had lived in the neighborhood longer than Daria. I checked their phone logs and asked the techs to check their search histories. No red flags. Furthermore, none of Daria's neighbors had made any calls or texts to Kevin Danziger.

Cross Security had contacts at all the major carriers and internet providers, and while everything I'd done was illegal, I didn't care. Danziger posed a threat. If I was right, he'd killed at least once already. He'd do it again. Unfortunately, I couldn't prove he and Reagan had any connection. And without that, it'd be hard to prove Kevin killed Reagan. I had to think outside the box.

After dinner, I left Daria in the capable hands of my coworkers. She wrote down where I was going and when I left, along with instructions on what to do if I didn't come back by a certain time. Even if Daria's memory wasn't the best, her phone would remind her what time I was supposed to return and what to do if I didn't. Then I headed over to pay Uma and Tom a visit. I didn't think they were involved, but at this point, I wasn't sure of anything.

Uma answered the door, wiping her hands on her apron. "What can I do for you?"

"I just had a few questions."

"Did you figure out whatever happened the other night?" she asked.

"Yes," I said, "which is what brings me here. Do you mind if I come inside?"

"Not at all." She stepped back, allowing me to enter. "Excuse the mess. We just finished dinner."

"No problem. I just had a few questions about your neighbors."

"We know all of them. Don't we, Tom?" she called into the den where Tom was watching sports. He ignored her, and she rolled her eyes. "What do you want to know?"

"What can you tell me about Ginger Kendrick?"

"She's always on the go. She spends more time away than at home."

"Is she close to anyone around here?"

"No. Her sister stops by a lot. Marlene, I think her name is. She always checks on the place."

"Do you know if she gave anyone a spare key to her house in case of emergencies?"

"She didn't ask us. I'm trying to think." She yelled into the other room. "Hey, Tom, do you remember who Ginger was talking to at last year's Halloween party?"

"I don't know. Which one was she?"

"She was the fairy."

"Oh, right. Um...I think she was talking to Abe Lincoln."

"No one was dressed as Abe Lincoln."

Tom grunted. "The one with the top hat and monocle."

"Mr. Peanut?" Uma called back.

"Yeah, fine, whatever."

She turned to me. "That was Kevin, I think. Ginger wanted him to do something. Water the plants or feed her cat or something. I can't remember. Her sister had broken her leg and couldn't do it. She must have given him a key."

"Kevin Danziger?" I asked.

"Yes." Uma smiled. "You met him. He's such a nice young man. He helps everyone out around here."

"Even Daria?"

Uma frowned. "We've tried, y'know. She seems friendly enough when we cross paths, but she's not much for socializing. I don't know how many times I've invited her over for dinner, but she never comes. She never comes to any of the holiday parties or neighborhood barbecues. I don't know why."

I had some idea. "Do you know if Kevin's home? I'd like to ask him a few things."

"He might be there. He might not. His weekends are unpredictable."

"Do you know if he has a girlfriend?"

Uma smiled. "Interested?"

"No, ma'am." For once, I was thankful to have my engagement ring hanging around my neck. "I'm off the market."

"Shame. You'd be perfect for my nephew."

"So Kevin's spoken for?"

"He's supposedly engaged, but I've never seen her."

"Good to know."

"Is there anything else?" Uma asked. "You didn't say much about the other night."

"Do you remember if any of your neighbors were already outside when the police knocked on your door?"

"I think the whole neighborhood was out at that point. The only one I don't remember seeing was Kevin. But he came out as soon as they knocked. He was rather agitated that night. Between us, all the flashing lights freak him out."

"Any idea why?"

"He never said, but it's pretty nerve-wracking. It scares me. I'm lucky I got Tom here. If I didn't have him, I don't know what I'd do." She walked me to the door. "Oh, hey, if you don't mind, can you bring this over to Kevin?" She handed me a container of cookies with a note attached.

"Sure."

Uma watched as I climbed onto Kevin's porch and rang

the bell. Kevin Danziger drove a black, late model sedan. I hadn't noticed it when I arrived, which meant he'd parked somewhere else or he was out. I assumed he was stocking up on lye, plastic sheeting, and duct tape, but that was probably because I watched too much TV. Satisfied, Uma shut her door.

Reaching into my pocket, I pulled out my lock picks, scanned the area for signs that Kevin had a home security system, hoped for the best, and let myself in. When I didn't hear the telltale warning beeps, I stepped inside and put the container of cookies down on the table in the foyer. Every one of the units was an identical copy of the others.

Since I was familiar with the layout, I slipped on some gloves, pulled my long, brown hair into a ponytail, and headed for the bedroom. Grabbing my phone, I photographed the clothes hanging in the closet and the items in his drawers. Underneath the bed, I found a pair of red sneakers, nearly identical to the ones Reagan wore. I snapped more pictures.

In the hall closet was a sledgehammer, long-handled axe, and toolbox. But they were clean and shiny. My gut said these were the tools Danziger used to bust a hole in the attic wall. If Uma was right, Danziger offered to housesit for Ginger during one of her trips. He copied her key and memorized her disarm code, so he could enter her home anytime he wanted.

Filing that thought away, I continued my search. Something in here had to connect Danziger to Reagan or Daria. I had to find proof.

Hurrying upstairs to Danziger's home office, I scoured his bookshelves. They were filled with true crime and criminal psychology texts. He had almost as many notebooks as Daria. I wondered if any of them were hers, so I checked each one. What I found was even more unsettling.

Danziger had been keeping tabs on her from the moment he moved in. He observed her routine, what time she got the mail, when she went out, who came to visit, how she traveled, and her lack of socialization. He'd been making notes on everything for years. Commenting on any changes he observed and speculating as to the cause.

When Daria started meeting Reagan on Saturdays, Danziger had become intrigued. His observations became more detailed. He'd seen Reagan spying on Daria. After that observation, Danziger's notes took on a new life. He recorded things he witnessed from inside Daria's house. What she ate. When she ate. How she took notes. How she functioned. When she created and worked.

Grabbing my phone, I photographed the pages. This would never be admissible, unless the police had cause to get a search warrant and discover it on their own. But I could use the information to guide them in the right direction. Plus, I didn't have time to read and review everything when Danziger could return at any moment.

While photographing the last thirty pages, I heard the door slam. He was home.

I'd spent enough time in Daria's house to know there was no second floor escape plan. My best chance was to find a place to hide, wait for an opening, and sneak out.

"I know you're in here," he called. "Come out. I won't hurt you."

I didn't move, afraid he'd hear my footsteps from the floor below.

"Alex Parker, I'm talking to you. I just spoke to Uma. She said she sent you over here to bring me cookies. They're on the table. My front door was unlocked, and your car is outside. Let's not play games. This charade is exhausting."

Palming my gun, I peered out the doorway. "I didn't mean to intrude," I called down the stairs. "But I really had to use the bathroom."

"Sure, if that's what you want me to believe."

My heart pounded in my chest as I slowly descended the staircase. He could justify killing me. I broke in and posed a threat. He had the right to defend himself. But I'd be damned if I didn't shoot back.

When I made it to the bottom, I found him sitting in the living room, eating a cookie. "Did you find what you were looking for?" He held out the container.

"Yep, the bathroom's right where I thought it'd be."

"Right, stick with that story. It's not the least bit unbelievable." He gently shook the container. "Snickerdoodle?"

"Did you poison it?"

He smiled. "We both know that's not my thing."

"What is your thing?"

"You know or you suspect. That's why you broke in. I take it you found my notebooks. But all that says is I'm conducting research for my next book. It's on the aftereffects of a near fatal attack at the hands of a serial killer."

"You didn't share your observations with the police. That could be viewed as obstruction."

"I didn't know the two were connected. How would I? I'm not a cop or a private detective. I'm just a nerd who writes papers."

"You partnered with Reagan so you could observe Daria up close and personal. Did you do that because you needed the access or because you needed a fall guy?"

"I don't know what you're talking about."

"You went to his apartment building."

"I went to see my fiancée. I work days. She works nights. We're lucky to get a few hours together here and there." He grinned arrogantly. "Everything you think you know has a logical explanation. Ask anyone who knows me. They'll tell you what a swell guy I am. Ask Uma and Tom. They love me."

"I don't think Reagan LaRoche would agree."

"Unfortunately, he's not around to say otherwise. Or am I wrong about that?" But the look on his face told me he knew damn well Reagan was dead because he killed him.

"It looks like you have one loose end to tie up. Are you going to drown me too?"

"Funny you should mention drowning. I'm sensing a theme here. Did you read my paper? Serial killers are fascinating creatures. They develop their own rituals. Their own code of conduct. They stick with it. They don't deviate. When they do, everything unravels. That's how they screw up. They become frenzied or rushed. They break from tradition, and they get caught."

"Or they get too cocky."

"Serial killing requires three victims."

"What's your number?" I asked.

He picked up another cookie and examined it. "A word of advice. You'll never find what you're looking for. It doesn't exist."

"What am I looking for?"

"Proof." He put the cookie down. "It's time you leave. I'm sure Daria needs you to keep her safe. But you won't always be there. You can't stop the inevitable. You can only delay it."

"We'll see." I backed toward the door, not taking my eyes off of him. "Enjoy your cookies while you can. You won't be getting those where you're going."

THIRTY-NINE

"I told you what happened. Danziger practically confessed to killing Reagan. He's planning to kill Daria. There has to be something we can do," I said. "I have photographs of his notebooks to prove it."

Lucca blew out a breath. "The bastard knows what he's doing. He didn't say anything specific. He implied it, but his statements are open to interpretation."

"He's the guy."

"I know. Unfortunately, he covered his tracks. He has a logical explanation for everything."

O'Connell rubbed his mouth, circling the living room. "We've spent the last few days going over every aspect of this guy's life. He's always been careful. I'm sure he and Reagan communicated directly, but that doesn't help us. Without a paper trail, this is nothing more than speculation. The cameras in Reagan's building show Danziger visiting on several occasions, but we never know what apartment he visited."

"What about prior to Reagan stalking Daria?" I asked.

"The saved footage only goes back ninety days," O'Connell said. "We took a look at Danziger's social media page, but without a subpoena, we can't tell when he updated his relationship status. But it looks legit. However, the interesting thing here is his girlfriend didn't move into Reagan's building until a few months ago."

"The girlfriend's involved," I said.

"I don't know. Money trail shows she paid cash, which is consistent with her business. We looked into Danziger's financials, but he always withdraws a healthy sum from the ATMs every week. He could have stockpiled it to pay for her apartment," O'Connell said.

"They're not dating," Lucca said. "She's hooking on the side. Danziger probably pays for her services, and when he needed an excuse to see Reagan, he upgraded her."

"Most likely," O'Connell agreed.

"So we flip her," I said.

O'Connell shook his head. "I've tried. But she's never been charged. Vice raids Cat Call every so often, but the club looks legit."

"Danziger's playing the long game. He's been stalking Daria for years. Why did he escalate now?" I asked.

"Another predator came sniffing around." Lucca held up a printed copy of Danziger's thesis. "He talks about that here. Killers want to establish dominance, but once they reach the pinnacle of their spree, they get reckless. They want to be challenged. And that's when they fail."

"It sounds like this guy should have a degree in psychology," O'Connell said.

"He double majored in it, but his post grad work is sociology," I said. "He probably figured psychology would give him away." We'd been hitting this at every angle for days. But we hadn't found anything that would stick. "Reagan LaRoche couldn't have been his first kill. It was too clean. The first time is always messy."

"One of his colleagues died in an accident back in Chicago," O'Connell said. "I spoke to the detective who investigated, but he didn't find any signs of foul play."

"Was Danziger a person of interest?" Lucca asked. O'Connell shook his head. "Danziger researched other serial killers, not just Andrew Holland." He skimmed the appendix. "I'll see if any witnesses or survivors remember speaking to Danziger. He might have terrorized them too."

"You should see if any of them died under suspicious circumstances," O'Connell said. "Danziger might not be emulating one killer. He could be emulating all of them."

"Don't just look into suspicious circumstances," I said. "Dead is dead. Danziger believes he's clever enough to get away with murder. He probably has a reason to think that, and it started long before he and Reagan ever crossed paths."

"I'll keep looking," Lucca said. He stared at the closed bedroom door where Daria was taking a nap. "How long can we keep doing this?"

"As long as it takes," I said. "She signed a contract with Lucien this morning. Cross Security will be at her beck and call until the threat's removed."

"He'll find another way," Lucca said. "Danziger won't give up. He's too smart. He's just like the killers he wrote about. He wants to be challenged. This is a game to him. That's why he confronted you. He wants to play. You're the Sherlock to his Moriarty."

"You need security to watch your back too, Parker," O'Connell said.

"Danziger won't make a move on me. I'm not his target. Daria is."

"Reagan wasn't either, but he killed him."

"Reagan knew the truth. He could have told us what we wanted to know. After we arrested Reagan, Danziger panicked. He waited for Reagan to be released, encouraged him to strike out against me, ensuring we were motivated to find Reagan, and then he killed him, tying everything up nice and neat."

"Do you think Reagan attacked you?" Lucca asked. "Or was it Danziger?"

"Timing fits for Reagan," I said.

"I'm looking into a few other possibilities," O'Connell said. "Reagan was pretty active on those dating sites. Gerhart said he thought Reagan had a date that night. We can't find any record of it, but he could have asked someone out in person, met with her, and afterward, went back to the office to drop off some stuff for the photoshoot."

"Do you think he accidentally left his phone behind?" I asked.

"It's possible."

"It's just a theory." Lucca opened the door. "Killers shouldn't be smarter than we are, but Andrew Holland was, and Danziger is too. Unless we find something he missed, we'll never be able to touch him until it's too late."

O'Connell studied me, watching as I glanced out the window every few minutes. "Do you think Danziger knows where Daria is?"

"How could he?" I asked.

"I don't know, but that hasn't stopped you from looking outside every two seconds."

I released the slats on the blinds so they fell back into place. "What do we do, Nick?"

"I don't know, but we'll figure it out."

"He's not like most criminals. He has no timetable. No reason to rush. He'll wait us out as long as it takes." I dropped onto the couch. "I told her she'd be safe. But that'll never happen."

"It will."

"You don't know this guy. He's thought everything out. We've spoken to everyone he knows. They all say what a wonderful guy he is."

"That's what he wants them to think."

"What did Ginger say when you spoke to her?"

"She didn't know anything about the hole in the attic. Last Halloween, the neighborhood did this elaborate Halloween setup. They had a big party outdoors. Danziger approached her and welcomed her to the neighborhood. He'd said something about how it was nice that he was no longer the new guy. She said he was friendly. He told her if she ever needed any help with anything to let him know. She had a three day work trip and asked if he wouldn't mind holding her mail for her. Somehow, he convinced her to give him her key in case of an emergency. When she got back, he gave her back the key, and that was that. She hadn't thought anything of it since."

"Now that she knows someone broke through the wall in her attic, maybe she'll rethink things," I suggested.

"Not likely. She has no idea when or how that happened. She hasn't been in the attic since she unpacked, but she knows the guys who did the work on her bathroom had to go up there to check the wiring and pipes, so if the hole had been there then, they would have told her."

"And she had the bathroom work done after Danziger gave her back the key."

"Precisely."

"He could have made a copy," I said.

"I'm sure he did. But unless you happened to see it hanging on his key rack with a label that read 'copy of Ginger's key' I have no way of proving it."

"He'd have some kind of logical explanation for it anyway."

"Do you really think this guy is that good?"

"We don't have shit on him. At first, I thought Reagan was just that good, but I had it wrong."

Daria opened the bedroom door, running her fingers through her thick mane. "Nick, right?"

"You remembered," he said.

"Finally." She looked around. "Where's Eddie?"

"He went to check on some things," I said.

"I guess there are worse places to be stuck. Honestly, this place is just as nice as my house. I could get used to living here," she said.

"You shouldn't have to," I said.

She snorted. "Regardless, I can't stay at my place, even after you catch this guy. It'll give me nightmares or trigger who knows what. I just want to find somewhere new. Somewhere safe."

"Would you mind taking a look at a few photos?" I'd shown her Kevin Danziger's photo before. She recognized him, but she hadn't been certain he was the man who attacked her. But I wanted to try again.

"Sure."

O'Connell laid out an array of six. "Do you recognize any of these people?"

She sat down and studied each photo, stopping on Danziger's. "He has soulless eyes. Without a soul, nothing can keep out the evil."

O'Connell glanced at me over the top of Daria's head, but all I could do was shrug.

"What about the man who attacked you?" I asked.

"He had the same eyes." Daria squinted at the photo. "Do you have any pictures without the glasses?"

I hadn't found any, but Cross Security had made a mockup. I held up the printed photograph.

She shivered, refusing to take it. "That's him. That's just how he looked in the mirror." I put the photo down on the table. "Doesn't he look like the Lightning Killer?"

They had the same hair color, but they wore it differently. With the glasses and oversized sports coat, Danziger didn't look particularly intimidating. But he hadn't dressed like that when he stalked Daria.

O'Connell scrunched up his face. "I sort of see it."

"It's the clothes," I said.

"You're right," Daria said. "Without the jacket, he looks stronger, more athletic." She picked up the photo and turned it over. "What did I ever do to him?"

"Nothing," I said. "This isn't about you. It's about some twisted fantasy this guy has. He wants to be the superior version of the Lightning Killer."

"How are you going to stop him?" she asked.

"We're working on it." But I had no idea, and Daria knew it.

She went back to the dining room. Focusing on her art was the only thing keeping her sane. Dr. Chen said it was a good coping mechanism, especially since most of the people in her support system, like her parents and Brin, had been asked to stay away. We didn't want any innocent bystanders getting caught in Danziger's web.

To be on the safe side, a patrol unit was keeping an eye on Brin. Daria's parents were too far away to be in any danger. We'd considered the possibility of having her stay with them, but Danziger wouldn't let geography stop him. After all, the Lightning Killer had conducted his spree over thousands of miles.

"She wants to move?" O'Connell asked.

"Wouldn't you?"

"Good point." He looked around the safe house. "How

does Cross feel about letting her keep one of his safe houses?"

"I think he suggested it. She has the money, so that's not an issue. Even if she didn't, have you seen the sculpture she's working on? It's incredible. Once it's done, she won't have to worry about money ever again. Celeste already brokered the deal."

"I'm still thinking about arresting her for something. I'm working with the DA to look into possible charges."

"Celeste was the catalyst. Without her, Reagan would be alive. But Daria would still be in danger. She just wouldn't know it. Maybe it's better this way. Danziger was always a ticking time bomb. It's just a matter of time before he goes off."

O'Connell grinned. "You might be on to something."

FORTY

Enacting O'Connell's plan required time and patience. Martin wasn't happy when I postponed my trip indefinitely. He was even less thrilled when I told him not to come home. But that was for his safety and mine. One thing was clear, if Danziger didn't snap soon, I would.

"We have all the pieces laid out," O'Connell said. "Cross Security swept Daria's townhouse. There are no hidden cameras or listening devices. The place is clean. The hole in the attic has been boarded up, but to be on the safe side, Cross Security installed motion sensors up there. No one can surprise us. Daria's townhouse is officially for sale. The sign out front has been hammered into the ground, and we've been sending undercovers in with the real estate agent to view the house. This afternoon, when the couple received the good news that the offer was accepted, Uma was standing on her front porch. By now, I'm sure she's spread the word that Daria's moving out and a new family is moving in at the end of the month."

"Did you hang a sold sign?" Lucca asked.

"It's swinging in the breeze as we speak," O'Connell said.

"Great," I said.

"Let's hope so." Lucca blew out a breath. "Do you think Danziger's going to fall for it?"

"We put him on a clock. He doesn't know where Daria's moving. If he wants to do this, he has to act before she disappears forever," I said.

"Misinformation is already circulating," O'Connell said. "Her agent has one story. Brin has another. Her therapist another. Her online store has a notice it'll be shutting down temporarily, and her P.O. box and website information have been changed to an out of state address. If anyone asks, the realtor's been told to say Daria is moving to a warmer climate. If pushed, she'll say South Carolina. With so many different stories, Danziger won't know what to believe or where to start. He'll act."

"We hope," I said.

O'Connell looked at me. "I still don't like this. You don't look anything like Daria. He'll notice the difference."

"Reagan wasn't the only magician. I have a few tricks up my sleeve. Cross has a lot of clients in the entertainment industry. He called in some favors. I can do this. Plus, the real Daria will be there during the day. Danziger won't realize we subbed in a decoy," I said.

"You hate playing decoy," Lucca muttered.

"No kidding, but no amount of makeup, wigs, and prosthetics will ever convince Danziger that you're Daria." I looked at O'Connell. "Do you have everything straight on your end?"

"We'll wait four nights before we do it. We don't want him to think it's a setup."

"Alex," Lucca put his hand on my forearm, "are you sure you want to do this?"

"Do you remember what I said when you asked for my help?"

"You didn't want to piss off a serial killer."

"It looks like that ship has sailed. I don't have a choice anymore. We're good, boy scout. Whatever happens, that's what we agreed."

"Yeah." He sighed. "But I'm sorry."

"Keep that in mind the next time you ask for a favor."

*   *   *

Our plan went off without a hitch. Daria wasn't pleased to be back home, but with so many friendly faces keeping an eye on her, she had no reason to worry. I spotted Danziger watching us from his front porch. He waved at me, the same calculating smile on his face.

I waved back. *Bring it, asshole.*

"Did he see you?" Lucca asked when I stepped inside.

"Yes."

"Good."

After it grew dark outside, Daria and I traded clothes. I donned the wig and put on the prosthetic face mask that the special effects expert had made. Then I painted my skin with Daria's makeup, put on a non-prescription version of her glasses, and looked at myself in the mirror. I didn't recognize me, which meant Danziger shouldn't either. But to be fair, I didn't look exactly like Daria either.

"It's dark. He won't be able to tell," Lucca said as he adjusted the wig on Daria's head. "Nick will take you back to the safe house. He'll make sure you're safe."

"What about you?" Daria asked me.

"I'll be fine. Lucca will be here. Officers are on standby. I'm trained for this."

She gave me a hug, which was uncharacteristic since she didn't like to be touched. That was something else we had in common. "Thank you."

A few minutes later, O'Connell showed up, knocking on the door and calling for me. "That's your cue," Lucca said.

When Daria went outside, O'Connell spoke to her, making sure she kept her back to Danziger's place. Then they headed for his car. She got in the front seat, and they drove off.

Lucca checked the time. "And so it begins."

Remaining in character, I packed a few more boxes, making sure to scribble notes in an empty journal every few minutes. O'Connell sent Lucca a text, telling them they arrived back at the safe house. We worked for another forty-five minutes.

"You should go," I said.

"I'll be nearby."

"I know."

He indicated the pinhole cameras which had been installed during one of the supposed open houses. "The police are keeping an eye out. The tac team isn't far away."

"Just go. I'll be fine."

"If he doesn't show, I'll be back in forty-five minutes. Any longer, and he'll know Daria's not here."

Lucca went to pick up dinner while a patrol car remained outside. After a call came in over the radio, the car pulled away. But Danziger didn't make a move. He must have sensed this was a trap. So we'd have to try again.

Which we did, the next day, and the next. By the end of the week, most of Daria's things had been moved out of her house. Only the furniture remained.

"He's not taking the bait," I said. "Do you want to call it?"

"I already called in our dinner order. Neither of us has eaten yet. We might as well follow through with the rest of our plans. Kelly got tired of not seeing me, so she took Grace to visit her parents. I have no reason to rush home."

"Neither do I."

"So dinner." Lucca grabbed his keys off the table. "Patrol car's outside, just in case. I'll be back soon."

While he was gone, I went out the back door to make sure Daria didn't have any lawn gnomes or wind chimes. The big maple tree loomed at the end of the property. In the dark, it looked ominous. Foreboding. A breeze picked up, blowing the raven hair into my face and getting it tangled in the stem of my glasses.

I carefully brushed the strands behind my ear, feeling the weight of the clipped on earrings as they jingled. On the bright side, I wouldn't miss having to dress like this. Giving the tree one last look, I went back inside and locked the back door.

Now that the house was nearly empty, I found it creepy. Picking up a journal, I wrote, *Creepy house.* Stifling my giggle, I put the pen down and went into the kitchen. A few bottles of water were all that remained in the fridge. I opened one and took a sip while I circled through the dining room, living room, and down the hallway.

Most of Daria's toiletries had been removed when she went to stay at the safe house, but a few nonessentials remained. Finding an empty box, I went back into the bathroom and knelt in front of the vanity. The first cabinet contained a few extra towels. I put those in the bottom of the box and opened the next cabinet.

A car engine sounded, followed by the whooping of a siren turning on. The patrol car wasn't supposed to take off. We'd already tried this trick. My phone vibrated, and I pulled it out of my pocket.

The text was from O'Connell. *9-1-1 received reports of a bank robbery in progress. All units responding. Hang tight.*

"Some night." I tucked the phone away, finished packing up Daria's extra cosmetics and toiletries, and went to grab the packing tape from the main room. While I was in there, I heard rustling near the back door.

Resisting the urge to reach for my gun, I moved closer to the door and peered outside. The breeze continued to blow, making the tree branches sway. For a moment, I thought I saw a figure moving around the trunk, but on second glance, I realized it was just a shadow. If the house wasn't creepy, that damn tree definitely was.

I tapped my fingers against my thigh, doing my best not to let my imagination run wild. The point of this wasn't to freak myself out. The place was wired. Even though backup wasn't on scene, they were close. But given the 9-1-1 call, I had to assume the tactical unit had been called away as well.

I didn't like this. A thud sounded in the kitchen, and I jumped. Flipping on the light, I didn't know what I expected to find, but there was nothing there. Opening the fridge, I found one of the water bottles had fallen over. I had no idea why. Ghosts came to mind, and I laughed at the ridiculous thought.

After checking the front two rooms and upstairs, I grabbed the packing tape and returned to the bathroom. I sealed the box and carried it out to the foyer. I picked up another empty box and went into the bedroom.

Daria had packed up all the icons and saints. But the curtains remained. Since I had no intention of sleeping in here, I stood on her bed and pulled down the rods. I'd just folded the curtain and tucked it into the box when I heard a noise out front.

I dashed out of the room and to the front door, but all I saw through the window was the neighbor across the street returning home. I'd never been so jumpy in my entire life. I sent a text to Lucca, asking if he was on his way back. While I waited, I finished packing Daria's bedroom, taped that box, and put it in the living room. The only room left was the guest bathroom.

Repeating the process there, I filled the box with towels and opened the mirrored medicine cabinet. Inside were several over-the-counter medications, a few hair supplies, and random toiletries. I hefted the box onto the counter, tossed everything inside, and closed the cabinet.

In the blink of an eye, I saw his reflection in the glass. He grabbed me. One hand went over my mouth, keeping me from screaming while the other wrapped itself around my middle.

"Shh," he whispered against my ear, "it'll all be over soon." I stomped down on his foot, but he yanked me backward, off the ground. Fresh pain shot through my bruised ribs, as my body contorted. I screamed, but his hand ensured the sound came out muffled.

After struggling against him to no avail, I bit down hard on his gloved hand.

He shook his hand free from my teeth. "You, bitch." He threw me into the tub. My back slammed against the hard porcelain, and my ears rang. The rough treatment had knocked loose my wig, which clung to the side of my head at an odd angle, taking the glasses with it. "What the hell is this?" He grabbed the wig, yanking it off my head.

"Surprise." I didn't reach for the gun hidden under Daria's baggy sweatshirt. Under these conditions, he might overpower me and use it against me. Instead, I rolled onto my outer left leg and kicked him with my right.

It knocked him backward, but before I could climb out

of the tub, he pounced, like the jungle cat from Daria's sculpture. He held me against the side of the tub while I scrambled and fought against him. I scratched at his arms and face, but I never touched skin, just the thick protective clothing he wore.

He threw a punch at my face, which connected with a lot more force than I thought he was capable of. Using the opportunity, he turned on the water and plugged the drain. "Where is she?" he asked. "Where are you hiding her?"

"You'll never find her." I smiled, tasting blood. "You should give up now."

"I don't think so." He grabbed the front of the sweatshirt and dragged me away from the side, laying me flat. The water from the faucet poured over my face, making it hard to see and impossible to breathe.

I knew there was no point in struggling against him. He'd done this at least once before. Instead, I reached beneath the hem of my sweatshirt, pulled the gun which had been secured to my body with an elastic band, and squeezed the trigger.

With all that water, I couldn't see what I hit, or even if I hit anything. I hadn't bothered removing the gun from inside the oversized shirt before aiming and firing, but the strength left Danziger's hands. I shoved him off of me and moved away from the flowing faucet.

Removing the gun from inside my shirt, I pointed it at him. "Put your hands on your head."

"Where is she?"

"Now." I climbed out of the tub and shoved him onto his stomach. I yanked one hand behind his back and grabbed the packing tape. Quickly, I looped it around his wrist several times before tucking the gun into the waistband of my pants and grabbing his other arm. Once he was secure, I noticed the bloody hole in the back of his shoulder. Flipping him over, I saw where the bullet had entered. "If you were smarter, you would have worn a vest."

He glared at me, his teeth chattering from the shock of the bullet wound. "You tricked me."

"I guess you aren't that brilliant, after all." I removed what remained of the prosthetic nose and attached mask and tossed them on the ground. I eased onto the floor, keeping my gun aimed at him while I called O'Connell. But with all that packing tape wrapped around him, Danziger wouldn't get far.

"Parker?" Lucca yelled from the front door. "Parker?" He ran into the bathroom. "Are you okay? I heard running water."

"You took so long getting dinner, I decided to take a bath. I just didn't realize I had company."

FORTY-ONE

I towel-dried my hair while O'Connell and Lucca filled out reports. "I can't believe that worked. Obviously, Danziger didn't bother reading his own thesis or taking his conclusions to heart."

"It was his last chance," Lucca said. "It's a good thing we didn't call it."

"Well, he did," O'Connell said. "There was no bank robbery. Danziger made the call using the mini-mart's phone. After Lucca left, he wanted to make sure the cops would be busy."

"It was a smart move." I put the towel down on O'Connell's desk. "Too bad he wasn't smart enough to realize I wasn't Daria."

"You looked the part," O'Connell said. "But I'm glad you were you and not her."

"That makes two of us," I said.

"Three." Lucca eyed the ice pack I held against the t-shirt O'Connell had given me to wear. "Are you sure you're okay?"

"The ribs have been better, but they've also been worse. It's nothing a little R&R won't fix." I scanned the statement I'd given, making sure it looked complete. "One thing is clear. We have our work cut out for us."

"We?" O'Connell chuckled. "What we? You're taking off tomorrow."

I skimmed CSU's report of the evidence found in Daria's attic. "I don't think Reagan ever entered her house. His prints were on the snacks, not on the ladder, the beams, or the floor. We didn't find any trace of him inside Ginger Kendrick's townhouse either."

"You think that was all Danziger?" Lucca asked.

"Don't you?"

Lucca shrugged. "Until he talks, we won't know for sure."

"Actually," O'Connell said, "I had a couple of unis bring in Danziger's girlfriend. She had no intention of cooperating, but when she was told she might be charged as an accomplice for attempted murder, she mentioned Kevin had another friend in the building he would visit whenever he dropped by to see her. She didn't know who Kevin's friend was, but she gave us the apartment number."

"Reagan's apartment," I said.

"Exactly. She remembers seeing Kevin dropping off a few things and leaving with others. Snacks and water bottles, mainly."

"Reagan was never in Daria's attic," I said. "None of the neighbors ever saw him in the area, just his car. The man Daria kept seeing waiting for her and watching her was Kevin Danziger. That's why no one ever reported anyone suspicious in the area. Danziger lives there. Seeing him in the backyard or lurking around Ginger's or Daria's townhomes wasn't odd, especially since he volunteered to assist his neighbors with all sorts of projects."

"That's what I'm thinking," O'Connell said.

"But why would Reagan make some kind of deal with Danziger?" Lucca asked.

"Reagan wanted to do Celeste's bidding. He wanted her to feature his art, and a part of him must have bought into her theory that forcing Daria to confront her past would enable her to get back to work," I said.

"Which it did," Lucca said. "But still, Reagan should

have reported it."

"We don't know what their deal entailed. But we know Reagan had been following Daria. Danziger saw it happening and confronted Reagan. Danziger might have threatened to go to the police, so Reagan told him why he was doing it. Perhaps Danziger said he'd keep an eye on Daria and take some photos of her art projects. Fear alone might have been enough to get Reagan to agree and not think too much about it," I said.

"We won't know more unless Danziger talks. His girlfriend doesn't know any details, but that might explain how Daria's earrings and hairbrush ended up at Reagan's place," O'Connell said. "Danziger must have planted them, figuring he'd get away with murder by framing Reagan."

"Do you think that was always his endgame?" I asked.

O'Connell shrugged. "You said it yourself. Danziger always thought he was smarter than anyone else. He had no intention of getting caught. He set Reagan up to take the fall. And since Reagan was stalking Daria, he made the perfect patsy."

"That would explain why Danziger killed him," Lucca said.

"I'd like to know for sure," I said.

"I'll see what I can do," O'Connell said, "since I'm assuming that wish fulfillment is a requirement for the title of favorite detective."

"You know it." I grinned. "Did you tell Daria the good news, Lucca?"

"I did. She's over the moon. She has a new apartment, courtesy of Lucien Cross. She doesn't have to live in fear. And she's literally about to become a multi-millionaire. Given everything she's been through, she deserves it."

"Amen to that," I said.

O'Connell laughed. "Maybe that's what all those statues and symbols were really for."

Signing my statement, I asked, "What else do you need from me?"

"That should be about it. We'll have some more forms for you to sign and you might have to go over this once more tomorrow, but everything else will come later, closer to the trial," O'Connell said.

"Good because it's about time I make good on one other promise."

*   *   *

"Can I refresh your drink?" the bartender asked.

I pushed the glass toward him. "Please."

"Coming or going?" a man asked, sliding onto the stool beside me.

"Coming, I think." I looked at him, finding his smile rather charming.

"Rough flight?" He eyed the glass in front of me.

"You have no idea." Between the pain in my side and my fear of flying, or rather crashing, I'd opted to down a prescription pain reliever before getting on the plane. In theory, that was great. In practice, not so much. I'd hoped it would knock me out so I could sleep the entire way. Instead, I spent most of the flight staring at the airsick bag and hoping I wouldn't have to use it.

"Most people drink before they board a plane, not when they arrive." He nodded to the bartender. "Put her drink on my tab, and give me one of what she's having."

The bartender gave him an odd look. "Are you sure, sir?"

"Absolutely." He smiled at me. "Are you waiting for someone to pick you up?"

"Are you offering?"

"I could be persuaded." He picked up his drink and took a sip. "That's not what I expected."

"What were you thinking? Straight vodka?"

"You never know." He slid a twenty to the bartender. "What brings you to California?"

"A 747."

He chuckled, rubbing his eye. "Smartass."

"Why are you here?"

"Business, but I could go for a little pleasure too. What do you say? There's a hotel right next door."

"You should take that ring off your finger before you proposition a woman in an airport bar," I suggested.

He looked down at the ring, running his thumb over the band. "You don't find this a turn-on?"

"Nope."

He drained the rest of his glass. "That's a shame since the one around your neck makes you even more irresistible." He reached out and ran his thumb across my cheek.

"How'd you know I was here?"

"When you changed your ticket, I got the notification since I purchased the original ticket for you. Why didn't you tell me you were taking an earlier flight, sweetheart?"

"I wanted to surprise you."

Martin leaned in. "I'm glad you did." He kissed me long and hard. "Are you sure you don't want to reconsider the airport hotel? With L.A. traffic, we're looking at about 45 minutes. I'm not sure I can wait that long."

I held his face close to mine, letting my fingers tangle in his hair. "Try."

He kissed me again, reigniting the electric tingle from the last time our lips met. "Let's get out of here." He scooped up the bag from where it sat between my feet. "Do you have any other luggage?"

"No."

"Good. We'll have a clothing optional weekend."

We made the drive from the airport to his beach house in just under forty minutes. Martin drove like a maniac, but that wasn't anything new. Thankfully, my stomach had settled before I got in the car.

"I want to show you the place," he said. He put my bag down and led me through the massive house. "Ta da." We stood in the midst of a giant game room. Table hockey, pool, pinball, and several vintage arcade machines filled the room, in addition to a large bar and several stools.

"No wonder you haven't come home." The pinball machine called to me, and I wandered over to it. "Did you buy this?" I pulled back the plunger and worked the flippers.

"The place came furnished. What do you think?"

"You should get one of these for your house."

He nibbled on my earlobe. "It's something to keep you

entertained when I'm working late."

When the ball slid past the flippers, I turned in his arms. "Are you telling me you have to go to work now?"

"No." He waited for me to put my hands on his shoulders before he lifted me onto the pinball machine. For once, I was actually taller than he was. I leaned forward, pressing my forehead against his. We hadn't been able to get enough of one another. "There are a million things I want us to do. Places I want to take you. Things I want to show you."

"Or we can stay right here, and I can kick your ass at pinball."

"I've been practicing. You don't stand a chance."

"No?"

"No." He stole a kiss while pulling the plunger back and launching the ball. But he was more fascinated with me than the game.

"You're going to tilt," I warned.

"One can only hope."

When making out on top of a hard surface stopped being fun, I pushed him away. "How about you show me the bedroom?"

"That I can do." He took my hand and guided me down the hallway.

* * *

The weekend flew by, as they tend to do. Martin brushed my hair back as I lay against his chest. "Why can't you stay longer?" he asked.

"I have work."

"I thought O'Connell made an arrest."

"He did, but there's always paperwork and other things to deal with. I should check on Daria and see how she's doing."

"I can't believe Cross sold her the safe house. He'll probably start moving real estate next."

"It's Lucien. He always has something up his sleeve." I looked at him. "When you were in the shower, I found the lease agreement. Maybe we should talk about that instead."

"I haven't signed it yet."

"But you had it drawn up for a reason. Six months, Martin. That's what it said. Is that how long you're going to be here?"

"I don't know."

I bit my lip, nodding. "It's okay."

"No, it's not." He inhaled. "I was going to wait until dinner. But you want to talk about this now, so we will." He played with the ends of my hair. "This is a great house. It's fully furnished. It's right on the beach. We have a pool and hot tub. And you like the game room." He smiled. "And the bedroom."

"Only because you're in it."

"Let's make this home."

"What?" I sat up. "You want to move here?"

"Not forever, but for a few months."

"How?" I blinked, convinced I was in the midst of a very strange dream. "I have a job. I can't just walk out."

"You wouldn't have to. A few weeks ago, Cross came here to look at property. He's planning to open an office since so many of his clients are celebrities who do a lot of work in L.A. You could oversee that."

"That's Lucien's decision, not yours."

"Alexis, he suggested it to me. He's making amends. He feels responsible that we're apart."

"He is responsible." I narrowed my eyes. "I'm a bartering chip, aren't I? He's dangling this over your head so you'll let him back in on the project."

"You are not part of the negotiation."

"At least not in black and white. I hate this. That manipulative prick."

"He's doing something nice."

"He's shipping me out to California."

Martin's face fell. "You don't like it here?"

"It's sunny."

"Most people think that's a good thing."

"Earthquakes. Sharks. Fires. Mudslides. Water shortages. Brownouts."

"Just think about it. We'll be together. This could be home too, at least temporarily."

"Do you really want to do this? This project means that much to you?"

"It's more than the project. It's the office and jobs. People depend on me."

I laughed, though it wasn't funny. "You and I do the same thing. We put everyone else first."

"If this is too big of an ask, I'll understand. I'll come home every weekend or you come here, and that'll be it. We'll manage. Every week. Not longer. It's too hard, especially when I never know if or when I'll see you again."

"What about Mark? He's like family to both of us."

"He made plane reservations the moment I told him I had courtside seats to several Lakers games. You can be sure he's coming to visit. He'll probably be here more often than you are once basketball season starts."

"When did you tell him about the tickets?"

"A month ago."

"No wonder he was so damn happy. I thought he got laid."

"In Mark's opinion, courtside seats are better. I, however, disagree."

"What about my grief counseling meetings?"

"We'll find you a meeting here. I'll go with you." He ran his thumb across my cheek. "You can fly back anytime you want. This isn't a prison sentence. You can come and go as you please. But I don't want to be without you for months on end, and you're terrible at sticking to the plan. So I'm making a new one."

"Okay," I said, wondering how my friends would react to the news.

His green eyes brightened. "Really?"

"How bad could it be?"

DON'T MISS ZERO SUM, THE NEXT ALEXIS
PARKER NOVEL

AVAILABLE IN PAPERBACK AND AS AN E-
BOOK

ABOUT THE AUTHOR

G.K. Parks is the author of the Alexis Parker series. The first novel, *Likely Suspects,* tells the story of Alexis' first foray into the private sector.

G.K. Parks received a Bachelor of Arts in Political Science and History. After spending some time in law school, G.K. changed paths and earned a Master of Arts in Criminology/Criminal Justice. Now all that education is being put to use creating a fictional world based upon years of study and research.

You can find additional information on G.K. Parks and the Alexis Parker series by visiting our website at
www.alexisparkerseries.com

Made in the USA
Columbia, SC
28 March 2023